SCROLL OF SEALS

A CHRISTIAN FANTASY ADVENTURE

THE HOLY WARRIORS' COMMISSION
BOOK TWO

TAMARA MAUDELLE

TAMARA SMITH

Cover Design: Etheric Tales and Edits © 2021

ISBN Print: 978-1-7372915-6-5
ISBN EBook: 978-1-7372915-4-1

Printed in the United States of America

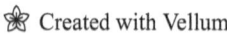 Created with Vellum

ACKNOWLEDGMENTS

To my fantastic mother, Collene: God took you to Heaven early last year, but you were always my number one fan and the best mom anyone could ever wish for. I miss you, Mom!

To my friends, Wendy, Marcia, and Chris: for being my Beta readers. You were constructive and caring and very helpful in assisting me in creating a better novel.

To my amazing sister, Jan: for being my Alpha reader and for your continued support and encouragement.

To my brother, Rick: for letting me bounce ideas off of you and for giving me valued advice regarding military equipment, maneuvers, and procedures.

To my dad, who died way too early in his life and in mine. I still remember your laughter and the twinkle in your eyes. You still inspire me, and I wish you were here to share my new writing adventure. I love you, Dad.

CHAPTER 1

I tried to shake off the drenching cold rain that threatened to seep down the back of my neck as I struggled to hide under a canopy of poison sumac—which was the only protection I could find at the moment. *Great! The last thing I needed was an itchy, oozing rash.*

"This has to be the worst weather we've ever encountered," I muttered to my team.

"You got that right, Mara," Aaron whispered in my earbud from some distance away.

It was difficult to see through the torrential rain amid these dense woods. This mission was a real pain, and I heard several muttered oaths from various team members inside my earpiece.

"Just stay put, mates," Edison returned, "until the rain lets up a bit. We don't know what we might be walking into."

I shifted in my crouching position, and my feet squelched and then slipped out from under me. Landing on my butt, I felt the cold mud in places that it was never meant to be. *Crap!* Using only one hand as my right hand held my Ka-bar knife, I tried to push myself back into position, but I slid back down onto my rump again, which ground more mire into my backside. During my undignified landing, my weapon bumped out of my hand and off to the side and luckily, within the middle of some underbrush. "Dear Lord, give me strength!"

"Mara, you okay?" my new husband asked with concern in my ear.

"I'm fine, Finn. My dignity is a little bruised by falling into the mud, but I'll be okay," I muttered.

I detected a few snickers tickling the inside my ear.

"What's that?!?!" I replied forcefully into the com.

The only responses were a few more guffaws and comments stating, "Nothing."

I finally returned to my original position and wiped my one muddy hand on my pants, and took a firm grip on the knife I'd retrieved from the underbrush.

Breathing hard and tapping my finger against my weapon, I tried to control my temper. *Breathe in and out, in and out.* At least my heart no longer boomed in my chest, and the irate finger slowed its drumming rhythm.

I arrived home early from my incredible wedding to this nightmare, which included being rushed into planning meetings, and then headed to this god-forsaken landscape to implement this mission. As usual, there wasn't much intel to go on, but our employer was God—and you don't say "no" to the Father Almighty. That's why He brought all of us back from death—His Chosen—to rid the earth of Lucifer, his fellow demons, and of course, Satan's minions—the myrmidons.

The smell. Even the rain, mud, and ozone from the storm's ferocious lightning couldn't disguise the stench of the myrmidons. There was definitely one heading my way. I gripped the knife in my right hand and pulled out another with my left. A sharp snap of a large twig broke under someone's foot. Glancing to my left, I spotted the demon lackey as he moved awkwardly in my direction. I waited until he lumbered by me, traversed a few feet away, and I slowly and carefully stood. Making sure my footing was secure, I crept forward and slashed him deeply across his back. He turned swiftly with a loud grunt and moved to shoot me with his rifle. I swung my right hand up and across, cutting the femoral artery in his upper arm. Moving quickly, I used my left hand to block his other arm, then ran a double slash across his throat. A swift kick to his solar plexus knocked him to the ground, and as I knelt on his chest, I realized he was already dead. The black slimy ooze of his demon blood ran from his lethal wounds to the rain-soaked soil of mud and earthworms.

"One myrmidon down, Edison. They're on patrol, so everyone watch your six," I communicated.

"Copy that," Edison replied.

The plan was for our team to merge toward a compound about four clicks from our current position. This was the meeting place of two demons—one major and one minor, along with two influential state senators. It was unknown whether these politicians were possessed by evil or simply corrupt. We wouldn't know until we reached the building and met them firsthand.

I joined up with Jasper, and he looked as disheveled as me. Mud covered one entire side of his body, with briar scratches up and down his well-muscled arms.

Raising my eyebrows, I stared at his body, and he replied, "Don't ask. This weather is as ornery as a constipated mule."

I chuckled at his joke and gave him a goofy grin as he glanced at my mud-soaked backside. Moving toward our destination, Jasper and I took out three more myrmidons, finally reaching the rest of our team members. They looked as miserable as Jasper and me.

"Xavier and Billie, you're in charge of the west entrance: Finn and Jonas, the south. Jasper, Mara, and Basheer, I need you to take the front. Aaron and I will handle the east side," Edison instructed quietly. "Remember, no shots are to be fired unless necessary. We need to kill the demons and take the senators alive, then gather any physical evidence they may have within the house. They could destroy the documentation and flee the scene if they get wind of our entry. There's no way to know what the demons have for escape routes."

We nodded in understanding and scanned the compound from the edge of the property's wooded area. Several high-tech security cameras had been spotted around the building using earlier satellite surveillance.

Aaron crouched down and pulled a laptop from a waterproof bag. He began to type, removed his satellite phone from the same carrier, and made a call.

"Poppy, it's time."

Aaron waited a few minutes, then pecked at the laptop keyboard. Within moments, he closed the computer, stuffed the phone and computer into the bag, and gave us a proud thumbs-up. The security cameras still worked, but the video now played in a loop.

"Basheer, it's your turn," Edison said.

Basheer pulled out a small device and flipped a switch.

There was a loud pop, followed by a crash as a tree fell within the woods to our right—with a little help from a small explosive. We watched as several outer perimeter myrmidon guards headed into the dense forest.

"Nothin' like a little distraction to clear the path for us young'uns," Jasper quipped in his sing-song southern accent.

Edison quirked a smile. "That's our cue, mates. Move-in!"

Jasper, Basheer, and I crept toward the front entrance. Basheer went in one direction, and Jasper and I in the other. Two more myrmidons stood guard around the corner, and we took them out quickly. I spotted Basheer, and he'd taken out another from his side. As we neared the door, there appeared to be only two more guards. Jasper signaled us, and we gave our silent acknowledgment. We scuttled behind the tall ornamental bushes toward the entrance, which was located behind the demons.

I stabbed the one closest to me with a quick jab in the middle of his back, and when his knees buckled, I slit his throat from behind. Jasper eliminated the other one, and we proceeded to the door. As Basheer picked the lock, we felt a presence. We swung around, and another myrmidon appeared out of nowhere and was about to fire his rifle at Basheer at close range. Jasper swung his arm up to shove the demon's shooting arm away from us, but we were too late. *Boom!* The rifle went off, albeit over our heads and into the air. But the damage was done, and now our enemy would know something was afoot.

"Dang, nab it!" Jasper cursed under his breath.

I heard other mild expletives through my com.

"We have to move fast before too much damage is done," Basheer whispered urgently.

Putting our knives away, we raised our rifles and entered the foyer. Demon guards came at us from every direction. We dove for cover and fired in earnest. The noise was deafening, but we had to defend ourselves and the rest of the team. After several minutes, the thunderous din finally ceased.

In my ear, I heard, "Sound off." It was Edison. To my relief, everyone answered.

"You all know your orders. Get moving!" Edison barked.

Jonas, Basheer, and I began clearing the house. We knew where the main meeting room was located, and Jonas, Edison, and Finn were to gain access to that space as quickly as possible. We heard a few more shots from somewhere in the building, and once our section was cleared, we made our way to the meeting room. As we entered, the place was in chaos. Computers had been destroyed, reams of paper were burning in the fireplace, and two men were dead at the table.

"The demons! Where are they?" I hollered in frustration.

"Stay calm, Mara. Aaron, Billie, and Xavier are on their tails and will report in. In the meantime, we must salvage all the intel we can find. Team, get to work," Edison ordered.

"Copy that," I replied.

My hands shook and my jaw clenched at the possibility the demons could have escaped. One laptop had minor damage, so I stuffed it into my bag. Finn tried to pull some of the documents from the fireplace, but there wasn't much that hadn't been badly damaged.

Jonas and I approached the two dead men at the table. They'd been shot through the head, execution style.

5

"These are the two senators," Jonas said. "I'm assuming the demons decided these guys weren't worth the trouble of taking them along during their escape, but they didn't want them found alive by us either."

"I concur, Jonas," Finn replied. "I have what appears to be a map— at least, what's left of it. We'll see if our lab can do their magic and pull whatever intel they find."

Hearing a noise from outside the door, we raised our weapons.

"It's us, team," Aaron yelled from the safety of the hallway. We lowered our weapons.

They were a muddy mess and covered in cobwebs.

"I'm so sorry, but they got away," Xavier replied. "Unbeknownst to us, there are several mazes of tunnels beneath this building and all over the property. The demons are long gone."

Finn rubbed his furrowed brow with a weary hand and said, "It's not your fault. We had no way of knowing about the tunnels. There wasn't enough time."

Edison stood from his position of leaning against the fireplace mantel. "I agree. Let's place the Holy Fire bombs and get the bloody heck out of here."

I lowered my head and said in a quiet and defeated voice, "Copy that."

After returning to the base, there wasn't much to review regarding the previous mission. The burned piece of map that Finn had retrieved from the fireplace wasn't helpful either. It was an edge piece of a standard map of the Middle East with no "X" marking any specific spot. We still had no clue as to what these demons were planning.

That evening, Finn and I discussed this problem at length during dinner.

"None of this makes sense," I said with a furrowed brow.

"I know. But we have to have faith, Mara," Finn replied, covering my hand in comfort.

"I suppose. I'm sorry I'm such a wet blanket tonight. Let me stare at your handsome face for a while. That always lifts my sour mood." I winked at him and set my elbow on the table with my chin in my hand. Flashing him googly eyes, I ogled him with a lovelorn look. This man still amazed me with his rugged, handsome good looks. His short, thick, curly black hair, sparkling green eyes, and cleft chin always drew every woman's eyes in each room he entered. He had the body any other man would envy…tall and muscular with broad shoulders, a narrow waist, and muscles that bulged through his tight black T-shirt. I exhaled a long, loud sigh and ran my stockinged foot up his shin.

"You're playing with fire, gorgeous," he replied in his Irish-lilting accent. "Stop looking at me like that. I feel like a piece of meat." Finn laughed when I made a chipmunk face at his comment.

"I know. Isn't that exciting?" I giggled and returned my foot to rest under my chair.

"Awe, now I'm disappointed," Finn winked. "Oh well, we need to put Gracie to bed anyway. She's fast asleep in her chair."

As I glanced at her, she was, indeed, out like a light. I threw a crouton at him and blew him a kiss. "You're right. Let's get the poppet to bed. I'm also beat, Finn."

CRACK—BOOM! I cringe as the late afternoon storm's lightning strike hits something nearby, and I feel the shock through to my toes. The cold stinging rain blinds me as I run through the dense woods while my feet slide precariously on the slippery undergrowth. I keep running, then trip over a fallen log, and I struggle to breathe more oxygen into my over-stressed lungs. My heart races frantically in my chest, and I hear the rapid thump, thump, thump echoing in my ears. I regain my footing and begin sprinting once more. But to where, I'm unsure.

"Jonas!" I scream in my head as I try to connect psychically with my brother. Where is he, and why isn't he responding? Jonas shouldn't be far from my location, but I can't sense him anywhere. I hear several

of my pursuers closing in. Obviously, I'm being herded into a specific direction, but there isn't anywhere else to run.

"Mara, there's no use trying to escape because we will capture you. We already have your brother. Just stop and make it easy on yourself." The voice comes from one of the men on my six and far too close for comfort. I want to shoot at those hunting me, but I don't know Jonas's location. I can't take the chance that I may inadvertently shoot my brother.

As I continue running, branches, twigs, and foliage whip and scrape against my skin. My exposed hands and face are now so cold I can no longer feel the pain of the cuts and slashes.

The incessant rain is still dangerously impeding my progress. I fall again into the slippery undergrowth, regain my footing, and try to peer through the downpour to find an adequate hiding place. But, as I squint to look through the deluge, I know I'm trapped. Several men in fatigues are ahead of me, waiting for me to advance to their position. I come to a dead halt since many rifles are pointed in my direction.

"It's time to stop running," a deep voice yells behind me. Raising my arms in surrender, I turn around to face the man speaking to me. He's carrying a large yet strange-looking weapon. It isn't a standard rifle, but something I've never seen before. It is matte-black in color and has an extensive square firing mechanism attached to the top gun rail. He raises the weapon to his shoulder, aims, then fires. Whirr! Whirr! I hear this deep rumbling sound, then feel something strike my body. Darkness envelops me, causing me to fall to the ground. There's instant nausea, and my brain feels like it's shaking in my skull. Then blackness.

~

I JERKED awake in terror and gasped as if I'd been running a marathon. Glancing in Finn's direction, he stared at me, attempting to discover what had roused him from a deep sleep.

8

"Mara, are you okay?" He rubbed a rough hand over his eyes as if trying to clear them.

"Yes—I think so. It was a frightening dream, and I know it was supposed to be important—but about what, I haven't a clue."

I described the nightmare in detail, and his eyes grew wider with every description I provided.

"Holy cow!" he said and pulled me close in comfort.

"I know. But what could it possibly mean, Finn?"

"I haven't a clue. We'll have to address it with the team at our next meeting. In the meantime, hopefully, the good Lord will provide more answers."

"Yes. God willing," I whispered into his shoulder as I shivered at what this dream meant. Although, I had a pretty good idea, and I knew Finn wouldn't like it—not one bit.

CHAPTER 2

*A*fter we had returned to the base from our honeymoon, Finn moved in with Gracie and me, and we converted the third bedroom into an office for him, but there was a full-sized pullout bed if we had company. It was nice that he could spend more time at home. Finn could use the apartment office instead of being away on the meeting floor finishing the plethora of paperwork necessary for a base this large.

I continued to have the same recurring dream about being chased through the woods. No part of it had ever deviated from the original nightmare. Finn and I hoped God would give more information, but nothing else had been revealed in my dreams.

Gracie was settling in well with the new routine and was giddy that Finn was now part of our family. We hadn't received any news regarding the pending adoption, but we knew it was a waiting game. We prayed we'd be approved and this beautiful, intelligent, loving child would officially become our daughter. It seemed every day, we loved her even more. Gracie was kind, thoughtful, caring, and intelligent, with a witty sense of humor, even for a four-year-old.

When not on missions, the Chosen were required to find suitable work on the base. I decided to be tested to determine which job would best fit me and my talents. After receiving the results, I was perplexed about the career I would enjoy, but it would also need to benefit the base and its people. I excelled in computer logistics and programming, psychology, animal caretaker/rehabilitator, and other areas beyond my education and training. Finn and I discussed my options, but I knew which career I preferred. However, it wouldn't benefit the Chosen or the running of this facility. Finn said he wanted me to be happy with whatever I pursued.

I loved working with animals, and God gave me the gift of being able to communicate with them. I wanted to rehabilitate injured, abused, or neglected animals, but they weren't generally allowed on the base. Only cats or smaller pets were permitted since there wasn't an area for dogs to exercise or to "do their business." So, upon further reflection, I decided to pursue counseling base members and assisting our facility veterinarian. I'd already begun training in both careers, and God gave me the knowledge and expertise I needed to excel. My new jobs kept me busy.

During our time of settling back into the base, we had an urgent meeting which was led by Edison Kincaid. He was one of the three Principals that designed and ran the Chosen's underground command center hidden in the middle of Idaho. Edison had a quick wit, was Australian to the core, and had a matching charm to boot. He was a big man with a full head of sandy-colored hair, intelligent gray eyes, a neatly trimmed mustache and beard, and a booming laugh that was highly infectious.

My new husband, Finn, was also a Principal, and he and Edison worked together in planning and implementing our missions. Helen Bouchard was the third Principal, and she handled the logistics of keeping the base fully staffed and running smoothly. My entire elite team was in attendance, which included my two older brothers, Jonas and Aaron.

It was good seeing my team, and they appeared happy and ready to start a new mission. Billie, who was hard-core military, was sitting next to me. But instead of her short, shocking blue hair, it was now a bright shade of purple. Jasper was wearing his usual cheerful, friendly smile and greeted us with his southern drawl of a hello. He was a large, handsome man with dark eyes and matching exquisite skin. Over the past several months, Jasper had become one of my favorite team members and was like one of my family.

Xavier, whom we dubbed "The Silencer" because he rarely said much unless he felt it was necessary, sat at the back corner of the table. He had the regal look of a Native American, with his long graying hair kept in check by a ponytail, and his face was strong with a square jaw, intelligent brown eyes, and thick black brows.

Basheer, our talented pilot who was Lebanese, was also in attendance. He worked hard to understand our American sense of humor and was a compassionate, intelligent, and giving man.

There was a brief discussion as our team said how much they enjoyed our wedding and the week of vacation on the island of Aruba.

Chuck, who had joined us on our previous missions, had returned to his place on the Delta team. Naturally, he would be missed, but we understood that he had only been with us to complete his military training.

A new face sat at the other side of the meeting table. This man was handsome, in his late twenties, with short, thick, dark hair and dark skin, and his eyes were a warm brown shade that seemed full of mischief. He was well-muscled, in excellent physical shape, and as tall as Finn at six-foot-four. His charming smile was infectious, which enhanced his striking good looks.

"Okay, mates, let's get down to business," Edison commented in his delightful Australian accent. He prayed for the good Lord to guide us, then continued, "I want to introduce the new team member. This gentleman is also one of God's Chosen, and his name is Armand Baptiste. He's kindly transferred from our Western European base to join our group here in the States. Armand has several degrees, but his specialties are Archeology and Theology. His knowledge as a Historian is also a significant asset to our team."

Armand stood as he addressed the group. "*Bonjour.* I'm honored to be here. But please call me Armie." He greeted us in French, then continued in English, decorated by his beautiful accent. We introduced ourselves, and he shook everyone's hand and took his seat.

Edison spoke again, saying, "Thanks for joining us, Armie. Now, on to business. Something big is going down, but at this time, we're unaware of who or what it involves. Kaiko, our prophet, has advised us that we must stop whatever this new demon is planning. The only intel we have now is what Kaiko has told us. This monster is looking for a sacred object that could change the balance of power in Hell's favor. Our watchers are going through massive data as we speak, trying to find anything that could give us a lead on this demon or what it's after. Mara has advised us that she's had the same recurring dream about her and Jonas being captured by unknown assailants. Have you had any new visions or dreams that could give us a clue as to what's on our horizon?"

I wrinkled my brow and relayed what I had seen in my dreams, but I couldn't advise my team what it meant. "I wish I could tell you more, but that's all I have at the moment."

Finn spoke, his Irish accent more prominent due to his frustration. "So Kaiko couldn't provide any additional information? We need a lot more to go on."

"Negative. She said Archangel Gabriel hadn't told her anything else but that it would come. I suggest our three psychics review satellite images, news feeds, blogs, or anything else that might trigger more information." Edison looked at my brothers and me with questioning eyebrows.

"We'll do whatever is needed," Jonas said.

"Jeez-o-Pete and tan my hide with a willow whip! Is it just me, or do all y'all hate how we're never given enough information?" Jasper's loud voice echoed through the room, and he shook his handsome head and glared at the team. "We're fighting a pre-Armageddon war here, dang-nab-it!"

My eyes widened into saucers at his outburst, which was uncharacteristic for this kind and gentle man. "Jasper, yes, we all feel frustration, but there isn't anything we can do until God reveals what we need to know," I muttered kindly.

"I'm sorry, Mara, but I don't know how all y'all are so calm about this. It thoroughly gets my bearded goat." Jasper abruptly stood, which caused his chair to spin behind him, and he turned to stomp from the room. He muttered, "I'll be back once I calm my highfalutin anger."

Aaron spoke quietly once Jasper left the room. "He's right, you know. It burns my butt too." He ran a hand through his dark, curly hair and glared at me with his blue-green eyes. I still found myself staring at him occasionally in wonder because Aaron was the spitting image of our dearly departed father.

In a no-nonsense, deep, and authoritative tone, Xavier replied, "Stay the course, my good friends. Faith is one of the most difficult trials for all of us, and the devil would love nothing more than to make us doubt the Father. When has He ever not come through for us?" One dark eyebrow raised critically in everyone's direction and we nodded in return. "I'll go speak with Jasper. He's been dealing with some personal issues lately and we must show him patience." Xavier stood and quietly left the room. This man always had a quiet nobleness about him. I could imagine him dressed in a Native-American ceremonial outfit chanting to the heavens for good weather and bountiful crops for his tribe. He was an inspiring man.

There were several hushed moments before anyone uttered another word.

"Uh-hmm. Let's take a fifteen-minute break, and hopefully, Jasper and Xavier will rejoin the meeting," Finn said.

After our break, the two gentlemen did return, and Jasper made a quiet and sincere apology.

"There's no need to apologize, my friend," Jonas replied. "You were only speaking aloud about what the rest of us were thinking."

The remainder of our team concurred, and we continued the meeting.

"*Excusez moi,* I'd like to speak with Mara after this meeting to review her recurring dream. I would need as much detail as possible," Armie quipped, and I returned his request with a nod.

Finn continued, "On to another subject. Kaiko said that it's essential that the Chosen take out as many myrmidon hives as possible. We have begun our investigations and located seven within the U.S. Our four other allied bases worldwide have also been notified of our prophet's request, and they're on board and preparing to begin their assaults. She also said that every team member on the base must have scuba training and UDT, which stands for underwater demolition training. The training sessions and times will be messaged to each of you within the week." We stared at Finn with stunned expressions. "I know, it's bizarre, and she just told us today, but we can do this. I've never had this training, so we'll all be in the same boat—sorry for the pun. We'll meet again to review our myrmidon targets and possible strategies. Any questions?"

The team shook their heads in response and the meeting adjourned.

Finn and I met with Armie, I relayed all the details of my dream, and he kept nodding his head. He tapped his finger on his cheek as he listened with a pensive look in his eyes. When I finished, he took my hand in his, kissed the back of it, and said, "*Merci.* I'll think about this information and what it may imply. Please let me know if you're given more intel, *belle femme.*" He then gave me a smile and a wink and looked at Finn. His grin disappeared, and his eyes reflected sorrow as he departed with a nod. I turned to look at Finn and saw a flash of jealousy and a hint of anger in his eyes.

"Finn, stop. I've already read him, and he doesn't have a devious or lecherous bone in his body. His flirtations are innocent, and he doesn't even realize he's doing it. I saw his gorgeous wife and three children in his mind. All of which he truly adores. Don't let him get your goat, my love—there's no reason. Besides, you know none of us can commit any sins. Especially the major ones." I didn't tell Finn that when I probed Armie's mind, a shield was in place. He was protecting something deep in his psyche, but I knew it wasn't anything sinister. But it still made me wonder what was so important that it had to be protected.

Finn visibly relaxed and a tender smile came over his face. "You're correct. I'm being ridiculous and I'm sorry. I'll also apologize to Armie. It was rude of me and I know I hurt his feelings," Finn offered contritely.

"Thank you. Let's go back to our place. Gracie is with Kaiko's mother for her schooling session, so we have the apartment to ourselves. Now, what could we possibly do?" I tapped my foot as I glanced at the ceiling, feigning deep concentration. Fingering one of my long, red curly tresses, I batted my eyes at Finn.

Finn started to speak like a crusty old pirate, "Blimey, I believe I've turned my lovely lassie into a nasty wench. Arrrggghhh! You know exactly what I was ponderin'. Shiver me timbers, don't hornswoggle me, lass, or I'll make you eat cackle fruit, then toss you off into the briny deep into Davy Jones's locker. Arrrggghhh!"

He continued talking like a pirate from the elevator and back to our apartment while he mimicked a limp as if he had a peg leg. I laughed so hard, tears streamed down my face. But the mood changed once we closed the door behind us. We had the entire afternoon to ourselves and would take advantage of our alone time. After enjoying each other's company for most of the afternoon, we took a well-deserved nap. In hindsight, I should have thought twice about sleeping.

I'M DREAMING AGAIN. I see Finn standing before me, and we're both laughing with joy as we frolic in the turquoise-colored Caribbean Ocean. We're now lying in the soft sand, enjoying the warm sun and tropical breeze, but the dream takes a drastic turn, and the scene changes. I'm

moving through underground tunnels that don't appear to lead anywhere in particular, but I seem to know where I'm supposed to be headed. There are gunshots in the distance as well as men yelling in Hebrew. But the cacophony echoes through the massive tunnels, giving me no direction as to where it's coming from. Now the images appear to fast-forward, but I'm still moving through a maze of more tunnels. The pictures slow again, and I turn around another corner and come to a dead end.

Stopping quickly, I stare at the strange writings on the wall before me. Several small squares are indented in the stone, about three inches in diameter, and are etched with unusual symbols. After pressing several tiles, the floor gives way, and I fall, but it feels like I'm careening down a children's slide. After a few minutes, I slow to a stop and end up sitting on my rump on a hard, cold floor. Darkness surrounds me. After returning to my feet, I run my hands along the damp stone wall, trying to find my way in the inky blackness. An intense light appears out of nowhere, and I discover I'm in a massive chamber. Looking to my left, I spot hundreds of ancient crates stacked everywhere.

Then turning to my right, I'm drawn to what appears to be a larger container. It's by itself, with nothing else stacked near or on top. I move closer as if mesmerized. There's some writing on the crate's cover, along with several symbols. As I sidle closer to this bigger crate, holiness and peace surround me. An image of an object appears in the back of my mind within the dream—a scroll, maybe? There are more symbols on the parchment, but these are different from those at the entrance to this place. As I try to reach for this image, I feel something about to attack me, and the hairs stand up on the back of my neck. I turn quickly to see what's causing my alarm...

I JERKED awake and protested in frustration, "Dang it!"

"What?" Finn uttered next to me, blinking his eyes and trying to focus on my face.

"I had the strangest dream. Of course, I didn't get to finish it...as usual." I explained to Finn what I had seen in this vision. "Initially, the tunnels were large, made of cement block, and the ceilings were arched. There were even wooden walkways and handrails. They were well constructed, but as I explored them, they became narrower and more primitive. I can still see them in my mind, and I've no clue what's in the large crate or what any of the writings mean."

"What about the smaller crates? Did you see anything written on them or maybe any symbols you recognized?"

"Let me try and attempt to enter the vision again, and maybe I can access the room." I closed my eyes, thinking about the chamber, and felt myself return to the vision.

EVERYTHING BEGINS *to come into view again. Concentrating on the crates, I realize most of them are so worn with age that it's impossible to make out any definite images. I continue moving down the row of boxes of every shape and size. But they're tightly sealed with no visible markings on the outside. Looking around the large room again, I finally see something clearly defined on the opposite wall. A significant symbol resembling a plus sign is etched deeply into the stone. As I peer closer, I realize it's more than that. The outer points of the plus are flared outward, and it looks so familiar.*

I PULLED myself out of the vision and related what I had seen to Finn. He squinted his eyes with puzzlement at what I had described, but he didn't know what it meant either. We would call another meeting of our team tomorrow morning to advise them about my latest dream. At least it was another clue to our next mission.

LATER THAT AFTERNOON, we enjoyed a family dinner. Gracie delighted in telling us what she'd learned today about how bears "hidernate" in the winter, then wake again in the spring. Finn and I giggled at her word misuse, then politely corrected her. Asher, my young gray and white Maine Coon cat, was thrilled to sit at the table, and he listened intently to our conversation. I wondered if he simply enjoyed being in our company or understood what we were saying. We pretended not to notice when Gracie handed him chicken pieces from her plate.

That evening after watching television, we prepared Gracie for bed, read her a bedtime story, said our prayers, and tucked her in. We each gave her a goodnight kiss, and Asher snuggled next to her, which was his usual position by her side. He usually stayed with her until she fell asleep, then moved to our room later in the evening.

I called my mom before bed to update her on our latest news. She also regaled how wonderful her house looked since returning from our wedding in Aruba. Mom had no idea we sent a large construction crew to work on her home while she was away. Finn and I arranged to have several things upgraded in her home, which included a larger rear deck, a new on-demand water heater, updated kitchen flooring, and the wooden barn repainted. She was thrilled and couldn't stop thanking us for our thoughtfulness and how we shouldn't have done it.

"Mum, you're worth it, and we're so pleased you love the changes. You deserve it, and we hope we can come for a visit soon," Finn said to her in an assuring tone. "We love you dearly, Mum."

"We sure do. Gracie misses you too. You won over our precious child," I assured my mother.

"Please give her my love. She's such a wonderful girl, and I'm thrilled to have her as my delightful grandbaby. I was thinking of redecorating your old room, Mara. I thought it would work well for little

Gracie when she visits," she replied happily. I told her it would be great and Gracie would love it.

After retiring to bed, the vivid dreams returned.

A HOT SUN is shining from above, and as I gaze at the vista, I'm surrounded by old buildings made of blocks of stone, palm trees, sand, and some strange looking grasses. As I look around, I focus on one building in particular. It's a mosque, and it's made of white stone, but the top dome is colored green, and there's a turret on the right side of the building. Many men are moving about me wearing long robes, and the people appear to be of Middle East descent. As I scan the area once more, I see the ocean. The land juts out like a peninsula, and a cement wall runs along one side of the area along the ocean's edge. This scene fades to black and another greets my vision.

I'm in the caves once more, but everything around me vanishes. Looking at the sizeable lone crate, I sense that this container holds a human body—and one of great importance. As I continue to concentrate, no further information is given.

After waiting a few moments more, an ancient document appears before me. It looks like a map of some kind. Seven spots are clearly marked at different locations within the map's grid. As I try to focus harder on the ancient parchment, everything blurs, and the map quickly closes into a tight scroll. No matter how hard I try, the document won't open again.

A rich, haunting voice speaks loudly and clearly in the deep recesses of my mind. Terror and awe move through me because of these utterances, and I know it's not to be ignored. "You are not to know what is held within. Only the Lion shall gaze upon this rune. The Order of Solomon's Temple must spirit it away for safekeeping until the Lion comes to fulfill the prophecy of the Will of God."

21

∾

I SLOWLY OPENED my eyes and thought about what I'd seen and heard. *Who or what is the Order of Solomon's Temple?* I stayed in bed for several minutes contemplating this information, then rose and went to the kitchen. After finding a pen and paper, I jotted down exactly what the voice imparted in the dream. These words were too important, and I didn't want to take the chance that I wouldn't remember them perfectly by morning. I turned off the lights and returned to bed.

"Is everything okay?" Finn whispered in concern.

"I'm fine. Go back to sleep." I moved close to him and snuggled against his warm, muscled bare chest, inhaling his clean scent.

Asher let out a hoarse meow in response to being disturbed as he slept at the foot of the bed. I decided to wait and tell Finn in the morning about the vision and silently thanked the Lord for the dream and message. *His command would be obeyed, but what would be the cost? The possibilities were endless and, of course, horrifying. What was this map for, and why was it so important?*

CHAPTER 3

*a*fter breakfast, Finn walked Gracie to Kaiko's mother for daycare. Finn returned and I relayed every detail of the previous night's dream. He said he would call a meeting for this afternoon. Finn and I already had a meeting scheduled this morning with the other base principals, and we made our way to the bottom floor of the underground facility.

Edison Kincaid and Helen Bouchard were already waiting for us as we entered the conference room.

Finn said, "Thanks for meeting with Mara and me this morning. This is actually Mara's idea, so I'll let her begin." He handed thick folders to both Edison and Helen.

I addressed the Principals. "Finn handed you detailed proposals on the ideas I'll present today. But before you peruse the paperwork, I'd like to give you a synopsis of what I'm proposing. After careful thought and consideration, I'd like to discuss these ideas with you. As you know, the base has exactly seventy-two children within its walls. Currently, school-aged children are homeschooled by their parents or other adults who kindly volunteered their services. The younger ones are being tended to by babysitters—if the parents are lucky enough to find them. I propose we provide daycare services, build physical school rooms and hire teachers. After reviewing the facility's personnel, we have plenty of qualified people to fill these positions. In addition, Finn said there's a full wing empty on Level Six that would provide adequate space for this essential endeavor. Do you think this is a viable venture?" I stopped speaking to gauge their expressions as to whether they thought this was a good idea or if I should be locked in a loony bin.

Helen spoke first, though her expression gave nothing away. "That's a fabulous idea. You're correct, Mara. Quite a few of our Chosen are actual schoolteachers, and many of our other staff are well educated in many subjects. I'm sure several of the parents would probably love to continue teaching the base children on a larger scale. What do you think, Edison?" Helen stopped and stared excitedly at him.

"I believe Mara has a great idea and I wish I'd bloody thought of it. But how would we get this all started? We would need a committee of some kind and someone to run it. Any ideas, Mara?"

"I've already spoken with someone who would love to take on this project. Kaiko's parents, Gloria and Marshall Riley would be excellent to head the committee. They're certified teachers and are well-loved by the children and the base community. I spoke with Father Faraj too. He has contacted the other religious leaders at this facility. They said they'd love to help regarding the religious education side."

"Let's take a vote," Finn stated, then continued, "All in favor of pursuing the first proposal, say 'Aye.'" Everyone's hand went up and they agreed to the proposal. "Okay, Mara, tell them your second idea." I looked at Finn and he winked at me in encouragement.

"This may seem more daunting and expensive. A huge section next to the hydroponics bay on Level One is not being used." Peering at them, I took a deep breath, then continued. "I propose using this section to create a large park." Edison and Helen were about to object, but I held up my hand to stop their protests.

"Wait a moment before you oppose my idea, and please let me finish. I've been sensing the negative impact of being underground for long periods from everyone living in this base. The special lighting that was installed was a step toward trying to alleviate this issue, but it still exists. People need sunlight, nature, and fresh air. All the things God provides us to thrive, and our children also need this. I've spoken with Jasper, and he's sure it can be done. He said he would use the same natural sunlight from the outside and even knows how to vent in fresh air directly from the surface. There are miniature trees with minimal root systems that Jasper has developed. Artificial turf could be used, and many flowering plants would also be added. I would suggest including a playground for the children and even an area for a dog park. We need dogs here, don't you think?" I stopped speaking and wondered if I'd pushed too far. When I talked to Finn yesterday, he loved every idea and said the base could afford it. But I wasn't sure the other Principals would be on board.

"Mara, I believe you have three avid fans before you," Edison said praisingly. "Finn and Helen, would you like to discuss this privately, or do you want to decide on this second proposal now?" Finn and Helen agreed to vote immediately. The proposal was approved, but they requested this project would also need a committee. They would require time to review the written submissions and the corresponding analyses.

I thanked them profusely and said I would begin establishing the committees. After I hugged Helen and Edison, Finn and I left the room. I whooped for joy as we walked down the hall toward the elevator.

"Finn, I'm dancing on cloud nine. Thank you for encouraging me to do this. I can't thank you enough, too, for doing all the legwork for the written proposals. The cost analyses, budgets, etc., were beyond my education." I stopped him as I grasped his hand, then wrapped my arms around him.

"You did most of it, love. You were a fast learner. Although, you'll have a large task ahead of you, and so does everyone else involved. I'd love to help if you need any more assistance." His bright green eyes gazed into my excited blue ones and I smiled happily. "I know you can do this." He kissed me sweetly and I hugged him again.

"I still don't know how we can afford everything around here. Finn, you honestly can't tell me how all of this is funded?"

He looked at me, raised his dark eyebrows, and whispered, "It's a secret. But you'll find out when the time is right."

"Hmm. Being cryptic again? Are you in cahoots with the good Lord?" I smiled again and palmed his behind.

He laughed, then quipped in his Irish accent, "I'll never tell, my sweet lass."

We picked up Gracie from the Marshall's place and took her to lunch at the American fare restaurant. My brothers Aaron and Jonas would also join us for a meal. We sat down and Gracie was so excited to see them. Both of my brothers crossed their eyes in that hilarious way that made her laugh with glee. We kept the conversation light and refrained from talking business. After our meal, we ushered Gracie back to her schooling, and the four of us took the elevator to the meeting floor.

Finn brought the meeting to order, said a gathering prayer, and I advised our entire team about the dream I had last night. They listened intently, then their eyes opened wide in surprise as I mentioned the voice that had spoken to me.

"Y'all serious? Heavens to Betsy, those caves must have been terrifying," Jasper blurted. His handsome face stared at me in shock, his dark eyes flashing with interest. "Any idea whom this voice might have belonged to?"

"Nope. Not a clue. I'm assuming an angel of the Lord," I theorized. As I sat waiting for more questions from the team, I felt unease from someone in the room. But I wasn't yet able to identify the culprit.

Basheer spoke up, saying, "You heard people speaking Hebrew, but that doesn't necessarily mean the location is in the Middle East. There are caves like you're describing in many places around the world, so we'll need more information and pray it will be forthcoming."

"I concur, *mes amis*. I will delve into this information and see if I can find the most viable locations. Your description of this desert locale sounds familiar, and I'll search my databases and see what I can find. As to the caves, you say this was a hidden vault, and a plethora of items were stored within this place? Do you know who the body may have belonged to, *mon cher?*" Armie inquired with an arched eyebrow.

I thought about it briefly, then responded, "Not specifically. However, it was someone of significant importance—and I'd say, blessed. But I didn't feel this document belonged to this person. Though why it was placed with this specific figure, I couldn't say. Regarding the scroll, I'm positive it's an ancient map. However, I've no clue what the seven different symbols mean. I wish I had more information to give you."

As I stopped speaking, I felt the same unease again, but now I knew who it was. I casually glanced at Armie, and it was unquestionably him. As I tried to read his mind once more, I felt his surprise, agitation, and a bit of trepidation. There was still no way to penetrate his psyche any deeper, but I also knew it wasn't right for me to invade his thoughts.

"Let's move on, mates," Edison urged. He turned on the large computer screen on the wall and clicked a few keys on his laptop. "According to reliable watchers, several mercenaries have been hired by a powerful yet unknown entity. We're assuming this is the demon our prophet warned us about. As you know, he's after something important, but what this item is or why he wants it is still a mystery. At this time, we only have intel on two of the mercs he's hired for this upcoming job. This first man is an American by the name of Simon Maharis. He's an ex-Army ranger with ties to the Russian mob and is an expert tracker and sniper." The photo of this man wasn't clear, but he had a shaved scalp, was in his early forties, lean but well-muscled, and portrayed the image of a charming, grinning boy-next door.

Edison displayed a photo of the second man. This mercenary was of Middle East descent with a strong, hard-looking face, jet-black hair cut close to his scalp, and a ruthless expression. He was in his mid-thirties, with a thin frame, and had a trim mustache and beard.

Edison continued, "This second man is Saalim Hadid, and he's the one who worries me the most. He was active-duty military with the United Arab Emirates for many years. This man is well-trained and has been reported as ruthless and good at everything he does. This includes recon, tracking, demolition, and information extraction, which means torture. But four years ago, he went AWOL, then off the grid. But we have it on good authority that he's been working under contract for someone important. We think it's the demon. Our watchers spotted both of these men and nine others in Belize. They arrived on different flights within the same day, then departed promptly the next day to parts unknown. There's no information as to who they met while visiting Belize. We're attempting to locate them again, but we're hoping our Gatekeepers can provide this intel now that we have their names and photos." Edison looked pointedly at my brothers and me, and we nodded in understanding.

"Mates, I believe we have a lot of work ahead of us. Let's begin our research, and we'll also consult with our prophet. Does anyone have other questions, comments, or concerns?" Edison asked. Everyone shook their heads, and he concluded the meeting.

Edison, Finn, Helen, Jonas, Aaron, and I stayed behind after everyone else left the room. Edison handed my brothers and me copies of the two mercenaries' photos. I traced each face with my fingers and took a few minutes to concentrate on them. My brothers did the same. After several minutes, we set the photos aside.

I gave everyone in the room my psychic impressions. "These two men aren't possessed by evil. Of that, I'm sure. Regarding Saalim Haddid, he did a lot of work for an underground revolutionary group in Yemen, though not as a hitman. I don't see him as a cold-blooded killer. He was more of an intelligence gatherer and did minimal work as an enforcer. But he's no longer with this group. Someone of great power hired him, but Saalim doesn't know who pays his salary. Edison, your analysis is incorrect. This merc is not the one we have to worry about. This man's conscience has been in flux regarding the misdeeds he's committed, and he wants out of this life. But he greatly fears his new employer. He knows not to question or leave his current boss in fear of being assassinated."

I continued, saying, "The one we need to fear more is Simon Maharis. Beneath the charming exterior lies a very ruthless and cunning individual. He enjoyed his work with the Russian mob, which included being an enforcer, human trafficker, and hitman. No job is too slimy for this mercenary and he likes hurting people. The money offered by this new employer was too enticing to refuse. What scares me about this guy is his intelligence, which seems to be off the scale, and I get hints that he's involved in something dark and dangerous—outside of simply being a merc. He doesn't appear to be in charge of the mercs either, and he also has never met the one who pays him. I can't seem to go any deeper into his mind, though. Jonas and Aaron, did you get any other information on these two men?" I peered at them, hoping they had more to add to my assessments.

Aaron spoke up, "I agree with Mara. Maharis is the dangerous one. I wish I could get a sense of who they work for. My impression is that his employer has hired an intermediary that handles all communications with these mercs. I feel an intense evil when I think about their employer, but that's all I can get at this time. No locations come into view either, which is frustrating. As Mara has said, I can't delve any deeper into Maharis's psyche either. Did you get anything else, Jonas?"

"I'm afraid not. But it seems this demon keeps moving around, never staying in one place for long. I also agree with my siblings' judgments regarding these two men. Nothing was coming through as to their thought processes. But this isn't surprising since the Chosen can't always get mental connections with laypeople. It's hit or miss, and if this demon is smart, he won't hire anyone that can be easily read. He must know that the Chosen, especially the Gatekeepers, are highly psychic. It makes sense that he'd try to hire people not predisposed to telepathic intrusion. This could be a real problem in gaining the intelligence we require."

"I agree, Jonas. Should we try once more?" I asked my brothers.

"But let's only attempt to get current or future information from their minds." They agreed, and we began concentrating on their photos once more. As I dove deeper into their psyches, a shield blocked my way, and I tried several more times and finally gave up. As I pulled out and gazed at my brothers, I thought they had the same issue. When I peered at Finn, Edison, and Helen, they had the strangest look.

"What is it?" I asked in puzzlement. They didn't answer, then I heard it. Jonas and Aaron were humming a tune in unison.

I glared at my brothers, and they both answered, "What?"

"Why are you both intoning that song?" I asked incredulously.

Jonas answered with irritation, "What song? I wasn't doing anything."

Finn piped in, "Yes, you were. All three of you started humming together while concentrating on those photos. I believe it's the children's tune, 'The Wheels on the Bus Go Round and Round.' "

"I was too?" I inquired in a stunned voice.

"That's affirmative," Edison said, still baffled.

I thought about it momentarily and then blurted out in shock, "This demon has chosen these specific mercenaries for a reason. He has placed a block against any psychic intrusion using this simple tune. This devil knows exactly what he's doing and how to stop us from reading his non-demon crew. I have to assume someone's past is set in stone in their minds, so that's how we obtained this basic information. But deeper memories can be blocked, and current events are always subject to change and can be hidden by extensive training with mind control. How on earth are we going to get around this dilemma?"

Everyone sat in silence, pondering this major wrench into our investigation. Unfortunately, it appeared no one had an answer at the moment.

Finn finally spoke up, "I think we may have to hope the good Lord will provide help on this problem. In the meantime, is there anything else we need to address?"

"Yes," I replied. "I'd like to clarify that these three dreams are all related to this demon's plans. I assume God will continue to provide more clarification as to my visions and maybe even help me to see more of them. I'll keep you advised if I learn anything new."

Finn nodded and said, "Okay then. Let's close for now, and we'll continue researching this hellion. In the meantime, we must continue our pursuit of these myrmidon hives and their eradication. Our Beta team has taken out a hive in Maryland, and the Delta team is on its way to Georgia. I'll also keep you apprised on this front as well. Thanks again, my good friends."

After our meeting, I walked away with a knot in my stomach. That recurring sense of dread left a bitter taste in my mouth. Now we've added this frightening merc named Maharis into the mix. *Who was this guy, and why was it when I thought of him, my vision only perceived a vivid hue of a bloody red wall?*

CHAPTER 4

The following day, I met with Jasper and the Rileys. They agreed to head up the committees that were required for the projects and would also seek volunteers to fill the committee seats. They were excited to begin these important endeavors, and I asked if they'd kindly keep me apprised of their progress.

After speaking with my new project managers, I volunteered at the veterinarian clinic at the base. Dr. Joanne Sanderson, who was the resident vet, had kindly granted my request to be a liaison between her and the patients. I spent the morning assisting with a Siamese kitten who was to be spayed and communicated with the feline, keeping her calm, secure, and content. All-in-all, I was pleased I could alleviate an animal's stress during a frightening time at the vet's office.

After having lunch at home, I snuggled into the lounge chair and began thinking about the visions. We desperately needed more information, so I decided to concentrate and see if God would work through me once more.

An overwhelming blackness consumes my vision. My spirit is moving, so I simply wait, hoping my perspective will clear. Ahead of me, I see specks of light. Then thousands of stars and colorful planets of every size surround me. Moons and suns encompass the planets. As I maneuver at great speed again, I enter through vast and colorful nebulas and many galaxies. There's even a "whooshing" sound, plus pings and sparks, but I find this odd since I'm traveling through space. Isn't the cosmos a vacuum—so how can this be? After several minutes, I approach another giant planet ahead that has three moons and one sun. My spirit descends to this world through several layers of its atmosphere, then I'm soaring above mountains, oceans, large land masses, and lakes. I fly lower now toward strange-looking animals grazing the lush green fields. Up ahead is a vast and unforgiving desert with more bizarre-looking creatures roaming the barren landscape.

I progress toward an extensive mountain range and up to the top of the crest of the highest peak. There are massive layers of ice and snow. As I peer closer, someone is moving over the mountain. This person has the stature of a giant, and upon his back are folded wings of transparent glowing filaments. More of these beings join the first and begin chanting toward the heavens. As I observe this awe-inspiring scene, tears of joy fill my eyes, and I wonder if I should be witnessing this astounding miracle. A loud boom cracks across the sky and a flash of light breaks through the snow and ice, then arcs to the ground beneath. The beings, which I believe are angels, continue chanting praise, then a blue fire burns where the savage light beam has struck the ground.

A distinct voice echoes in the recesses of my mind, speaking the language of the angels from the beginning of time. "These are My words to which My judgment shall be witnessed. Protect them as you would Me, your God. The Lamb, who shall return as the Lion, will execute My divine plan, and those who I created in my image shall be judged. At the time of My pronouncement, there will be seven seals for seven punishments, and only the righteous shall be given salvation.

Hear Me now, let no one lay their stain upon My edict. Only those of My choosing shall approach it until the Lion returns to do My bidding."

The blue flame dissipates, and what is left is a glowing closed scroll. The outer covering is imprinted with the words of the angels, and a raised gold seal protects its contents against unworthy witnesses.

MY EYES blinked open in amazement, then tightly closed again as I sobbed with tears of overwhelming emotion. I moved to the floor and prostrated myself before God as unworthiness consumed me. Even though I heard familiar voices calling to me in the distance, I yelled at them to let me be. Other voices inside my head whispered songs of love and assurance, and my turbulent emotions ebbed to a normal rhythm.

I was still lying face down on the floor when I opened my eyes and saw my dear husband's tearful gaze. He was lying on the floor by my side, rubbing my back as he whispered tender and consoling words. I smiled at him and then uttered, "Hello."

"Mara, sweetheart, are you okay? You scared us to death."

"I'm so sorry. Wait—us?"

"Aye. Your brothers are here too. Don't forget that the three of us are connected with you. Your turbulent emotions sent us a fire alarm and we ran over here ASAP." Finn still stroked my back and he then asked, "Can you get up now?"

"Yes. I'm okay."

Finn helped me to my feet, and as I looked up, my brothers' faces were before me, ashen with fear.

"Jonas, Aaron, I'm so sorry. But trust me, I didn't expect to experience a vision like this. I need to sit down for a few minutes." Finn led me to the sofa, and Asher ran over from his hiding place and curled his body tightly onto my lap, not taking his gaze from my face. "I'm fine, baby." I stroked his soft fur and kissed him. Finn pulled me into his arms and I laid my head on his shoulder.

"Take all the time you need, Mara. But, I have to ask, did this vision come to you out of the blue?"

I shook my head in denial, then replied, "No. I wanted to try and obtain more information on the object we're supposed to find. But I never expected anything this intense."

My brothers each took a turn kissing my cheek and sat at the other end of the sofa. I blew my nose several times into the tissues Finn handed me and thought about the recent vision. Several minutes passed, then I pulled away from Finn and began relating all I had witnessed in minute detail. I asked Aaron to record my account so none of the information would be forgotten. When I finished, there was silence except for Asher's purr.

"Wow! I mean—wow!" Jonas exclaimed in awe.

"Exactly. What can one say after hearing such an astounding account?" Aaron asked as he rubbed his hands over his face.

"This was the most glorious vision I've ever witnessed. It was God speaking with his angels and giving them instructions. The planet I saw did not resemble Earth, so I wonder if it was Heaven or maybe it was this planet millions of years ago. Who's to say? But the Seven Seals from Revelation? That is definitely a 'wow.' At least now we know what this demon is after. Why does he want it? But does it matter? All we know is that we must keep it from him at all costs. We need the current location of the scroll." Sitting in silence again, we pondered this surprising new information.

"Mara, please stay here and rest, and I'll gather the team for a quick meeting." I began to protest at Finn's suggestion, but he stopped me, saying, "We have your account on this recording. I'll play this for the team, then we'll meet again once everyone has had the time to digest your vision." I consented, and he gave me a quick kiss. "Aaron and Jonas, please stay with your sister until she's recovered."

They both agreed, and Finn pulled out his phone to assemble the team as he walked toward the door. As he turned back with one last look in my direction, he was obviously angry. His eyes were now guarded, brows slightly lowered, jaw clenched, and I physically felt the tenseness within his gait. I hoped we could discuss his anger once he returned from the meeting. But he didn't come home as he said he would, and I tried calling and texting him, but he didn't answer. A few hours later, he messaged me with a terse, "I'll be back in time for supper."

Finn did return by dinnertime as Gracie and I were about to sit at the dining table. After he washed his hands at the kitchen sink, he kissed Gracie on the top of her head, then sat down to join us. He chatted animatedly with her about her day and only glanced at me when necessary. Tears pooled in my eyes, but I quickly blinked them away. Obviously, he was still upset but hid it well from Gracie. After dinner, we watched television as a family, but I had no clue what had been on the TV. We put Gracie to bed and then returned to the living room. I closed Gracie's bedroom door, and Finn began turning out the lights.

"Finn, stop. We need to talk about what's going on here. Please."

He halted as he was about to turn off the last light in the room and lifted his head to peer at me.

"Let's go to bed, Mara. It's been a long day."

"No. Finn, I know you're upset with me, and we must discuss it. You've been punishing me all afternoon, and I've no clue what I did to deserve it. I love you and refuse to allow anything bad to fester between us." The tears threatened to spill over again, but I angrily brushed them away and sat on the sofa. "Please sit and tell me what I did that made you so angry." I couldn't look directly at him, fearful I would cry.

He sat down but stared straight ahead, saying nothing. I waited, hoping he would open up. Finally, he turned to face me.

"Yes, I'm angry. Look, I know these visions are who you are now, and I also understand their importance in the battles we must undertake. But I find you reckless when you deliberately initiate one when there's no one around to look out for you. It scares me to death when I find you lying on the floor and wonder if, one of these times, a vision might even take your life. Do you know how terrifying it is for me and everyone else who loves you?" Tears were in his eyes as he said these heartfelt words, and guilt consumed me.

I grasped Finn's hands, kissed his cheek, and replied, "I'm truly sorry. You're correct; it was foolish of me. I'm used to doing whatever I want, whenever I want that it didn't occur to me how these visions could affect the ones who love me. But as you said, these visions are part of our lives now. How do we rectify this, Finn?"

"None of us can control visions that happen spontaneously. But I ask that you let me or your brothers know when you plan on initiating one. Someone should always be with you in case we're needed. Please promise me you'll agree to this, Mara." Finn tightened his grip on my hands.

"I agree to your request. Again, I'm sorry I scared you, and I'll also apologize to my brothers tomorrow. But Finn, when you're upset with me, please don't walk away, then punish me for hours afterward. It doesn't accomplish anything—especially when I had no clue what I'd done. I understand if one of us is angry and needs to cool our tempers before we talk, but if we're having a problem, it should be discussed as soon as possible. Does any of this make sense, and are we good now? I hate when you're upset with me." I looked pleadingly into his gorgeous green eyes, and he gave me that wink that made my knees weak.

"We're good now, and I hated being upset with you too. You're right; I shouldn't have let it fester in me so long—and I think I *was* trying to punish you. I'm sorry too. Please accept my apology." He was sincere, and I gave him a thankful smile. I was relieved this mess had passed.

He grinned at me and gave me a hug and a noisy kiss on my cheek. "Now, let's get to bed because I'm suddenly exhausted. I'm even too tired to make love to you tonight, my sweet. Rain check for later?" Finn stood and offered his hand and pulled me up.

"What? Are you sick of me already? I knew it would happen, but so soon?" I faked being hurt, snorted loudly, and punched him playfully in the arm. I commented in a more serious tone, "I'm tired too. Oh, by the way, I have an early training session tomorrow on how to fight with those Ninja Sai knives. Would you have time to take Gracie to daycare?"

"Not a problem. After I drop her off, I'm going to the gym for a workout. So, you'll learn how to use those things, huh?"

"Yup. I feel I'm being guided to learn another skill, so why not? *Ayyy-ya!*" I did a quiet imitation of a Ninja warrior yell and threw in a few exaggerated Karate chops with my hands. Finn smirked at my antics and took my hands in his, and his expression grew serious.

"By the way, Mara, I know I never told you that I have an FAA license to fly single-engine airplanes, but I'd like to become licensed to fly twin engines as well as helicopters. I've been thinking about it and would like to complete my education. What do you think?"

"Wow, I had no idea you could fly an airplane. That's so cool, Finn. You should continue your education if that's what you want to do. It would also be useful if one of our mission pilots becomes injured—though, I sure hope that never happens to anyone on our team."

"Good thinking, love; that's also an added benefit." He released my hands and continued, "I became a private pilot when I was in my early thirties in my previous life. It was always something I wanted to try, but I learned that I enjoyed it. I have to say, it's been a while, so it may take a few hours to get the hang of the single-engine again."

"Finn, with your talents and smarts, I know you'll fly right through it." I snorted at my pun, and Finn chuckled so hard he snorted too. We laughed again, and he stopped before me and caressed my cheek with his finger.

"I really love you, Mara." His eyes grew dark as he stared deeply into mine. "You know that, don't you?"

"I do, and I love you too, my handsome Neanderthal." I leaned in and kissed him soundly. Then pulling away, I screwed up my face into a chipmunk impression and clacked my teeth together.

Finn laughed, made his caveman face, bent over, then staggered like a drunk gorilla to our bedroom. I stifled my giggles as I turned off the last lamp and followed my delightful primitive beast to bed.

Thankfully, I had a dreamless night for a change, but I still woke up tired and was reluctant to get out of bed. Sighing, I kissed Finn as he slept, checked on sleeping Gracie, and left early for my training session.

My trainer was patient but thorough, and I enjoyed learning to use the Sai knives. The lesson was over in two hours, and as I bowed to my trainer, I caught sight of Finn and several others watching me from the doorway. I put the two weapons in their protective cases, grabbed my bag, and headed to the door.

"Mara, my Lord in Heaven, is there nothing you can't do? By the end, you looked like you had been using those knives all your life," Finn commented and hugged me.

"Thanks, Finn. God has given me the ability and knowledge to do these things. I'm amazed too. My trainer said I'd need a few more lessons and should be fully adept with these weapons. Hopefully, I can finish the training next week. I'm heading home to take a shower and grab a quick bite. Then afterward, I'll meet you at the pool to start our scuba training. I have to admit, I'm somewhat nervous about this."

"Love, you can do it. God wouldn't give you something you couldn't handle. I'll be learning along with you, Aaron, Basheer, and Xavier. We're lucky we have Jonas, Edison, and Billie, who are pros at scuba and underwater demolition and can teach us everything they know."

"I'll be there, Finn." I gave him a quick kiss and returned to our apartment.

The lessons at the swimming pool were fun, and I enjoyed the training. We had excellent instructors, and it wasn't long before we were adept at the equipment as well as maneuvering underwater when carrying the weight of the oxygen tanks. After a couple of hours, Edison called a halt and said we did a great job and would meet again in two days for one more lesson. We would then travel by boat a few miles from shore and conduct a deep-sea ocean dive.

"The pool is easy with this equipment, but the ocean is a different animal. You add tides, choppy waters, murkiness, sharks, etc., which can be harrowing for your first time. Take your showers and change, and we have our team meeting in one hour. See you there," Edison said.

When I left the water, I felt like a beached whale. Finn smiled knowingly as he and my other student team members felt the same. But after a shower and a few prayers, I felt better. Grabbing another bottled water and a power bar, I headed to the meeting. I scowled with distress as I rode the elevator to the meeting floor. *We had to discover what God needed from us, as I knew we were running out of time. But where was this artifact, and would we find it in time?*

CHAPTER 5

Our meeting was in full swing, and we discussed my visions and how we should interpret them.

I spoke up, saying, "As far as I know, we must find this scroll that somehow relates to the Seven Seals of Revelation. This scroll appears to be a map, but my gut says this doesn't matter. We're not to view it without being chosen specifically by God. We're not even allowed to touch this sacred object. And in that same vision, I have no clue who the voice was talking about regarding the Order of Solomon's Temple. Hopefully, the Lord will also provide the identity of this Order. Also, we don't know where the scroll is located. How much time do we have before the demon and his mercs find it? These things are currently unknown. Our only information is that it's underground in some type of cave system. We can assume it's in the Middle East, but that's only an educated guess. So where do we go from here, my friends?" I felt something coming from Armie again, and it drove me crazy. He looked as if he had been struck in the face. *What had I said that caused his shocked expression, and what was he hiding?*

"I believe the key to everything is the mercs. But this demon chose well when he hired them. How do we get past their defenses? Mara, can you and your brothers try again?" Finn inquired, rubbing his forehead in frustration.

"We have no choice. They have the information, which are the only leads we have. Pass me their photos again—especially the one of Maharis." Edison handed it over, and I cleared my mind and let down my outer psychic walls. The rest of the team murmured amongst themselves as I delved into the mind of this mercenary.

I SEE some of his recent past again, which doesn't tell me much, so I move forward in his mind but hear the nursery rhyme again. For some reason, I can't seem to budge it, no matter how hard I push. Lowering another significant protective wall from my psyche, I move in closer. Bingo! I spot him and realize he's now in San Francisco at a well-known major hotel. As I continue watching the scene before me, a malicious intrusion enters my psyche, and I freeze in place.

"MARA! DANG IT—STOP HIM!" Two voices screamed inside my head, and I fought hard to heed their warning. It felt like I was swimming in quicksand and sliding deeper into the muck.

What is wrong with me? I shouted inside my head, and then I felt a slam and a bang as a massive wall went up in front of my vision.

"Mara! Come out of this, now!" I heard Finn's frantic voice as I blinked my eyes and focused on my husband. My chair had been turned around, facing away from the table, and the merc's photo had been torn from my grasp. Jonas and Aaron were beside me, holding my hands. Finn knelt in front of me, his expression filled with terror.

"What happened?" I asked urgently.

Jonas spoke up, "Sis, the demon had a grip on your mind and

attempted to take you over. Aaron and I had to enter your psyche and build a major wall. Are you okay? Please tell us you're fine!"

I blinked, shook my head, and rubbed my face in frustration. "Umm, yeah. At least, I think so. The demon entered my mind? Dang! I had to lower one of my major walls to get further into the merc, but I still had another one up. This demon must be fierce." Finn wrapped his arms around me and hugged me in relief. After a minute, he finally let me go. I then turned my chair around to face the table and the other team members. My friends looked petrified.

"I'm okay, honest," I murmured. "We've learned something here today—and it was a hard lesson. Although, we at least discovered one of the merc's locations." I gave the team the current whereabouts of Maharis.

"Mara, did the demon obtain any critical information from you?" Edison asked as he leaned forward in his chair.

I took a few minutes to search my mind for possible information leaks and replied, "No, I don't believe so. My major wall has our base, personnel, and private information behind it, so I think we're safe. Jonas, Aaron, how long was he in my mind?"

"Barely a few seconds," Aaron said. "We felt him as he tried to enter, then we saw your body and face freeze, then your mind. You still blocked him, but he tried everything to penetrate your final wall. We're quite sure we blocked him in time, so we agree with your assessment."

"That's a relief. Are we done here? I think Mara needs a break," Finn responded with concern.

"No, Finn, I'm fine. There's something else," I spoke up but was cautious about discussing the next subject. I inhaled a deep breath and spat out the information. "Through my link with Maharis, I saw that the demon and the mercs need Jonas and me to find the scroll. They know the basic location but need us to locate the exact hiding place. They require our skills to get to the artifact."

"Son-of-a—" Finn started to swear. "Why would they need you, and how do they even know about the two of you and your skills?"

Jonas, Aaron, and I looked at each other and came to the same conclusion.

"Okay, I'll give my two-cents worth," Jonas said. "I think information from the three of us was obtained when we tried to rescue Isabella. When all three of us jumped into that mid-level demon's mind, he may have transmitted the Gatekeepers' abilities to other demons. The three of us had previously discussed this possibility after that mission, but we had no evidence that our assumptions could be correct. Until now, that is."

Everyone at the table was deep in thought as they digested this information. We politely waited until they were ready for further discussion.

"So—the demons of Hell know about the Gatekeepers' skills. Man-oh-man, doll, is this what you're sayin'?" Billie asked in her strong New York accent, and her purple hair appeared even brighter than before.

I said, "That's our educated guess, which we believe to be true. But that's all they know. Although I have to say, they'd find out eventually. Look how many demons we've already killed using our skills. It was only a matter of time."

Finn replied, saying, "She's correct. They'd have discovered the Gatekeepers' talents after all their battles with evil. It's irrelevant. Our issue now is how to get to the scroll before the demon. Obviously, they know more than us."

"The thing is, they need us as much as we need them to find this thing. Maybe we can work it to our advantage," I said contemplatively.

"Go on..." I had piqued Finn's interest, as well as everyone else in the room. I told them of a possible plan that may help us find the scroll. As I continued relaying my idea, Finn's eyes flashed with anger.

"Mara, you've got to be joking! Not a chance and no way on God's green earth!" Finn barked, jumped to his feet in frustration, and stomped across the room.

"Do you have another idea, Finn?"

He was about to protest again, but Edison stopped his objection with a wave of his hand. "Mara's plan is a good one. Is it dangerous? Yes. But it could work. Let's mull over this proposed idea for twenty-four hours, and maybe someone can develop something better."

We waited a day, but no one could think of another viable plan. I even tried with Finn in attendance, to gain more intel through another vision. None was forthcoming. I knew in my heart we had to implement what God had foretold in my dream, but I was also aware it could ultimately be a foolhardy and suicidal mission.

CHAPTER 6

My scuba team finished training out to sea within the next couple of days. It was indeed harrowing but also intriguing. We were also taught how to attach explosives to the hull of ships. Edison even had us do a night dive, which was quite an experience but not enjoyable. At least I now had the training and should do well if it was required on a mission.

A few days later, our teams took out two massive myrmidon hives. One had been in New Jersey and the other in New Mexico. Our next target was Wyoming. This was a much smaller hive with approximately ten myrmidons, so Jonas and I said we could handle this mission. We made our strategic plans and flew into the targeted location.

The myrmidon hive was in an isolated area surrounded by approximately twenty acres of heavily wooded forest. Before we proceeded to their hideout, Jonas and I said the St. Michael prayer and asked for his protection and guidance.

We left our vehicle and trekked to the myrmidons' location. I would've found the scenery beautiful with all of the golden-colored leaves of fall if it hadn't been for the damp chill in the air and the approaching storm clouds. My palms sweated, and my heart raced, but I did my best to hide my trepidation from Jonas, although I knew he felt the same.

According to my brother, who had spirit walked into the compound, seven myrmidons were on the lower level, with three more in the basement. We carefully approached the building and entered to begin our assault. The air reeked from the myrmidon's rotting stink, and we could sense their locations. God gave us every skill needed to find and destroy evil. We fired our automatic weapons and didn't stop until this floor was cleared.

"You okay, sis?"

"Perfect."

We proceeded to the top of the basement stairwell, gave each other a nod, and carefully descended the stairs. As we reached the bottom, we didn't see any myrmidons but continued our search. I halted as I felt the heavy, oppressive weight of evil. One lackey tried approaching me from behind, but I twisted my body around, dropped to my knees, and fired two shots at my quarry's forehead. He dropped like a stone, and I returned to scan every room. As Jonas and I neared the rear of the basement, we killed the last two myrmidons, who we found hiding behind an ancient boiler. The place reeked of dead minions and the acrid smell of gunfire.

Our next job was to eliminate the remains. We gathered their bodies together in two piles, one on each floor. I pulled out a small, hand-held flame thrower device and set each pile of bodies on fire. Once the low burning blue holy fire enveloped the demons, I tossed the flame thrower on top of the heaps so it would also be destroyed. We waited until all the evidence was eradicated, leaving only a small blue fog that surrounded what had once been the devil's lackeys. After praying for God's protection and assistance, we returned to the main floor, scanned the building mentally, and agreed the property was still clear.

"Remember, Mara, we have to discharge all of our special ammo before we leave this cabin, then put in the other clip with the standard semi-automatic rifle rounds."

"I wish we didn't have to do this, Jonas." But I agreed, and we reluctantly emptied our weapon clips into the plasterboard of one of the inner walls of the cabin.

"Okay, let's move out." I gave Jonas a look of resignation, and we walked out the cabin's back door. We moved in the direction where we'd parked our vehicle approximately four miles out.

Jonas and I remained quiet as we started our return to our transportation. It was raining heavily as the storm had reared its ugly head. The wind picked up, and the golden leaves hanging on to the tree's limbs lost their tight grip and blew precariously to the damp ground below.

"Jonas..." I whispered to him through my mic, and we crouched low to the ground, our rifles raised. He felt it too. Something was coming for us, although it wasn't evil. But it was ominous. We crawled over to a large tree but had no idea who was tracking us. They were directly ahead, but then we heard something from our right.

"Dang, it!" Jonas mentally swore, and I couldn't help but hear it in my mind. "We better split up. Watch your six, and I'll see you on the other side," Jonas said and winked at me as he took off at a low run to the south, and I ran to the west.

As I jogged, I knew this was the vision I'd been seeing over the last month. I continued sprinting in earnest, tripping over a couple of fallen logs. After picking myself back up, I started moving again.

Crack—boom! I cringed as the storm's lightning strike hit something nearby, and I jumped at the intense noise. The rain pelted my skin like ice, and I tripped over another fallen log. I panted, trying to catch my breath. This was all playing out exactly like my dream.

"Jonas!" I screamed as I tried to connect psychically with my brother. *Where is he, and why isn't he responding?* Jonas shouldn't be too far from my location, but I couldn't connect with him. Several of my pursuers could be heard several yards behind me and were following me at an alarming rate. I knew I was being herded in a specific direction, but there wasn't anything I could do to alter my situation.

"Mara, there's no use running from us because we will capture you. We already have your brother. So stop and make it easy on yourself."

These were the exact words from my vision. I let the scene play out again before me, and I dreaded the moment that I'd be knocked unconscious—and it happened all too soon.

OH, my head! It felt like it was splitting in two, and nausea rolled through my stomach. My body shivered from the intense cold and shock, making my teeth chatter. I tried to open my eyes, but they felt heavy and wouldn't respond to my command. After trying once more, they finally lifted. The brightness made my head pound harder, and I tried to place my hand over my eyes, but they wouldn't obey either.

Trying to focus on my surroundings, I noticed I was in a small bare room, and Jonas sat ten feet across from me, apparently unconscious and bound to a metal chair. His hands and feet were tightly fettered to his seat with zip ties. His handsome face looked pale, bruised, and scratched, and he was soaking wet. His thick, short blond hair was plastered to his scalp. But to my relief, he appeared to be breathing with no visible significant injuries.

"Jonas!" I said aloud, trying to awaken him. I tried using our psychic link again, but he still didn't stir.

My hands and feet were also bound to a metal chair with the same restraints. My head still ached, but the nausea was ebbing. I tried wriggling my hands and feet, but they were held fast to the chair that was attached securely to the floor. My limbs felt numb, and my hands and feet tingled as if they'd been asleep. Of course, all my weapons and the remainder of my gear had been taken.

I continued to assess my surroundings. The walls were made of cement, but the room didn't appear underground because of one window behind Jonas. It was boarded up, but I could see the fading daylight between the wooden slats. Iron bars were across the boards, so we couldn't escape by removing the wood from the window frame.

There was an old wooden table against another wall with a lamp, some syringes, vials, a bottle of alcohol, and cotton swabs. *That doesn't look promising.* There was a small bed on each side of the room. Each one had a heavy metal headboard and footrail, including a handcuff and ankle chain. I noticed a door to my left and one behind me. The one on the left was made of steel with a combination keypad lock. The other one was a simple wooden door that had no locking mechanism. A small fuel oil furnace was the only heat source in the room.

Listening intently, I heard two men talking outside the room, but I couldn't determine what they were saying.

"Oh, crap! I think I'm going to hurl," Jonas slurred. He was stirring and trying to return to full consciousness. Turning in my direction, he looked toward me with a barely focused gray-blue stare. "Mara?"

"Yup! I would've preferred a room with a better view. Is this the best accommodation you could afford, Jonas?" I was trying to keep the panic out of my voice.

"Uh, sorry about that. You know I *am* saving to buy an estate on the French Riviera."

After giving Jonas a wry grimace, I said, "What the heck did they hit us with? I feel lousy."

"I believe it was a sonic weapon. I didn't know it had been refined to work this well without killing the target," Jonas replied

"Lovely," I retorted with sarcasm.

I snorted out loud but now heard voices coming near the outer door. There were four beeps, the door clicked, and two huge men entered the room. They wore military clothing and masks, and each man carried a set of fatigues and boots.

"Ahh. Our sleeping beauties awake." This was said by a white man with an American accent. The two men walked toward the table and dropped the clothing, and then each one picked up a syringe and a vial. They each filled their syringes and strode toward us.

The man who'd been speaking, whom I named Rocco, saw the panicked look on our faces and said, "Don't worry. This injection is for the aftereffects of the sonic weapon. It'll make you feel much better, you'll see."

Rocco rolled up my sleeve, quickly cleaned my arm, and injected me with the antidote. Jonas was getting the same treatment from the other guard.

"It should take about ten minutes before the medication takes full effect," Rocco said.

As the two men were leaving the room, Jonas and I tried to see what numbers they punched into the keypad to unlock the door. But they were efficient at blocking our view.

After they departed, I asked Jonas within my mind, "You getting anything from them yet?"

"Not much. Only stuff from their childhood, then that darn school bus song was playing in my head. I don't think we've traveled far since we were knocked out. According to my body's time clock, it's only been about two hours. That's all I know at the moment. You?"

"I read the same thing, then that song started in my head too. They're not possessed by evil, but we both already knew that. I hope this shaking will stop. It's hard to concentrate with my teeth clattering like a rattler's tail," I said with frustration.

About fifteen minutes later, a couple of our captors returned. This time it was Rocco and a tough-looking woman. They were both wearing their face masks. Luckily, Jonas and I felt better, except for freezing to death.

The hulk of a woman grabbed a stack of clothes from the table, walked toward me, and said in a thick German accent, "Okay, *frëulein*, you're going first. You get to take a hot shower and a change of clothes. Behave yourself, and everything will go smoothly for you. At least, for now." She cut my zip ties, grabbed my arm, and steered me through the wooden door. It was a bathroom with a sink, a toilet, and a shower stall.

The room had no window, but the shower contained towels, soap, and shampoo.

The woman still had my arm in a vice grip as we walked toward the shower. She turned on the water, looked at me, and said, "Okay, girlie, use the toilet, then strip, shower, wash your hair, and get warm. We don't want our prisoners dying from exposure. At least, not yet." Releasing my arm, she backed up to sit on a stool in the corner of the tiny bathroom. She kept her hand on the pistol at her hip.

I followed her orders to a tee. After I undressed, I noticed she stared curiously at the Holy Trinity tattoo on my upper left arm—the mark Jesus had given me when I died and went to Heaven. The shower felt wonderful, and I spent much time warming up my freezing body. Once the shaking subsided, I bathed, dressed, and walked to the sink and mirror. There were several scratches on my face, and I used the antibiotic ointment tube on the counter. At least my lips were no longer blue, and my teeth had stopped chattering.

"A comb, brush, and deodorant are in the cabinet below. I expect you to continue to behave yourself, and we'll get along fine," the huge Amazon woman said through her mask. *This was one tough cookie.* She would be difficult to crack—if it was even a possibility. I entered her mind briefly. The scene before me was a child playing on a rope swing, and then a large woman walked out of a house, wiping her hands on a dish towel. She told the child it was time for dinner, and they returned inside. I sped forward in her mind, and then, "The wheels on the bus go round and round..." *Dang nabbit!*

I put on the clothes provided and was surprised they fit. After drying my hair, Lt. Amazon grabbed my arm again and steered me from the room. She sat me back in the metal chair and restrained me again using more zip ties.

Rocco guided Jonas to the bathroom for his turn at warming up. After they returned, he was also retied to his chair, and the two guards left us once more.

"Why the royal treatment?" I asked Jonas.

"Because they must really need us," he replied worriedly. "But that's a good thing. At least we have value at the moment."

I continued our conversation telepathically. I didn't want our captors to hear the remainder of our discussion.

"Jonas, I didn't get anything from that hulk of a woman. Just that freakin' song. Did you get any intel?"

"Nope. I detest that tune, Mara. I only know they're mercenaries. He's taking orders from someone powerful, though, which we know is the demon. I don't know how much they know about us, so we'll have to wait and see what happens next."

At that moment, the door clicked, and Rocco stepped back in, along with the first guy. I decided to call him Igor. There was no denying he was the "persuader" of the duo—he had a slimy look and even walked with a slight limp. *Peachy.*

Rocco said, "Now that you're both comfortable and not on the verge of death from hypothermia, we can start our discussions." He looked pointedly at Jonas and me and tried to give us a friendly smile. He failed.

Jonas spoke up, "So why do we have the distinct pleasure of your company?"

"You'll find out in due time. However, let's quit the pretense. We know you are Jonas and Mara Patrick: Brother and sister and two of the infamous Chosen Ones. Jonas, I know you can travel outside your body —spirit walking, I believe? Your special skills are of value to us. We need you, Jonas, but not your sister. She's here to make sure you do as you're told, so behave yourself," Rocco said, and he looked at us with a raised eyebrow as if asking for our compliance. Neither of us gave any indication of emotion or cooperation.

"So, what is it you need from me?" Jonas asked.

"Eager, are you? You're going to find something for us, then retrieve it. If you don't, that man over there will have fun with your sister."

Igor gimped over to me and punched me hard in the stomach. I uttered a loud "oomph" and doubled over in my seat.

"You son-of-a—!" Jonas yelled at Rocco.

"Now you know where we stand. Trust me when I say this man is well-versed in information retrieval and talented in torture techniques. That's a small warmup, if you will, of what this talented doctor can do. I'll leave you to think about what I've said," Rocco finished, and the two men left the room.

"Mara, are you all right?"

I tried to catch my breath, then whispered to Jonas, "Lovely." I hoped the agony would subside quickly, but I used my mind to block the pain. It took a few minutes, but the terrible ache finally dissipated.

"I'm okay, Jonas," I said as I carefully sat back in the rock-hard chair. "It's just my butt is falling asleep. Couldn't they give us softer seats?" I snickered, trying to ease the look of fear on Jonas's face.

"Hang in there, Mara. We'll get through this together," Jonas uttered compassionately.

"Yes, we will," I returned with a nervous smile. Turning away from Jonas, I wanted to hide my pained and fearful expression from his gaze. Doubt and frustration ran through me, and I didn't want Jonas to be aware of my negative feelings. A sense of dread filled my body because I knew something terrible was about to happen, but I had no clue what it was. A brief moment of terror flashed in my mind, and I could only pray that whatever happened to me, I would survive the upcoming nightmare.

CHAPTER 7

I jerked awake and glanced at Jonas, and he was asleep. Unfortunately, I had the dream about the caverns again that had been plaguing me the past few weeks. That feeling of impending doom was still in the back of my mind, and I did my best to dispel the fear.

I could no longer see daylight through the boards covering the windows, so it must be after dark. One lamp was lit in the corner of the room, providing adequate lighting.

"The dream again, eh?" Apparently, he hadn't been asleep as I had thought.

"Yup."

"Anything changed?"

"Nope. I guess that's reassuring." I sighed, then silently asked what time it was from the second person in my mind.

"Just after nine in the evening," was the response.

"Thanks," I replied. "Do you know where we are yet?"

"Affirmative," said the warm voice I knew so well.

I heard a noise from the other side of the door, and our two captors entered. That inkling of fear entered my mind again, but I quickly swallowed it and hid all emotion from my face.

It was Rocco and Lt. Amazon. They brought food and water and gave us another bathroom break.

As my guard took me into the restroom, I asked her again what this was about. I continued to relay simple questions to her, hoping to push her mind into relaying quick images I may intrude upon. She didn't answer my questions, so I tried again.

"Come on, can you at least tell me where you're going to take us? I mean, who on earth am I going to tell?"

She blinked hard and then gave me an angry stare. I shrugged my shoulders and began washing my face. I drifted into her psyche, and there it was again, "The Wheels on the Bus Go Round and Round...." I rolled my eyes after hearing that dreadful song, and it was apparent I could retrieve nothing from her mind.

"Hurry up, princess. I don't have all night," the huge woman squawked.

After cleaning up, she guided me back into the room and had me lay on one of the cots. She cuffed me again—one hand to the headboard and one ankle to the footrail. At least the chains were long enough so I could move a little bit and even sit up. She tossed some blankets over me, and it was now Jonas's turn. He and his guard returned a few minutes later, and he was chained to the other bed. Our captors left the one lamp on and departed the room, with the door locking securely behind them.

"Comfy?" I asked with a smirk on my face.

"Kiss my butt," he replied, blowing me a brotherly kiss across the room.

I moved my mind to Jonas and the other person riding my thoughts. "I didn't get anything from the Amazon. Just that crappy tune."

"Okay," Jonas responded quickly.

"Message received" was the answer I had been waiting intently to hear.

I continued, "We're tucked in for the night, and we'll touch base with you in the morning. Let's pray we get more intel. This is getting tedious, even though we're being treated quite well."

Then the voice replied, "Hang in there. We're here if you need us, but in the meantime, stay safe and sleep tight."

"Will do. Catch you in the morning," I responded, turning my mind to Jonas. "You get anything from Rocco?"

"Just that horrible song! I can't read him at all—I hate this!" he retorted loudly in my head.

"It's okay, brother. We'll get more—this much we do know. Let's get some sleep," I reassured him.

"Roger that, sis."

THE NEXT MORNING came all too soon. We were given another bathroom break and served a quick breakfast. Lt. Amazon was still guarding me, but there was a new guard for Jonas. It was Maharis. Even with his mask, it was apparent it was him. Rocco and Igor also walked into the room, carrying a coat and a pair of wrist and ankle restraints.

Rocco said, "Jonas, you're being taken elsewhere so we can test your so-called skills. Remember—we have your sister. If you don't cooperate at any time, all I have to do is contact my friend here," he indicated Igor, "and he'll take my displeasure out on your sister. Do we understand each other?"

My brother nodded, and he was re-shackled and escorted out the door. Maharis stared at my face, gave me a strange look, and departed the room.

As I sat in bed, I contacted the voice in my mind and told them the mercs were taking Jonas to be tested. I was alone but would be fine until their return.

"Mara, we're here and watching them transport Jonas. A couple of the team will follow them and make sure he stays safe. Are you positive you're okay?"

"Yes, I'm fine. Just take care of Jonas."

"You got it."

I heard the door lock click and Maharis walked back in. He was carrying a tall plastic tumbler of soda and a couple of cookies. He set them on the little table beside the bed within my limited reach.

"I brought you something cool to drink and a treat. Don't worry—your brother will be fine, and he'll return in a while. Enjoy." He gave me a smile from under his mask, trying to make me think he was a wonderful, sweet captor as he walked out the door.

This merc gave me the creeps. When he was around, I experienced emptiness, violence, and death. There was something atrociously wrong with this guy, and I wished I could figure him out. *Hmmm.*

Glancing at the nightstand, I wanted to taste the drink and cookies. But as I reached for the soda, it moved away from me as if by magic. I tried to grab it again, but it slid farther away from my hand and skidded off the table onto the floor. *That's so weird.* Shaking my head, I leaned back again. I might as well get a little more sleep while I waited. Then closing my eyes, I remembered how this all started.

BACK ON THE base about a week ago, we had the second meeting regarding my plan to obtain the intel on finding the scroll.

"Mara, this is not going to happen. I won't allow it!" Finn growled.

I scowled at Finn, ignoring his outburst, and began explaining my thoughts. "Both the demon and our team need the location of the scroll. We know they have an approximate destination, but not the exact one. So, we must assume they need Jonas to spirit walk to find it. Also, we must surmise they need me as a bargaining chip to persuade Jonas to do what they ask. They need us, but we also need them.

"I propose this—we let them succeed with the kidnapping. Jonas, Aaron, and I have a strong psychic bond, and we can communicate with each other over long distances. I hope Jonas and I can obtain intel from the mercs once we're taken because we'll be physically near them. It should be easier for us to delve into their minds if we're one-on-one. But, even if we're unable to get the intel at that time, we know they'll have to take us to the approximate location of the scroll, then they'll use Jonas to find the exact site of the chamber. Aaron, you and the rest of the team will remain close by. Jonas and I will communicate with Aaron through our psychic bond."

"Hell no! This plan of yours is insane and exceedingly dangerous. Mara, how do you propose we allow the mercs to kidnap the two of you? And, it certainly can't look obvious, or they'll know the jig is up," Edison growled in exasperation.

"The dream I keep having is the key. I dreamt it again last night, and it provided more information. I now know the location of this kidnapping, and it'll take place in Wyoming when we're sent to take out the small myrmidon hive. Jonas and I will go in, take out the hive, and then return to the woods. This is where we'll be kidnapped. The rest of the team must stay out of the way and let it happen."

Finn kept running his hands through his hair. His face was turning red, and his eyes glared back at me. "This is still too risky," he barked.

"Finn, this is what is meant to be. I had this dream about the forest on several occasions. I'm sorry you hate the idea, and if it was you being taken, I'd find it abhorrent as well. But this is the path the good Lord has chosen. Trust me, I'm terrified of it too, but it must be done! Stop being a protective bull elephant and get in the game!" I was also getting angry, and my breathing became labored with frustration.

"Finn's right, Mara. This proposed mission can, and probably will, go sideways, and the risks are too high. It's downright ludicrous. It's not happening—at least not while I'm alive!" Aaron spouted.

"I agree, mate," Edison concurred. "This isn't a plan that any trained military leader or personnel would agree to implement. There are too many unknowns, and I can't endorse it."

"That's bull!" I yelled in return. "We have no choice. It's our only plan, and no one can devise an alternative."

"I agree with Mara," Jonas replied quietly yet firmly. "I'm willing to take the risk and believe it's what's meant to happen. I'm in."

Finn and Edison swore loudly at Jonas's statement.

"Look, cupcake, it's not that we don't believe in your visions or understand your side of this, but it's a foolhardy plan. Of course, I believe that you and your siblings are graced by God's gifts, but it's a shmegegge plan. I agree with the nay-sayers," Billie said with conviction.

Xavier spoke up using a much louder tone than his typical soft timbre, "Mara has the only viable idea. Of course, it's risky, but God gave her this information on more than one occasion. Are we to ignore what the Father is showing us? My vote is in favor of this mission."

The arguing amongst the team grew louder, and I'd never seen my people this angry. Even Basheer and Armie were arguing with one another.

A loud, insistent gavel banging against the table finally halted the verbal cacophony. Once it was quiet, Finn threw the gavel down and glared at me with accusing eyes.

"As one of the leaders of this base, I, in no uncertain terms, forbid this foolhardy proposal to be set into motion. Do you understand me, Mara? I repeat—I *forbid* you from even thinking about doing this mission. And that goes for anyone else who thinks this is a feasible idea!" After barking at me and the team, Finn shoved his chair back so hard, it bounced off the wall behind him and flipped over onto its side. He turned, marched from the room, and slammed the door behind him.

No one said a word. Instead, angry, frustrated, and shocked expressions stared at the closed door.

I'd never been this infuriated, so I stood up, excused myself, and exited the room. Spotting Finn pacing heavily down by the elevator, I heard him muttering incoherently to himself.

"Finn McKenna!" I yelled down the hall in exasperation.

"What?!" He turned to face me with his hand on his hips and standing at full height—using his stature as an intimidation tactic.

I halted directly in front of him, toe-to-toe, and I also put my hands on my hips.

"You *forbid* me?!" I stressed each syllable by punching my finger into his broad chest. "You *forbid* me? Who do you think you are?" My voice echoed loudly in the hallway, but I kept my temper in check. I stepped back a foot and continued my tirade. "This is not up to you—even if you are one of the leaders of this base. It's up to God and the Gatekeepers. We do what *He* tells us, and this is *His* command. Do you think Jonas and I *want* to be chased, knocked out, and kidnapped? I'm no idiot. Do you think I'm unaware that this plan is fraught with unknowns and danger? You're using your heart and not your head, Finn. Remember when we promised not to let our relationship interfere with God's plan? Tell me you recall our pact."

He stared stubbornly at me, and I turned away with a loud "Lord in Heaven, give me strength." I strode to the hallway wall and sagged against it. Looking toward the meeting room, my team had gathered outside the doorway and, unfortunately, witnessed our tirade. I glanced down at my feet in exhaustion.

Hearing Finn pacing the hall again, I continued to stare at my shoes. But after several minutes, his feet appeared within my line of vision and were a few inches away, facing mine.

"Mara..." I didn't return his gaze. "Mara..."

Raising my head, I peered into his bright, apologetic eyes. "What?"

"I'm sorry." He pulled me into his arms and held me close. I buried my face against his chest and leaned heavily into him. "You're right. I merely can't stand the thought of anything or anyone harming you. Again, I truly apologize." I felt a couple of trembles move through Finn's body, and it broke my heart.

I leaned back and took his face into my hands. "I know, baby. It's not what I want either, but what's meant to be. We can speak with Kaiko if it makes the team feel better about this decision; however, I know I'm right about this."

Finn leaned in and kissed me. He turned to the team and said, "Let's get back to the meeting, my friends."

After we retook our seats, the faces that returned my gaze were calm and apologetic.

Edison stood and faced the group. "Mara is correct. We were wrong to doubt her, and this plan must be carried out to the letter. I made the determination against it because of my extensive military training, and in using that knowledge, a mission like this would never have been approved. And I know most of you who also had this training based your decision on the same criteria. However, we're no ordinary militia group, nor do we work for a government run by men and women. As Mara said, we work for the man upstairs, and that, my friends, changes the entire game and how it's run. Shall we proceed with this mission? All in favor?"

The room was silent. All I could hear was the whir of the air conditioning entering the room through the air ducts. Then slowly, one by one, everyone's hand went into the air.

Edison exhaled a calming, relieved breath and said, "Alright— onward and upward, mates. To begin, how do we slip the details of this myrmidon mission to the demons? We need them to know when and where Mara and Jonas will be so they can carry out the kidnapping. Bollocks—sorry, it still seems odd to be planning my people's abduction."

"I'll have to connect with this Maharis guy again. Before you protest, my brothers will be in there with me for protection, and I'll connect with him just long enough to make the demon think he stole it from my mind. Let's do this today, directly after this meeting. Well, what does everyone say?" I held my breath, waiting for the team's response.

They all reluctantly agreed.

Edison said, "I suggest you take the minimum weapons required for this mission. Ensure you don't have any of our special ammo on you when you're caught or anything else the demon could analyze and find a defense against."

"Good idea, Edison. We'll make sure we empty our weapons, destroy the holy fire flame thrower, and only carry a generic knife blade. Also, we should have regular ammo on us, so they don't wonder why we aren't armed when we're captured," Jonas said.

Everyone agreed.

Directly after the meeting, my brothers and I connected mentally with Maharis. We heard that terrible song, and with Jonas's and Aaron's help, I released the next mission's details to him in the hope he would forward them to the demon. The plan was now in place.

I DOZED OFF, but something woke me, and I heard alarms going off in my head. When I opened my eyes, terror filled my mind, and I screamed. Maharis stood over me, ripping off my shirt. I struck him with my free hand, but he swore loudly and punched me hard in the jaw. Apparently, I blacked out, and as I was coming to, I heard him talking as he ripped off the remainder of my clothes.

"You were supposed to drink the soda I gave you. My cocktail would turn you into a zombie—you'd feel everything I do to you, but you wouldn't be able to move a muscle. But, what the hell, I like my women to fight me while I take 'em!" He squeezed my breasts, and I cried out in pain. He took that opportunity to shove his tongue down my throat. I continued hitting and punching him with my free hand until he held it fast.

I bit his tongue and he slapped me hard in the face. He lifted himself, pulled out a knife, and I cringed in terror. He moved to cut off what was left of my clothes that were held fast by the hand and ankle cuffs. With my clothes gone, he dropped his pants and underwear and was about to move into position.

"You vile pervert! This is not going to happen! Get off me, you filthy pig!" Twisting my hand from his grasp, I screamed in terror and anger as I kicked, punched, and slapped at my attacker. He grabbed my one free wrist again and held it against the other. The weight of his body was now on top of me again, and I could barely move or breathe.

In the middle of this entire episode, I could hear two voices in my head, screaming at me and asking if I needed help. But the only word that would come to my mind was "No!" and I screamed it loudly in my head and verbally at my attacker. The repeated word "no" was my automatic response to Maharis's violent onslaught. Even though he had me tightly pinned, I continued to scream, swear and tried frantically to do anything to stop what was about to happen.

"No!!!" I bellowed but realized I needed to communicate with my team.

"I need my team now!" I yelled frantically in my head after I finally got my brain to work correctly, hoping Aaron and Finn would come to my aid. As I kept physically fighting Maharis, his mind completely opened to me. I caught glimpses of some horrific things but also saw the intel we needed on the artifact. However, I was too terrified to take it all in.

The monster on top of my body was about to rape me, and I tried every evasive tactic my trainers had taught me. But my restraints held me fast, and I couldn't get enough slack to implement any of the moves. I was in big trouble and began to panic as I knew the horrific violence was about to happen.

I finally screamed aloud, "St. Michael, save me!"

At that instant, there was a "whooshing" sound, and a warm breeze brushed against my body. A vibrant scent of gardenias and roses replaced the stench of Maharis's sweat. Suddenly, my would-be rapist was lifted off me and tossed like a ragdoll against the opposite wall, which knocked the wind out of him. I saw a flash of an angelic form of great height and strength, with dark auburn hair and deep, penetrating green-gold eyes. His immense presence filled the room. He wore some type of iridescent armor that glowed with a strange light. St. Michael gazed at me with a look of intense Godly love and compassion, then he nodded his head and was gone as quickly as he had appeared, but the pungent odor of flowers still lingered.

Banging and yelling could now be heard at the door, then Finn and Billie burst through. They came rushing over to me, but Maharis was regaining consciousness. Finn's face was filled with rage as he turned and charged over to Maharis. He lifted him to his feet and pummeled him mercilessly. Then Finn moved behind him and put the man into a deadly chokehold and was about to take his life.

"Billie, get these restraints off of me. I have to stop Finn from killing that monster." Billie worked quickly, dispensing my cuffs, and wrapped a blanket from the bed around my naked body.

Finn now had Maharis on his knees. The would-be rapist's face turned red, and he was about to pass out due to the lack of oxygen.

"Finn, you have to stop. We need him alive!" Finn didn't hear my voice as he was still enraged to hear anything but the blood pounding in his ears. I rushed over to him, knelt beside him, and worked frantically to get my dear husband to look at me.

I touched his face and said urgently, "My beloved husband, stop choking this man. He can't die yet. Please, Finn, let him go."

He finally focused on my face and released Maharis, who was unconscious, but hopefully still alive. Finn reached out and gently touched my badly bruised face, then took me into his arms. Our bodies shook, and we held on to each other until the trembling dwindled to an intermittent shiver.

Billie came over and checked to see if Maharis was still breathing. She nodded and said, "Finn, get Mara to the bathroom. I'll bring her a change of clothes and the first aid kit. Aaron, Edison, and I will tie up this putz and stuff him into the truck. Now get movin'. We don't know if any more of these mercs may appear."

Finn helped me to the bathroom, where we waited for Billie's return.

"Mara, oh my Lord in heaven, Mara. I've never been so terrified, my love." He kept kissing my face and stroking my back.

"Finn, I'm okay, just shaken up. Oh my, I'm going to be sick," I gasped as I turned to the toilet. Finn stayed at my side until the nausea finally passed. I sat down on the closed toilet.

"Why is it you always witness me tossing my cookies?" I said, trying to lighten the mood.

"Just lucky, I guess." Finn tried to grin but missed by a mile.

There was a knock on the door, and it was Billie. "You okay, kiddo?" Her brow was furrowed in concern.

I nodded and thanked her for the clothes and first aid kit. She left the room, and Finn closed the door and stared intently at my face. He knelt before me and used a cold washcloth to wipe my bruised skin and bleeding lip. I felt myself starting to shake uncontrollably again.

"Finn, please hold me. I desperately need your strength," I whispered tearfully. He stood and drew me deep into his arms. Burrowing as close as possible, I began pulling his willpower into my mind. I felt him shiver, but it passed, and I held on until my quivering subsided. Eventually, I pulled away and reached up to caress his face.

After tending to my cuts, he helped me dress, put on boots, and we left the building. As we exited the door, a dead body was on the ground. It was the man I called Igor. He had been killed by someone who had shoved an ice pick deeply into one of his eye sockets. It was a pretty gruesome sight.

I looked at Finn with a raised eyebrow.

"It wasn't us," he replied, then continued, "I assume the scum in that room did it. He wouldn't want anyone to know or interfere with what he had planned for you. We took care of the other two mercs near the road. Don't worry; they're not dead, just unconscious and tied up."

Billie and Aaron were waiting for us as we walked to the truck. Aaron had to give me a long, reassuring hug, and he didn't want to let me go, but he eventually released me.

"What about Jonas?" I asked worriedly.

"He's safe. The rest of the team extracted him as soon as we knew you were in trouble. They'll meet us at the airport," Billie replied. "Are you sure you're okay, girlfriend?"

"I'll be fine. Let's go home," I said and gave her a small smile.

"Copy that," Billie concurred, fluffing her purple hair.

"Where is Maharis?" I asked.

"Don't worry, chickee. We stowed that yutz into the back of the truck. He's trussed up tighter than a five-pound egg up a three-pound chicken's patootie." Billie smiled as she replied, clicked her tongue, and gave me a wink.

Finn helped me into the truck and gave me an ice pack for my jaw, which I gratefully accepted. He pulled me close to his side and continued glancing at me until we reached the airport. After making sure I was comfortable on the plane, he went back out and helped the other team members carry Maharis into the back of the jet. I caught a glimpse of the monster and noticed he was bound up like a Thanksgiving turkey with rope and duct tape. The silver adhesive was also wrapped around his naked waist and hips, so it would be interesting when the tape was ripped off his private parts. I had to let out a giggle as I relished the thought.

CHAPTER 8

Sitting in my seat on the plane, I watched as my remarkable team members approached me, each needing a hug. Jonas was the last to embrace me, and when he did, he didn't want to let go. After moving back, he sat beside me, stared apologetically into my eyes, and took my hand. Finn stood a few feet away, allowing my brother to speak with me.

"Mara, I'm so sorry for what happened to you. I could feel your terror and tried to get you to answer me, but you kept saying 'no.' Those mercs still had their guns trained on me and I didn't know what to do. I had no idea…" He glanced away as his eyes filled with tears.

"Jonas, none of us knew this would happen," I whispered.

I raised my voice so every one of my team could hear. "It's no one's fault except Maharis. I hope you all know what I say is true, and I'm safe because of this wonderful team of mine. Thank you for being there for me." My eyes also teared up as I gazed at my good friends.

Jasper piped up, scratching his head in confusion. "Mara, how in tarnation did that snake in the grass get chucked to the other side of the room while you were tied to that bed? I'm pert-near sorry to ask, but I'm dying to know."

"God came through on that one. I asked for St. Michael's help, and he gloriously appeared, picked up Maharis, and tossed him across the room like the piece of dirt he is. This wondrous Archangel was the most beautiful being I've ever seen." I described everything I witnessed, felt, and experienced, and my team listened in awe. They were surprised, too, about how the drugged soda had miraculously moved away from my grasp.

Billie spoke up, exclaiming, "God protected you from being drugged as well? And the flowers—so that's what we smelled when Finn and I entered the room. I couldn't figure out why the scent of luscious flowers was so overwhelming, and I've never smelled anything so amazing in my life." Billie was embarrassed because she'd been talking like a schoolgirl, which belied her tough exterior.

I spoke quickly to cover her unease, "It *was* glorious, wasn't it? I have to say, I recognized it from my trip to Heaven. There's nothing like it on Earth."

"Okay, everyone, we need to buckle into our seats and get this plane in the air," Basheer instructed as he headed toward the cockpit.

Once airborne, Finn handed me another ice pack and told me to keep it on my cheek and jaw. He said my face was turning a lovely shade of violet.

"You *do* look good in purple, though." He leaned over and kissed me gently, trying to avoid touching the cut on the side of my lip.

"Flatterer."

Edison walked toward us carrying two more ice packs. "These are for you, mate." He gestured toward Finn's hands, and I noticed the scrapes and bruises on his knuckles.

"My goodness, Finn!" I gently stroked the back of his damaged hands. "Do they hurt?"

"Nah. They're fine. Thanks for the ice, Edison."

Finn's good friend nodded in acknowledgment, squeezed Finn's shoulder, and returned to his seat.

As I gazed into Finn's eyes, he knew I wasn't anywhere close to feeling normal. So many emotions rolled through my head, and I was also trying to process what had happened to me. We both knew I was in shock, even though I could still act normal with everyone else.

"It's okay, love. It'll take time, but it will get better. Right now, I'm going to get you a small nip of whiskey because it'll help calm your nerves," Finn said, and he walked away and grabbed us both a drink.

After he returned, he downed his whiskey and set it aside. He was looking straight ahead, and his hands trembled.

"Finn?" I took his hand, but he wouldn't return my gaze. "Finn, look at me."

He turned his head, and what I saw in his eyes said everything. I got up, settled onto his lap, and snuggled close to him, burying my face in his neck. Finn wrapped his arms tightly around me, and I felt his body shaking gently as he cried with grief, sorrow, anger, and relief.

I murmured reassuring words as he released his pent-up emotions. He was calming down now, but I continued to snuggle and stay close to his warmth. After several minutes, I handed him tissues, and he tried to wipe away the telltale sign of his tears.

"Mara, I've never felt so helpless or scared. Aaron told me he knew you were in trouble, but you kept repeating that you didn't need help. I was beside myself, and I almost beat up poor Aaron, trying to get more information from him about what was happening to you. But he didn't know either, poor guy. Then you finally told us to come, thank the Lord. I wanted to kill that maniac."

I understood what he was saying and how awful it had been for him and my brothers. "When I was being attacked, all I could think of or say was 'no!' It was simply a panicked response to the possibility of being raped. I know you thought you'd kill that man, but you didn't, and that's what's important."

"I love you so much, Mara. My heart aches with the thought that I could have lost you today. We always wonder that someday one of us could be killed by a demon, but not by some deviant human."

"Yeah, who'd a thunk it?" I snorted at Finn, and he finally gave me a happy chuckle. "Are you okay now? You know, you don't always have to be a superhero, right?"

"Aye, love. Although, it's fun having you think of me as one." He gave me a wink and gently kissed my bruised cheek. I was about to move from his lap to my seat, but he held fast, refusing to let me go. "Just stay here for a little while longer, Mara." I smiled at him and nestled close again.

After we sat silently for a while, Finn said, "I'm having Gracie stay overnight with Kaiko's family, Gloria and Marshall. She doesn't know we'll be home today, so you'll have some time to recover. I'll need you to see a doctor as soon as we land." He quickly held up his hand as he knew I was about to protest. "No arguments, my dear. It's happening. Then, I'll make an appointment for you tomorrow to see Brianna. You'll need to talk with someone about the attack." He raised one of his dark eyebrows at me, daring me to argue.

"I know you're right and agree to do as you ask. I love you and adore you for taking excellent care of me." I kissed him gently but groaned as my lip hurt at the contact.

"What are we going to do with Maharis? I'll need to probe his mind for more information," I asked Finn.

He looked down at me with confusion. "I thought you found what you needed from him—the relic's location. What more could you possibly want?"

"He didn't have much information other than it was in the Middle East. I saw that mosque from my vision, so I hope Armie or Basheer can help. The demon didn't reveal anything further to the mercs, so we must hope God will give us that unique intel. It's something else which I'll discuss with you later. Finn, please tell me what we will do with him for now."

"We'll take him to a safe house about an hour from the base. He'll be blindfolded, so he won't know where he's being held. Don't worry— he'll be under heavy guard until we decide what to do with him next. You'll need a few days to recuperate, and then you can take a crack at him. I must tell you, I don't want you anywhere near him again. I don't like this idea, Mara."

"I don't either, but I must get this additional critical intelligence from him. It's too important. Don't fight me on this—not now, please," I begged him tearfully, as I was too worn out to argue.

He gave me a sweet smile, caressed my hair, and replied, "I won't. We'll keep him on ice until you're ready to read him. I only insist that I be there. Agreed?"

"Agreed. I insist that you're with me too." I gave him a weak smile, leaned into him, and closed my eyes to rest. Finn was correct; the whiskey helped.

When he finally let me return to my seat, he held my hand for the remainder of the trip and never left my side. Once we returned to the base, he even walked me to the doctor's office, where I saw Dr. Helena Rodriguez. The doctor took a skull x-ray and was satisfied that my jaw wasn't broken and that I had no severe injuries.

"Mara, you've incurred severe bruising to your jaw, and it'll turn quickly to an ugly, large, vivid purple color. You needn't be alarmed because, as you know, the Chosen heal very quickly. Almost twice as fast as the average person," Dr. Rodriguez informed me.

"What? I didn't know that. Did you know about this fact, Finn?" I asked incredulously.

"Yes, I did. I'm sorry, love. I thought you knew. Something always gets through the cracks. I'll make a note that all of the Chosen are told of this newer development. We also believe that we age at a much slower rate too. How's that for a fountain of youth?"

My jaw dropped as I heard this new information. "This is intel I can honestly get behind."

Dr. Rodriquez smiled widely and sent me away with a bottle of mild sleeping pills, and told me to take over-the-counter meds for pain.

We finally settled into the apartment in the late afternoon, and I took a long, hot shower. Wiping the steam from the mirror, my once bright blue eyes looked haunted and bloodshot, and my long, curly golden-highlighted red hair was dull and lifeless. My heart-shaped face was drawn, and a giant bruise covered almost half my face.

"Lovely. So much for God's perfection, Mara. You look like death warmed over," I murmured to my frightful reflection.

Finn fixed us a light dinner, and we relaxed by watching television. He stayed close by my side and remained attentive, even though I reminded him I was okay.

At bedtime, Finn insisted I take the prescribed sleeping pills. I finally gave in because I was too tired to argue. He helped me to bed and climbed in beside me. Asher had also been glued to my side all evening as if he knew what I'd been through. I said several prayers to the Lord for being with me this day and thanked St. Michael for his miraculous help.

Finn had been correct. I was afraid I'd have nightmares, but the pills helped me sleep deeply through the night.

Finn was already out of the shower when I woke up the following day. I went to rise from the bed, but every inch of my body hurt. After slowly climbing off the mattress, I shuffled to the bathroom. Finn was already shaving, bare-chested, and dressed in his khaki pants. I loved watching him shave and how the strong, smooth muscles moved through his upper back and shoulders as he lifted his arms with each stroke of the blade. He looked at me through the reflection of the vanity mirror.

"Don't be scared, love, but your face is now a vivid shade of plum. I'm very fond of plums."

I stood beside him and gasped at what I saw. It was a deep purple color and covered my entire left cheek and down to under the jawline. It didn't seem painful, but I felt the ache once I opened my mouth to reply.

"Hurts to speak? We'll get food into you this morning, then you'll have to down a few pain pills."

"I'll need to cover this up so I don't scare Gracie. I still have that heavy special effects makeup I used for the Hotel Demente mission.

That should do the trick. My entire body hurts this morning, so I'll soak in the jetted tub."

"Good idea. I'll keep an eye on you if you don't mind." He kissed my unbruised cheek and stroked my back.

After filling the tub, I piled my hair on top of my head, removed my pajamas, and was about to get into the water, when I heard Finn say my name in a quiet, surprised tone.

Walking back to the mirror, I stared in surprise. I'd never seen so many bruises on my body before. They were everywhere—wrists, arms, shoulders, neck, breasts, stomach, thighs, and ankles. As I turned around, there were even a few on my back. After facing the mirror again, I sobbed.

"Oh baby, it's going to be fine. They'll heal quickly and you'll be just fine. Shush now; I'm here. Please don't cry, Mara—you're killing me." He picked me up, carried me to the tub's wide edge, and sat down with me on his lap. Finn continued talking to me in soothing tones until the tears finally ebbed, and I was left with the hiccups.

Finn handed over several tissues so I could wipe my eyes and blow my nose. "I'm...so...sorry. I don't know...what...got into me."

"You've been through a horrifying experience, and I guess a good cry was what you needed." He kissed me gently over my entire face. When he was done, he gazed into my eyes and chuckled.

"What?"

"You have shaving cream all over you, my sweet."

We both looked back to the mirror, and he was correct; our faces were covered in white foam. Our reflections looked ridiculous, and I saw one colossal dollop sticking out from the tip of my nose. I giggled, then guffawed with abandon. This triggered Finn, and he laughed loudly too.

He gazed at me again and whispered sweetly, "I'm sorry for what that imbecile did to you. I wish I could make it so it had never happened." His eyes were filled with sorrow and pain, breaking my heart.

"I know you hate what happened as much as I do. But it did, and by the grace of God, I wasn't raped or killed." I shivered in fear as I made this statement. "Thanks to you, I know I'll be fine as long as I have you, Gracie, my brothers, Mom, and my wonderful friends. You too, Asher." Asher had walked in and also sat on the tub's edge, totally uncaring that his tail had submerged in the bath water.

Finn stood with me in his arms, then gently set me into the bathtub's warm, swirling jets. He grabbed a washcloth, wet it in the bathwater, and wiped the shaving cream from my face.

"Thank you. I love you so much; you know that?" I whispered.

"Aye, I do. And I love you too, my sassy wench. Argh!" I giggled again at Finn's pirate impression.

My body felt much better after the long soak, and I did an excellent job covering the giant bruise on my face. The makeup had worked well, and I hoped Gracie wouldn't notice anything amiss. Luckily, she didn't. Finn and I greeted her with immense joy, and she jumped from lap to lap, soaking up the hugs and kisses. She had to tell us everything she did while we were apart, and we spent several hours together, playing games and conducting an imaginary tea party.

I had to leave for a short time for a session with Brianna. It was a good idea, and I was glad Finn insisted I speak with her. I felt better afterward and would continue seeing her three times a week until I thought the therapy was no longer needed. However, she explained that I'd probably have PTSD with some flashbacks and nightmares. But we would handle them if and when they arose.

Later that afternoon in the apartment, Finn took me aside and said, "I have a great idea. Tomorrow is Friday, and the weather is supposed to be unseasonably warm for fall in this part of Idaho. Why don't we take a few buses and transport all the kids and their families to Overlook Park? We could have a picnic, and the kids could enjoy the amazing weather and soak in some sunshine. What do you say?"

Overlook Park was located on the facility's above-ground property, and the employees developed it for our personal use. A small playground had been built for the children. There were even picnic tables and grills installed. It wasn't used often because it was about an hour from the base, but it was a beautiful park, nonetheless.

"Finn, that would be amazing. The fall colors are in full swing too. But can we organize it in such a short timeframe?"

He gave me that raised eyebrow again that he did so well and looked at me as if I'd grown two heads.

"I know. You can do anything when you put your mind to it." I snorted loudly and eagerly nodded my head.

He kissed me gently and said, "I'll send out a base-wide message and make all the arrangements. Everyone needs this right now."

I gave him a big smile but winced as the movement hurt my bruised cheek. After rubbing it gently, I replied, "I totally agree. I can't wait!"

That evening, Finn and I both read a bedtime story to Gracie. She laughed joyously when Finn read the part about the silly alligator. After saying goodnight, we returned to the living room sofa, and I flopped down in exhaustion.

"Phew. I'm beat. I don't know why I've been so tired lately."

"Mara, you have a lot of healing to do, so it isn't surprising."

I turned to look at him and noticed he stood staring intently at the large seascape painting he'd purchased for me a few months ago. Puzzled, I rose from the sofa and wrapped my arms around him from behind, stating, "I still love that painting and I could stare at it all day."

"Hmm," was his only comment.

I stepped back from hugging him and moved to his side. Gazing at the painting, I looked back at him again. His expression was one of puzzlement.

"What is it, Finn? Does it look different?"

"Aye. But I can't put my finger on it."

"I told you! You didn't believe me when I mentioned it on the flight to Aruba," I exclaimed, stabbing him in his upper bicep with my index finger. "Ha!"

He looked at me, grinned, kissed me lightly, and turned to stare at the painting again.

"I swear," I began, "it's changed again. How can that be? When you first gave me the painting, there were three coconuts on the palm tree. Before we left to get married, there were six. There are still six, but now the seagulls are gone. What's going on here, Finn?"

I turned and gave him a suspicious glance with furrowed eyebrows, then asked, "Are you doing this? Pulling a prank on your poor, innocent wife?"

He turned to me and held his hands up in surrender. "Love, it's not me. I swear. But who is doing this, and how is this person making these changes? What a conundrum." Finn pulled out his phone and snapped some photos of the painting. "I want evidence so we'll have proof if the painting changes again."

"Why, Sherlock, I'm quite impressed with your detective skills. I wish I'd thought of that." I walked to the coffee table, grabbed my phone, then pulled up photos of the painting I'd taken when we returned from our honeymoon.

"It doesn't work, Finn. I took this photo when you first gave me the painting so I could send it to my mom. When I pulled it up on my cell right before our wedding trip, the painting changed on my phone. I took another photo upon our return, but let's see if the seagulls are in that one." I pulled up the latest photo, and we both stared at it in amazement.

Finn spoke up immediately, "They're gone! What in blazes is going on?"

"Beats me. Is it divine intervention, or is something afoot with the serial prankster? You know, the one who gave me the raccoon eyes from my binoculars, your mysterious itching powder in your bloomers, the thousand tennis balls in Jonas's locker, and last but not least, the farting machine under Aaron's chair in the conference room."

Finn laughed out loud and scratched his head in consternation. "You got me there. We'll have to devise a way to monitor that painting without anyone knowing we're looking. But for now, I say we hit the hay." He took my hand and led me to the bedroom.

As I removed my heavy makeup to prepare for bed, the bruise was starting to fade. Finn even commented that it was already looking better. The marks on my body still seemed prominent, but I hoped a good night's rest would speed up the healing process.

I fell asleep quickly, but all too soon, I had a nightmare about being attacked by Maharis. Feeling myself being shaken awake, I was now staring into Finn's worried face.

"Mara, thank the Lord. You were thrashing around and starting to scream. It was the attack, wasn't it?"

I nodded as I felt tears streaming down my face. "It was so real— like it was happening all over again." Finn snuggled me close and whispered soothing words of comfort.

After a few minutes, I pulled away, realizing my nightgown was soaking wet. I quickly changed, drank water, and returned to bed.

"I'm afraid to go back to sleep, Finn. These must be the nightmares Brianna warned me about."

"I'm so sorry, sweetheart, but you have to try and get some rest. You're exhausted. Take a couple of those sleeping pills, and I'll turn the bedside lamp on low for the night. Do you think that'll help?"

"I hope so." After I took the medication, Finn drew me close to him, and I stared at the lamp for a while but eventually drifted back to sleep.

"Mara, it's me. Isabella. Can you see me?"

I'm looking around, trying to view her in the heavy fog of my dream. She finally appears before me, looking beautiful, happy, and peaceful.

"Isabella. It's good to see you again."

"You too, Mara. But I have to say, I'm sorry for what you had to endure."

"Thank you, Isabella. I was surprised that the attack wasn't in any

of my visions. But I suppose I wouldn't have gone through with it had I known what would happen."

"The Lord knows this as well. What transpired was meant to be so you would discover the relic's location. But it's also important that the terrible carnage in the wake of that man's life must be revealed. You know what I'm talking about, Mara. I know you don't want to face it head-on, but you must. Please continue what you started so the families of the dead may have their answers, and many future innocent lives will be saved as well. But be warned, your attacker's haven is exceedingly dangerous to humanity, and you must take great care when you delve into his den of horrors."

"Isabella, I don't understand."

"My dear, you will. But for now, you must face your attacker, lower his defenses, then take what you need. Once this is accomplished, your fear will be cast aside, and the soulless man will no longer have power over you. But when you do this, stay vigilant and keep your barriers in place. The powerful demon still lurks behind the soulless' man's mind, so keep your brothers near."

"How much time do we have to find the relic?"

"There is no urgency at the moment. The demon is unsure what to do next now that he has lost the Gatekeepers. He is scrambling to ascertain his next move. You'll be told when the time is right to extract the holy object."

Thank you, sweet Isabella."

"My dear, Mara, I'm only the messenger. I've been blessed by His generous love and given the task of delivering this dire instruction. Remember this, the mirror image of the soulless man is just as dangerous as the first. Until we meet again, my child...."

"Wait, what do you mean...Isabella?" I ask her, but she's gone.

~

I SLEPT DREAMLESSLY through the remainder of the night, and the next morning in bed, I told Finn what Isabella had said.

"You understood what she was telling you?" Finn asked with some confusion.

"Yes, I believe so, but I'm at a loss as to her parting words. I know I have to interrogate Maharis, upset him enough so he lowers his defenses, then enter his mind and retrieve what I didn't want to see while I was attacked. At the same time, I need to be shielded from the possibility that the demon that hired him may try to enter my psyche again. Piece of cake," I added with sarcasm.

"Crap! Will we ever be done with this lunatic? We still have him at a safe house, but I hoped to have him picked up by my FBI contact tomorrow night."

"Finn, we don't have enough on him. He would simply get a slap on the wrist for my attempted rape. That's even if we get him to court and I testify. We don't have any forensic evidence with the proper chain of custody. Real, viable evidence is what we need. If the glimpse of what I saw in his memory is any indication, that man has committed some seriously heinous crimes. I have to say, I'm terrified to see what they are, but we've no choice—he's a violent individual who has to be stopped permanently."

Finn leaned back against the headboard and clasped his hands behind his neck. With knitted brows, he contemplated everything I had divulged.

He finally spoke up, saying, "Mara, you know I don't like this, but I understand it has to be done. Your safety is my utmost concern, and you'll be protected. When do we have to do this?"

"Tomorrow. The sooner I get this monster out of my life, the better. We'll need to speak with everyone today, especially my brothers, and make sure we're all on the same page. I'll need a few things I'm hoping your FBI contact will be able to provide. Our entire team should also be notified about what I had seen on the general location of the relic. Maybe they can narrow down a more precise area." I relayed to Finn what I would need from his FBI friend. He grimaced with disgust at what I wanted from them but agreed to my request.

"I'll contact everyone this morning and get the ball rolling. In the meantime, we have a wonderful day trip to enjoy. By the way, love, your face is healing nicely. It's already a beautiful shade of dark sunshine and no longer the juicy plum color." He leaned over and kissed me sweetly on the lips.

As he moved back to retreat off the bed, I grabbed the waistband of his pajamas and pulled him back toward me. Wiggling my eyebrows suggestively, I pulled him close again, kissed him deeply, and caressed his muscled chest in delight.

"Mara, are you sure about this?" he inquired in a gentle, concerned whisper.

"I believe so. I mean—I want to. Can we take it slowly, though?"

"That I can do." Finn got off the bed, locked the bedroom door, and we both divested ourselves of our pajamas.

Finn stayed true to his word. He gently kissed every bruise he encountered on my body as if trying to heal them with his loving lips. I panicked when he started to take things further. But Finn gave me time and let me take the lead.

From that moment forward, all my reservations and fear left me. We were back to being Finn and Mara—how it had been before.

Afterward, tears welled in my eyes as I laid my head on Finn's bare chest. He must have felt the moisture because he put a finger under my chin and looked into my face.

"Mara?"

"I'm okay—just happy and relieved that the monster didn't ruin this beautiful part of our relationship. You're incredibly good to me, and I don't know what I did to have God bless me with such a special, caring, and loving husband."

"I love you too. But please don't cry because it breaks my heart." He gently ran his hand up and down my back, and we were happy being close to one another.

"You handsome rat! You know, it's all your fault that I'm addicted to you." I snorted slightly, then reached over and pinched him in the hip.

"Ouch! You frisky wench." He chuckled with pleasure and continued, "I'm glad my lovely bride is back again, along with her beautiful smile. But now, we have to get out of this bed. Gracie will be up soon, and I have to contact the team, then we need to prepare for our trip to the park."

"Oh, shoot! I almost forgot," I muttered, and we both scuttled off the bed and into the bathroom.

Finn and I were surprised by the turnout when we boarded the buses. We took four vehicles to the park, and everyone was excited to join the outing. When we arrived, the children piled out with glee and ran as fast as their little legs could carry them. Everyone smiled at their jubilation, and we unloaded the food and supplies for the day's outing.

It was a beautiful day. The sun shone brightly, and it was unseasonably warm. The trees' leaves glistened in the light with their bright fall colors. I could smell the exquisite scent of the drying leaves under my feet and raised my face to take in the warmth of the sun's rays. Living underground for long periods made me appreciate God's blessings of fresh air and warm sunshine. Standing still, I closed my eyes and continued to soak in God's glory. *I missed this!*

"Finn to Mara, come in, Mara," Finn whispered.

"Sorry. It's just so healing to be within God's gift of nature," I said.

He kissed my cheek and whispered, "I couldn't agree more."

As the adults sat at the tables watching the children frolic and play, two squirrels and a chipmunk jumped on our table and ran over to me. They chatted away, and I laughed joyfully as they climbed onto my shoulders. The other adults stared in awe as I pulled out a bag of shelled peanut halves lying on the table and began hand-feeding the little animals. Jonas and Aaron also fed them, and the little minxes were delighted with their new friends. Once they filled their cheeks until they were about to burst, they tittered a bit more, then bounded off the table and up a giant oak tree. Finn smiled and shook his head in wonder, and everyone else laughed at his amazed expression.

"You never cease to surprise me, Mara. Animals adore you," Finn said with a chuckle.

"I know. It's bizarre, but I love it," I said, giggling with glee.

As we continued our conversation, a voice persistently whispered in my head, and it wouldn't be silenced. Jumping to my feet, I called everyone over. The adults and children joined us, and I instructed them to join hands.

"Why don't we all sing, 'He's Got the Whole World in His Hands.'"

Our group started to sing the song, and I waited for what would happen. I urged the children to sing louder as they thanked the Lord for this exquisite day. Their voices resounded through the forest, and it was glorious.

It started. The trees began swaying left, then right, in tune with the music. The children briefly stumbled on their words when they witnessed the sight, and the trees' movements slowed, but I urged them to keep singing, and they chanted the song loudly once more. The trees gently swayed in unison again, and then a swarm of Swallowtail butterflies began circling us, along with many vibrant-colored cardinals. It was as if the birds were also singing their praises to the Lord. The butterflies swirled and flitted among us, and the children danced with them. God's precious little ones continued to sing to His glory.

The fall-colored leaves swirled gently around us as the trees moved, like gold, orange, and red showers from Heaven. The breeze flitted around our bodies, and the leaves weaved a choreographed dance as if they were also exalting the Lord above.

As I watched the adults, their faces were filled with joy and awe, and it took my breath away.

Before long, the music ebbed, and so did God's afternoon entertainment. The large trees finally stopped swaying, and all that was left of the movement was the rustling of the leaves that held steadfast to their limbs, defying autumn's assault in preparation for winter.

The butterflies and cardinals made one final swirl around the children, gracefully swooped upwards, and disappeared over the trees' canopy.

Not a word was spoken when it ended, but none was needed. The children's faces reflected wonder, and the adults were stunned and amazed.

After several minutes, I said, "That, my sweet children, was a gift from God, and He loves and cherishes every one of you. Remember what you've witnessed and tell all who will listen of His miracle. You're blessed, indeed. Now go and play and enjoy this glorious day."

The children laughed with delight and did as I asked. They played, danced, giggled, and ran until lunchtime. The adults gathered around and talked excitedly about the miracle of the trees. Afterward, we ate grilled hamburgers and hot dogs with all the trimmings, including sweets for dessert and freshly squeezed lemonade.

The older children played again after we ate, but the younger ones were worn out, and we laid blankets on the soft ground for them to nap. But Gracie insisted on sleeping in Finn's arms at the table, and he smiled contentedly. We talked about anything and everything.

"This was an exciting day, and I'm thankful God gave us that unbelievable miracle. I have to say, too, I see why you insisted on adding an indoor park to the base, Mara," Jonas said, smiling widely at the children.

Aaron also grinned and said, "I agree. God's gift of nature is incredibly healing to the mind, body, and spirit. I'm glad we did this, and I'll always treasure the Lord's fantastic show."

"By the way, Mara," Jonas piped in, "you won't believe the number of people who have volunteered for your projects. The way everything is looking, the indoor park and schoolrooms will be completed fifty percent ahead of schedule. It's unbelievable. Shipments of supplies have been coming in daily, and we've been able to acquire everything we would possibly need. You should see Jasper working in the park. He's like a child in a candy store—I've never seen him this happy."

Kaiko and her parents sat with us, and Gloria commented, "We have all the teachers we need now for the school and the daycare center. The curriculums are almost completed as well. The classrooms are nearly finished, and the children and parents are excited for classes to start."

"I'm happy this is all working out, and I can't wait to see everything completed," I exclaimed. Finn winked at me and smiled.

We were startled as children yelled in panic as they ran toward us. Gracie woke up, wondering what the commotion was about. Finn put her on the ground and asked her to stay with Gloria.

He ran to the children, asking them why they were upset. They pointed to a direction just to the edge of the park area where a dog stood, his teeth bared as he snarled in our direction. Finn told the children to return to their families, and he was about to reach for his gun. I calmly approached him, telling him not to pull his concealed weapon.

"Let me approach the dog. He looks like he's starving and is afraid of us. Give me a chance to communicate with him," I advised Finn. He looked at me, gauging my determination, and nodded in agreement.

"I'm going to watch your back, Mara," Finn advised.

"I know."

I slowly approached the dog and heard his warning growl again. He was a medium-sized mutt that appeared to be a cross between a retriever and a shepherd. His ribs showed through his thinning fur, and my heart went out to him. I slowly neared him but stopped about ten feet away. Standing quietly, I connected with him. His mind resisted, but I continued my psychic touch until I finally felt his response. Kneeling on the ground now, I waited for him to approach. He took a step back and then sat down on his haunches. Communicating with him again, I felt him lowering his fear. He stood back up and took a few steps toward me, then several more.

The pup was now only a couple of feet away, and he stopped, lowered his body to the ground, and belly-crawled until he was directly in front of me. The poor thing whined and whimpered, then nudged my hand with his nose. I slowly raised my palm, and the dog licked my fingers in response. Stroking his thin body, I murmured gentle and reassuring words. As I stood, he turned around and looked back toward the woods. I peered again into his mind and saw what he was trying to tell me.

I turned to look at everyone in the park and yelled back to them, "It's okay now. This dog won't hurt anyone. He understands we won't harm him; we're all part of his pack. Jonas, would you and Finn please approach us?"

Finn and Jonas came forward and stood beside me. The dog did nothing but rise and lick each of their hands.

"There's a female with young pups just beyond that tree line. I've already communicated with her, and she's not fearful or aggressive, so you won't have any problems with her. But she's emaciated too, and we need to get both of these dogs and the pups to the vet at the base. Jonas, would you be willing to find another person to assist you in taking them back?"

"I'd love to. Are you sure the dogs will get on the bus?" Jonas asked with trepidation.

"I'll tell them what will happen and not to be afraid, and where they're going, there will be food, water, shelter, and protection. On the way back, you can connect with the dogs so they know they can also trust you." I communicated this information to the canines, and the male sat back down, looking at us with hope and gladness. I scratched the dog's head in reassurance.

Jonas returned to the group at the park and Aaron volunteered to help. They then went into the woods, carrying a box, and after several minutes, came back with another mangy, emaciated dog and a box that held three puppies. The female was a smaller dog with a dirty, scruffy multi-colored coat and looked like some kind of terrier. The male dog followed them as they climbed into the bus.

"Mara, do you want to go with them?" Finn asked.

"No. Jonas and Aaron will take care of them. I'd rather stay here so Gracie can continue to play, and I'd like to get to know everyone."

Finn took my hand and we returned to the picnic tables. During the next hour, we both preceded to introduce ourselves to the people at our outing whom we hadn't met previously. At the last table, I sat next to a young woman with a beautiful six-month-old baby boy. The mother smiled at me and introduced herself.

"Hi. I'm Tiana Murphy, and this little man is Darius." She shook my hand, and I grinned widely at her and cooed to her precious child.

"I'm Mara, and this is my husband, Finn. It's great to meet you and your lovely boy too." Darius reached out his chubby arms to me, wanting me to hold him. "May I?" I asked with anticipation.

"Sure." She passed me the precious boy, and I held him close and kissed his little cherub cheek. "You're so blessed, Tiana. He's amazing." The little boy jumped up and down on my knees and babbled in his secret baby language.

"I have two more children over there. My husband, Otis, is in the blue striped shirt playing with my other son, Jamal. He's eight—my son, that is." She giggled with embarrassment. Tiana pointed to a tall, striking man playing with several children, including Gracie. "That's my six-year-old daughter next to him. Her name is Nia."

"You have a lovely family, Tiana. You must be so proud," I commented. She then asked if we had any children, and I pointed to Gracie and told her about the pending adoption.

"The two of you must be on pins and needles. I'd be a nervous wreck having to wait for that kind of answer," she replied in commiseration.

"We are, but we trust in the Lord that He will make the right decision for Gracie. It's all we can do," I answered in a hopeful voice.

Gracie called to Finn and he joined the group in their game of tag.

"I think Gracie has found a new best friend in Nia," I noted as I watched them giggling and hugging each other as they shared a secret. I couldn't help but smile at their quick and endearing friendship.

"I agree," Tiana replied. "They're so cute together."

Tiana and I became instant friends like we'd known each other forever. Even Finn and Otis were in deep conversation and got along well. We talked for over an hour before Finn said it was time to head home.

After returning to base, I hugged Tiana, and we agreed to meet for lunch soon and would arrange several playdates for our daughters.

We returned to our apartment with Finn carrying Gracie, who was sound asleep on his shoulder.

"Finn, would you mind if I check on Aaron, Jonas, and the dogs?" I asked.

"Sure. I can get Gracie her dinner and then into the bath. Take your time, love."

I called my brothers, who were both in their apartments with the animals. They informed me the dogs and puppies were fine, just underweight. Their bloodwork was normal, but the heartworm tests wouldn't return until tomorrow. They'd been given baths at the vet clinic and were tick and flea free.

I first stopped by Aaron's place. The mother and pups were settling inside a large dog bed amid an even larger pen. The veterinarian had clipped the poor dog's matted fur after being bathed, and she was white with a few random black and brown spots. She was adorable, and so were her puppies. They looked just like her.

Aaron had moved his furniture around to accommodate his new roommates. He even had an area in the kitchen where several puppy pee pads were placed in one corner.

"Mara, I decided to call her Lizzie. The pups—I guess I'll leave the names up to those who adopt them in the future," Aaron said.

"I like the name. It fits her." I petted Lizzie while she drowsily tended to her nursing puppies. "I have to say, I don't envy you having to take her topside every time she needs to take care of business."

"Yeah, that won't be fun, but they're worth it." He smiled with satisfaction.

I hugged Aaron and left to visit with Jonas.

Jonas had a comfy dog bed set up for his new pet too. He named the male dog Diesel, and they were already best friends. Diesel followed Jonas everywhere he went and stayed close on his heels.

"Jonas, does he know to go to the door if he needs to relieve himself?" I asked.

"He sure does. It makes me wonder if he belonged to someone. But I can't worry about that right now. I want to get him well. By the way, Diesel isn't the pups' father—he's already been neutered."

"I guess that's a saving grace. Oh, by the way, you need to remember his feeding schedule. Don't forget your next appointments with the vet too. He needs constant monitoring until his weight is back to normal."

"Yes, Mom," Jonas replied in a mocking tone.

"Butthead," I murmured and snickered out loud. I hugged him and strolled out the door.

"Mara, Aaron, and I will take care of you tomorrow. You'll be safe with us. You know that, don't you?"

"I do, Jonas, and thanks. It's just that I'm not looking forward to seeing inside the mind of that pervert. Ugly doesn't even begin to describe what I saw in there. May God be with us," I replied sadly, giving him another hug.

"He will, Mara. You can count on it." He hugged me back and kissed me on the top of my head.

When I entered the apartment, I heard giggling from the bathroom and saw Gracie soaking in the bathtub with Finn sitting on the floor, reading her a story. Even Asher was taking part, sitting on the side of the tub. He attacked one of Gracie's toys floating on the bath water's surface.

"Well, don't you two look happier than little pink piggies in a mud patch?" I asked, and Finn chuckled.

"You like pink piggies, Mommy?" Gracie asked in childlike wonder.

But I couldn't respond because I was shocked at her calling me "mommy." It was the first time she'd ever called me anything but "Mara."

Finn looked at me with widened eyes, and I sat down next to Finn, wearing a huge, silly grin.

"I like rats better," I commented as I winked at Finn, then said, "You called me mommy, Gracie. Are you sure, sweetheart? You know you don't have to." I moved closer to her, grabbed a washcloth, and gently washed away a smudge of dirt from her chin.

She looked at me with her lovely dimpled smile and replied, "I know I had a mommy before, but she's in Heaven, right? So…" She furrowed her brow in a child's thoughtful expression, then continued, "I would like to call you mommy and daddy. Please—with a cherry on top?"

Finn and I smiled brightly at her and answered quickly that we would love it if she did. She giggled joyfully at our answer, then started singing "Pop Goes the Weasel" to Asher. The cat stared at her and elegantly reclined on the tub's edge as if mesmerized by Gracie's crooning.

"I'll get dinner started for us, Mara." Finn stood, and as he turned, I saw tears of happiness slip down his cheeks.

Later that evening, after Gracie was put to bed, I took another soak in the jetted tub. Finn was brushing his teeth but stopped to watch me undress and climb into the frothing water.

I turned to look at him and retorted, "You're a lecherous man, handsome, but I wouldn't trade you for anything." He grinned, winked, then licked his lips like the big bad wolf.

"All the better to devour you, my dear." He walked over and knelt behind me. I moaned as he massaged the knotted muscles and tendons in my neck. I was enjoying his loving touch.

"Daddy, I need a drink of water, please." I jumped as I heard Gracie's voice and the soft knock on the other side of the locked door.

Finn lowered his head in defeat and muttered, "We're now officially parents, my dear." He kissed me and strolled out the door to tend to our lovely daughter.

After my soak, I examined my bruises in the mirror and was thrilled they were barely noticeable. As Finn walked in, he commented on how much better they looked, then stared at the large one on my face.

"Hmm. It's now a bright shade of a juicy lemon. Delicious!" He ran his hand down my naked back, and I swatted him playfully with a towel. "Come on, my sweet. I'm simply admiring your rosy cheeks," he admitted as he leered at my butt.

"Ha, ha. Very funny." I grinned back at him as I put on my night-gown. "As much as I would love to continue what we started in the tub, I'm exhausted, and we have a big day ahead of us." I looked at him through the mirror; my eyes were dark, worried, and apprehensive.

Finn turned me toward him and gently stroked my bruised jaw. "I'll be with you every step of the way. He can never hurt you again." He pulled me close in a warm embrace, and I nestled against him.

"Thanks, Finn. I needed that."

"By the way, my FBI friend will bring what you requested to the safehouse tomorrow. Do you honestly think you'll need those awful things to break through Maharis's barrier?"

"I'm afraid so. As gruesome as they may be, it should make him release that incessant block running through his mind when he's around the Gatekeepers. We better get everything we need from him tomorrow. I don't want to go into that pervert's mind any more than necessary."

Finn nodded and led me to bed. After falling asleep, I had another night terror, but Finn was there for me. After I changed out of another sweaty nightgown, I returned to bed, silently said a rosary to the Holy Mother, then slept through the remainder of the night, held closely in my husband's protective arms.

CHAPTER 9

The next day came all too soon, and when my alarm went off, I kept hitting the snooze button. After three snoozes, I tossed the offending alarm across the room and pulled the pillow over my head to quiet the insistent *buzz-buzz*.

I had no sooner fallen back asleep when I felt a hand on my shoulder. Finn's cheerful voice spoke into my ear. "Come on, sleepyhead, it's time to rise and shine."

"Go away! I need more rest! You can handle the morning routine." My voice sounded muffled from behind my pillow, and I turned away from Finn's direction.

"Mara, get up. I know you're tired, but we have to get moving." He pulled the pillow from my head, and when I turned to look at him, I gave him a murderous glare.

"Bugger...off!" My voice ground out each word, and Finn's eyes grew wide with surprise.

"What's with you today?"

"I'm in a foul mood; that's what's with me!" After seeing the exaggerated raised eyebrow on Finn's face, I said. "I'm sorry. I don't know what's wrong with me this morning. Sheesh!" I finally got out of bed and stomped to the bathroom.

Behind me, I heard him mutter, "I think the honeymoon is over..."

Preparing for our day, my mood improved. We ushered Gracie to Gloria's place and met with Jonas, Aaron, and Billie at the motor pool. Our entire team had been notified of today's mission, but Finn had advised them that they weren't required for this mission. But Billie wanted to join us—I assumed because she felt protective of me regarding my attempted rapist.

We reached the safe house an hour later and greeted the two Chosen men from our Delta team who were taking the current shift of watching Maharis. They guided us to a room where two people waited.

Finn said, "My team, this is my FBI contact, Rashidi Khaled. He prefers to be called RK. Sitting next to him is his partner, Jada Marsalis." Both people at the table stood up and we shook hands.

RK was approximately six foot six with short, thick jet-black hair and a well-trimmed mustache and beard. He was long and lean with serious, intelligent obsidian eyes. When he smiled, his face lit up, and as I glanced into his mind, I discovered this man had seen far too many tragedies in his career. Finn told me previously that RK's family was of Egyptian descent and that he and RK had been friends for some time. I liked the FBI agent and was pleased to finally meet him.

Jada was younger than RK and was lovely with her exotic good looks and kind, smiling brown eyes. Her dark, wavy hair was kept in check by a barrette, and she gave me the distinct impression she was a newer FBI recruit.

"It's a pleasure to meet you. Finn speaks highly of his team, and I hope you know all of your secrets are safe with Jada and me." RK nodded as he finished his welcome and handed me a large manila envelope.

"Mara, this is what you asked for, but I have to say, I still don't understand why you would want them. Though, I'm sure I'll soon discover the reason."

"Thank you, RK. I hope you know how much we appreciate everything you've done for us and what you may be asked to do in the future. Today, we'll attempt to find information on Maharis's past crimes and, in turn, obtain irrefutable proof as well. Even though our techniques are considered unconventional, they're generally successful. At the beginning of the session, my brothers and I will endeavor to place a deep wall within Maharis, so the demon will no longer have access to him. My brothers and I will then work together to obtain as much intel as we can find within his mind. I'm sure he'll call my brothers and me every vile name in the book to demean and distract us from our task. We'll enter the room alone, and it may take time for us to accomplish our goal. Are there any questions?"

"Finn said we're not to interfere unless it's requested of us. Shall we get started?" RK raised his eyebrows in question.

Our entire team, including RK and Jada, held hands and asked for God's guidance and protection, then concluded with the St. Michael prayer. As I glanced at Jada, she was surprised by our supplications yet pleased.

Finn hugged me close and whispered how much he loved me and gently caressed one curled tendril of hair that slid out of my French braid. I held his face between my hands, stood on tiptoe, and gave him a lingering, reassuring kiss.

I turned to Jonas and Aaron and said, "Remember, you'll probably see everything I see. It may get nasty in there, and nothing can prepare you for the ugliness. Aaron, you've never seen this part of the evil that men can do, not like Jonas. If it becomes too much for you, leave the room. Jonas has the skills to keep the wall in place."

Taking a big breath, I made the sign of the cross, and the three of us entered the room where Maharis was being held.

Maharis was blindfolded and shackled to a metal chair. It was attached to the cement floor by a robust one-foot chain welded to one of the legs so the chair could only be moved a few inches. There was a steel table in front of him that was also secured. Three empty seats were placed across the table from him. The only other object in the room was one roll of silver duct tape lying on the floor near the door that I had requested ahead of time. There was a sizeable one-way mirror against the other wall where my team could watch our interrogation.

The man who had previously attacked me sat silently but diligently tilted his head, listening to our every move. Jonas moved behind him and removed his blindfold. Both sides of his face were black and blue, and one eye was swollen shut. I knew this resulted from Finn's handiwork directly after my assault.

We walked to the other side of the table and stood silently, examining the man across from us. Dropping the sealed manila envelope on my side of the table, I stared at him, and he appeared smaller than what I'd seen in my night terrors and, actually, a little pitiful. I kept my expression neutral, not letting this deviant read anything from my face.

"Ahh, it's you. I'd recognize those big knockers anywhere. Did you come back for more, you little whore? I have to say, you had the sweetest little—" Before he could say any more, Jonas had him and his chair down on the ground and had the boot of his foot just short of crushing the pervert's windpipe.

I strode over to get the duct tape, started unwinding it, bent down, and wrapped it around his mouth and head, silencing anything else he might have to say. In my mind, I messaged Jonas and Aaron, and they put Maharis back into a sitting position.

My brothers and I sat across from Maharis and stared intently at him. He tried to speak, but the duct tape was doing its job, so he then attempted wriggling around to free himself from his bonds. But he was held firmly in place. He breathed hard, and we could hear his angry inhales and exhales rushing through his flaring nostrils.

As I moved into his mind, the music began, "The wheels on the bus go 'round and 'round...." I tried several ways to get into his psyche, but the irritating tune continued. Glancing at my brothers, we decided to implement phase two of our plan.

Sounding bored, I said, "Well, well, well...you poor thing. Look at you, so impotent. Oops, did I say that?" My brothers and I laughed hysterically, and Maharis's face turned beet red with fury.

Staring at him, I continued, "Seriously though, I do feel bad for you. How long has it been, Maharis? Don't you miss those young, nubile bodies—taking everything you want from them, then casting them aside and going on to the next?" I looked into his mind again and saw a flash of the horror of his crimes. The music was still there, but it ebbed to a quieter cacophony.

"I know how much you miss this. Would you like a peek to feed your insatiable hunger?" I pulled the photos from the envelope and placed one before him. His eyes grew wide, and his breathing quickened.

I scanned his mind again, and the music was fading.

Pulling out another picture, I slid it next to the other. I did my best not to look at the photos and silently instructed my brothers not to either, but they were hard to miss. The pictures were police shots of dead, naked, mutilated young men and women.

Maharis couldn't look away as I placed another one before him. He was now in a state of excitement, totally focused on the heinous photographs.

Then, I moved in for the kill. The music block in his mind was gone, and I dove into this maniac's psyche and memories. Connecting with my brothers, we placed an impenetrable wall to block the demon. This barrier should stop the evil one from ever infiltrating this man's mind, thus halting access through this rapist to any of us. Once it was in place, I accessed Maharis's memories. I tried not to focus on his killing spree because the ferocity of this man's crimes was beyond anything I could have imagined. Out of the corner of my eye, I saw Aaron abruptly leave the room, and a quiet "I'm sorry" could be heard in my mind.

I continued probing, moving quickly beyond the actual rapes and slaughters being committed and focused on locations and possible victim names. Moving deeper, I felt a quick, intense evil trying to enter Maharis, but our block was effective, and he was unable to get through.

Delving deeper, there was something up ahead that I needed desperately, and I made my way quickly toward it. This was it. I made sure every detail was drilled into my memory. As I tried to get more, nothing else would show itself. This must be all I was allowed to find. After pulling out of this psychopath's brain, I leaned back in my chair. Turning toward the mirror, I nodded to my people watching the scene. As I gathered the photos, Maharis mumbled protests when I placed them back in the envelope. Jonas and I stood and glared at the horrible man across from us. He was still in a heightened state of excitement and was intently focused on the envelope in my hands. Raising his eyes to mine, he stared at me with such intense hate that it permeated the room.

I walked around the table, and he followed me with his eyes. I stood before him, then bent over and whispered into his ear. "You'll never get to touch, rape, or mutilate anyone again. You're now wretchedly impotent and useless; not even a maggot will have anything to do with you. You're nothing—just a useless…little…man."

His rage, along with his excitement, was impossible to miss. I turned as if to walk away but swung back with a high, forceful kick and knocked him and his heavy metal chair back to the floor with a loud bang. Jonas winked, and we strolled quietly from the interrogation cell.

Aaron sat on the sofa in the other room with his head between his knees. Billie was rubbing his back in a comforting gesture.

"Is he okay?" I asked Billie.

"Yeah, he's fine. It must have been pretty ugly in there."

"That's an understatement," I muttered.

Finn, RK, and Jada walked out of the observation room and strolled toward Jonas and me. Finn asked one of the Delta team guards, "We need to talk elsewhere. Is there another more private room in this place?"

"Yup, over here. It's already set up for you." The guard led us down a hallway to a room with a large table and several chairs. There was a carafe of ice water and several empty tumblers. I poured a large glass, drank it all down, and swallowed another. Jonas did as well.

I looked directly at Finn and asked, "How long were we in there?"

"The two of you were in his mind for nineteen minutes. Mara, are you sure you want to do this now? Both of you look like death warmed over."

"Yes, I'm sure. Jonas?" As I studied him, I wondered if I looked as bad as he did—ghostly pale and as if we hadn't slept in months.

"I'd rather do this now and get it over with."

I nodded and began relating what I had seen in Maharis's psyche. "First of all, this man is exactly what my spirit guide had said—he's soulless. He has the typical traits of a psychopath: no conscience and doesn't give a rat's butt about what anyone thinks or feels. His sense of grandeur also fits the profile, and he even thinks he's a god. I'm not a forensic psychologist, but these thoughts constantly roam around in his head. I'm not saying all psychopaths are soulless, but he assuredly is. Why he has no soul? Unfortunately, this man was conceived through incest, and this deviant mortal sin runs through three previous generations of his family. His two siblings were born with extreme deformities and died immediately after birth. Maharis was the only surviving child of his incestuous parents.

"On to the even uglier part. He has killed thirty-nine innocent young men and women. He likes his victims between the ages of eighteen and twenty-six and has rarely deviated from these numbers. They're symbolic to him, but I don't know why or even care. His abductions were conducted mainly here in the U.S. and usually on the west coast, although he did kill a couple of people while he was overseas in the military.

"He took his time selecting, photographing, and stalking his victims. Once he captured one, he would drug them, then transport his quarry using a semi-truck he inherited from his grandfather. Every person he kidnapped on U.S. soil was taken to an old abandoned orchard in northern California. There's a rustic, run-down house on the property as well as a huge barn. He took all his victims inside this building. I believe he had a couple of special rooms under this barn where they were used to store the orchard's fruit."

I had to stop for a minute as I was feeling sick to my stomach.

Finn squeezed my hand and advised the others at the table, "She needs a break. Can we get her a cola?"

Jada nodded and left the room.

I took a few deep breaths while pulling mental strength from Finn. Jonas had also taken my other hand, and as I looked at him, he gave me a reassuring, shaky smile.

"I'm sorry, RK. When I entered Maharis's mind, I did my best to quickly sidestep what he did to his victims, but I guess I still witnessed a little too much."

"Don't worry about it, Mara. I'm still stunned by everything you and your brothers can do. Please, take your time and only continue when and if you're ready," RK replied compassionately.

Jada returned and handed me a couple of ice-cold sodas. I thanked her and drank one in relief, letting the sweetness slide down my parched throat.

I exhaled a large breath and began again.

"His room of torture won't get us much, so I won't discuss it. The space we need is also located on the underground level below the barn. I have to say, he was always well-organized and kept excellent records. Everything you need to identify his victims is in this room. Photos, dates, locations, and—" I trailed off and took several more gulps of the soda. My hands shook, and I couldn't make it stop. Finn and Jonas took my trembling hands in theirs again.

"He also took trophies, or mementos, from each victim. Everything is neatly cataloged and displayed in this place, including photos and videos of the rapes, tortures, killings, and dismemberments." I finally stopped, sat back in my chair, and finished the last of the soda with a still trembling hand.

No one spoke for several minutes, then RK said, "My Lord in Heaven! I'm so sorry you witnessed all this filth, Mara. I've seen a lot in my career, and I can imagine what you must be feeling. At least I never had to see inside the minds of the monsters I chased and captured."

RK's words touched my heart, and I read his sincerity. However, when I peered at Jada, her eyes were skeptical. She gave me a hard stare, and I knew she wanted to roll her eyes at my story, but she was too polite to do so. I understood she had no reason to trust me—other than the word of her partner.

I spoke up again, "There's an area of his mind that confuses me, and I don't know what it means—although I think it's important because the demon seems to have a heavy hand in what Maharis had been working on in this location. I saw glimpses of some animals in cages and even his human victims being contained in this same manner. If I had to guess, I'd say they were lab experiments. But what kind of tests? I haven't a clue. I must remind you that this man is brilliant, and whatever he's been working on in that lab could be inherently dangerous. That's all I could get from him, though I wish I could give you more."

The room was quiet as everyone digested the information.

RK finally broke the silence, "I suggest we keep this lab danger in mind when we go after this man's hideout. Mara, do you have the specific location of this orchard?"

"Not an exact address, no. I never saw it in his mind. However, I do know he owns it, but I don't think it was ever in his name—maybe it was under another. But there's no need for us to chase our tails. Hopefully, I can find it by simply following the landmarks I saw in his memories. That means a road trip for us."

Jonas directed a question to me, "Mara, do you know why we kept seeing Maharis's reflection while we were in his mind? Why did he appear to be looking into a mirror? I saw this three times."

"I viewed it too, Jonas, and frankly, I haven't a clue. Maybe he's simply that much of a narcissist. Hopefully, it doesn't mean anything," I answered.

Jada asked, "What did he take as mementos, Mara?"

I lowered my eyes and softly answered her.

"That son-of-a..." Finn blurted, unable to contain himself.

"Mara, are you sure? I mean, that's truly abominable," Jada exclaimed in shock.

"I'm sorry, Jada, but yes."

Even RK didn't look so good and was sickened by the information. But he cleared his throat and said, "If what you say is true, Mara, we certainly won't have any issues putting this monster in prison for several lifetimes."

"That's where you're wrong," I retorted loudly, then continued explaining, "Prison is not where we're going to put him! Maharis has many nefarious friends and even some in prestigious positions."

"But he can't possibly get off of all these counts of first-degree premeditated murder! That's impossible, Mara," RK blurted.

"Oh yes, he can—and he will! I saw his future as well, RK, not only his past. He won't get off of the murder charges, but he *will* escape. No matter what prisons you incarcerate him in, he vanishes from them. I've looked at several scenarios, and he gets away and begins his spree again. We will *not* let that happen! RK, you must keep him locked up in safe houses until we know how we will deal with him."

"Then why is it urgent that we find his killing site and the evidence if we don't put him on trial?" Jada demanded.

"We need the evidence to locate the bodies, identify the victims, and return them to their families. Haven't they suffered long enough? And don't forget the labs—we have no clue what kind of science project this creep was developing."

"She's right, Jada," RK admitted. "I understand you haven't seen what the Chosen can do, but I have. God specifically selected them to do these amazing things, and we can't ignore what they're saying. Let me prove that this killing zone exists, and then we'll go from there. What do you say?"

Jada thought hard about what RK had said, then she stared at me, her brows furrowed as she contemplated her decision.

"Okay. I agree to see *if* this orchard exists and *if* the evidence is there. But all bets are off if we don't find anything."

"Sounds fair to me," I said.

We left the table and all I wanted to do was go home. A raging headache was banging against my skull, and the exhaustion was overwhelming. I stopped at the bathroom, splashed my face with cold water, and swallowed some aspirin. Returning to the front entrance, RK and Jada had just stepped out the front door, and I stopped cold when I noticed Maharis standing by the wall, chained securely to a large beam. His feet were also shackled, his mouth still taped, and the man could only move a few inches. He was staring out the front window. The two Chosen guards stood near him, keeping an eye on their captor but unconcerned that Maharis was fixated on something outside.

As I approached the door, I moved past Maharis, giving him a wide berth. Reaching for the handle, I stopped suddenly, filled with intense rage. I turned like a shot, ran toward Maharis, lifting my body into a quick karate move, and kicked Maharis full force in the engorged region of his anatomy. He uttered a loud "whoomph" and passed out cold, his body sliding down the post and onto the floor. His arms were still above his head, chained to the post. The Chosen Ones stared at me questioningly and shrugged, then they both looked away as if they hadn't witnessed the assault.

Finn, Jonas, and Aaron eyed each other with painful expressions—as if they wanted to cover their groins with their hands in defense. Billie smiled widely, nodded her head in approval, and chuckled with glee behind her hand. I said nothing as we walked out of the house and climbed into our vehicle. RK and Jada's SUV was pulling away.

After several minutes, Finn finally asked, "Are you going to tell us what that was about, or is it a secret? Not that he didn't have that coming."

My anger had dissipated, so I was finally able to answer him, "Maharis was looking outside and watching Jada. He fantasized about what he would do to her as his next victim. I saw every bloody and gory detail of that pervert's idea of fun. That's exactly what I saw at the end of my mind-meld with that slug. If he gets sent to prison, he will escape, and Jada will be the next one he abducts, rapes, tortures, and kills. I was infuriated. It was instinct, and I decided to damage what he most adores." I turned to Finn and gave him a don't-mess-with-me glare.

He raised his hands in surrender. "I'm surprised you didn't kill him. I would have."

I heard the other three passengers say, "Me too!"

Aaron asked, "Why didn't you mention this in the meeting just now?"

"Because there wasn't any point. Jada is on the fence about us anyway. If we feel she needs to be told later, then we will," I replied.

"Mara's correct. I think Jada wants to believe us, but she doesn't yet. We need to give her time. Our biggest problem is what to do with Maharis. Any ideas, love?" Finn asked.

"Well, it's not up to us to take his life. But we'll be told how to handle or dispose of this demented individual. The end of his life is most certainly coming soon. That you can be sure of," I said, staring vacantly out the car window at the passing scenery. "By the way, Finn, why didn't you tell us that RK is a Chosen One? I know you said he was one of us, but I thought you meant one of the good guys." I looked at him questioningly with a raised eyebrow.

"Yeah, what's up with that? Why didn't you spill the beans?" Jonas asked accusingly.

"I know. I should have said something. But I figured you'd sense it once you met him," Finn said.

Billie snorted from the front seat. "Yeah, why in blazes isn't he with us at the base?"

Finn answered, "This is what he wants. A couple of years ago, he was shot twice by a serial murderer he was chasing and died on the operating table. He was legally dead for several minutes, but God sent him back as a Chosen One. RK decided he'd be more useful staying within the FBI ranks to assist in this war, and I believe he made the correct decision. Not all Chosen decide to join the teams. It's up to them how they want to fight within God's commission, which was RK's choice. He's hoping to build a Chosen team within the FBI—secretly, of course."

I pondered his words briefly, then asked, "How does Jada fit into RK's plans? We know she isn't a Chosen of God."

Finn shook his head and said, "I honestly have no idea. RK told me he has a gut feeling about her and thinks she'll be an asset to the team he's building. He's always had good instincts about people, so I trust his judgment."

I furrowed my brow, then replied, "I believe he's right. There's something special about her, but I can't put my finger on it. I guess time will tell."

CHAPTER 10

*A*fter returning to our apartment, I sat heavily on the sofa in exhaustion and closed my eyes. At least my headache was better.

I felt Finn's stare, but I was too tired to return his gaze. "My sweet, why don't you take a hot shower and then go to bed for a few hours? I can retrieve Gracie, bring her home, and entertain her for the afternoon."

"That sounds like Heaven, but when I close my eyes, I see those terrible images. I think I'll go to the pool and swim several laps until that monster is out of my head. Although, I'll take you up on your offer of picking up Gracie. I wouldn't be good company for her until I recover from this morning."

"Do whatever you think will help. I want my smiling, exquisite wife back again." He leaned over and kissed the top of my head and caressed my healing cheek and jaw. "You better get moving before you find that you can't."

I was thankful I had the large pool to myself and swam laps until I couldn't make another stroke through the water. Drying off the best I could, I pulled my clothes over my suit and returned home. As I walked into the room, Gracie ran over and embraced me. I knelt and held her close, taking in her love and childlike enthusiasm.

"I missed you too, pumpkin. Are you having fun?"

"Oh yes. Daddy and I are playing pretend. We're in a castle and I'm the princess. Daddy is the frog." I looked at Finn. He was crouched on the floor on all fours, flicking his tongue in and out.

"Ribbit!" I chuckled at Finn's imitation as he bounced around the floor. Even Asher was in on the action. He began jumping in the same motion as Finn.

"I'm so glad you're having fun. I wish I could join you, but Mommy needs a shower. You two enjoy yourselves." I kissed the top of her head, then kissed Finn and Asher.

After I finished my shower, I sat with a towel wrapped around me on the closed commode, wondering how I would get my nightgown on, then walk to the bed. By the time I struggled into my panties, I couldn't make another move. My body felt like it was filled with lead weights, and as I stared toward the bathroom door, I thought I would cry. *Dang—I hate this!*

Finn walked into the room and saw me looking exhausted and unable to stand.

"Oh, baby. I was worried about you and I was correct. Let me help." He assisted me into my nightgown, picked me up in his arms, and carried me to bed. "Now, sleep for as long as you need."

I mumbled something incoherent and was out like a light.

A few hours later, I woke to a darkened room and glanced at the bedside clock. It was after nine. I must have slept for over seven hours, but at least I felt better. After putting on a robe, I entered the living room, where Finn, Gracie, and Asher were watching television.

"There you are, sleepyhead. You *do* look more like my lovely wife," Finn complimented me with a bright grin. As I sat on the sofa with them, Gracie climbed into my lap. I hugged her and held her close. She was already bathed, in her pajamas, and getting sleepy.

"She wanted to stay awake until you got up because she was worried about you," Finn informed me.

"I'm doing great, Gracie, and thank you for your concern. You're very thoughtful, sweet pea." I gave her another squeeze and a tickle. She laughed joyously, and I loved hearing her spontaneous giggles.

"Mara, I kept your dinner warm. I'll bring it in and you can eat in front of the boob tube," Finn generously offered and brought me my supper, laying it on a tray table.

Gracie was already asleep in my lap, so Finn gently picked her up and carried her to her room, and tucked her in for the night.

The meal was delicious, and I didn't realize I hadn't eaten for several hours. Once I finished, Finn took care of my dishes and the tray.

I thanked him profusely, and he replied, "It's my pleasure to serve you, my lady." He spoke in an elegant British accent, then bowed royally. I peered at him with raised eyebrows, and he responded, "You have to realize that Gracie turned me from a frog to a prince. I'm now royalty and well-to-do. Would you now like tea and crumpets?" His accent was more pronounced but with a cockney flair. I laughed joyously at his humor, pulled him down next to me, climbed onto his lap, and kissed him passionately.

"You're my prince, Finn. I love you."

I moved suggestively against him, but he stopped me with a gentle hand, replying, "I love you so much too, but I have something to show you."

"I can hardly wait," I cooed suggestively.

"That's not what I meant, you little vixen. Give me a minute." He set me beside him, walked toward his office, returned with a closed office box, and set it on my lap. A label on the top said "Grace Eliana Garcia." I carefully opened the carton and found a well-worn stuffed animal, a receiving blanket, booties, a baptismal dress, a lock of hair in a baggie, and many photographs. As I looked at the pictures, there were many of Gracie from birth until her mother died when she was three and a half years old. There was also an exquisite one of Gracie with her mother. It looked as if it had been taken professionally. Now I knew where Gracie inherited her beauty. Her mother was apparently of Latino descent with glowing olive skin, expressive dark eyes, and thick, dark curly hair. She had been a gorgeous young woman and loved her daughter immensely.

"Finn, where on earth did you find these things?"

"I didn't—it was RK. When they closed that horrible orphanage where Gracie lived, they found paperwork for a couple of storage units. There were boxes and boxes of the children's personal items in those places."

I scanned her birth certificate and exclaimed, "Finn, Gracie's birthday was two weeks ago and she just turned five! We missed it."

"Really?" he asked and then looked at the date on the certificate. "Don't worry. We can arrange a party for her—maybe within the next few weeks?"

"That would be great. We can invite her new friends—she'll love it! We'll have to decide on decorations, a cake, gifts, invitations—the whole shebang!"

"Sounds like fun, love."

"Gracie will be thrilled to have these things from her mother. This is incredible, Finn. I'm ecstatic it was found."

"I agree. It's great that Gracie will have some personal possessions from her mother's life. I'll return the box to my office, and we can discuss this with her after Mass tomorrow."

After Finn returned to the room, he pulled me back onto his lap, and I laid my head on his chest, listening to his heartbeat and inhaling his enticing, sensual scent.

"Are you ready for bed? I think you're falling asleep again," Finn whispered.

"Mmm-hmm. At least tomorrow is Sunday, and we can sleep in for an entire extra hour, Finn."

"It sounds like heaven to me."

. . .

WE ATTENDED Mass the following morning, but I told Finn that I needed to speak with Father Faraj after the service. A large group of us were to meet for brunch at one of the restaurants, and I told Finn I'd catch up with them after I spoke with our priest. Finn smiled, kissed me, and guided Gracie out the church door.

Father was gracious and listened intently to my concerns. Afterward, I asked him to join us for brunch and he graciously accepted. We gathered at a large table piled high with various delicious foods.

Our mission team and our new friends from the picnic joined us. Gracie was thrilled to have her new best pals with us as well. Even Father joined in the fun, and he made us laugh with his cute jokes.

After returning to the apartment and changing clothes, I settled Gracie down to watch an animated movie. Finn and I sat in his office and decided how to approach our daughter about the things we found that belonged to her birth mother.

"Mara, may I ask why you needed to speak with Father?"

I blew out a breath, then replied, "It was about yesterday. I felt I had to confess about losing my temper with Maharis. It's been bothering me since I attacked him in the vestibule at the safe house. Not that I didn't think he deserved it, but he's still human, and I shouldn't have let my anger get the best of me. I knew it was a sin and needed to confess it and be absolved."

Finn contemplated what I said, but a silly grin formed on his face.

"What? It's not funny, you rat!" I had no clue what he found hilarious about my reconciliation.

"No, it's not your confession. It's just that everyone at the base is talking about what you did to that psychopath and how they all wished they'd had the opportunity of kicking that idiot in the bollocks too."

"Everyone knows? Oh my gosh, Finn, how embarrassing." Heat flushed my face and I covered my cheeks with my hands.

Finn pulled my hands away and gave me a sweet and tender kiss. "Love, no one is laughing at you—they're proud of you. I must say, your restraint is envied by everyone. Many people said they probably would've killed the nutjob. You did well, Mara. I understand how you felt you needed to confess losing your temper." He began to chuckle again, and I hit him over the head a couple of times with a throw pillow, giggling too.

"Ouch! Watch it, woman; you'll have to confess again for husband abuse." He chuckled once more with a glint in his eyes, then pulled me into his lap and kissed me passionately. At the end of the kiss, I laughed again.

"What?" Finn asked.

"I just realized something. During the confession, I related to Father Faraj what had transpired. I explained how I reacted by assaulting the murderer in his nether regions, but Father repeatedly turned away from me while he was finishing the rite. When we were done, his eyes were watering, and I couldn't figure out if he'd been crying or had a severe allergy problem. I now realize he'd been trying to hide his laughter."

"Oh my. I would've loved to have been a fly on the wall in the confessional," Finn replied, still chuckling at my circumstance.

"You handsome rat! There's a devious side to your nature." I playfully pinched him in the ribs, and it turned into a fun-loving wrestling match. I squealed in delight, and our game became something more serious and loving.

A WHILE LATER, we sat with Gracie and showed her the box of her birth mother's things. She loved the photos, although we kept one aside for later. We also explained that we discovered her birth date and would celebrate it within the next few weeks. She was overjoyed and said she couldn't wait. We spent the rest of the day as a family, enjoying a nice dinner, and then played games until Gracie's bedtime.

As Finn and I prepared to turn in for the night, I said, "We need to address when we should head to California to find Maharis's killing site. Do you have any ideas?"

"I've spoken with RK, and we're considering going on Wednesday. Will that work for you?"

"Yes, I think so. That gives me time to prepare mentally."

"Goodnight, my sweet." He caressed my cheek and fingered one of my red tresses. "You amaze me, Mara. Do you know that?"

I snuggled against him and smiled like a Cheshire cat in satisfaction. "What a lovely thing to say. Thank you. And you never cease to amaze me, too—in every way imaginable."

"You're insatiable," he crooned, then kissed my neck.

"It's all your fault. You're irresistible, and I can't keep my hands— or anything else away from you." I chuckled deviously and began a trail of kisses across his beautifully muscled chest.

"Argh!" he growled in his pirate impersonation.

I giggled, then replied in a whisper, "Any time, my crazy, gorgeous peg-leg pirate."

CHAPTER 11

The next couple of days were enjoyable but busy. However, I couldn't shake the exhaustion and the moodiness.

On Monday, our team met to discuss the upcoming mission and who would be involved. RK and Jada would meet us at the airport, along with a couple of their trusted forensic scientists. The plans were made, and we'd leave early on Wednesday morning.

Finn and I had lunch together, and he spoke up when we were served our food, "I've scheduled our flight for tomorrow morning, and RK, Jada, and their team will meet us with vehicles at the airport in Oakland, California. We'll take Highway five north, per your request. Then we'll leave the navigation up to you."

I frowned momentarily, then said, "That'll work." I tilted my head, thought for a couple of minutes, then shook off the feeling of trepidation.

"Mara, I see your thoughts bouncing around in your beautiful head from over here. Is there something wrong?"

"I...don't know. As we get closer to the trip, the feeling of foreboding grows stronger. This shouldn't be a dangerous mission—disgusting and horrifying—yes, but not dangerous. So why do I feel this way? I see Maharis's reflection again when I think about him. It's bizarre."

"I trust your instincts and we must follow them. Also, I'm enforcing full gear get-up in case there's any danger. I'll contact our team as well as RK. On another note," Finn continued, "do you think Aaron should join us on this mission? I have reservations. He still seems shaken about what he saw in Maharis's mind."

"After seeing Aaron earlier today, I agree with you—he needs to sit this one out. He pretends he's back to normal, but we both know that's untrue. I told him to see Brianna to talk about his experience inside that nut job's head, but he blew it off. He might listen if you're the one to tell him to see the doc because he respects your authority."

He nodded at my suggestion and replied, "I'll talk to him and see what I can do. If that doesn't work, I'll make it an order, but I prefer he sees her voluntarily. Forcing him may make him push back harder against getting help. I must say, though, knowing Aaron, he'll go if we keep a united front."

"Thanks, Finn. I feel better already. Now let's enjoy our 'Death by Chocolate' dessert."

THE NEXT DAY, we landed in Oakland and were greeted by RK, Jada, and the two forensic experts, Ron and Craig. Our Chosen team consisted of Finn, Jonas, Edison, Jasper, Billie, and me. RK had two large black vans waiting for us, and we stowed our gear in the back. I'd drive the first van, and Jonas would take the second. RK rode with Finn, me, Jasper, Billie, and everyone else would take the second vehicle. RK questioned us about what threats may be before us on this trip. I explained my trepidation and what I saw in my mind about Maharis, who was continually looking into a mirror.

RK's eyes were thoughtful, and he said, "I did a deeper dive on Maharis, and I still couldn't find anything legit on him before the age of twenty-eight. The birth certificate on file from his military days turned out to be fake, albeit a good one. So, we have nothing on his siblings, parents, grandparents—I mean, zilch. We're on our own on this one. Hopefully, when we find the orchard, we may be able to conduct a trace on the property."

"This guy is a mystery," I agreed. "When we arrive at the location, I'd like everyone to stay in the vehicles while I scan the surrounding area. I doubt I'll be able to find much because I can usually only feel demons, but it's still worth a try."

"Roger that," RK replied. He phoned Jada in the car behind us and relayed my request.

We drove for several miles, and I knew we were on the right course. After two hours, we stopped at a diner for a break which included lunch. It was good to stretch our legs and get a bite to eat. The conversation was light and we even joked around. I liked RK's two forensic specialists. They were also kind, although a little too serious.

Jada was another story. She was barely civil to me, using short and abrupt answers when spoken to and, at times, glared scornfully in my direction. I tried to keep my annoyance at bay, hoping after a while, she'd begin to believe what we were doing was real and necessary.

After lunch, we climbed back into the vehicles, filled up the tanks at the gas station, and returned to the expressway. I began to feel an urgency that I needed to exit the interstate. Clicking on the turn signal, I exited and stopped at a crossroad. Checking the mirrors, I spotted Jonas's vehicle directly behind me. I sat quietly, waiting for divine direction.

Everyone in the vehicle was silent, and I felt their eyes on me as to what I may do next. My mind immediately pulled me to turn east, so I followed my instincts. We traveled this road for ten miles, and I knew I had to turn north again. Slowing the vehicle at a crossroad, I waited a few moments but didn't take the turn and drove east again until the next corner. This wasn't right either. After driving another two miles, I knew I should turn. Jonas followed closely behind, and we were headed north once again. The landscape grew denser and less inhabited.

I recognized the area from the mind of Maharis, but not enough to confidently drive anywhere specific. Slowing the vehicle again, I knew we had to turn off onto a westbound road. This next track was rough, but I knew it was the one we needed. I carefully maneuvered around the potholes but drove for another ten minutes. Eventually, I slowed the van until I came to a stop. It was quite dark because the trees were dense along this road, but I knew we had to turn again.

Spotting a downed pine tree about ten feet ahead, I knew the driveway was close. Putting the van back into gear, I drove to the tree and stopped again. I stepped out of the vehicle, leaned against the hood, and scanned the area, hoping God would tell me what I needed to know. Finn, RK, Jasper, and Billie exited the car and came to my side. They didn't say a word and waited for my next move.

I looked right, then left. There were a lot of downed limbs along this road, and so much of it looked the same, but I knew different. I walked across to the other side and began pulling limbs away from one area. The others followed my lead and dragged the brush to one side. There it was—a narrow dirt driveway. RK walked over to a dilapidated post. He uncovered it, and there was an old sign that had flipped upside down on its rusted nail. "Runyon Orchards" was all it said.

"Let's go," I said quietly, and we climbed back into the vehicle. RK radioed the car behind us, and we drove down the long and narrow, winding driveway. As we traveled forward, we saw hundreds of old fruit trees. We turned another curve, and I spotted a clearing ahead that included a huge old farmhouse, several outbuildings, a few old trucks, tractors, and the giant barn I'd seen in my vision.

"Tell the team in the second vehicle to wait and ask Jonas to scan the area," I instructed RK.

Clearing my mind, I began to search the property, but I stopped and grabbed Finn's hand. He knew I needed his support simply by the haunted look in my eyes.

"This is definitely the place," I whispered. Then taking a deep breath, I continued, "I see the horrifying darkness of his heinous crimes, the blood, the screaming...." I trailed off because I had to push quickly past the horrors of this place, and Finn squeezed my hand in comfort. "We all know that's the barn, but I'm sorry to say, I can't gauge with certainty if any other people are on this property. I know there aren't any demons here, but please confirm this with Jonas. If he agrees with my assessment, we'll have to do this by the book."

Jonas couldn't determine if there was anyone else on the premises either. RK said we'd start with the house and make sure it was clear. Then we'd move to the dreaded barn. We exited our vehicles, and we let RK take the lead, and he gave us the orders. He requested that Billie and I, as well as the techs, stay behind and for me to continue scanning the area. We inserted our earbuds, donned our Kevlar vests, and checked our weapons. RK's advanced team slowly approached the house in combat formation.

Billie and I kept our eyes and weapons trained on the surrounding landscape, ensuring our team stayed safe while they approached the farmhouse. Their communications could be heard as they entered the building and went from room to room, floor by floor. We heard the word "clear" as they traversed the house.

"Son-of-a..." was blurted into my ear, and RK apologized and said he was fine. His foot had fallen through a loose board in the third-floor attic. Several chuckles were heard in response, and we were finally told they were exiting the house.

Billie and I continued scanning the entire area, and we didn't see any other activity.

"This place gives me the heebie-jeebies," Billie muttered. I grimaced in response and agreed with her comment.

Our team returned to the vehicles, and RK reported, "I didn't see any evidence that anyone had been in that house for quite some time. How about everyone else?"

The others agreed.

I spoke up, "I guess we need to move on to the barn, though I have to say, I feel a sense of impending doom within that building. But I don't know if it's from the residual violence by Maharis or if there's a new danger. I'm sorry I can't be more forthcoming."

"I agree, Mara. I'm not getting anything else, either," Jonas said. "However, I'm seeing that horrible mirrored reflection of Maharis again."

RK instructed Jasper and one of his forensic techs to stay at the vehicles and watch our six. Then he advised us on how we'd enter and approach the barn. We could tell there were four obvious possible entrances: one set of double doors on the main floor for large machinery, a service door at both the front and back of the building, and a smaller one on the second floor for the hay elevator. We decided to forgo worrying about the elevator hatch.

We split up into teams and entered the lower doors to the premises. I was with Billie and RK, and we would enter through the large machinery doors. The massive doors squealed loudly as we slid one of them aside on its upper rail. Upon entering, we heard a loud fluttering of wings as several pigeons were startled from their perches in the upper loft, and they flew out of several broken side windows. Finn and Edison whispered that their two teams were inside the barn.

This building was so full of machinery, hay, straw, pitchforks, shovels, pails, etc., that we couldn't see any farther than ten feet. It was also dark except where the sun's rays slipped through cracks in the wood at the upper west side of the barn. The barn smelled of mold and old wood, and the dust tickled my nostrils, and I struggled not to sneeze. We moved forward only a few feet at a time, carefully scanning each area.

"My team is heading to the loft," Edison murmured through our earbuds.

"Copy that," RK replied quietly.

"Copy," Finn said as well.

Our team moved in farther, but we halted and crouched quickly when we heard a rustling to our right. We waited, then RK moved toward the sound and realized it was only a giant rat. RK grimaced, and we continued our sweep. It was tricky maneuvering around the equipment, and we did our best not to knock anything over and remain as quiet as possible.

"Finn here. I believe we've found the entrance to the lower level. Once you've cleared your section, head to the northeast corner."

"Will do," RK answered. He nodded at us, and we continued forward.

"Wait," I said. Stopping in my tracks, I remained still. RK and Billie kept scanning their surroundings. Some dirt drifted from the floor above us through the wooden floorboards and landed on our heads. RK rechecked his phone and discovered Edison's team was moving above us.

I still gave the signal for my team to stand where they were. Something was directly below us, and I could feel death and blood in my bones.

Addressing the team, I whispered, "The torture chamber is below, people. I also just saw a flash of Maharis's image again. Everyone, please be careful."

Edison's team muttered, "Clear" from the upper barn level, and they descended the loft ladder. We cleared the main level and then merged at Finn's location.

Finn's rifle was pointed down at his side as we approached, then he aimed it toward a hatch in the floor. "On the southeast side of the barn, we found another door that leads to the basement."

RK nodded and said, "In that case, let's split up and enter through both entrances. Jasper and Ron, I need you to leave the vehicles to cover the two entrances to the basement. Jasper, find a vantage point and cover the basement door at the south. Ron, join us at our location, find a hiding place near the lower-level hatch, and cover us from there."

The two men replied, "Copy," and we waited until they were in place.

RK, Billie, Finn, and I were to enter through the hatch, and the others were to use the other cellar entrance.

RK signaled Finn, and RK stood at the door, his rifle raised, waiting for Finn to open the hatch door. Finn swung it open quickly, but luckily the stairway was empty. We realized it was well-lit, so someone was still paying the electric bill.

Finn took the lead and began descending the stairs, staying vigilant and sweeping his rifle back and forth. The rest of us followed behind. I was the last one to descend the stairs, and I nodded to Ron, who was off to one side on the main floor, keeping a sharp eye on the basement hatch. He returned my nod, and I moved down the steep stairway.

We made it to the bottom, and it smelled dank with decay and something else that must have been rotting fruit. Finn made a few motions to us, and we traversed down the cement corridor. It opened into a broader space that split into two more hallways. Finn looked at me with a questioning brow. I nodded, closed my eyes, and concentrated. After a few moments, I opened my eyes and pointed to the hallway to the left.

"Billie and Mara, please clear the hallway on the right and its adjacent rooms. We'll wait and guard this area until your return," RK ordered, and we did as he had instructed. Finding nothing but rooms filled with rotted fruit, we returned to RK and Finn.

The four of us now moved down the hallway I had pointed to earlier. Periodically, we heard updates from Edison's team, but they hadn't found anything yet. Our team continued, but I whispered, "Stop." We approached three doorways, and I said quietly, "The killing room is the third door on the right. I don't know yet about the trophy room."

Our team cleared the first two rooms as we moved down the hallway. RK opened the killing room door, and he and Finn cleared the area. As we looked around at this horrible place, it was exactly as I had seen it in Maharis's mind. The room was cement, and I first noticed the bloodstains on the walls, ceiling, and floor. Even though the smell of bleach filled the air in this room, you could still detect the unmistakable odor of blood and death.

In the center of the room was an anchored large metal surgical table.

Off to the side was a steel tray on a rolling stand. A variety of several instruments were on this tray, still covered in blood, and who knows what else was adhered to their surfaces. A large drain was in the center of the floor that was still wet from a recent washing. There were also large hooks on one wall where chainsaws, hatchets, and handsaws were hung. At least these appeared to be cleaned. To the right was a large double utility tub that had also been permanently stained with blood. A curled up green garden hose with a sprayer was rolled onto a hook by the tub. Next to the wash area on the floor were many buckets stacked inside one another that had once been white but were also stained a dark reddish-brown. RK walked over to a large double-door metal cabinet and opened it to see what was inside. To our dismay, there was a plethora of sex toys of every size and nature. RK quickly closed the cabinet and turned away in disgust.

"Let's get the hell out of this animal's torture chamber," RK growled, and we quickly piled out of the ghastly cell of death.

When we returned to the hallway, our faces were pale, and we had a sick look in our eyes. But, being God's solid, well-trained soldiers, we continued moving forward with stoic resignation. As we turned the corner, it opened into a large area piled high with stacks of stained, empty fruit crates. We heard a quiet scuffle coming from ahead, and we raised our rifles. It was Edison's team.

RK said, "Edison, please take your team back down this hallway to the first door. That's the killing room. I need Craig to begin taking photos while my team finds the trophy room, then we'll report back. Be forewarned; it's a real hellhole. The rest of us will make sure this barn is completely clear." Edison nodded, and they passed us and went on to the killing room.

We continued down the last hallway that hadn't been cleared. Only three doorways remained, one on each side of the hall and one at the end. The first one we opened was a crude bathroom, so we left it and traveled to the second door.

After signaling to Finn, RK threw open the door, and Finn stood to the side, ready to shoot at whoever may be on the other side of the entrance. Finn nodded to the rest of us, and we entered the huge space. There were rows and rows of metal shelves filled with canned fruit and vegetables. We split up and took each aisle, scanning for hostiles.

Maharis's reflection appeared before me again. *Dog gone it! What does it mean?* I kept moving until we met at the other side, where the shelving ended. This was the trophy section. Along the back wall were more shelves to one side with glass jars of unmentionable items. Each container was meticulously labeled and numbered. Along the right side was a peg board on the wall with carefully logged photos of each victim, labeled and numbered. There was another shelf to the right with dozens of video tapes tagged with each victim's name. In self-defense, I had to block my mind because every killing played over and over like some horrible snuff film. I fell hard on my knees, and Finn was there, wrapping his arms around me as I gathered myself together.

"You okay, Mara?" RK asked with concern.

"Yes…just give me a minute." I saw another flash of Maharis, and I stood up in fear.

"This room is clear," RK said. He moved a few feet away toward one of the canning shelves and was about to speak to the other team, and I saw a terrifying flash in my head.

"RK—look out!" I screamed.

At that moment, a hulk of a man came barreling out from behind one of the fruit storage shelves straight at RK. The attacker raised a lethal-looking knife and aimed at the agent's back. RK tried to sidestep quickly, but he wasn't fast enough. The intruder stabbed him in the back of his right shoulder. RK twisted his body around, and they both went down in a tangle of flailing arms and legs as each man struggled to win the fight. The assailant was now on top, grunting, growling, and drooling, and RK was losing the skirmish. Finn and I were already there, trying to pull the man off him. By this time, Billie had returned from another sweep of the other shelves and struggled to wrench the assailant from RK. But trying to dislodge this maniac was like attempting to move Mt. Rushmore.

"We have to stop him! He's crazed with terror!" I screamed at Finn as I raised my gun, but Finn was faster. He deftly moved so he wouldn't inadvertently shoot RK, then fired his pistol twice into the crazy man's back. RK shoved the man's body away, and it rolled over, landing face up, but the attacker was still alive. This giant man sobbed loudly from terror and pain, looking desperately for someone to help him.

As I moved to approach him, I was surprised how he was the spitting image of Maharis, but this man was more heavily muscled with a fleshier-looking face. Finn blocked me from getting close to the assailant, but I shook my head and told him he wouldn't hurt me. Finn gave me a puzzled stare, nodded, then kept his gun trained on the man as I knelt beside him.

"It's okay. We're your friends and we won't leave you. You're safe now, I promise." I spoke to this man gently, trying to calm the frantic crying and ease his shock and panic. Our attacker was grunting, and I realized he couldn't speak. He tried to grab my hand, but Finn attempted to intervene.

"Finn, it's okay. He's mute, so he can't communicate. Plus, he knows he's dying and needs comfort," I said. Finn stayed close by but let the man take my hand. I delved into his mind and saw many images, including some that were heinous; I had to shove them aside. Then I reassured this dying poor soul, which calmed him. It was only a few moments before the hand gripping mine went limp, and the eyes imploring me for help turned into a blank stare. His spirit left his body, moving around the room, and I felt its intense sorrow. It proceeded upward, and his despair was replaced by immense joy as it ascended toward the heavens.

"He's gone," I replied in sadness.

Billie was helping RK, but he said he was fine, and she and Finn helped him sit upright. His face was bruised, but I was more concerned about the stab wound. Billie knelt behind him and examined the bloody injury.

"You were lucky, RK. It doesn't appear that anything major was severed." Billie removed the med kit from her vest and began treating RK's wound.

"It hurts like hell, but then they always do. This isn't my first, and I'm sure it won't be my last." RK tried to laugh but missed by a mile. He hissed when Billie applied the antiseptic.

"You want something for the pain? I have morphine," Billie asked.

"No. Just give me acetaminophen—I need to keep my mind clear." RK took the tablets without water, and we helped him to stand. He staggered slightly, but righted himself, then grabbed his weapon from the floor and returned it to its holster.

"Where in Sam Hill did Maharis come from, and how on God's green earth did he escape from custody?" RK barked in anger.

"He's not Simon Maharis," I replied softly. "This man is—or should I say was—his identical twin brother. Let's get this job done, and I'll explain later. I don't feel any more danger from another human or demon, and I'd prefer to spend as little time as possible in this house of horrors." I gave RK a pleading look, and he nodded in agreement.

Finn said, "We have one last room to clear. RK, are you up to it?"

"Let's go," he said, and we approached the last door.

As we arrived within a couple of feet of the room, we noted a hallway that led both left and right of this enclosure, but they were dead ends. It was lined with windows, but the interior was dark. As we neared the door, our bodies were blocked by some unseen force. No matter how hard we tried, we couldn't step any closer.

"What's going on?" Jada asked with disbelief.

"I don't know," Finn replied. "Jonas, can you see anything through the windows?"

Jonas pulled out his laser flashlight and shined it through the glass. He scanned it back and forth, and as he moved along them, he still couldn't get closer than two feet.

When he finished his scan, he said with remorse, "It's a lab." He looked at us and shook his head in grief. "It has four rooms. The first tiny one is the changing room, and the second is the disinfecting cell. Then there's the actual lab, and through to the back is where he kept his subjects."

We all cringed and immediately took several steps back. But Jonas stayed where he was and began running the light along the seams around the door and walls surrounding the room. There were also massive vents and pipes leading into the lab.

RK said, "It looks like he did his due diligence. This room has its own air treatment and filtration system. Not that I know much about labs either, but that's my two-cents worth."

"What do we do?" Jada asked.

"Luckily, God stopped us from entering," I replied.

"I'll have to call in a hazmat team, and they'll handle this lethal situation," RK said.

I felt a sudden sense of foreboding, and within my mind, God sent me a dire warning. "No! We have to take care of this ourselves. We can't let our government, or anyone else for that matter, get a hold of this diabolical monster's research. Who knows what he was working on and how far he got, but we can't let this weapon leave this place. It's what God wants."

"Mara, are you sure? Because now we have to figure out how to destroy this lab without taking down the entire barn," RK said.

"I'm positive."

Finn and Jonas discussed possibilities, and then Jonas said, "We do have these new Blue Fire timed grenades that might do the trick, but we have to get them inside. There's a hazmat suit in the entry room of the lab."

"I guess that's what we'll have to do," Finn replied. "I'll go in and set up the bombs."

I was about to object, but Jonas interrupted, "Finn, you don't have any biohazard experience. I do. I'll go in and set the bombs. While I'm at it, I'll try to find his research data."

I insisted we say a prayer of protection then Jonas approached the door. He paused within two feet of the entry again, and we wondered if God would let him through. But Jonas took another hesitant step and was allowed to enter the anteroom. He closed the door securely behind him, and we watched as all three rooms lit up like a Christmas tree. We gasped when we saw the latest technology in biochemistry and engineering. It was amazing, yet terrifying. He donned the suit, checked for leaks, and entered the disinfecting chamber.

After Jonas left the second room, he entered the lab. He moved to the computer, found some spare thumb drives, and backed up several files. When he finished, he walked into the back chamber, and we tried to see what he was doing, but from our vantage point, we lost him. After several minutes, he walked out of the subject room and gave us a thumbs-up. Then moving to the center of the lab, he set the other grenade. When Jonas set the timer, he re-entered the disinfecting cell and was sprayed from every direction. The green light flashed, and he moved to the entry space, removed the suit, and walked out to join us.

"They're set. We have five minutes, then it will go "whoosh." We're safe here, but God's holy fire will destroy everything in the room. I was also able to find several data files and backed them up. At least we have his research so we can figure out what he was working on," Jonas said.

His face looked pale, and I asked, "Jonas, are you okay?"

"Yes. The specimen room was pretty ugly. He used several poor animals, and there was a cell for a human, but luckily, it was empty."

I crossed myself and said, "Dear Holy Mother of God."

The room then exploded in a "whoosh," as Jonas said. The rooms were filled with blue fire, and we waited for what would happen next. After several minutes, the fire dissipated, and all that was left was a dense, royal blue fog. But we could see that all of the contents in the rooms had disappeared, including the cabinets, counters, refrigeration units—absolutely everything.

Jada stared through the glass in stunned silence. She finally turned to me with raised eyebrows, and I said, "Don't ask—we don't know how it works, but God does, and that's all that matters."

"I guess we're done with this portion of the mission," Jonas said. "We just have to deal with the rest."

"Jonas is correct. We need to return to where we left our attacker, and I'll call in the rest of our team so we can finish this horrible job," RK said with remorse.

The remainder of our team had arrived at our location, wondering what had happened. I could tell by the look on their faces they were also shocked at seeing the man who looked like Maharis.

"Okay, team, we have a job to complete. Ron and Craig, get the rest of your gear from the van, and let's get this over with."

They both said, "Copy that."

RK spoke again, "Finn, I'll let you take over. I'll handle my team, and you can take care of your end of things." Finn nodded, squeezed RK's good shoulder, then ordered Billie, Edison, and Jasper to assist RK's team.

"Finn, I'd like to go up top and see where the victims' bodies are buried on this property," I said shakily. "To tell you the truth, Jonas and I need to get out of this basement. We can only shield ourselves for so long." Jonas's face was devoid of color, and I knew he was also working desperately to keep the visions at bay.

"Take Jada with you, Finn," RK ordered.

"I'm…fine. I don't need to go up top…I can help," Jada stammered, obviously also feeling ill at what she'd seen in the trophy room and the torture chamber.

"Go!" RK barked. Jada nodded and followed Finn, Jonas, and me back to the top. We exited the barn, returned to the vehicles, and sat down for a few minutes. I handed Jada a soda and told her to drink it.

"Trust me, the sugar helps," I said as I handed her the ice-cold soda. Jada gulped it quickly, and everyone else enjoyed theirs as well.

After several minutes, I replied, "Jonas, take the property's north side, and I'll take the south. Let's start around the buildings, and we can move out from there. You and I both know the bodies are here somewhere. We can both feel them."

"You got it, sis."

"Jada, you can come with me if you like. Finn, would you mind assisting Jonas?"

"Sounds like a plan, love."

CHAPTER 12

*J*onas and I searched the property by the house and the outbuildings, but we had no luck. I knew the bodies were here but weren't near the home. Looking around, we noticed three roads leading off the estate. I assumed these tracks led to different fruit orchards. Sure enough, we saw three distinct rusty signs. The first was the one we used to enter the property, and it said "Exit." The other two had signs that read "Tree Orchard" and the other, "Berry Fields."

"Jonas, did you feel the victims when we drove onto the property?"

"Nope, not nearby."

"Me neither, so we better check the other two roads. Jada and I will head toward the tree orchard." We climbed into the first van, and Finn and Jonas took the second vehicle toward the berry fields.

I could feel Jada watching me as I drove, but I ignored her and concentrated on finding the burial site. After stopping the vehicle a few times, I exited the van and stood silently, hoping to find Maharis's victims. We were getting farther away from them—not closer.

Climbing back in, I glanced at Jada. "There's no way they're near this road," I whispered in frustration.

A shout from Jonas came through my earbud, "Mara! They're here; I know it. But I need you to find the precise location."

"We'll be right there," I responded. Turning the van around, I sped back down the lane, then turned down the other one that led to the strawberry fields. We approached Jonas's vehicle, and he and Finn stood off to one side. I parked, and Jada and I rushed over to join them.

This wide-open field was sporadically covered with old strawberry plants—way past their prime. I felt the victims, but yet, something wasn't quite right.

"You're correct, Jonas. They're certainly close by, but..." I said, trailing off. I waited and let my mind wander. Scanning the field and moving back and forth with my eyes, something caught my attention. The movement was toward a wooded area to the right of this parcel.

"Over there!" I began walking as if in a trance to the direction where I had seen something—but what, I wasn't sure. Jada, Finn, and Jonas followed my lead as I moved along the edge of the field by the wooded tree line. I stopped when I saw it—or should I say him. It was a wisp of a shadow of a young man. He was motioning to me, and I ran toward him. As I neared him, he disappeared into the woods. Halting, I turned and entered the same area where he'd vanished. It was a man-made path, and as I continued, it opened into a wide-open shrine. Many crudely made crosses and cut wildflowers had been placed everywhere. As I examined the ground, it was apparent this was the burial site. There were several rows of raised mounds of dirt. Most were old and overgrown with grass; others were fresher and relatively new. Each grave had been given a simple wooden stake that displayed a number.

"Finn, call the entire team and tell them to get here ASAP. They won't want to miss this," I replied, and Finn contacted them. He headed out to the van to wait for the remainder of our group.

As I watched the scene before me, ghostly apparitions appeared individually. They said nothing but stood huddling together; gazing at us with happiness and hope at being found.

We waited because I didn't want to speak with the victims until the remainder of our team arrived to witness what was to come. After several minutes, I heard them approaching and told everyone to hold hands. The FBI team appeared puzzled, but they complied.

"Don't break the link; you'll be amazed by what comes next," I said.

Reaching for Jada's hand, she pulled it back, eyeing me strangely. "Trust me. Take my hand, Jada." I took Finn's hand on the other side, and everyone else joined in. Jada thought about it for a moment, then she tentatively clasped mine.

She was still eyeing me, so I said, "Jada, look over there." I pointed ahead of us. She gasped at what she was now witnessing. Other amazed words were spoken by the rest of the FBI team.

"What is this?" Jada croaked in a whisper.

"The victims. They're filled with joy at being found and only want to ascend to Heaven. They now know they can move on to the Father," I cried with relief.

As I glanced at Jada, there were tears in her eyes. "It's wonderful!" Her voice was filled with awe and astonishment.

"Yes, it is," I replied.

The same young man I'd seen previously moved toward us, smiling happily. We stood still as he came to stand before me.

"You came. We were afraid you wouldn't find us. Can we now leave and move on to what has been calling us?" he asked with sincere hope.

"Yes, you can. But, before you go, do you know if these are all of his victims?" I asked, wanting to ensure we had found every body.

"They're all here except for two, which were his parents. He burned them years ago in the old furnace at the end of this road. Their spirits left long ago, so you can do nothing for them. There were three more in Afghanistan that he killed while he was deployed. They have already moved on," he said.

"Thank you, Ephraim, is it?" I asked.

"Yes, and you're welcome. You'll tell our families about us, return our bodies to them, and tell them we're joining our holy Father in Heaven?"

"We will do all that you ask of us, Ephraim."

"Thank you!" he replied joyously, then returned to join the other spirits waiting for him.

Jada was about to pull away, but I told her to wait. She turned back to the spirits scattered along the back of the graveyard. I counted thirty-four of Maharis's victims in this burial ground. If I added his parents and the three people he killed in Afghanistan, that equaled the thirty-nine victims I saw in Maharis's mind at the safe house.

A bright light started to move from the trees above and descended to the victims' spirits below. As it approached them, the beam turned into thousands of intense colors that aren't normally seen by the human eye. These were the marvelous hues I'd seen during my trip to Heaven. The view was spectacular as it surrounded the ghostly apparitions. We heard joyous music and saw hundreds of white doves swirling around the spirits in harmony with the music and the colorful lights. There was a strong scent of flowers in the warm breeze that was only known in the heavenly realm. This wind gently buffeted us as it swirled and danced around us and the ghosts. What was even more strange, this breeze never lifted any dirt, leaves, or debris as it flitted around the entire area. There was one bright, instant flash of colorful beaming rays, and Maharis's victim's ghosts were gone, raised to the glory of Heaven.

Everything around us was back to normal, and we disengaged our hands. Jada sat hard on the ground, along with RK and the two forensic scientists. I heard them crying in amazement at what they had witnessed. The rest of our team was grinning with our usual awe at what God gave us—a brief glimpse of the glory of His Heavenly Kingdom.

"Heavens to Betsy, the Lord above always knows how to give us a show!" Jasper declared in his charming accent. "Praise Jesus!" He began pacing, shaking his head and smiling with amazement.

After a while, our teams returned to the vehicles. RK rode with us back to the barn, and we asked how he felt after being stabbed.

"I'm fine; the pain is down to a dull roar." He quietly chuckled. "By the way, after you left the trophy room, we found where Maharis's brother had been hiding. There's a false panel behind one of the shelves. This shelf is connected to the wall, revealing a small hidden room inside. It looked like this was where this man spent most of his time. There were children's books, toys, a small cot, a sink, and a toilet. We missed this hidey-hole. No one is to blame—someone would have had to carefully examine each wall to have found it. I'll have my team do a more in-depth sweep.

"On that note, Finn, you and your team should bug out and return to base. I need to call the remainder of my trusted colleagues to handle this case. It'll take my agents several weeks to process this site. Mara, you can count on my team to contact the families of the victims as well as return the remains to them for proper burial.

"I suggest we use Maharis's brother's body and I.D. him as the original Simon Maharis. It'll take a little finagling, but it should wrap this case up in a tidy little bow."

Finn thought about what RK had said and spoke up, "That sounds like a plan. This will also give us time to figure out what we'll do with Simon Maharis."

"I agree," I replied. "It's best to let the FBI take this case over and do what's necessary. By the way, when I touched Maharis's dying body, I was able to extract quite a bit of information. Simon Maharis is actually Karl Runyon, and his twin's name is Amos Runyon. Their great-great-grandfather owned the orchard, who started the family tradition of incestual relationships—it's all so disgusting! We pretty much know all about Simon, or should I say Karl.

"But Amos is a whole other story. This poor man was born with many physical and mental issues. I don't know much about developmental disability, but I would say it was somewhat severe. Although Amos could accomplish basic functions to care for himself, he couldn't speak or read. He followed his twin brother around like a puppy dog and loved him dearly—although he hated that his brother tortured and killed people. After Simon murdered and buried his victims, Amos cried over their mutilated bodies and then decorated the burial site with flowers and crosses. After he witnessed all the atrocities committed by his brother, it drove Amos further over the edge—straight into madness. There was no saving him, but at least now, he's with our dear Father in Heaven. Amos is now at peace."

We returned to the farmhouse, and RK assured us they would handle everything needed to process the scene. I thanked our FBI team members, and the rest of my team returned to the van, simply eager to leave. During the return drive, everyone was quiet.

Edison finally broke the silence and said, "I thought our job was messy and disgusting, but I wouldn't trade what we do for what RK and his agents must endure. The things we witnessed in that barn were off the charts of horrible and nightmarish. Mara, you and your brothers saw what this maniac did to those poor victims? I'm so glad I didn't have to witness such heinous atrocities. I'm sorry, mates, that you had to see that."

"I agree, Edison," Jasper replied. "I don't know how all y'all do what you do either—I certainly would never want to see inside his plumb-crazy head. Trust me when I say I was glad to skedaddle out of that hellhole. That place made me feel as nervous as a long-tailed cat in a roomful of rocking chairs. I hated it!"

We chuckled at Jasper's assessment and southern turn-of-phrase, lightening everyone's mood. When we finally arrived in Oakland, we stopped for a meal, boarded our plane, and returned home. Our expressions were strained with mental exhaustion, and we were glad to be back at the base.

Finn and I entered our apartment. Asher greeted us loudly with a yowl, and we plopped onto the sofa in relief. Finn reached over and held my hand as we tried to process the nightmarish experience of this day. We sat for a while, taking turns petting the cat, then Finn adjusted his position, reclined on the sofa, and pulled me next to him. It felt good to sleep against my husband, and we were out like a light, with Asher snuggled on top of Finn's head.

A while later, someone nudged me, and I felt a kiss on my forehead.

"Wake up, Mara; it's time to get moving."

I mumbled something rude but opened my eyes and saw Finn's smiling face with Asher still asleep above his head. "Sorry, Finn, I hope I didn't call you anything too disgusting." I grinned back at him and kissed his cleft chin.

"Nope."

We sat up, which caused Asher to squeak with disdain at the interruption, and I scanned the apartment.

"Good, the maid was here already. That was such a great idea to hire someone to clean this place a couple of times a week, Finn. They even do our laundry and grocery shopping. I love being spoiled like this."

"Oh, you've got to be kidding!" Finn barked in aggravation.

"What?"

"Look at the painting!"

I peered at the seascape, and it had changed again. We rose from the sofa to take a closer look.

"Yee-gads, unbelievable!" I screeched as I perused the seascape.

There was now a very obese, naked, wrinkled old man standing by the beach chairs, facing our direction. Someone exaggerated the size of his private parts, and the geezer smiled as if he knew exactly what section of his anatomy had our undivided attention. There was also a wrecked dinghy along the shore and shuffled footprints that ran from the boat to where the octogenarian stood. On the left side of the painting was a giant ostrich. His body faced the ocean, but the artist had the animal's head pushed down between the animal's knees, and he was looking at us upside-down. The ostrich's eyes were huge, long-lashed, and comical, and we had to laugh at the spectacle.

"Who is doing this, Mara? I mean, it's cunning, crafty, and hilarious."

I laughed loudly, almost snorting with glee, then stuttered, "I... don't...know. But it's so funny, Finn!"

He laughed hysterically too, and we stood there for several minutes, enjoying the comical display.

"I must say, seeing this painting made my day," I said, still twittering.

"Someone has a bizarre sense of humor, but I like it," Finn agreed, with mirth still filling his expression.

"We need to go pick up Gracie, but what do we do about this old man's...well-endowed attributes?" I asked with glee.

"Hmm. How about a simple sticky note for now? Hopefully, Gracie won't notice, but if she does, we'll have to explain the physical difference between men and women. She's five now, so I think she would understand if she doesn't already. We have a brilliant child on our hands."

"We most certainly do. I find it pretty terrifying too—in a couple of years, she'll probably be smarter than the two of us put together."

"By the way, love, RK said we should have an answer regarding the adoption within a couple of weeks. He also said everything is going well and thinks we have it in the bag." Finn smiled widely as he told me the good news. I squealed at his announcement and kissed him fervently.

"Let's go pick up our daughter from daycare, Finn. I've missed her."

"Me too, love. Me too."

CHAPTER 13

That evening, we invited Jonas and Aaron over for dinner. I was still worried about Aaron and hoped the gathering would bring him some cheer. Gracie was also pleased that her uncles were coming for a visit.

After their arrival, we invited them in and offered them a drink. Gracie played with Asher on the floor, and Jonas followed me into the kitchen to help me grab the beers. We strategically left Finn with Aaron alone, hoping Finn could convince him to participate in private counseling with Brianna. We waited several minutes, then decided we had procrastinated long enough and entered the living room. Finn gave me a nod and a wink, and I sighed in relief. Aaron looked happier as well. Whatever Finn had said to him must have made him feel better.

We sat on the sofa visiting for a while when Jonas swore loudly in astonishment. "What on earth happened to that beautiful painting?" He abruptly jumped off the couch and hurried to the picture on the wall. He removed the sticky note that covered the old man's unmentionables, and gales of laughter erupted from his mouth as he scrutinized the new addition to the once-lovely artwork. Aaron stood beside him and guffawed at the scene before him.

"Why did you two add these hilarious characters?" Aaron asked incredulously.

Finn and I watched my brothers in suspicion, but we couldn't detect any deception on their faces. I even tried to read their minds, but I only saw laughter. *Hmm, they still could be hiding something, but if they were, I couldn't tell.*

I gazed at Finn and shrugged, communicating that I couldn't gauge whether they were the painting tricksters.

"We didn't do it," Finn said, then continued, "and we have no clue as to who's the culprit. There's a prankster afoot. No one has figured out who pulled all those other jokes on us, either. Don't worry; we'll figure it out...one way or another." He smiled with an "I'll get 'em" look and took a swig of his cold beer.

"I have to say, this old man is hilarious," Jonas replied as he snickered once more.

Luckily, Gracie had been in the bathroom when we were discussing the painting, and she still hadn't noticed the naked old man. Finn and I sighed with relief and hoped she never would.

Later in the evening, after I put Gracie to bed, we were sitting in the living room and had just finished playing cards. We each enjoyed a few beers and were feeling a bit tipsy. We played charades for a time and had a ball—of course, being a little drunk helped the hilarity.

I stood up to take my turn at the game and wobbled a bit on my feet. "My goodness, we're zonked, aren't we? I think we've had enough alcohol."

Jonas and Aaron said it was late when the games were over, and they should get home. Finn and I walked them to the door, and just as Aaron was about to exit, he glanced at the painting once more, then stole a quick look at Jonas. It was so brief, I almost missed it. In that split second, I saw Aaron's mind and found what I needed.

Jonas spoke from the other side of the open door, "Goodnight, you two, and good luck with your flying classes tomorrow, Finn."

"Thanks, Jonas, I appreciate it. Good night," Finn said.

Locking the door behind them, I turned to Finn as I grinned from ear to ear and danced a jig.

"What's going on? You look like the cat that ate the canary." He pulled me into his arms and stared into my eyes.

"Hee, hee! I know who's been pranking us with the painting," I crooned in a sing-song voice.

"Who?"

"You just had dinner with them, Finn."

"Your brothers? I couldn't see that they gave anything away as to their culpability."

"I didn't either until they were walking out the door; they quickly exchanged a mental 'we got 'em,' and I caught it. Those conniving little dirtbags. This explains everything—like how our phone's photos keep changing. Aaron is a whiz at anything electronic. They could also easily get in and out of our apartment without leaving a trace on any of the security feeds or data records," I muttered as I pursed my lips, thinking about their antics.

"We'll get them good for this," Finn said as he pretended to twist his fingers against his upper lip over an imaginary mustache. "Okay, Watson, we need to get proof."

"Hey, why do *I* have to be Watson? I'm Holmes, my good man. You're Dr. Watson," I said indignantly, imitating a British accent.

"Touché. Now that we know they can track everything electronically, I think I can get a hold of a nanny cam. It can be connected to our computer, so Aaron can easily find it and think he's stopped us from catching them. Then we can add another self-contained small camera hidden inside the bookshelf. He shouldn't be able to find that one. I can view that camera's SD card on one of Edison's private laptops. We should be able to catch them both in the act."

"That sounds like an excellent idea, Watson. The game is afoot," I responded, still using a terse British accent, then giggled at the look on Finn's face. "All right, that idea deserves you being called Sherlock Holmes. Feel better?"

"Aye, love. I'll take care of planting the cameras tomorrow. I know I can get everything from Edison, *Watson*." Finn gave me a comical glare, and I kissed him in return. He chuckled and slapped me on my behind. "But for now, let's go to bed. I'm too old to drink that much liquor—as you said, I feel positively snockered."

I fell asleep that night and didn't experience any more night terrors. However, I slipped into another vision.

Moving through a dense mist, I wait until it finally clears. I'm now in a medium-sized building, and as I move along the entryway, I see a security guard at the front desk and one more at the elevator door, and it's obvious they're low-level demons. Glancing at the computer screen at the reception counter, there's a large picture displayed. It's the atom symbol, and the center dot within the atom is used as the "O" from the name of "Ottswater Pharmaceuticals" within the logo.

I move toward the elevators and see a directory. Aviana Ottswater, President and C.E.O. is listed, and she's located on the top fourth floor. The other levels are administration, and the sublevels are shown as laboratories. My spirit is now slipping down to the lower floors. I'm traveling from door to door down a hallway, and there's a sense of doom and terror. Stopping at one entrance, I realize this is a room of death. Moving inside, even though I try to will myself to stop, I continue forward and see two people in hazmat suits working at the counters, and one of them lets out a wail. I see she's pierced her finger with a needle, and the look of terror on her face chills me to the bone. Her colleague sees her injury, hastily approaches the exit, departs the room, and presses an alarm. The injured woman frantically scrambles to the door, but it won't open. She bangs in fervor, pleading for the person on the other side to let her out of the lab. But her colleague shakes her head with tears in her eyes.

As I watch the injured woman, she scurries over to a phone and begs the person on the other end of the call to let her exit, but no one will help her. The woman sits down hard on the floor, and I watch in horror as she begins to bleed uncontrollably from her eyes, ears, nose, mouth, and from the puncture wound. She convulses wildly, rolling back and forth in agony, and then vomits a bucket of blood. She's delusional now and rips off her mask. Her face is no longer recognizable. The skin has turned to massive blisters and blood spills from these as well. Her body releases one massive shudder, then becomes still on the cold, unforgiving floor.

As I JOLTED AWAKE, I spotted Asher walking on my stomach, and he moved to stand on my chest. He let out a loud and angry squeak, staring intently into my face. He howled again, which woke up Finn.

"What on earth is he hollering about?" Finn asked in frustration, blinking hard at the cat.

"I don't know. I'll check." I climbed from the bed, and Asher dashed to the bathroom. Following him, I realized we must have lowered the toilet lid, and he needed to relieve himself. "Sorry, baby. And I thank you for not using the floor as your toilet." I lifted the lid and he jumped up and did his business.

Returning to bed, I told Finn what Asher needed and said he could go back to sleep. Finn had to get up early for another day of flight training. I would tell him about my strange dream later.

CHAPTER 14

The following day, I told Finn about my dream.

"So, it must relate to the lab we saw in Maharis's barn," Finn said, puzzled.

"I guess so. I'll contact Edison this morning and tell him what I dreamt. Hopefully, he can learn as much as he can about this company, then we can discuss it at our next meeting. It certainly doesn't bode well. Now, about you…how much longer do you have in your flight training?"

"Basheer is an excellent instructor, and barring any unexpected missions, I'd say another week. Are you missing me?"

"You know I am. By the way, I'm having lunch with Tiana today, and she's helping me plan Gracie's birthday party. Do you have any requests?"

"Nope. You're a genius at everything, so I'll defer it all to you. Just let me know when and where I need to show up."

"Ha! That was devious—compliment me so you can get out of doing any of the work. I know how you men think, but I love you anyway, you handsome hunk!" I kissed him before he walked out the door to flight training.

"You know me so well, gorgeous!" he bellowed back.

AFTER DROPPING Gracie off at daycare, I spent the morning working at the vet clinic, then I met with Tiana. I hugged her and we sat down to eat and began the party planning.

Tiana looked exceptionally lovely today in an elegant, fuchsia-colored blouse and navy slacks. Her silky black hair was styled in sleek waves that complimented her high cheekbones and large, expressive dark eyes.

"Tiana, I want you to know how much I appreciate you helping me with all the party plans."

"I love doing it, and Nia and Gracie have become instant best friends—just like you and me." Tiana smiled and reached across the table to squeeze my hand.

"Aww! I feel it too. I don't know if it's because we're both Chosen Ones or simply a cosmic connection. I guess God only knows," I said. "Before we go any further, I must know how you became one of God's chosen."

"I was born with sickle cell anemia. The symptoms weren't too bad as a child but worsened through my teen years. I seemed to get better when I went to college, and that's where I met Otis. We fell in love and married. We wanted children, but I didn't want to give birth to a child with sickle cell, so Otis was tested, and he doesn't carry the gene— thank the good Lord above. Since we discovered our children wouldn't inherit the gene, I insisted we have kids as soon as possible because I didn't know when the flare-up would happen or if it could even take my life. The symptoms worsened dramatically when I became pregnant with my youngest, Darius. I carried him for eight months until my health deteriorated rapidly, and I had to have a C-section. During the surgery, I died. That's when the angel appeared to me in Heaven and asked if I would return and do God's will. Now my family and I are here, and we're thankful for this second chance."

"Tiana, I'm so sorry. But I'm delighted God chose you and you're now back with us." I had tears in my eyes as I grabbed her hand in comfort.

"Me too. I'm as healthy as a horse and love living here among the other Chosen. This base has been a Godsend—no pun intended. I'm a geologist and a civil engineer, and my husband is an astrophysicist. Although I have yet to understand what our roles are within the scheme of things, we help whenever we're called."

"Wow! I don't possess skills anywhere near your capabilities. Don't worry, I'm sure you'll be needed, and I have to say, quite soon. Hmm. I don't know how I know that, but I do."

"I sure hope so. We're both helping with your projects—the park and school—which we're so excited about. It's been a hoot! Okay, you have to tell me your story."

I relayed how I became a Chosen One, my current role, and how Finn and I met.

"Talk about 'meant to be,'" Tiana replied in wonder.

"We're all so blessed, aren't we?" I asked.

"You got it, girlfriend."

"Tiana, do you mind me asking you something personal?"

"Not at all. Shoot."

"Have you encountered any bias, racism, or discrimination while you've lived on the base?"

"I'm glad you asked, and I'm delighted to say that I haven't. This is the first time we haven't had to deal with it. In our previous lives, we faced it frequently. We lived in the heart of Chicago and it was a constant battle. I worried about my children every day. Darius was bullied for being a child of color and also because he stuttered. I know many people deal with bias, but I wanted my children to be free of that burden. Living on the base—it's like a whole new world." Tiana's lovely face lit up with happiness, and it made me smile with joy.

I sighed in relief and said, "I'm thankful you and your family have found peace here. I don't know why it can't be like that everywhere.

Sometimes I think the devil wants to keep feeding the hate, making us attack each other."

"I agree. It's such a sad world we live in," Tiana replied.

I squeezed her hand in consolation and smiled kindly. "It is, but we're trying desperately to remedy it. Okay, on to the party. We haven't decided on a location, but I was wondering, do you think the park could be an option? I know I'd have to speak with Jasper, but it would be a good test run. Tiana, what do you think?"

She pursed her lips and thought about my suggestion. "You know, I think that's a great idea. Why don't you let me ask Jasper, as I'm seeing him this afternoon? We're finishing the irrigation system on the last of the planting beds, so I can ask him then."

"Sounds like a plan."

After lunch and parting ways, I stepped into the elevator and texted Finn to tell him I loved him and hoped his pilot training was going well. He immediately responded that he was having a great day. As I read his text, my eyes blurred, and my mind started floating. Knowing I was entering a vision, I tried to block it, but it was persistent. I leaned against the back of the elevator and tried to focus on my phone as I dialed Finn.

"Hey, babe!"

"Finn—about to have a vision. In the main elevator heading to the apartment floor. Please…come…" I couldn't say any more, as I could no longer see anything around me, and I slid to the elevator floor. The last thing I heard was Finn's voice calling my name.

It's hot and humid as I'm wading through something that's slowing my progress. When I look down, I'm standing in a swamp, and I can smell its rot and decay. I also feel the sweat running down my body. Looking up, I see a heavy canopy of trees layered in Spanish moss, and the sun's rays

are filtering through, giving me a more detailed view of my location. I'm breathing heavily, not only from the oppressive humidity but also because I'm running from something terrifying. I peer at the arms stretched out in front of me and realize I'm looking through the eyes of a man. The skin is shockingly pale, young, and muscular, with well-shaped hands that are scratched and bleeding. I hear sounds from behind me, then I smell the stench. Twisting around to look at what is approaching, I spot at least twenty myrmidons. The person I'm in moves forward, trying to run through the rancid water, but slips over a snarled branch. About ten feet ahead, I see an enormous cottonmouth snake slithering through the water, but luckily, it's heading in the opposite direction. My mind leaves his body and moves several feet away, and I watch the scene before me.

The man regains his footing and is about to run again, but he discovers these strange beings have surrounded him. "Y'all stay away from me, ya hear?" His yell is frantic yet commanding, and I can hear a French accent within his southern Creole drawl. This handsome, young, blond-haired man pulls out a large bowie knife and waves it frantically at the creatures. I feel his terror because, in his gut, this man knows these unknown enemies are emanating pure evil. Turning to his right, he sees an alligator advancing on one of the beings. He waits for the kill, which happens so fast that the enemy never sees the strike as the alligator pulls him under the water. The other evil things ignore the plight of their comrade and move forward again to the young, innocent man. I try to scream at him to turn around, but I can't warn him, as I'm not physically here. Oh, dear Lord in Heaven, this is a Chosen One of God!

"Mara! Talk to me."

Focusing my eyes, I spot Finn's face in front of me. He smiled widely when he realized my vision had ended and helped me to stand. I was still in the elevator, and a few people stood outside the lift door, staring at me with concern and fear.

"It's okay, my friends. That's what I get for drinking a bottle of tequila for lunch." I laughed as Finn assisted me from the elevator.

"She's kidding, folks. She's our resident psychic, and her visions sometimes happen this way. Thank you for your help and concern." Finn said graciously. The people stated they were glad I was okay and went about their business.

After entering our apartment, I apologized to Finn.

"There's nothing to forgive, love. I'm thankful you called me so I could be there for you."

"But I pulled you from your training. Though, I'm glad you're here for me. Finn, there's another new Chosen One, and we have to rescue him ASAP. He's in grave danger."

"What? Kaiko said we had all of the Chosen. I wonder if something has changed?"

"I don't know, but it doesn't alter the fact that he's in way over his head. The myrmidons are determined, and they have massive numbers. They won't fail in grabbing this new Chosen of God. And we have to move fast on this one, Finn."

"You got it. I'll call for an immediate meeting and we'll find this poor soul and bring him home. We'll also need to discuss the pharmaceutical company you saw in your dream."

"Finn, hold off until I get more intel on the Chosen One. We don't know who this man is, when this is to take place, and the exact location. I must attempt another vision hoping God will provide this vital data."

"Now? So soon?"

"Yes. I don't have a choice, Finn." I moved to the sofa, sat down, and patted the seat next to me. He sighed, ran his hand through his thick hair in worry, and joined me on the couch.

"I'm here for you, Mara. But please, be safe." I squeezed his hand, and we prayed for the Lord's guidance and protection.

It wasn't long before I was deep into the vision and extracted the information I needed. It was the same one I had in the elevator, but this time, I did my best to rewind everything to what had transpired before the myrmidons arrived on the scene. It was more difficult than I had anticipated—especially narrowing down the location. I was given the date and time, but I still couldn't ascertain the precise address of this newly Chosen man's home.

After pulling myself out, I told Finn what I'd seen, and we were ready to meet with our team. Time was of the essence, and we had little to spare. He contacted our people, and we would meet within the hour.

OUR TEAM WAS GATHERED in the meeting room, and I relayed what I had seen in the first dream regarding the drug company.

"The C.F.O.'s name was Aviana Ottswater, and the company's name was Ottswater Pharmaceuticals. But what they were hatching in their labs was very lethal indeed. I'd say it killed the lab technician within a few minutes," I said gravely.

Edison said, "I've researched this company and it's generally on the up-and-up. However, within the last five years, things got a bit shadier. They lost their U.S. government contracts two years ago, but I'd bet dollars to doughnuts they work for someone else. I would also hazard a guess they're well-funded. This type of research is not cheap, and according to their recent financials, they're well in the black.

"This is where it gets interesting. Now that Mara discovered Simon Maharis's real name, I found more history about him. Namely, his education information. He received his chemistry degrees from the Moscow Institute of Physics and Technology. As Mara has said, this man has a genius I.Q. The U.S. hired him out of college, luckily snatching him away from the Soviet Union, but he left to join the military. But when I dug deeper, I found that he currently works for Ottswater. There's our connection, mates. We have to assume Maharis was working on the lethal virus for this company."

"Holy, schmolly!" Jonas exclaimed. "Is this what we're dealing with? So, either the demons want it or are making it. Either option is terrifying."

"I agree," Finn replied. "But we have to assume a demon runs Ottswater. We must also assume it's the same demon that wants the Scroll of Seals. This gets deeper and deeper. But for the moment, our current objective is saving this young man from Mara's recent vision. Mara, I'll let you give us the details."

"Thanks, Finn. We must rescue this newly Chosen man of God before the myrmidons find him. And trust me, they are many in number. I would say at least two hundred will be in pursuit of this person, whose name is Leonide Lavolier. This Chosen One's return date and time is tomorrow at approximately two-fifteen central. The site is the Atchafalaya Basin in Louisiana. I don't have his precise location because he lives in this large bayou, and his home has no physical address. Edison, I hope you can get me a detailed map of this enormous basin. Hopefully, the Lord will lead me in accessing the exact site of Leonide's cabin."

Edison nodded and began researching maps on his laptop.

Aaron scratched his head in confusion and asked, "Are we sure this is a new recruit of our Lord? Weren't we told that He had finished his selection?"

Finn responded, "A few minutes before this meeting, we consulted our prophet. She relayed that God had indeed sent us another. As you know, a couple of our Chosen were killed by myrmidons several months ago, so we assume the Lord wishes to replace them, and our prophet agrees with this conclusion. That being said, we better jump on this latest intel. It's a lot to plan in a short amount of time."

Jasper whistled, then said, "Jiminy cricket! That's for sure. I wish we had more time to prepare."

I spoke again but hesitated to relay the additional data I'd seen in the vision. "There's something else you must know...and this will be the most difficult thing for us." I stood and then paced the room.

"Spit it out, chickee," Billie said coaxingly.

"*Mon cher,* please don't keep us in suspense," Armie replied.

I glanced at my team, inhaled a deep breath, and continued. "According to my vision, our only hope of rescuing Leonide before the assault of the numerous myrmidons is to grab him immediately after his return from death." I paused and bit my lip. "So...we'll have to be sure to arrive before he dies—out of site, of course, and wait for God to send him back."

The usually quiet Basheer spoke up, "That doesn't sound so bad, my dear."

I cringed and said, "That's just it. This poor Leonide dies from being attacked by an alligator. He makes his living by hunting the bayou, and he's usually careful at his craft, but this day, he's careless and...well, you can guess the rest."

"*Mon Dieu!*" Armie exclaimed. "Now I see the dilemma. We will have to watch this vicious animal tear apart the poor man?"

"I'm afraid so." I winced at the thought and continued, "Leonide must die, and we can't interfere with God's plan. Nor can we be within his sight as he perishes. It would be horrendous if he witnessed us watching him being attacked, and we didn't attempt to save his life. It will be horrible for everyone involved, but this is what's meant to be, my friends. If we wait too long after his return, then the demon's lackeys will descend, and there's no way we can defend ourselves against this horde. We have to grab him as soon as he returns and get the heck out of there. I would suggest we immediately sedate Leonide because there won't be time to provide any explanations to the poor man."

Finn spoke up, "I agree. First, we must tranquilize him, then get him out of there and onto the chopper."

Everyone was quiet as they digested the intelligence. After several minutes, the team discussed possible scenarios and plausible mission strategies.

"Mara, I have a detailed map of the basin for you. I'll put it on the overhead screen," Edison said.

Moving over to the monitor, I ran my hand over the map and concentrated on Leonide. It took several minutes, but I finally honed in on the man's home. Edison marked the location, and the team worked together to devise the mission details. After ninety minutes, the plans were in place, and we were to meet at the hangar early tomorrow morning.

CHAPTER 15

Our team was on the Huey chopper and on our way to Louisiana. Jasper contacted a friend of his who also lived in the area. His name was Gaspar, and he'd be our guide and lead us through the dense and dangerous bayou.

We dressed appropriately for the swamps and slathered ourselves with camo paint and plenty of insect repellent.

"Those thirsty skeeters will eat you alive out there, so all y'all make sure every inch of you is covered," Jasper advised.

We landed at a small airport and met Gaspar. He provided us with two vehicles that could easily navigate this wet and lush terrain, and we drove as close to our target's home as the landscape would allow.

"We will have to walk from here. Leonide's place is about a half mile east. Follow my lead, stay watchful for snakes and gators, and y'all do just fine." Gaspar had a prominent Creole accent, and listening to his melodic words was a joy.

Xavier stayed behind with the vehicles in case the myrmidons appeared. Basheer was waiting at the airport with the Huey. We hoped we had enough time to bring Leonide out of this swamp before the demon's lackeys appeared.

As our team moved forward, there was a well-defined path, although areas of denser vegetation made it difficult to watch for predators. But after several feet of trekking through the swamp, I had trouble breathing because the humidity was so oppressive. South America was humid, but this was worse. I slowed my breathing, hoping this would help me draw in more heavy, stifling air. I heard Billie swear a blue streak behind me, and as I turned, she had just killed a gigantic water moccasin.

"I hate schlepping through this wet, ugly, and slimy vegetation. Hey, Mara, you have the gift of talking to these slimy creatures. Can't you tell them to stay away from us?" Billie asked in frustration.

"It doesn't seem to work with these pesky insects and leeches," I complained as I slapped at several mosquitoes trying to land on my arms. "Although, I think the swamp is quite beautiful. It's a whole new world: the Spanish moss hanging from the Cypress trees, tons of colorful, sweet-scented flowers, beautiful cranes majestically strolling through the underbrush, and a plethora of every type of butterfly and dragonfly. Now the leaches on my boots—not so much."

Finn and Aaron chuckled in my earpiece, and Jasper commented, "They're a pain, but you get used to 'em."

I felt the hairs rise on the back of my neck while Gaspar raised his hand into a fist, silently bringing us to a halt. We crouched briefly, and I watched Finn signaling to the team.

Crap! There were myrmidons ahead. Finn motioned to Jonas and Edison, and they nodded in compliance. The two men moved to the right and stealthily vanished into a dense area of trees and vegetation. We waited twenty minutes, then heard thrashing, grunting, and groaning. Several minutes later, Jonas and Edison appeared with wide grins and myrmidon blood on their knives. We smiled back, and they replied quietly that we were clear to proceed.

"Jasper, stay here and watch our six," Finn instructed. Jasper nodded and moved to a concealed location to lay in wait.

We were nearing Leonide's home, so we stayed just within view of his place. Watching for any movement, we finally saw him as he came out of his back door, laden with fish nets, buckets, a rifle, and a large knife on his belt. He wore ragged pants, an old stained t-shirt, and a ball cap facing backward. I estimated his age to be around his late sixties. He was of medium height with a lanky build but was heavily arthritic. The man moved with a stiff gate, and his hands looked gnarled and painful. Moving forward, he followed a path, and Finn signaled for us to stay behind him but out of Leonide's sight.

Before we continued, I whispered to the team, "Remember, this poor man has to die, and we can't interfere with God's plan. He mustn't know we're here, and we don't move in until we're sure he has died. Does everyone understand?" I heard my team's reluctant agreement as we followed God's next Chosen One.

Leonide stopped by the water just beyond the path and scanned the area for alligators and snakes. Luckily, the deafening sounds of insects and birds covered any noises we made as we followed him. Our team was about twenty feet away from the man when we hid behind several trees laden with Spanish moss and dense foliage. Crouching low, we waited in trepidation for the devastating and fateful moment of the poor man's demise.

We watched Leonide as he shuffled down a short, dilapidated dock to a small watercraft secured by a thick rope. He piled his supplies into the boat, released the line, and started the outboard motor.

It never occurred to me that he may take his boat farther into the swamp, well beyond our sight. I glanced nervously at Finn, and he shrugged and motioned we would wait.

Luckily, Leonide didn't troll far, and we then saw the bobbers where he had set previous traps and fish nets. He stopped the boat and turned off the motor. He pulled up a bulging net that was filled with crawfish. He hollered in delight, then hefted it into the boat, dumped his catch into the buckets, and secured the lids. His hat was caught by a low-hanging tree branch, which revealed he was balding on top, but what he had left of his graying hair was pulled neatly into a short ponytail. He grabbed his cap and placed it securely back on his head.

Something caught my eye above his boat. A giant black snake dangled from one of the overhead Cypress tree limbs and quietly dropped behind him into the dinghy. I grabbed Finn's arm, and he warned me to stay silent, but it was horrifying to watch. Leonide stiffly turned to his left and swore loudly in French as he spotted the cotton-mouth. He grabbed his large knife from his belt and attempted to kill the snake, but his arthritic legs couldn't move fast enough. Instead, he tripped over one of the buckets and fell overboard with a loud splash.

My team and I watched in horror as we witnessed the slithering movement ahead of him in the water. This twelve-foot predator was advancing toward Leonide's position. There was only a brief glimpse of a nose and a slight swish as the tail swayed back and forth, gently moving the water in a rippling dance of impending doom.

Leonide's head appeared above the water as he frantically tried to grab the boat. But his gnarled hands wouldn't cooperate, and he kept losing his grip. The poor man roared in pain as the predator's razor-filled jaw clamped onto one of his legs. Leonide fought hard, but the alligator started spinning him into a death roll, and they both disap-peared under the murky and perilous water.

"Please, God, take this man swiftly," I whispered in prayer under my breath.

A couple of moments later, Leonide was pushed above the water by the terrifying reptile, and the old man quickly gasped for air, but the alligator pulled him back under. We glanced again at each other but waited for what would happen next. As we watched, the swamp water turned blood red, and we caught glimpses of the predator moving away, swimming deeper into the swamp with Leonide's mutilated body.

"What now?" Aaron asked in a pain-filled voice.

"We wait," Finn said grimly.

Our team stayed still, but after several minutes, there was a bright display of kaleidoscope colors, the strong scent of flowers, and a sound of crackles—like thousands of sparklers being lit simultaneously. We watched as the dance of sparks and colors flickered onto the shore, and there was another bright flash, then, all was quiet. Lying on the ground near the shore was a naked young man whom God had returned from a torturous death.

"Go!" Finn ordered.

We moved in quickly and surrounded Leonide. His body was now young and healthy, and the gnarled, arthritic joints of his body were smooth and pain-free. He was a handsome young man with ashen skin that had yet to see the intense rays of the Louisianna sun and was full of muscle. He now had a full head of thick blond hair, and his expression was of pure innocence. Jonas pulled a set of fatigues from his backpack, and the men started dressing him.

"Is he alive yet?" I asked.

Finn checked for a pulse and nodded. "Luckily, he's still unconscious, but he won't be for long. Billie and Mara, check out his place and ensure no one is inside." Finn pulled out a vial, syringe, and alcohol, then sedated Leonide. He re-checked his vitals, nodded that he was stable, and Jasper and Aaron assembled the portable gurney.

"Roger that," I said, and Billie and I returned to his cabin. A loud howl greeted us as we entered, and an enormous hound dog barred our way. I immediately connected with the animal, and he sat back down and howled once more. Kneeling before him, I said his master was fine, but we needed to leave this place quietly. He seemed to understand and followed us around the cabin. Billie grabbed a few of Leonide's personal photos and other small items and stowed them in her backpack.

She turned to me and said, "What do we do with the dog?"

"He has to come with us. He'll die if we leave him here alone."

Billie gave me a cynical look, then shrugged her shoulders. "Let's bug out."

I contacted Finn and said we had an eighty-pound, four-legged, long-eared passenger.

Finn didn't reply for a moment, and I wondered if he'd heard me. He finally said, "Of course you do. Okay. Get back here ASAP."

"Copy that," I replied.

When we returned, the team peered skeptically at the dog but understood I'd never leave it behind. Finn and Aaron placed Leonide securely onto the gurney, and we started our trek back toward our vehicles. The dog, whose name I discovered from his collar was Doob, stayed close on our heels and remained quiet.

"Enemy incoming!" Xavier reported through our earpieces.

"How many?" Finn asked.

"From Poppy's satellite images, she says seven are headed my way. But there are too many for me to take out alone. And Finn, she also said there are at least twenty-five or more coming from the south and are moving in your direction. Due to the oppressive heat within the swamp, she couldn't get an exact count from the satellite imaging."

Finn nodded and said, "Billie, I need you and Jasper to return to the vehicles ASAP and assist Xavier."

"Copy that," Jasper replied from this hidden location.

"Will do." Billie nodded to Finn. She would meet up with Jasper, and they'd head back to assist Xavier.

"Let's move deeper into the brush, then we'll set him down to prepare for battle. Stay vigilant, my friends." We each prayed to the Lord as we waited for the incoming hostiles. The team surrounded Leonide and faced outward with rifles and knives drawn as we scanned every direction.

"Gaspar, whatever comes at us, just kill. But only use the weapons we gave you, or you won't survive. Understand?" Finn asked. "The quickest way to kill them is to shoot them through the head or cut their throats." Gaspar gaped at Finn in fear, but he clearly understood his direction.

Finn re-checked Leonide's pulse as we waited, and he was stable. Rapid gunfire was heard in the direction of our vehicles, then shouts and more shots. There's the smell—that terrible, odiferous, nauseating odor that always warned us of their impending arrival.

I pulled out a pair of Nepalese military kukri knives that I had specially made by our talented monks. The Sai knives had their use, but I found they only worked well when fighting mortals. However, the kukri knives were sharper, deadlier, and easier to carry and wield. I'd been practicing for weeks with these blades and knew they were my weapon of choice when battling myrmidons. Their strong curved blade and short handles worked perfectly for me, and the custom-made leather grips and small hand guards gave me a tighter hold and more protection.

Finn nodded to me but preferred his K-bar knife and handgun.

Doob growled and bared his fangs as he knew evil descended upon us.

"Here they come," Jonas whispered.

We heard rustling and a few primal grunts. The stench grew stronger, and we waited for them, anxious to take them out. The first one appeared before Aaron, but my brother was prepared. The demon lackey charged Aaron with a long knife, but Aaron was faster, blocking the blade with his own. My brother shoved him back and spun his body around, which gave him more momentum. He launched into the air as he high-kicked the myrmidon, which caught the demon in the throat, breaking his neck. The rest of them descended on us, and there must have been at least thirty. We never expected this many.

"Jonas, Aaron, call on your spirit animals!" I yelled and hailed my glorious white wolf, Spirit, as he instantly appeared from the woods and grabbed another demon by the neck. Spirit ripped off his head then he ran on to the next monster. I caught a glimpse of Phantom and Charlotte, but I had no time to gauge their battle strategies. One of the biggest myrmidons I'd ever seen descended upon me. My knives were ready, and I held my stance, letting him approach. His human yet demonic face leered in glee as he came closer, obviously assuming I was an easy kill.

He snarled and lumbered toward me, whipping his massive blade toward my neck. I ducked in response, but my sudden move caused him to lose his balance, and he rocked on his feet. Taking advantage of his stumble, I jumped up and caught him high in the chest with my feet, causing him to drop to his knees. Before he could recover, I sliced him several times around his head, and he screamed in agony. But as I moved away, he grabbed my leg and tossed me onto the ground before him. Losing no time, I twisted around to my back, swung my legs up, wrapped my knees around his giant neck, and tightened my legs. Then swinging the weight of my body upwards and to the side, I thrust him flat onto the ground. After I quickly released my leg-lock, I flipped him over by grabbing one of his lumbering arms and pinned it behind him with such a sharp, awkward movement I heard the "snap" as the bones in his upper arm and shoulder shattered. Then quickly gathering both knives together into my hands, I shoved the two blades into the back of his skull. The heinous black demon blood oozed from the gaping holes.

Quickly rising, I moved on to the next myrmidon. This one was smaller and lankier but appeared more agile. He took a run at me, which I quickly sidestepped, taking the opportunity to cut a deep crease across his back as he went by me. The demon screamed in rage, then turned to race at me again—his knife waving in anger and trying to cut me at any possible angle as I spun away. His fury couldn't be denied, but that was his worst mistake. It made him sloppy as he wielded his blade. I blocked his long knife with my shorter one, then spun around and buried my second blade into his back, deep into his spine. He dropped like a stone, but I still had to finish him. Taking out my gun, I shot him in the back of his head.

I whipped around to take on the next myrmidon, but all I saw was Jonas killing the last one. Dead myrmidons were everywhere, and I frantically searched for every one of my team. Thankfully, they were all still standing, albeit covered in that foul-smelling demon blood. Hearing a growl, I spun around, but I only saw Doob ripping out the throat of an already dead demon. The old hound wanted the last word.

"Doob! Come!" I ordered. The dog trotted over to my side in exhaustion, and I gestured to him to return to his master. Leonide was still on the gurney, untouched and still sedated.

Our spirit animals stood majestically off to the side, their coats blackened here and there by demon blood. My brothers and I thanked them for their love and protection and wished them a safe journey to wherever they were headed next. They stood for a few more minutes, assuring themselves we were safe, then they turned and strode away, vanishing into thin air.

I looked for Gaspar. He stood beside Aaron with a confused yet triumphant look on his handsome face. He nodded to me and said, "Y'all have a lot of explaining to do, Mara."

"You'll get your answers, my friend. I promise," I replied with a smile.

"Is everyone okay?" Finn asked of his team.

They responded they were fine, and we returned to Leonide's litter as we waited for instructions. Standing beside Finn, I saw a deep gash on his upper left arm.

"Finn, you're not alright." I began pulling away the material stuck to the bloody cut, and he tried to shoo me away.

"Mara, I'm fine. It can wait until we reach the vehicles. Nothing important was severed." When I examined the wound, there was no gushing bright red blood, and it didn't appear severe. I nodded, then kissed his cheek, stained with demon blood.

"Yuck!" I replied and wiped my mouth on my sleeve.

"Xavier, how is it your way?"

"We're clear. But stay vigilant on your way back," Xavier said.

"Copy that," Finn replied.

We picked up the stretcher and started again on our return trip. Gaspar stayed ahead of us. Aaron remained at the back to watch our six. I kept a steady eye on our flanks as Finn and Jonas carried the litter.

Jonas contacted Xavier and advised him we were approaching the clearing. Xavier acknowledged him and we made it to the vehicles. As we loaded Leonide in the SUV, we received an urgent message.

"Alpha team, this is Watcher Four. We have incoming at Lafayette Airport—approximately two hundred hostiles have arrived. We recommend you use the Baton Rouge Airport. It's approximately eighty-seven miles from your twenty. Do you copy, Alpha team?"

Finn replied, "Copy that, Watcher Four. Confirmed new destination of Baton Rouge Airport. Thanks for the intel, Watcher Four."

"There are two others with the hostiles—Saalim Hadid and the Amazon woman. I thought you'd like to know. Watcher Four out."

"Copy, Watcher Four," Finn replied, shaking his head in frustration. "Basheer, did you copy these transmissions?"

"Yes. I've already departed Lafayette and am headed to Baton Rouge." Basheer gave us the gate number where the Huey would be waiting.

Finn confirmed the gate number and typed in the coordinates of the Baton Rouge Airport in the vehicle's GPS. Leonide was loaded, and two of our men had to heft the heavy hound dog behind him. Doob refused to leave his master's side. He laid his head on Leonide's thigh and kept a vigilant eye on his best friend. Doob knew his master looked different, but his scent was the same. He loved Leonide.

Once we boarded the chopper, I insisted on cleaning Finn's wound and discovered it wasn't serious. I attached a bandage and said the docs at the base would have to tend to it upon our return. Finn made a few disgruntled comments but finally agreed when I gave him a stern and fierce stare.

CHAPTER 16

*a*fter arriving back at the base, we transported Leonide to the infirmary. The doctors checked him over and found he was in perfect health.

Everyone went to the locker rooms to shower and change, then Finn, Jasper, and I returned to the infirmary. The doctor treated Finn's injury, which required more cleaning and a few stitches, and he was to take an oral antibiotic.

We then stayed by Leonide's bedside, waiting for him to regain consciousness. Finally, after a half-hour, he began to rouse. I spoke quietly to him, hoping it would calm him and he would wake without the feeling of terror and confusion.

His eyes popped open, and he bolted up in his bed. He swore in French and stared at us in bewilderment.

"It's okay, Leonide. You're safe and we're here to help you, so please don't be afraid," I said quietly with reassurance.

"Whom might you be?" he insisted with disbelief, his eyes wide. I feared he'd jump off the bed and run out the door.

"My name is Mara, and this is Jasper and Finn. We found you and brought you to this location for your safety. Everything will be explained in time," I said calmly. "We've been in your position, so we know how you feel." At that moment, Billie walked in with Doob in tow. The hound trotted over to his master, reared up, and placed his giant paws on Leonide's bed.

"Doob! Wutch ya doin' here, boy? Tanks for bringin' my dawg here whit me. Dat was mighty kind," Leonide said in his thick Cajun accent. Seeing his dog eased the newly Chosen one's fear, and a grin returned to his face. But, as he looked at his bare arms and hands, the confusion returned.

Finn smiled and said, "You're welcome. We couldn't very well leave your best friend behind. Leonide, a lot of information will be forthcoming, but first, we must tell you what happened. What is the last thing you remember, my friend?"

Leonide's face reflected concentration, and he tilted his head as he thought deeply about Finn's question. "I'd have to say, being in dat fishin' boat and pullin' in my traps." He turned his head again, and his eyes widened in shock. "Lawd have mercy, da gator! I went down in da drink, den I felt oodles of pain. Shore did!" Realization covered his handsome face, and he stared at us in terror.

I spoke quickly, "Yes, that happened, Leonide. I'm sorry to say that the alligator killed you. But God brought you back, and you're as healthy as a horse."

"You can call me Leon. But what's whit my arms and hands? I had awful bad arthritis, so what's whit dis?"

"Leon, when you returned from the dead, God created one of his miracles, and you're now young and healthy." I stood and picked up a hand mirror from a table. "Take a look, my handsome friend."

Leon hesitated to take the mirror, but his avid curiosity won, and he grasped it and slowly raised it to his face.

I thought he'd be terrified, but he only said, "Now, dat's what I'm talkin' bout. Looky dat dare—I'm a handsome devil." He grinned into the mirror, turned his head back and forth, then opened his mouth wide to look at his teeth. "All my chewers is back. Don't dat beat all!"

He lowered the mirror and turned to look at us. "But why did dis happen, y'all?"

Finn stood and came to Leon's side. "My friend, you've been through a lot, so we'll provide the answers you require soon. But from all that we've experienced when we returned to a new life, recalling our trip to Heaven took a few days. Give yourself time, and you'll remember too. Trust us. We need you to rest and recover for the next few hours."

Jasper said, "You can call us anytime. This phone has our numbers, so we're at your disposal. Like Finn said, rest and dream. This is where you'll receive God's messages and remember your time in Heaven." Jasper showed him how to use the phone, and we left Leonide to rest.

Finn and I returned to our apartment and plopped on the sofa in exhaustion.

"That was a successful and enlightening mission," I said, laying my head on Finn's strong shoulder.

"Indubitably. It was amazing watching God bring a man back to life and into his former young body."

"Uh-hmm," I replied, closing my eyes and making my body relax for a moment. I knew we had to pick up Gracie shortly, but I needed this downtime.

After several minutes, Finn nudged me, waking me from my light slumber. "Come on, love; we must pick up our precious little girl."

I sat up and glanced at my watch. Then realizing I'd been asleep for almost thirty minutes, I jumped off the sofa and was about to head to the door with Finn, but my steps halted as something caught my eye.

"You've got to be kidding!" I giggled with delight, and Finn walked over to see what had tickled my funny bone. I pointed to the seascape painting.

Finn gasped and joined in my laughter. "How on earth did they manage to switch it in such a short time?"

"They must have done it...while we were in the infirmary with... Leon," I said between fits of chortles.

We moved forward to get a better look. There was no area of the painting that didn't have something added. The naked old geezer was still there along with the silly ostrich, but now there was a juggler, a mime, several monkeys, a gorilla, a goofy donkey, a Viking warrior, two sumo wrestlers, and a submarine telescope protruding from the sand. A World War II Japanese fighter plane, an alien spaceship, several cherubs, and a fiery dragon with enormous googly eyes were painted in the sky. In the water, a Loch Ness monster was moving smoothly along the shore, and in his gaping mouth was a giant smoking cigar.

There were two characters who resembled Finn and me near the palm trees. Finn was portrayed as a caveman stooped over with an exaggerated brow, jawline, and giant feet. He wore a tiny loin cloth that hid his private parts and was covered in thick body hair. I was dressed as a geisha, but my face was turned into another caricature: bright red lips, giant doe eyes, and a flaring hook nose with a gigantic wart.

"My dear Mrs. MacKenna, what an enormous nose you have." Finn snorted and smacked me on my behind.

"La-di-da! Look who's talking, Mr. Hairy-Big Foot-He-Man!" I lightly punched him in the arm and smacked his hind end in retaliation. We chuckled with glee and stared again at the hilarious painting.

Finn uttered a loud "aha," and then strolled to the entertainment center. Reaching around some CDs, he pulled out a small camera. "Let's see if we caught them in the act." Finn connected the camera to another phone he had hidden in a large drawer under a pile of old magazines. After turning on the cell, he plugged in the camera and waited for the video to load.

"Bingo!" I yelled in triumph. "There they are, the little imps. I'll get them for this!"

We watched the video as Aaron and Jonas pulled down the previous painting and hung the current one. The two laughed so hard that Aaron had to run to the bathroom for fear of peeing his pants. This made Jonas chortle even louder and landed on the floor in hysterics.

Asher was in the frame and he sat watching my brothers' antics. I swore that cat had a massive grin on his face.

Listening in, we heard Jonas yelling to Aaron in the bathroom, "They'll never figure this out. I can't believe you thought of this, Aaron. It's priceless!"

Aaron returned and stood with Jonas in front of the painting, reveling in their hard work of pranking us. "Finn and Mara still haven't a clue. We got away with it, brother! When should we replace this one with the original?"

"Let's wait awhile. We need them to stew a bit as they figure out who instigated these hijinks. I bet they never will, though."

They high-fived each other, laughed again, and we heard them say they better get out of there because we could arrive home at any moment. They grabbed the previous painting and swiftly disappeared from the frame. We heard the door close behind them.

"We have to get them back, Finn, but it has to be huge. What can we do?"

"Hmm. Let's think about it for a while. I'm sure we can create something spectacular and very public, love." He kissed me on the cheek, and we went to pick up our precious daughter.

THE FOLLOWING DAY, I spoke with Jasper, and he said he was taking Leon under his wing and would guide him through the newly Chosen process. He also said Tiana had finished the arrangements for Gracie's birthday party, which was set for tomorrow at the recently completed park.

I called Tiana and thanked her profusely for handling everything for me.

"Mara, you already said what you would like, so all I had to do was make the arrangements."

"I know, but what you did was beyond the call of duty. It was a lot of work, Tiana, and I can't thank you enough." I babbled loudly as I thanked her.

"Aww. I know you would do the same for me. You were out saving the world, so it was the least I could do. All that's left is making sure the park is decorated and then getting the birthday girl to the party—tomorrow at three in the afternoon. All the guests will arrive at two-thirty, so we're set for the surprise."

I thanked her again and said we'd be there on time.

That afternoon, our entire team gathered for a meeting. It was good to see everyone again, including Armie. He was his usual charming self, but at least Finn wasn't bothered by Armie's sweet-talking nature.

Finn started the meeting with our usual prayers and said, "Thank you, everyone, for a job well done. We only had a few hiccups with our extraction yesterday, but it was successful and with no severe injuries or casualties. However, it was surprising that the myrmidons had two of the mercs in tow. We're assuming the demon wanted any Chosen of God he could lay his hands on. I would have to assume he's desperate for any edge when it comes to acquiring the Scroll of Seals. Our prophet recently advised that it's all coming to a head, and we'll have to be ready to leave for the Middle East at a moment's notice."

Billie spoke with confusion, "What are we waiting on? Why haven't we schlepped ourselves over there when we first received the data on the scroll?"

A few of the other team members agreed with Billie's statement. Finn held up his hand and said, "I know. Trust me; I get what you're saying. But according to our prophet, we do everything in God's time—not ours. Apparently, some things have to happen in proper sequence before attempting to intercept the scroll and the demon. We can't make any moves until we get the go-ahead from the Lord's messenger."

The team nodded in understanding and continued their discussion. I glanced at Armie and had that strange feeling again—he was hiding something, but what? His mind was closed to me, and he appeared aware that I knew he was protecting his thoughts from my probe. When he returned my gaze, he lifted an elegant eyebrow as if telling me to behave myself and that he would reveal his secrets when the time was right. I nodded back at him from across the table in acknowledgment, and he gave me a respectful yet quiet, two-finger salute.

Edison spoke, "With the arrival of the two mercenaries yesterday, we attempted to put a tail on them when they left Louisiana. Our watchers followed them until they reached JFK. But from there, we lost the mercs in the shuffle. They're professionals and know how to blend in and lose a tail. With that being said, we do have the intel Mara received when she and Jonas were kidnapped. Armie, would you like to tell us what you discovered?"

"*Oui,* thank you, Edison. Mara told us about the location she saw in Maharis's mind as well as one of her visions. Her description was as follows: an arid desert, yet an ocean nearby. There were old buildings made of stone blocks, palm trees, some strange-looking grasses, and sand. Mara also observed a mosque. It was made of white stone, but the top dome was colored green, and a turret was on the right side of the building. She said there were many men in long robes coming out of the mosque, and they appeared to be of Middle East descent. Near the ocean, the land jutted out like a peninsula, and a cement wall ran along most of one side of the area, along the ocean's edge. After conferring with Basheer, reviewing many satellite images, and speaking with several military analysts, we agreed on this location." Armie pulled up photos on the overhead screen of the same mosque I had seen in my vision. The other pictures were of the peninsula and a labyrinth of tunnels.

Armie continued, "This building is called Al-Jazzar Mosque, and it's quite famous. It's located in Acre, Israel." He pronounced the city "Auckruh." "These tunnels were built during the Crusades in the twelfth century by the Knights Templar. As we speak, more tunnels are being discovered, and I'm sure they are still digging. I have to assume that God is holding off until someone gets closer to unearthing the specific chamber we're looking for."

"I agree," I said. "It makes plausible sense, and these photos precisely match what I saw in my visions. I believe God will guide us to the opening of these tunnels—either by visions or maybe not until we reach Acre itself. If it's the latter, we must pray that God helps us locate the chamber before the enemy finds us."

Several of my team looked at me as if I had grown two heads. I get that look a lot, but not usually from my team.

"What?" I asked.

Jonas ran a frustrated hand across his forehead as if he had a nasty headache. "Y'all telling us that we have to fly by the seat of our pants again? I hate to think we have to secretly enter a Middle East country under the radar. We'd have to be on the lookout for mercs, myrmidons, unfriendly locals, and the demon himself while finding the entrance to a hidden chamber located miles under a city. Piece of cake!"

"I know it sounds insane, but that's usually our M.O. We should be used to it by now," Finn replied.

Edison swore, and everyone else shook their heads in frustration.

"My dear friends, it can and will be done. And the Chosen at our base in the Middle East has, and will continue to be our valuable ally," Armie said quietly with assurance. "Let's not jump the proverbial gun just yet. We still have time, and I'm sure the good Lord will provide more intel because He always comes through, n'est pas?"

"He's right. Have faith, mates. Keep praying for guidance; I'm sure we'll be provided with more information to help us succeed on this upcoming mission. Is there anything else you'd like to discuss?" Edison asked.

"Oui. I do have one other subject. Leonide must join us on this upcoming mission." Armie made this statement with authority, and by the look on his face, he was determined we acquiesce.

Finn stood in surprise. "You've got to be kidding! He's green, Armie, and he's only starting to remember his trip to Heaven. What about his military training? He still doesn't know much about us and what we do here. That's impossible."

"No. It isn't, Finn. Leave it to me, and I'll see he gets his full training within half the normal timeframe. I *will* need assistance from several of you, but it can be done—and it *must* be done. Leonide is essential in this next commission. Mara, I'm sure you'll soon be aware of this also."

I stared at Armie, concentrated on Leon, then the scroll. There was something to what Armie had said, but I couldn't decipher the reason. At least, not yet. The team was staring at me again, and so was Armie. He raised his eyebrows at me, but this time in a plea of agreement.

"Armie is correct about Leon, but as to why, that's still unknown to me. Hopefully, this will also be made clear soon." I nodded to everyone, and they looked back and forth between Armie and me. Then they gazed at each other and grinned as they gave in to our surprising recommendation.

"If you both say we need him, then we better get his training started," Finn agreed with a reluctant sigh. "Armie, Jasper, Edison, and Billie, I'll leave it up to you to prepare Leon and bring in anyone else you may need. And may God have mercy on us."

The meeting adjourned and as we exited the room, Finn peered at me in confusion. "Did you know about us needing Leon in the Middle East mission?"

"Actually, no. But when I thought about him and the scroll, I felt a sense of urgency that he must be there—I know it's weird." I made a rude noise and poked him in the chest. "Come on, big guy, we need to finish our preparations for Gracie's party. What do you say we finalize the event planning, my handsome caveman?"

Finn hunched over, furrowed his brow, grunted, and offered me his arm. I also stooped over, answered his grunt, grabbed his arm, and we both ambled like drunken gorillas toward the elevators.

THE NEXT DAY WAS BUSY, and we were excited to see the park. Finn and I gasped at the view as we entered the area. It was breathtaking, and it looked like a typical city garden. The wooden sidewalks were in place, the sod was laid, and the planting beds were completed and filled with bushes and beautiful flowers. I could feel the sun shining from above through the skylights, and the dwarf trees threw enchanting shadows across the ground. There were a couple of large open areas where people could throw a ball or maybe even play a game of croquet.

A small stream of water weaved its way around the entire park and ended up in a small pond with a fountain. I loved the added touch of lampposts set strategically throughout the area. This place could be used at night, which was a bonus.

Jasper jogged over and grinned from ear to ear. "Well, what do y'all think? The kid's playground is to the right, and the dog run is located to the left at the rear and is fenced in." The children's area included several colorful climbing objects, a large swing set, a slide, and a play-house. We strolled along the walkway to the rear of the giant park that led to the dog section. A fancy fence with a gate surrounded it, and it looked like it had sod installed there as well.

"How are you handling the issue of the pup area? I mean, how do you keep it clean?" Finn asked delicately.

"We're using genuine hardy grass, and everyone must pick up after their dog. We also figured out how to safely neutralize and disinfect the drainage bed under the sod. So don't worry, there won't be any ammonia accumulation from the canines' urine."

"Jasper, I thought you weren't going to use sod since it would be too heavy," I interjected.

"We were able to construct and install a few more beams on the lower floors to support the added weight. Plus, we found grass that required less dirt and water. So it was a win-win," he replied.

Jasper's excitement was infectious as he continued, "We're hoping to develop the correct ecosystem to allow for live beneficial insects like butterflies, ladybugs, and the like. Maybe even some birds, but those things are on our wish list."

"How on earth did you accomplish all this in such a short timeframe? It hasn't been that long since you started. It's become an awe-inspiring park," I said incredulously.

"Thanks! I think so too. We've been moving fast because many people volunteered their services."

"Good heavens, my man, how on earth are all of you figuring this out?" Finn asked in bafflement.

"You know how, Finn…." Jonas smiled widely again and pointed to the heavens.

"How does the stream work, Jonas?" Finn asked.

"The stream uses the same water that's run through the hydroponics garden. It comes in through a small waterfall on the east side of this room, along the wall between the hydroponics section and this recreation area. This water is cleaned and recycled as it moves into the park and is sanitized again when it returns to the hydroponics bay. We wanted two small ponds—one for the children and one in the dog area to cool off or play in the water. Of course, a drip irrigation system runs under the flower beds, trees, and shrubs. The breeze was just added because it can get hot here during mid-day." The cool, delightful light wind wafted around us as we gazed at our surroundings.

I couldn't help myself and hugged Jasper. "You're one amazing man." I had tears in my eyes as I surveyed the beauty of it all.

"Shucks, Mara, we're simply having fun. Come on; I need y'all to take a gander at the schoolrooms."

After taking the elevator, we strolled to the schooling and daycare wing. After entering the first space, I was delighted they used my suggestion of placing a photographic mural on an entire wall in each classroom. In this area, which they called the ocean room, the mural was of an underwater ocean display. The giant photo was striking, and the colors were rich and lovely. The Rileys walked in as we gazed at the artwork.

"Mara, Finn, we're so glad you're here. Well, what do you think?" Gloria prodded as she proudly stood with her husband, Marshall.

"Oh my gosh, Gloria, it's stunning. The desks are all here, along with the textbooks and whiteboards. Are all the other rooms completed too?"

"Yep. We have all the teachers lined up, and the curriculum for each grade is in place. Since the children have already been tested to determine their proper grade level," Marshall replied, "classes will begin immediately."

"The two of you outdid yourselves, and I know the children can't wait to start. I'm sure the parents are ready, too," I said happily.

The Rileys guided us through the remainder of the rooms, and each one had a distinctive mural. Even the daycare area had a wall painted with zoo animals. We thanked them, and Jasper hugged me and said he had to meet a lady friend for lunch.

AFTER RETURNING from the education wing, Finn, Tiana, and I spent the morning putting the final touches on the party decorations in one of the park's grassy areas. As we worked, I could hear birds singing in the trees—even though it must have come through hidden speakers. I felt and smelled the sweet scent of the outdoor breezes, and I basked in the warm sun as it filtered through the gigantic skylight. It was pure bliss.

The guests were arriving, and it was time for Finn and me to leave and pick up Gracie from Bible school. We would take her home and have her put on her new party dress. She only knew we were having a few friends together to celebrate her birthday, but she had no clue about the party. Gracie was excited after donning her new frock and laughed delightedly at her reflection. It was a hot pink dress with plenty of lace and sparkles. She had matching lace socks, patent leather pink shoes, and a tiara on the top of her head.

"Come on, pet. We have to get a move-on. Your friends are waiting for your arrival," Finn said, grinning from ear to ear. He picked her up, hugged her, and carried her to the door.

After we exited the elevator, she asked where we were headed. She thought we were going to Tiana's apartment to celebrate with her new best friend, Nia.

"Come inside, my lovely girl," I said. We walked through the double doors to the park, and everyone yelled, "Surprise!" Gracie was positively giddy. But what delighted her was seeing Nana. Finn had arranged to have my mom flown in for Gracie's party. When she spotted her grandma, she rushed over as fast as her little legs could carry her and threw herself at my mom. They loved each other so much that I cried at their reunion. After several minutes, my mom told Gracie she should go and play with her friends and they would see each other later.

My mom would stay in our spare room and remain with us for three more days. We even had her bring her Bichon dog, Sadie, to visit with us, much to Asher's consternation. However, a few hours after my mom arrived at our apartment today, they became best friends, and Asher even shared his cat bed with her.

All the children amassed together, explored the park, then went to carouse on the playground. The adults gathered around several picnic tables, and we also prepared food on the portable grills. It was a delightful party, and everyone had a great time. Gracie loved the food, her gifts, and the huge pink birthday cake. The party ended a few hours later, and we returned to our apartment.

Gracie was tired but happy. Mom went to her room because she said she would like to nap, but we knew she wanted to give us time alone with our daughter.

We asked Gracie to join us on the sofa. There were two more gifts for her—just from Finn and me. Her eyes widened as she gazed at the bright wrapping paper, and I handed her the first one.

"Before you open this, Gracie, we want to tell you something," I replied sincerely. "Your daddy and I want you to know that we love you and are so blessed that God brought you to us to be our daughter. We also want you to know that we can't ever replace your first mommy. She loved you dearly, and I know she still watches over you and will always remain in your heart." Finn nodded in agreement, then bent over and kissed Gracie. "That being said, go ahead and open your present."

She ripped off the paper as Finn held the heavy gift. After the paper was gone, she stared transfixed at the photograph. It was a large portrait of Gracie as a toddler on her mother's lap. In the picture, Gracie's mom was gazing down at her precious child, and the love reflected in her mother's eyes couldn't be denied.

Gracie reached out a hand and lovingly traced her mommy's face in the photograph. We watched as several expressions flitted through Gracie's eyes—confusion, recognition, love, loss, then back to love again.

"Mommy..." was all she said. She leaned in and kissed her mother's face in the photo. "It's mine?"

"Yes, my sweet, it is. If you like, we'll hang it in a special place in your room," Finn said as he kissed her again and put her on his knee. "Would you like that?"

"Oh, yes!" she squealed and hugged us both.

"Okay, baby, we have one more gift." I handed her a smaller package, and she held it gently in her lap. "Go ahead, open it," I muttered.

She was more careful this time and gently removed the paper. When she looked at what was revealed, she was puzzled. It was a framed certificate of adoption.

"Can you read it, pet?" Finn asked.

She tried, but some of the words were too difficult for her.

"Gracie, honey, this certificate says you're officially our daughter. That means no one can take you away from us, and we're now your real mommy and daddy. Your new name is Grace Eliana McKenna." I was now crying, and Finn also wiped tears from his eyes.

"Really and truly? I'm all yours, and you are mine?" she asked with incredulity in her sweet voice.

"Really, truly, and pinky swear." Finn held up his pinky and she wrapped her finger around his. She seemed to understand what this meant, and she cried with happiness. We held her close and told her how thrilled we were that she was legally our little girl.

That evening, Mom, Finn, and I spent a lot of time with Gracie and played all her favorite games. Asher insisted on taking part in the family night too. He kept stealing the game pieces off the board, making Gracie giggle with delight. Sadie insisted on following Asher during his antics until they both decided to settle down for a nap on the sofa.

After putting Gracie to bed, Mom and Finn sat on the sofa, and I decided to catch up on my emails. I was delighted that one of the communications was from our wedding photographer, and she had sent several proofs for us to review. As I scanned the pictures, I discovered our photographer had done an excellent job of memorializing our wedding day. But as I viewed the following photo of Finn and me with Mom, I gasped out loud, then sobbed in earnest.

Finn and Mom ran over to me, and Mom said, "Honey, what's wrong?"

I tried to explain through my tears and blubbering, and then I pointed to the photo. Finn and Mom gasped loudly, and Mom started to cry too. They stared in shock as they couldn't believe what they saw. The picture was of Finn and me standing with our arms around each other, Finn in his tuxedo, and me in my wedding dress, and Mom stood beside me with pride. But what was so amazing was that my dad was beside Finn with the same expression of joy and jubilation.

Mom's tears subsided, and she croaked, "How can this be? Your father's in the photo, looking the same age as when he died, and he's wearing a fabulous suit. This is incredible!"

"God must have done this," Finn exclaimed with awe. "Go through the rest of the pictures, love. We have to see if there are any more of him."

I did as Finn requested; indeed, there were three more of Dad. One photo had been taken of my mother, but Dad stood proudly beside her. The second one was of the entire family, including Gracie, and Dad was posing proudly next to Aaron and Jonas. The final picture was of all the Patrick men—Jonas, Aaron, and Dad.

"Wow!" I couldn't think of anything else to say.

Finn repeated what I said, then asked, "It's astounding that he's in these photos, but how did the photographer center the pictures properly? Could she see your dad too?"

I replied, "I didn't read her email notes—let me pull it up and see what she said."

As we perused the message from the photographer, she said the usual pleasantries, but then she inserted a note. "I guess this is a strange comment, but I don't remember the older man being at the wedding or how he turned up in the photos. Stranger yet, I don't know how the pictures were accurately centered and why I didn't cut the poor man out. There's no explanation, either, as to why he's in some photos and not the others. I think I'm losing it, Mara and Finn. I hope you know this man, but if not, I can remove him using my software if that's your preference."

The three of us laughed happily and thanked the Lord for His miracle.

Mom said, "How do we explain this to our extended family and friends? I guess we'll have to display these special photos where no one else can see them."

"I agree, Mum," Finn replied with a massive grin. "So that's your dad, Mara? He's a mighty-fine-looking man."

"We think so too." I grinned pridefully and said, "Oh my gosh, I must forward these pics to Aaron and Jonas." I immediately sent them, then called my brothers and told them to check their emails. They hooted with joy, and I heard heavy emotion in their voices.

"Mara, this is unbelievable! I can't wait to receive the printed photos and put them on my wall." Aaron laughed again, and Jonas boisterously agreed. We talked for several minutes more and finally said our goodbyes.

"This has been the most amazing wedding present ever." I stood and hugged Finn and Mom, tears still filling my eyes.

"It is indeed, my dear daughter. God is good. I'm going to bed and say many thankful prayers to our Lord and Savior. Goodnight, my precious children." Mom gave us another hug and a kiss and retired to her room.

Finn pulled me into his arms, and I held on in happiness. I gazed up at him, and he smiled and passionately kissed me. "We're exhausted, love. Let's turn in, and we'll also give special thanks to the man upstairs. He certainly has given us so many blessings."

"Yes, He has," I replied, and we walked hand in hand to bed.

Unfortunately, I began to dream…

CHAPTER 17

*T*here is a large landscape covered in a deep mist. The fog clears, and I view the dry, arid location I remember from Maharis's mind. The mosque comes into view, then I move toward the land along the ocean and see a long block wall along the water's edge. I'm now moving toward the city and down behind an alleyway.

My travel halts in front of what appears to be a small market or store inside a tall stone building. This structure is below an old church. As I gaze around the entrance, it's littered with junk—old dolls, toys, furniture, and kitchenware. Moving through an old wooden door, I advance into the room where more discarded items are strewn about the area.

Focusing ahead, another entrance awaits me, and I float to and through the door, and I'm now in a large circular room with a vaulted ceiling. There's an arched tunnel ahead of me, and I again move toward and through the space. These tunnels aren't lit, but for some reason, I can see everything clearly. Continuing again, there's another narrow archway, but this one leads downward. Following the long stairwell, I finally approach the bottom. Four tunnels lead in separate directions, and I'm pulled toward the second one from the right for about a *hundred feet. More tunnels are now in front of me, and I'm drawn to the one on the far left. I travel another hundred feet but halt suddenly, turn left, and face a cement block wall.*

As I gaze intently at the wall before me, it looks like regular large blocks of stone, so what am I supposed to see? Symbols begin to take shape and they glow under my stare. The images appear to repeat in a specific pattern, like a combination. It's a doorway. I'm about to press the blocks in the given sequence, but I'm being pulled away and brought swiftly to another location.

Looking around me, I see nothing but a colorful array of light and hear a familiar voice. "Mara, are you there? It's me." As I peer through the fog, I see the beautiful face of Isabella. But instead of her lovely smile, her expression is grave and sorrowful.

"Hello, Isabella. I'm happy to see you again, but I have to say, you don't look as if you're bringing me glad tidings."

She lowers her head slightly, glances left and right, and looks at me again. "No, it's not great news, but it's something you must know. The time is swiftly approaching for you and your team to find the artifact. Within nine days, one of the archaeology teams will discover the hidden chamber. I recommend that you leave no later than six days from now. Please stay vigilant, as the demon and his horde eagerly await your arrival in Israel. He has eyes everywhere, so you won't be able to hide from him. He'll be a constant threat, and he's eager to obtain the holy relic and kill the Gatekeepers who escaped his grasp.

"But that's not the only reason I'm here before you. It's regarding Maharis." She pauses for several moments as if waiting for something.

"Isabella?"

She raises her somber eyes to me again and says, "Maharis must be with you and your team on the upcoming quest to the caverns—specifically, the chamber where the scroll resides."

"Are you serious? We must drag this dangerous and violent man across the world and down into who knows how many tunnels and hope he doesn't kill us in the process. But why?"

"Mara, it's in that specific chamber where he'll receive his judgment. Maharis must decide his fate—our Lord and Savior or damnation. It will be his choice and his alone."

"I see," is all I can say at the moment regarding the shocking instruction.

Isabella frowns, lowers her head again, and clenches her jaw. She appears to be debating with herself, deciding how much she should tell me. After a few moments, she raises her gaze back to mine. "I have to warn you though, my dear. You'll see things that will horrify you, but you must continue to trust in Him. You'll try to influence Maharis, but whatever path this soulless man chooses, you must remember that it's ultimately his decision. I must go. I love you, my sweet Mara."

"Isabella...wait! I don't understand...what do you mean?" She vanishes from my view, but her voice still echoes in my head.

AFTER WAKING, I stared into the darkness of my bedroom. Finn's arm was across my stomach, and I slowly eased out from under his embrace. After padding to the bathroom, I closed the door and turned on the light. My reflection was shockingly pale in the mirror, and I turned on the faucet and splashed my face with cool water. I couldn't help but reflect on what Isabella had said and what it might mean.

What horrors will I see, and how will I possibly influence Maharis's decision about whether he goes to Heaven or Hell? And doesn't he have to be dead to receive final judgment from God? How does he die? Will I have to kill him, does someone else, or is it the Lord Himself that ends the serial killer's life?

I shook my head in consternation and then heard a scratching at the bathroom door. I turned the knob and Asher sauntered in, rubbed against my legs, jumped on the counter, and wrapped his huge paws around my neck. He peered at me questioningly, and I felt concern coming across his thoughts.

"Thanks, Asher, but I'm fine. I promise." His loud purring echoed in my ears, and I carried him back to bed.

The next morning, I told Finn about the visit from Isabella. He wasn't pleased, and I couldn't blame him.

"We should call a meeting with the team this morning to give them the latest news," Finn said with reluctance.

"Remember, we're taking Gracie to her first day of kindergarten today. She's so excited, along with everyone else. I'm ecstatic the base children now have an actual school."

Finn smiled, then said, "I agree. Amazingly, when all the kids were tested, they scored high scholastically. But homeschooling has them behind socially, so your idea of actual school rooms should quickly raise their social skills. Well done, love." He bent me over the back of his arm and kissed me passionately.

"Wow! That was potent," I replied, fanning my face. Finn laughed and said we'd better get moving. We had a long day ahead of us.

After proudly dropping off Gracie at her kindergarten schoolroom, we headed to our meeting. I told the team what I had seen in my dream and what Isabella had relayed about Maharis.

Everyone spoke at once, and Finn had to raise his hand in a silencing motion. "I know. It seems like an impossible task having to take Maharis with us. But we've accomplished more difficult ones than this. If we put our heads together, I'm sure we can devise a way to get him to the chamber."

Xavier cleared his throat, scratched his stubbled square jaw, and said, "Having worked with my tribe's shaman, I believe there are substances that can induce a hypnotic trance that we could use to keep him calm yet pliable. I'm sure we could work with our base chemists and physicians to develop something that will work. Let me handle it, and I'll report our findings."

Finn nodded and gave Xavier the go-ahead. "From Mara's latest vision, she has the precise location of where we will enter the cave systems. Basheer, we'll need you to connect with your contacts in

Israel. We'll require additional assistance to stay under the radar when we fly in and out of Acre. Transportation, preferably covered trucks, will also be needed to get to and from the city."

"I still have underground connections there, so it shouldn't be an issue. Don't worry, I'll see that this is accomplished and report back." Basheer nodded his regal head and jotted a few notes into his laptop.

"According to Isabella, we must leave in six days, so we better get our ducks in a row, mates. We'll meet again tomorrow morning at nine," Edison confirmed with a wry smile.

THE FAMILY GATHERED around the dining room table for a hearty evening meal. Mom's eyes sparkled with joy at having all her children surrounding her for a grand dinner. Gracie was in heaven at being able to sit next to her grandma and have her constant, undivided attention. We regaled stories regarding the pranks played on all of us, and Mom was tickled to tears.

"You know, we still have no clue who'd been the instigator of all those jokes. Is anyone ever going to fess up?" I asked my family, then glanced accusingly at each of my brothers and Finn.

Jonas retorted with indignation and said, "Why are you looking at us? It could easily have been you, Mara."

I snorted loudly in disdain, made a look of incredulity, then smiled with a coy grin. "*Moi?* I'm way too lady-like to take part in such frivolities." I uttered another piggish snort, then scratched my butt like I'd never learned table manners.

"Mara, honestly," Mom reprimanded. But she giggled so hard that she emitted a delicate and unrestrained snortle.

We roared with laughter again, and Aaron quipped, "Ha! Now we know where Mara gets it from!"

Gracie watched us in wonder, trying to figure out what was so hilarious. But she grinned anyway, joining in on the fun.

"Mommy, may I leave the table, please? I want to play with Sadie and Asher," Gracie asked kindly.

"You're excused," I replied and thanked her for being polite, especially since we had company.

After Gracie departed to her bedroom to play with the animals, I said, "Mom, Finn and I were talking, and we wondered if you could stay with us for another few weeks. Our team has a mission in roughly six days, and the following week will be Thanksgiving. We'd be overjoyed if you could remain with us during that time. Please say yes."

"Oh my, that's a long time, honey. You know I'd love to stay, and so would Sadie. But I'd have to check with my neighbor who's tending to my kitty, Peanut. I'll call her tomorrow and see what she says. If it's okay with her, I'll agree."

Finn smiled, clasped my hand lying next to his on the table, and said, "It sounds like we have a plan."

I kissed Finn, then turned my gaze to Jonas. "Have you decided what to do with your newly acquired dog, Diesel?"

Jonas seemed slightly embarrassed to answer. "Well, yeah. Diesel has become fond of me, so it only seems fair that I should keep him."

Aaron spoke up, "That's the only reason, brother? You don't want to disappoint the dog? And you don't have any attachment to him, though, hmm?"

Jonas shrugged his shoulders with indifference, then gave us a guilty Cheshire grin.

Aaron stood in triumph and yelled, "Aha! I knew it! Jasper owes me fifty bucks. I told him you'd keep the pup."

"Hey, wait a minute. How about you, Aaron? What are you going to do with Lizzie and her puppies? Well?" Jonas taunted as he poked Aaron in the chest with his finger in accusation.

Aaron sat back down, turned a bright shade of pink, then said, "Well…I'm not sure…."

"Aaron Michael Patrick—don't fib to your family," Mom chastised her son, yet she had a knowing smile.

"I'm keeping her—I can't help it! I've grown attached to Lizzie and would love to keep the puppies—but that would be impossible. They've just turned eight weeks old, and I need to find them homes. But they're so adorable, and I can't bring myself to let them go. I'm in a real pickle." He was whining, and it made me snicker.

"Aaron, Jonas, and I will help find great homes for them. Several people on the base have already asked me if you'll need someone to adopt the pups. I'm sure they'll let you visit them if you feel the need." I smiled kindly, and his shoulders lowered in relief.

"Thanks, you two. I'd be grateful if you would handle it. It's too much for me to be there when they get adopted." Jonas patted his brother on the back—a little too hard—then Aaron kicked Jonas's foot under the table. Jonas yelped and smacked the back of Aaron's head.

"Boys, stop it!" Mom hollered. Then she mumbled, "My Lord in Heaven, do they ever grow up?" Mom stared at the ceiling in frustration as she spoke to God. "You two young men now have to take care of the dishes. That's your punishment. I can't believe my sixty-something-year-old sons are fighting like teenagers. Now, get hopping!"

Aaron whined, "He started it!"

"Did not!" Jonas returned.

"Did too!" Aaron replied and stuck his tongue out at his brother.

Mom's only response was a steamy glare, which was all that was needed. They both jumped up, quickly gathered the dishes, and carried them to the kitchen. We heard them grumbling from the other room, and Finn and I hooted with gales of laughter.

Mom scowled, then yelled again toward the kitchen, "I heard that!" But as she walked away, she was grinning from ear to ear.

FINN and I were in the bathroom the next morning, preparing for our day. He stood at the sink shaving, and I couldn't help but enjoy seeing him dressed with only a bath towel around his waist. I had finished my shower, dried off, and wrapped the towel around my wet hair. Finn's gaze stared back at me from the mirror, and he ogled every move I made in my nakedness.

"You dirty dog. Are you enjoying the view?" I asked as I sauntered over to him and wrapped my arms around his waist from behind. I rained several kisses along his strong, well-muscled back and hugged him, inhaling his clean, spicy scent.

"Indubitably, my dear. How can I not behold your lovely nakedness?" He rinsed and dried his face and turned around to kiss me deeply. I moaned in obvious response. Finn pulled the towel from my hair and ran his fingers through my wet, long, curly tresses.

I giggled as he tickled my ribs and nuzzled my ear. "I can't believe the show Jonas and Aaron put on for Mom."

He pulled back slightly and peered into my eyes. "What do you mean, love?" Finn asked as he continued the trail of kisses down my neck.

"When they retreated to the kitchen last night after being scolded by Mom, I caught the two of them giving each other a high-five, and they giggled like naughty schoolgirls. They're two peas in a pod. Are you listening to me, husband?"

"Mm-hmm. Every word, my sweet. I watched Mum after they were scolded, and she walked away with the biggest grin. I'm sure their show was all for her benefit. It gave her a chance to discipline her two sons in a squabble that she hadn't been able to do before—never having raised Aaron along with the two of you. She's an amazing woman."

"Yes, she is. Now on to another subject...." After removing Finn's only covering, I murmured, "We have some extra time this morning, so let's take advantage of this moment, shall we?"

His only answer was a leering grin.

"I'll take that as a yes," I whispered, devouring his mouth again.

CHAPTER 18

$\mathcal{A}$s we rushed to our team meeting, we entered the room breathless and uttered several apologies. We were given mischievous, knowing looks. I quickly countered their obvious and dirty thoughts regarding our tardiness.

Embarrassed, I grinned and said, "It's not what you think, so get your minds out of the gutter." Everyone chuckled, and I continued, "Our lovely daughter did everything possible to delay us this morning. She's never behaved in such a fashion. First, Gracie refused to get out of bed, and then she insisted she wear her Halloween witch costume. And her *pièce de résistance* was her ongoing argument about what she wanted for breakfast." I flopped into my seat in defeat, then blew a long strand of hair away from my face.

There were several snickers around the room as well as knowing and understanding glances. Finn's usual devil-may-care look was also absent this morning, and he had a perpetual glower.

Jasper chuckled, saying, "I wondered why all y'all looked more overwhelmed than a five-legged cow on a tightrope."

Edison grinned widely, then replied, "After raising five children, with two of those as foster kids, I think I can offer my opinion. Now that your daughter knows she has a stable, permanent home, she can do as she pleases and will also start testing you as any normal child would. During the pre-adoption period, she probably thought she had to be the perfect little girl you would discard if she did anything wrong. Congratulations, mates—welcome to parenthood!" He laughed boisterously, and there were chuckles all around.

I glanced sheepishly at Edison and asked, "Will she act this way every morning?"

"Who knows? But I'm sure she'll now behave like any normal five-year-old child," Edison replied.

Finn and I stared at each other in horror. I knew our work was cut out for us with this precocious child, especially an intelligent one.

Finn sat straight in his chair, then said, "Let's get started. We have much to cover and little time to plan our mission." He began the session with the usual prayers to the Lord, asking for His guidance.

As the meeting progressed, my gaze was repeatedly pulled to Armie. Something was up, and I could feel his frustration and doubt. I finally caught his eye and gave him a questioning look as I realized what he'd been hiding.

Armie nodded at me, and during a lull in the conversation, he stood and cleared his throat. "If I may interrupt, *messieurs and mesdames*, there is something we need to discuss. What I am about to tell you must not leave this room, and I am trusting all of you with my life and identity." He looked at us intently, pursed his lips, and continued.

"I am related to one of the Grand Masters of the Knights Templar, which dates back to the thirteenth century, and I continue to carry on the legacy. That being said, God selected me to join your specific team to assist in retrieving the holy artifact. As Mara had said regarding the message she received in one of her visions, the only persons allowed to lay hands on the scroll are of His choosing—and one of those individuals is me."

"Let me get this straight—" I interrupted, "do you belong to the

196

Order of Solomon's Temple—the group the holy angels mentioned in my vision?"

"*Oui,* Mara. That is exactly what I am saying." Armie paused to let us digest this information and continued, "If anything unforeseen should happen to me during this upcoming mission, it is up to Leonide to take my place. Unbeknownst to Leon, he is also a descendant of the Holy Order. Once we complete this mission, he must return with me to a clandestine location, complete rigorous training, and be knighted. This poor man has no clue what God has in store for him—*if* he accepts the honor." Armie raised his eyebrows as he glanced at us, trying to gauge our reaction to this new information.

Basheer interrupted and asked, "Are you saying that you know the specific location of this chamber? I mean, the Templars are the ones who constructed these underground tunnels in Acre, correct?"

"*Oui,* my friend, the Templars did build them. However, I have no more information as to the location than the rest of you. To make a long story short, when the city of Acre fell in the late thirteenth century, many Templars were either injured or killed, and the rest fled for their lives. The Templars, the Hospitallers, the Teutonic Knights, and the troops of the King of Cyprus all fought the endless onslaught from the Mamluk armies in their efforts to take Acre as their own. Many on every side perished during this horrible war, including innocent women and children. The entire debacle of the fall of Acre was blamed on the Knights, and those captured were tortured and killed by the King of France and the connivance of the papacy. Thus, those who survived scattered to the four winds and had to stay in hiding for fear of death. Through the centuries, the locations of many of our hidden stores have been lost. We are continually searching to find and relocate all the precious artifacts entrusted to us by God."

"That's quite a story, Armie. Do you have a plan on how to get the relic out of Israel to a safe and protected site?" Jonas asked.

"I will have others waiting for my instruction once we retrieve the scroll. We have to figure out our exit strategy, though—and that will be the trickiest part of our plan."

"That's what our meetings are for, mates. Now let's get to it." Edison replied.

I quickly spoke, wanting to address an important issue. "Before we move on, I'd like to discuss something. We still don't have any pertinent intel on this current demon, and I'd hate to proceed on this mission until we know more about him. Finn and I spoke with our prophet, asking her for any information she may have on this monster. She only said it was up to my brothers and me to obtain the intelligence. What I propose is that we take the time now and try to gain access to this demon. I want to initiate a vision, and I'd need all of you to assist me. I'd also require everyone to protect me and my brothers as we psychically connect. Does everyone agree to assist?" I gazed at each person at the table, and they consented.

"Thank you. Jonas and Aaron, I'll need you to guard my mind while I attempt this. Jonas, would you trade places with Finn because I need the two of you to hold my hands? Then I'd like us all to join hands around the table, and whatever you do, don't break the link. My brothers and I will put up strong walls in your minds, so you shouldn't be affected by any of the demon's onslaught. All we ask of you is to continue praying while we delve into the vision. Are there any questions?"

Billie raised her hand. "What do we do if the demon does try to enter our minds?"

Jonas answered, "Aaron and I will know if that happens, and we'll immediately stop. The block will shield you from seeing anything in the vision, so you'll be protected from viewing the monster and, in turn, from him noticing you. Your continued prayers will also protect you from the demon's intrusion."

"Okay, I'm game," Billie said.

Nodding to our team, we joined hands, and I began by saying a prayer to St. Michael for protection. I used the holy angels' assistance to gain access to our current nemesis and the information that the demon may impart.

My mind drifts as I look for the location of the demon. Giant clouds of every color move by me and through me as I search through the mire of the psychic realm. I feel my brothers protecting me beyond my current field of vision, and for this, I'm grateful. The colors change from glorious heavenly hues to something dark and malevolent. Moving past them, I call St. Michael again and feel a web of love and protection around my mind. Thanking him, the menacing advances no longer affect me.

I continue until I see a large fortress hidden on a vertical, treacherous cliff. Going deeper, I enter the side of the massive stone building and discover a dark and ugly room—which I would surmise is a dungeon. Several myrmidons surround the outer perimeter of this space, and I try to see the figure pacing back and forth in apparent frustration and anger. There are three other beings in the room, and I assume they're lower demons, but there's a fog in front of my vision, and I find it difficult to focus.

"I can't believe your complete incompetence and lack of ambition! First, you lose the Gatekeepers, then my most promised follower, Maharis, and finally, the simple retrieval of a newly Chosen One is beyond your imbeciles' grasp."

"My lord, we're doing our best. Unfortunately, the Chosen are always one step ahead of us, so how would we know?"

The haze clears and I see the demon. It's a tall, voluptuous woman with thick, long black hair and vivid hazel eyes. She appears to be an extraordinarily stunning female to an average human, yet I only see ugliness, hate, and contempt. She turns quickly on her heel and stabs the lower demon through the forehead with a long, jagged blade that appears to be made of bone. Her target falls to the ground and dies a horrible death. The body on the floor shrivels up to nothing, and she sneers in contempt and then licks the brackish blood from the dagger.

She approaches the other minor demon, and he retreats in fear and waits for his impending demise by his master. But instead of killing him, she opens her mouth, and a long, blueish-green tongue darts out and strokes the man's cheek. The lick leaves a vivid black scar on the man's face, and he rubs the injury, hoping to ease the pain.

"Xerkamedes, I promise I won't fail you again. The town of Acre will be under our control within nine days, and there's no way the Chosen will escape with the relic."

While the subordinate speaks, I enter his feeble mind and extract what I need. I then try to gauge the major demon's status and intent, but entering her mind is like swimming in cement. I get nothing.

"You better see to it that the Chosen fail! I'm running out of flunkies, but I won't hesitate to send you back to damnation if you disappoint me again. And this time, your eternal resting place will be in the lowest level of Hell, not within the second realm of my kingdom where you resided previously." She moved to stand nose-to-nose with the demon man before her. I've no clue how she could move that quickly. He trembles in terror and is rooted to the spot. Xerkamedes is about to say something else to her servant, but she tilts her head and turns toward me.

"Who's there?" She backs up and scans the room. It's then that I glimpse the actual hellion. I can taste, feel, and smell its wretchedness. Retreating as quickly as possible, I still can't escape fast enough.

I CAME to in the meeting room, my brothers gripped my hands tightly, and I told them to release me. Standing up so fast, I knocked the chair over and hurriedly ran to the wastebasket in the corner of the room. Luckily, I made it just in time as I violently vomited up my breakfast from the morning. I could still smell the stench of the vile monster, and it made me throw up once more. Finn was beside me, holding my hair out of the way until I finished. As the nausea passed, I realized the room was unusually quiet. But I was exhausted and couldn't turn around to assess my surroundings. I leaned against the wall, waiting for my strength to return. Finn took me into his arms, holding me upright, which gave me time to recover.

"Finn?"

"It's okay. I'm here, love."

"I'm so embarrassed," I muttered into his chest. He stroked the damp hair from my face and rubbed my back.

"Trust me, your team understands. They politely left the room when you began hurling into the garbage." He chuckled softly, and I punched him gently in the shoulder. "I see my beautiful wife is back to her old self."

I retreated slightly and looked around the room. We were alone.

"Your brothers asked everyone else to leave so you wouldn't be too embarrassed by your projectile vomiting."

"Oh, stop it, you rat!" I smiled tearfully and hugged him in gratitude. "Would you assist me to the bathroom?"

"I can do better than that. Are you up to walking back to our apartment?"

I nodded in agreement, and he held me close as we returned to our place. Walking straight to the bathroom, I brushed my teeth, rinsed with mouthwash, and splashed cold water on my face. Finn sat on the tub's edge while I cleaned up, and I was thankful for his calming and protective presence.

Going into the bedroom, I changed out of my damp clothes into a pair of black jeans and a purple blouse. I sat on the bed as I retied my sneakers.

"Mara, wouldn't you prefer to rest for a while?"

"Thanks, Finn, but no. Could you tell the team to join us back in the meeting room? Wait, maybe we should postpone for a little while. I need to remove and clean the garbage bin—the room probably reeks to high heaven."

"I've already seen to it."

"You made someone else clean up my mess? Finn, that's awful—I would have done it."

"I know, love, but it's already been taken care of, so let it go. Are you sure you want to finish the meeting?"

"Definitely. I have to impart to the team what I learned in the vision because I gained a lot of intel for the mission. We'll need it to continue our plans."

"You got it. I'll text them now, and we'll meet again in an hour. That will give you time to take a break and get a bite to eat." Finn spent a moment typing on his phone, then checked to assure himself that our team had received the text.

I moved over to Finn, took his phone out of his hands, tossed it on the dresser, and gave him a long and passionate kiss. He was breathing hard when I released his lips. His eyes twinkled as he looked at me questioningly, then raised a frisky eyebrow.

"An entire hour to rest and eat? There must be something else we can do during the next sixty minutes," I whispered flirtatiously as I kicked off my shoes once more.

"You're feeling better, I see." Finn grinned widely, strode over to me, and picked me up, throwing me over his shoulder. Walking to the bed, he tossed me onto the covers, and I giggled with love and happiness.

"I love you, Finn."

"I love you too, my gorgeous, tantalizing woman."

CHAPTER 19

The team met again an hour later, and Finn gave me the lead to provide everyone with the information I'd discovered during the vision.

"First, I want to thank all of you for your patience this morning. I'm sorry you witnessed me losing my cookies into a wastebasket." I lowered my head in embarrassment.

"Chickee, don't worry about it. We felt bad that you had to experience the vile evilness of that demon. We're glad we didn't have to see that schmuck. You have our sympathy."

"Thank you, Billie. I appreciate you saying that, and I want all of you to know how thankful I am for your support and friendship." I was teary-eyed as I spoke to my friends, and it took me a moment to continue. Finn squeezed my hand in reassurance and I sent him a grateful smile.

Finn said, "Before we begin, I'm bringing our Middle East team leader, Yosef, on the screen to join our meeting. He and his people have been closely monitoring Acre as well as Tel Aviv, and it's due to their vigilance that we have viable intelligence. We'll meet with them when we arrive on site, and they'll continue to be our eyes and ears as well as our backup. They've been fully updated regarding our intel, and you can speak freely in front of him."

After bringing Yosef up on the large screen, introductions were made. This man was all military and had intelligent brown eyes and an infectious grin.

"Yosef, do you have any new data to provide?" Finn asked.

"Nothing new at the moment. We still have the same number of myrmidons and mercs stationed in Tel Aviv and Acre. At this time, they're still covering the popular entrances to the caves and have no idea about the one Mara discovered. Many of the myrmidons have been eliminated by my teams, but every day, new ones are brought in to replace them. But don't worry; we'll keep at it.

"I assume they have no clue about your early arrival, and let's pray it stays that way. But we'll remain vigilant, my friends, and keep you apprised of any changes."

"Thank you for the update, Yosef," Finn said, and Yosef smiled in acknowledgment.

"Now, on to why we're here," I continued. "This devil is a major one, and her name is Xerkamedes. This demon is currently portraying itself as a woman. She's approximately six feet tall, has long black hair, hazel eyes, and is a striking figure. I'll refer to it as 'she' for ease of description. When I tried to enter her mind, its demonic form over-whelmed me, and I had to retreat ASAP. I'm sorry to say I received nothing from her.

"But the minor demon in the room is another story, and I got massive intel from this one. His name is Maccafor, and he's the one who's been in charge of the mercenaries and is Xerkamedes' lieutenant. Our major issue is that they've infiltrated the city of Acre with approximately twenty mercenaries, not including the myrmidons that number around one hundred. We're lucky Yosef and his teams have already eliminated many of these soldiers and are monitoring their continued arrival into the city." I stopped for a moment, waiting for any questions from my teammates.

Yosef replied, "Regarding the mercs Mara mentioned, my teams have spotted and identified them. We have counted seventeen in Acre and four more in Tel Aviv. The ones in Tel Aviv are watching the airports, and those in Acre are monitoring everything else—especially all known entrances to the tunnels. But my team will neutralize most of them when you arrive in town for the mission. The less the demon is aware of our current presence, the better, so we will wait until the mission begins."

"Thank you, Yosef. Your team handling the mercs gives us a better chance of a successful mission—and for that, we're grateful," Finn replied.

I also thanked Yosef, then continued, "We're fortunate our enemy seems to think we're coming to Israel in ten days. That gives us a distinct advantage and a head start. My main concern is how we'll get in and out of the country without being noticed by Xerkamedes."

I returned to my seat and handed the meeting over to Finn.

"Okay, team. You heard her—we have five days to finalize our plans and begin our mission. So let's dig in."

After several hours of tossing ideas around, we finally had most of the mission plans in place. But a few details still needed to be ironed out, such as getting the artifact out of the Middle East as well as ourselves.

There were several minutes of silence as everyone thought about possible scenarios.

Edison's eyes lit up, and he said, "What about this? Finn, remember several months ago we were gifted with three forty-one-foot Interceptor boats? I know they're still located in the Mediterranean, which is to our advantage. We need a couple of people to transport the boats to, let's say, Tel Aviv. Yosef, can you hide our boats somewhere in a private port?"

Yosef replied, "I have a few ideas on where we may conceal them, but let me work on it."

Finn said, "It sounds like we may have a viable exit strategy."

Edison nodded to Yosef and displayed a map of Acre and Tel Aviv, which was south of Acre. "We already discussed leaving Acre after dark using covered trucks. If we take this highway down to the Tel Aviv Port, we can have the Interceptors waiting to get us out of Dodge."

The rest of us carefully considered the idea. Finn rose from his chair and began pacing the room, and after several minutes, he stopped and faced our group. "Yosef, can we use the Tel Aviv Port without getting killed?"

"I believe so. Of course, bribes will be needed, but that shouldn't be a problem. But it's still a crapshoot, as you Americans like to say. So, I also recommend you use the S97 Raider, but you must transport this chopper ASAP to the Middle East. You can use a private airstrip to get into the country with little danger. I would rather you have the Raider as a safety net when your team escapes through the port until they are out of harm's way and into International waters."

"Yosef, we'll leave it up to you to complete all this. Just keep us apprised. Basheer will see to it that the Raider is transported to Israel." Basheer nodded in agreement. Finn continued, "Now, my friends, regarding the boats, no one on our base, especially within this team, has had any training on the Interceptor. I suggest we send some of our people to the Mediterranean as soon as possible to learn everything about these specialized boats. And I mean everything—piloting, the electronics, and anything else that's needed. I expect whomever we assign to become experts on the Interceptor.

"A few ace pilots at our Western European base have been working diligently with these boats, so we'll have them teach our people. I'll contact them once we conclude this meeting. But in the meantime, I'll need four volunteers to fly over to their base and take a crash course on these unique boats. I'd like three from our team and one from Delta. Any takers?"

Aaron, Jonas, Xavier, and Billie all volunteered. "Aaron, Xavier, and Billie—you'll be leaving tonight. We'll keep you apprised of mission details and anything else you should know. Thanks, Jonas, but I prefer that only one Gatekeeper be a volunteer. I hope you understand."

Jonas nodded. "Copy that, boss. Understood."

I raised my hand with a question. "What is so great about these Interceptors, Finn?"

"Homeland Security is currently using them. It's a forty-one-foot aluminum boat with a foam collar and a state-of-the-art speed boat. It has four three-hundred-fifty horsepower outboard motors and can reach sixty knots. This baby moves like a dream and turns on a dime. It also has everything we need, including radar, satellite, night imaging, and electro-optical infrared sensors. Of course, we have also added a few extras too. The electronics are proprietary, so I chose Aaron—I'll leave it up to you to learn what you need to keep the boats running. One thing all of you must remember when you are in these boats, hang on for dear life. We'll be moving fast; if we turn quickly, you could easily be tossed overboard. Understood?"

We all nodded and laughed at the same time.

"Armie, how is Leon's training coming along?" Edison asked.

"Very well. God also chose wisely with this one. He's learning quickly—even faster than I'd hoped. Trust me when I say he'll be ready by the time we depart for the mission," Armie replied.

Finn smiled with pride. "Excellent! Xavier, where are we regarding Maharis? Do we know how we're to keep him sedated yet ambulatory?"

"As of matter of fact, yes. Our doctors and scientists have fine-tuned the medication, and it's ready for use. It's safe, but we need Maharis to test the proper dosage," Xavier replied.

"Good. I'll contact RK and give him a heads-up, as well as your number, Xavier. Would you also see that we have proper accommodations for Maharis when he arrives? Just make sure he's completely out for the move. We don't want him to know where he's going or where he'll end up."

"Not a problem, Finn. Don't worry; I'll see he's unconscious for the trip, and the brig is prepared for his short stay. Since I'll be out of the country training on the Interceptor, I'll find a medic on this base to handle Maharis and his transport for the mission."

"Thanks, Xavier. It sounds like you have it under control. What's next, team?"

Basheer stood after he closed his laptop and updated us on his part of the mission. "I'll have to depart tomorrow with the Raider. I'll use the C5 plane to transport the chopper, and I've already chosen the appropriate airport. I just contacted my selected crew, and everything regarding transportation and defense is now in motion."

Finn nodded, then replied, "Thanks, my friend. We'll also contact you regarding the mission details once you depart."

We finalized several more particulars and concluded the meeting. I waited for Finn afterward as he contacted our Delta team members. After he hung up, he smiled and said he had the final volunteer. "You'll be happy to know that one of the volunteers is our friend Chuck."

"That's great! I haven't seen him lately and wondered how he was doing," I said.

"Chuck is second in command in the Delta team now—so I'd say he's doing very well. In addition, he's a whiz in electronics, so I know he's an excellent choice," Finn replied.

"Heavens to Betsy! I feel like a proud parent!" Jasper said excitedly from the doorway.

"Me too," Finn agreed.

Mission preparation was in full swing at the base, and as Jasper would say, "We're busier than a moth in a mitten." Our four base members had already departed for the Mediterranean for their training on the Interceptor, and Basheer was on his way to Israel with the C5 that held the Raider helicopter. We were to leave at dawn on Monday.

Our Delta team had met with RK, where Maharis was being held. The serial killer tried to fight off our team members when they attempted to administer the sedative, but he was no match for the Chosen. After a few minutes, he was out like a light and then transported to our base. A brig had been set up on level eight, and we knew he was well cared for—which was more than he deserved.

On Saturday, we arranged a large meal for our family and would spend the afternoon together playing games. Aaron would be missed, but he called, and we video-chatted with him for several minutes.

He appeared to be in good spirits. "You've got to ride in this boat. It's awesome!" His grin was infectious, and he said, "Although I almost dumped everyone on the boat into the ocean. But man, can that boat fly and turn on a dime. I felt like a kid again."

We laughed at his enthusiasm and were thrilled he was having a great time.

"The boat team played a prank on me, though. They filled my wet suit pants with shaving cream, those goofballs. And I mean packed full. When I stepped in, I felt like a giant doughboy."

We all hooted and he laughed along with us.

"By the way, I want to come clean with all of you," Aaron said.

"What?" I asked.

"It was me, Mara, who put the black grease on your binoculars at our sniper training."

"Really? You did that? I never would have guessed it was you. So... you pranked Finn and Jonas too?" I asked.

"I admit to your prank, Mara, but the other two, I plead 'not guilty.'"

I blushed, then snickered and snorted.

"Mara, what did you do?" Finn asked, peering at me under lowered brows.

"I put the fart machine under Aaron's chair at the team meeting."

"Mara, seriously, it was you?" Aaron asked incredulously.

"I'm afraid so," I replied.

Finn cleared his throat and then spoke up. "Since everyone is 'fessing up, I put all the ping pong balls in Jonas's locker. I ran a large downward tunnel in the ceiling that fed the balls into the top of his locker. That's why there were so many of them."

Jonas hooted, then yelled, "Now, wait a minute; you ordered *me* to clean up every ball in the room and down each hallway. Mara's correct...you *are* a rat!" But Jonas hooted with glee, then smacked Finn's head with his palm.

Finn rubbed his scalp like he was wounded. I glared at Finn in reprimand, but he smiled with a devilish grin.

"Well..." Jonas drawled.

"Come on, spit it out, brother!" Finn prodded Jonas.

"I was the one who put the itching powder in your underwear drawer." Jonas snickered, then Finn started to chase him around the room, threatening to toss him into the garbage recycler.

"Boys, now stop!" Mom scolded in a booming voice as she hid a grin behind her hand.

They ceased running, but Finn still reciprocated by slapping the back of Jonas's head. They both laughed, then the two of them returned so Aaron could see them on the video chat again.

I said, "So we all are responsible for the pranks? How on earth did we each come up with these things around the same time and still be unaware that each other was doing them? It's uncanny."

Jonas started humming the theme from *Twilight Zone*.

"Stop it, Jonas. It's weird, don't you think?" I asked, stunned.

"What can I say...perverted minds think alike," Aaron hooted.

"Aaron, that's disgusting," Mom said.

"Sorry, Mom," Aaron replied, but he clearly wasn't the least bit remorseful.

Mom chortled, then commented, "You're all incorrigible, but I still love you." She kissed us all on the cheek and said to Aaron, "Baby, I've got to say goodbye. I promised to call a friend, and I never break my word. Goodbye, my dear. Stay safe, and remember, I love you dearly."

"Bye, Mom. I love you too," Aaron replied.

We all said our goodbyes and disconnected the call.

Our family played several games that day, and it was great to hear everyone's laughter. When we put everything away, I could sense the room's mood; everyone felt the same. It was happiness, joy, and oneness, yet there were undertones of melancholy and an edge of fear. Going on a dangerous mission always brings on the latter, which was hard to ignore. I guess it was the overwhelming sense of excitement and impending doom. Only God knew what was in store for us on any given assignment, and my entire family and all of God's Chosen understood our warring emotions.

Yesterday, I received a message from Jasper, and he invited Finn and me to join him at the indoor park tonight at nine. We had no clue what it was about, and his only instructions were to dress comfortably and bring an appetite.

It was nearing the time for Finn and me to head to the park, but we had to put Gracie to bed. After her bath, Gracie and I entered her room, she said her prayers, and I told her it was time for sleep. Gracie's alternate personality reared its ugly head.

"I'm not tired, and I'm not going to sleep." After she stated her refusal with glaring authority, she bounded out of the room and plopped down on the sofa. Finn watched in consternation, and I looked at my mom, pleading for assistance. But Mom feigned innocence and shook her head, leaving this problem up to Finn and me.

"Gracie, it's time for bed and there will be no arguments," I said sternly, and Finn also repeated my command in a soft tone.

"No! I'm not tired and want to stay up with all of you." She crossed her little arms over her chest in defiance and stared at the television.

I looked at Mom again, but she raised one eyebrow at me.

After returning my mom's look, I finally understood what I had to do.

211

Walking sternly to the T.V. remote on the end table, I turned it off with a decisive click. I stood before the belligerent child, bent at the waist, and stared into her eyes—just a few inches from her face. "Gracie Eliana McKenna, get your butt off that couch and into that bed. *Now!*" My tone was quiet yet unrelenting, and my eyes never blinked or strayed from her gaze. My finger pointed with fervor toward her room, and there was no denying my resolve.

She rose and walked over to stand in front of Finn. Gracie's stubborn posture changed; it is evident by her expression that she wanted to try another tactic. Her lower lip protruded, and her chin quivered. "Please, Daddy, can I pretty please stay up for a little longer?"

Finn glared at the child, "Gracie, we will not tell you again—get into that bed." Wow, the tone of Finn's voice even scared me. It was low, quiet, and terrifying.

Gracie's eyes grew larger in her face as she stared at Finn, then she tried an appealing look at me again. Both of our expressions meant business, and she knew it.

I then said, "You have ten seconds to get under the covers, young lady. One…two…"

Her expression changed quickly to surprise, and she rushed to her room and promptly crawled under the covers.

Mom walked over to us, hugged us, and said quietly, "I knew the two of you could do it. Nice job!"

"I learned from the best, Mom." I hugged her back, and Finn and I went into Gracie's room to kiss her goodnight.

WHEN FINN and I arrived at the park, Jasper waited outside the doors.

"I'm so glad you two could make it. The park is all yours tonight, but please lock it up when you leave. You two won't be disturbed, so enjoy my gift. Y'all have a good time, ya hear?" Jasper gave us a wink, dropped the key card in Finn's hand, and walked away.

We looked at each other questioningly and entered through the double doors. It was stunning.

"My Lord in Heaven, Finn. This is amazing! But how on God's green earth did they do this? We are in an indoor recreation area at night with the moon and stars overhead. A summer breeze is wafting around us, and the air smells like a sultry evening. Do you hear the crickets and katydids?" I was blabbing and knew it, but I couldn't stop. I was awed.

Finn stared at the night sky in fascination. "I can't believe he did it. Daylight, I can understand, but nighttime? You're correct, love; it's wondrous, to say the least."

We gazed at the park and began strolling along the walkway with delicate street lamps lighting our way. Hearing the night insects and the delicate trickle of the water feature at the back of the park was soothing. As we moseyed farther, we discovered a blanket, a small lantern, and a wicker basket in the large open grassy area. Finn and I sat down on the blanket, and I opened the basket. There was a bottle of wine, glasses, fruit, cheese, and other appetizers. There were even chocolate-covered strawberries. Finn poured the wine, and I spread out the food. Everything was delicious, and we savored every bit of Jasper's thoughtful gifts.

"Let's enjoy the night sky, shall we?" Finn asked when we finished our meal. He turned off the lamp, and we laid down side by side on the blanket and gazed at the sky.

"The moon and stars have moved since we arrived! It's like they're following their orbit. Jasper and his team are miracle workers!" I smiled with joy and grabbed Finn's hand in delight.

"That they are, my sweet."

We both gasped as we witnessed a falling star. I couldn't contain myself and giggled with glee, and Finn watched me with love as I continued to stare at the night sky. "Finn, look! Now there's a meteor shower!" Finn glanced at it, but he turned back to gaze at me.

"I'm perfectly happy watching you, my gorgeous wife." He leaned down and kissed me passionately.

"Flatterer!"

We heard a loud "pop" and looked up again. Fireworks were being displayed overhead, and we gloried in all the different displays of colors and sounds. After the myriad of vivid hues quietly finished, Finn and I gazed at the glowing full moon and the twinkling stars.

"This feels like we're back at Mum's house when we sat on her front bench, enjoying the warm, romantic evening."

"I agree, Finn. That was the day before you proposed. I'll never forget those days we spent with Mom, Jonas, and Aaron. That was the start of us all becoming a real family when Mom finally met her first-born son, Aaron. I still cry with joy when I think of it. I'd never seen Mom so happy."

"Me neither, my sweet."

Finn and I stayed on that blanket for a couple of hours, simply enjoying being together under Jasper's re-creation of God's night sky. Life is good when you learn to appreciate what the Lord has given you, no matter how large or small, and for this, we must never forget to thank Him.

THE NEXT DAY WAS SUNDAY, and we attended Mass together. Instead of Sunday school for Gracie today, I wanted her to join us as a family for church. Mom cried joyfully when she saw the angels during the conse-cration, and Gracie stared in childhood wonder. My dear daughter almost yelled out loud, and I quickly quieted her, and she couldn't tear her gaze away from the altar. After the consecration, she wiggled in her seat excitedly because she couldn't contain her enthusiasm. When Mass was over, she asked many questions about the angels, and luckily, Mom took over and calmly answered every query as thoroughly as she could.

When the family sat down to brunch, it was eerily quiet. Worry furrowed our brows as we thought about our upcoming mission.

Gracie politely left the table to play, then Mom said, "Trust in the Lord, my children. He wouldn't send you on a fool's mission."

"We know, Mom," I said quietly. "It's just…it's more difficult now that we have a child to think about."

"I understand what you and Finn must be feeling, Mara," Jonas replied. "My goodness—Mom, I can't imagine what you must be going through when your children embark on these harrowing missions. How do you keep it all in perspective?"

Mom thought for a few moments, thinking about Jonas's question. "Being a parent keeps you in a constant state of worry about your children. But faith in God seems to put it into perspective, Jonas. You must all know that as humans, we have no control over anything in our lives, and as you have gotten older, you must have also understood this."

We nodded in agreement, and she continued, "So, you have to give everything in your life over to Him and always ask Him to guide your every decision and journey. Your father and I learned this a long time ago. Of course, we would still worry, but trusting in the Lord eases that burden to a more tolerable degree."

"Thanks, Mum," Finn said, squeezing Mom's hand with love and appreciation.

"You're very welcome. Now, I think I'll see what your precious child is up to."

"Mom, wait. There's one more crucial thing Finn and I would like to ask of you," I noted with urgency. "We were wondering if anything should befall us on this upcoming mission, God forbid, would you look after Gracie for us? Even if you feel raising another child may be too much for you now, would you at least look after her interests? This occurred to us last night, and we realized we hadn't made any provisions for her—which was stupid. We thought of you, Jonas, and Aaron, but we could all be killed on a mission. You're our best choice, Mom."

She sat back in the chair and said nothing for several moments. Then she raised her head and replied, "I'd be honored! But you have to understand, I'm no spring chicken, and I could also return to the Father at any time. But if it will ease your mind for this upcoming mission, I would gladly accept this responsibility of caring for our precious

Gracie. Then after the mission, we can discuss this further and weigh all our options." She stood back up and gave us one of her beautiful smiles.

Finn and I rose from our chairs and hugged Mom. "We feel better already. Thanks, Mom, and we love you dearly," I sniffled.

"You are very welcome, my babies. I'll check on Gracie and see if she wants to play Candyland."

CHAPTER 20

We met at the airport hangar just before dawn the next day, and it would be a long flight. Basheer was in place with the Raider and would wait for our instructions. Xavier and Chuck would remain with the boats, and Aaron and Billie planned to meet us in Acre at the safe house.

Maharis was being loaded onto the plane, and he'd be restrained at the rear of the aircraft. He was heavily sedated, which made me feel better. Luckily, I felt nothing at seeing him again. There were two I.V.s attached to his gurney that led to his arms. Grayson from our Beta team would be Maharis's medic, and he'd accompany us on the long flight to keep a close eye on him. Grayson was a huge man who could have been a linebacker, and he reminded me of the actor Dwayne Johnson. He had a bald head, a strong, square jaw, and dark penetrating eyes. He was as sweet as a kitten with us, but I knew he could squash his enemy like a bug and wouldn't have any issues controlling his patient. As we neared our destination, Grayson would give Maharis the prepared "zombie" cocktail and would continue to monitor and drug the serial killer on this entire mission.

It would take us two days to reach our destination, which included refueling. We were taking one of our faster jets and our schedule would be tight. The flights were long and tedious, but we spent the extra time reviewing our strategies and any possible contingencies. After finally arriving at a small military airport, we were met by Yosef, the leader of our Middle East base team.

We shook hands with our fellow Chosen warrior, who updated us with new intelligence. Luckily, not much had changed.

Yosef guided us to a quiet hangar and said, "We have a building where your team can hold up until nightfall, located only a block from your designated tunnel entrance. The two mercs—the Amazon woman and Saalim Hadid—are concerning as they have already arrived in Acre. Unfortunately, they are early, and that troubles me."

Finn stroked his chin in thought and peered questioningly at Edison. "Any thoughts?"

"Sorry, no. We will have to hope God will provide the answer."

"I agree," Finn replied.

Yosef brought us a change of clothes that matched what the locals wore. After changing, we climbed into the vehicles he provided and were driven to the safe house. Since we were taking two cars, we split up into two different routes and would arrive at different times. We must blend in and try our best to appear as Acre natives. Finn, Jonas, Yosef, and I arrived first and casually entered the building and traversed the stairs to the top floor. Aaron and Billie were already on site. Xavier and Chuck would wait near the Interceptors, and several of Yosef's team would be nearby if needed. Edison, Armie, Leon, Grayson, and Maharis would arrive in the second vehicle in a few minutes.

When everyone arrived, Yosef showed us that we could see the building with the tunnel entrance from one of the upper floor windows. He also advised us that a few of his team were watching the surrounding area and this building. We would wait for nightfall before leaving for the tunnels. Yosef bid us farewell, and we'd stay in contact with him and his team through our earbuds.

Yosef had seen to everything. All our weapons were already here, including my trusty knives. The oppressive heat within the building was already taking its toll on me, and I hoped I'd soon acclimate. Even my teammates tugged at their clothing to cool their bodies from the stifling desert climate.

There was food and water, but we ate sparingly while waiting for darkness. Finn checked in with Basheer, and he was ready and waiting with the Raider at a concealed and private location. Two of Yosef's team also stood guard over Basheer and the chopper.

I glanced at Leonide because he was fidgeting. "Leon, how are you doing?"

"I'm shakier than a rattler's tail, but I'll be fine, Mara. Thanks for askin'."

Armie nodded at me and gave me a reassuring wink, letting me know Leon would be under his watchful eye.

As I glanced at Maharis, he did look like a zombie. His stare was blank. When he stood, he swayed slightly and had to be guided while walking.

Finn watched my gaze and said, "Grayson, are you sure he's under control?"

"Yep. He's as tame as a pussy cat. If we run into trouble, I have more full syringes, but his next injection isn't due for another two hours. So don't worry, I've got this covered."

Finn nodded and turned to me.

"Mara, do you think you can induce a vision? It would be helpful to know if the demon or any of its lower minions were also here. The more we know, the better."

"I agree, Finn. Jonas and Aaron, I'll need your protection again."

"You got it," they answered.

I sat on an old sofa, closed my eyes, asked for the Lord's protection, and let my mind wander.

FOR A FEW MOMENTS, all I see is darkness. Then, thinking I should pull out, I notice a bright tunnel and realize I'm in the caverns. But these are the ones the tourists have been viewing, not the hidden ones from my previous vision. I watch as people mill about, but I spot several myrmidons. As usual, the people don't notice them, and even when one twenty-something man bumps into the demon lackey, he merely looks around in confusion, wondering what has knocked him into an elderly Hispanic woman. The young man apologizes and moves on.

My gut instinct tells me this is happening in current time. My spirit moves on, and I wonder why I'm being shown this scene. For some reason, I'm following this one myrmidon as he moves down the wide-open tunnel, turns a corner, and joins one other. Two mercenaries are in deep discussion, while down the narrow hallway, the myrmidons are banging on the rock wall with mallets.

"She said it's down here somewhere, so I suggest we keep checking the entire wall in this passageway. This would go faster if these disgusting automatons would stop disappearing," one mercenary says to the other.

"I hate this! I know we're getting a lot of money for this, but I want out of this hellhole and away from this she-demon."

"I agree, but do you want to go against this horrific monster? Because I sure don't." They both shake their heads in frustration, then stand straight as their conversation is interrupted.

Another man approaches them, and by the uniform he's wearing, he's one of the tour guards. "No one is allowed back here, gentlemen. Please return to your group." The sentry repeats his order in several languages.

The two mercs nod and walk out of the darkly lit tunnel. The guard never notices the myrmidons, but the demon flunkies at least wait until the sentry departs before they start banging on the walls again.

I float through the barrier and onto the other side. This passageway leads to the cavern, which contains the relic. The wall separating the two passages is thin and crumbling; even a minor hit could cause it to collapse. I take a closer look at the stone blocks and memorize the patterns.

As I decide to return to the relic location, I feel a demonic presence. But it isn't entering my mind; I assume it's near the vicinity of these caves. I know I should try to hone in on its location, but I'm leery, wondering if it's a trap. Just lingering long enough, I try to gauge a direction. It's not in the relic room, but I'm sensing it's somewhere above the tunnels.

I float out of the hidden passageway and return the same way I came. Following the path of the tourists, I move upward and out. Xerkamedes is nearby, but I only need a sense of her location and must refrain from falling into a possible ploy. After several moments, I discover she's hiding two blocks from the storefront of our secret tunnel entrance. The building looks like all the rest within the city, except there's a shockingly bright blue door, and along the outer door frame is a smear of bright red blood. I feel death inside this house, and it's not the demon herself. She's slaughtered the entire family of this home. Grief fills my mind and I wail inside my head. All the children—it's horrifying!

Xerkamedes knows I'm here! Jonas and Aaron quickly block her as I pull out.

Finn was staring at me and my brothers, and he sighed in relief once our minds returned to the present.

"We just got out by the skin of our teeth," Jonas said as sweat dotted his brow.

"Mara, could you have cut it any closer?" Aaron asked in fear.

"I'm sorry...but we had to know her location—the monster," I replied angrily as a tear slipped down my cheek. "She murdered the entire family within her hideout. The poor little children. She'll pay dearly for this!"

"Mara, honey, you need to focus," Finn said quietly. "You can't take her on if you're upset. As you've said, it only gives her the edge."

"You're right." I straightened my posture and returned my mind to the mission. "They know the location of one of the hidden tunnels, and the myrmidons are using mallets to try and break through from the other side. They're getting close and the wall is fragile. Time is definitely of the essence."

Finn looked out the window and then returned to stand with his team. "It'll be dark in another thirty minutes. We might as well change into our gear, check our weapons, and get ready to rock and roll."

"Copy that," we replied.

WHEN DARKNESS FELL, we were set to make our way to the store that held our entrance to the tunnels. We rechecked our communications and we were good to go. Peering out the lower floor windows, we scanned for enemy combatants. We spied two people walking down the narrow alley behind the adjoining building, but it was apparent they weren't malevolent. Splitting up, we crept to the storefront, using our night vision goggles. It was only a block away, so reaching the storefront that led to the catacombs didn't take long. We spotted Yosef's team, and they signaled that all was clear. The rest of our team arrived and we entered the building.

"Two of Yosef's men are on the adjoining rooftop with sniper rifles, so they'll let us know if we have any incoming," Finn said.

I led the team into the storefront and walked toward the back through the wooden doorway. We were now in the large room with the vaulted ceiling. My team and I traversed through the large archway that would take us to the stairwell. We removed our goggles and turned on our flashlights. With each step we took down the stairs, the years of collected grit, sand, and silt swirled around our feet, leaving a cloud of dust in our wake. Traveling down the winding steps, we halted at the bottom, and I closed my eyes.

"Which tunnel, Mara?" Edison whispered.

"Just a minute; I'm concentrating on the remnants of the vision." After several moments, I opened my eyes again. "It's the second tunnel from the right, and we follow it for approximately two hundred feet."

Armie eyed me critically and said, "Mara, I hope you're sure about this. When the Templars built these tunnels, the majority of them led nowhere or circled back to the beginning. The wrong tunnels could also be an endless maze."

"I'm positive, Armie."

"I trust you, my sweet," Finn whispered. "Let's move. Mara, lead the way, and Jonas will cover our six."

The tunnels were damp and I could smell the musty mold. All I could hear were our feet shuffling, but I kept a vigilant eye up ahead, and my AR15 was poised to fire if required. I counted my steps and knew we had traveled the correct distance.

It opened into a wide area again, and more tunnels were before us. Finn pulled out a small marker and put a cross mark at the top of the tunnel entryway we had just departed. The writing could only be seen by our red flashlights, so anyone else that may try to get out of these catacombs wouldn't be able to spot them.

Moving to the tunnel on our far left, I was about to proceed again, but I stopped, shaking my head.

Finn asked me in trepidation, "Mara, what is it?"

I turned around and addressed my team. "The myrmidons are just on the other side of this tunnel's wall to our left. They're testing the entire surface, trying to break through to find our catacombs. We need to be silent while we pass through. You'll hear their mallets when we near them, and please be sure to shine your flashlights toward the floor. These walls have cracks, and I wouldn't want them to spot our beams." My team nodded in understanding, and we quietly advanced into the long channel. We heard tapping against the wall to our left when we moved about fifty feet. Sure enough, we could smell and feel the evil of these lowliest demons. Luckily, as we moved another seventy feet, we could no longer hear their banging.

We traveled another seventy-five feet forward, and I stopped and turned to face the wall to my right.

"Now what, *chérie*?" Armie asked.

I didn't answer but stared intently at the blocks on the wall. Swinging my rifle over my shoulder, I used both hands and glided them over the blocks. I could feel several different patterns, but I couldn't decipher them. Tilting my head, I backed up a few feet. Then I let my mind drift as I gazed at the wall, and I began to see the symbols as they glowed and the patterns emerged. I watched for a few minutes, then pressed each block in the order shown to me. A door swung open.

As we peered through the opening, I heard Edison cuss, "Bloody heck, more tunnels?"

Several team members groaned, but Finn shushed everyone. "Just let Mara do her job."

I cringed because I didn't remember these tunnels. The team entered the large area and let me think—which I appreciated. But suddenly, we heard distant gunshots and yelling in Hebrew. Everyone pulled up their guns and aimed them at all possible threatening locations.

We then heard a voice in our earbuds. It was Yosef.

"Alpha team, we're taking out several myrmidons and a few mercs. We don't know where you are, but we aren't taking any chances. You're covered."

Finn answered quietly, "Copy, Yosef. Thanks for the heads-up."

After hearing the gunshots and people yelling in Hebrew, the memory returned of one of my earlier visions. But I don't remember this part—my vision had fast-forwarded until I reached another door.

"Finn, I don't know where to go from here. This part wasn't in any of my visions," I said in frustration.

"Then we'll have to figure out another way. Give yourself time, Mara. You'll be given what you need." He squeezed my hand in reassurance and kissed my forehead. I appreciated that my team gave me time to solve this problem.

After considering my options, I said, "Everyone needs to pray for guidance." My team nodded, and we held hands and prayed quietly. I kept my eyes open as our supplications continued and scanned each tunnel, moving my eyes from left to right. But nothing appeared. Tears came to my eyes in frustration as I felt I'd let my team down. I closed my eyes again and prayed harder for His assistance. It was then that I sensed a brush against my right leg. Looking down, I'm stunned. It's the cat I had during my childhood that I loved dearly. He looked up at me with clear green eyes and winked affectionately.

"Look!" I gasped. My team glanced at the tunnels, but they saw nothing. "No—look at my feet."

"Well, lookey d'are. Where did dat come from, girlie?" Leon asked.

"It's my childhood cat, Bo. I'd say the Lord sent him to guide us through these tunnels," I replied in awe. Reaching down, I picked him up and snuggled him close. He wrapped his huge paws around my neck and purred so loudly that it echoed back and forth through the chamber.

"That's Bo, my sweet? Now I see why you loved him so dearly. He's magnificent," Finn murmured.

"Isn't he?" My black and white tuxedoed Maine Coon cat had been sent by God to lead us to the relic. I kissed him fondly and reluctantly set him back on the floor. He went to each of my teammates and rubbed around their legs, purring as he went. He turned and walked away, leading us to the third tunnel to our left. We followed closely, and Finn marked every opening we entered and departed. Continuing to follow Bo, we encountered two other tunnels until we reached the wall I recognized.

Bo returned to me and asked to be held by reaching up his long body and wrapping his paws around my thigh. I picked him up, pulled him close, and buried my face in the silky soft, fragrant fur. "I've missed you so much, my love." He chirped and rubbed his face against mine. I kissed him again, and everyone also wanted to pet the precious boy. Even though I knew his task was completed and he had to leave, it wasn't easy to let him go. Tears ran down my cheeks as I slowly returned him to the floor. Bo weaved around everyone's legs again, then trotted to another long tunnel. At this entrance, Isabella appeared, picked up Bo, and held him to her chest. I heard everyone gasp as they laid eyes on her, and she smiled, turned, and disappeared.

I was crying now and Finn pulled me close. "It's okay, love. You now know that our beloved pets get to go to Heaven, and we'll see them again. That was such a blessing, don't you think?"

Nodding into the front of his shirt, I finally backed away, and Jonas also pulled me to his side and kissed my forehead. "I remember him well, Mara. We all loved him dearly, but Bo was your baby. Amazingly, the Lord gave you this stunning gift." I returned Jonas's hug, stepped back, and dried my eyes.

"Thanks. You're both correct; I feel blessed. But now, it's time to finish what God sent us here to do." I approached the wall, and the three-inch etched stones were again before me.

"When I push these blocks in the correct order, a section of the floor will give way, and I'll slide down into the chamber. Don't worry; it's a safe fall—like a slide in a playground. I'll go first. It'll take a minute or so once we reach the chamber for the lighting system to illuminate. So stay still and wait." Everyone responded with their understanding of my instructions, and my team stood back and waited for the floor to open.

I pressed the blocks, the section under my feet gave way, and I slid downward. Wishing I could whoop out loud as I careened along the descent, I waited for the ride to stop. It was only several seconds until I slowed and slid gently to my feet onto a stone floor. The room was black as pitch, and I knew I'd better move as the next team member would appear soon. I felt along the cold wall, shuffled sideways, and waited. Finn's muffled chuckle was followed by his feet touching the ground. Then Billie was quietly giggling as she touched down behind Finn.

I heard a loud click, then there was a flash of light, and the chamber was now suffused with a soft yet bright luminescence. I had to blink quickly, allowing time for my eyes to adjust to the sudden change. The remainder of my team descended the slide, followed by Maharis, then Grayson. Edison checked on Maharis, and he was still catatonic.

Armie moved forward and knelt in reverence. We all followed his lead. He finally stood and we did as well. We spread out and gazed at everything before us. Foot-wide channels ran along the outside of this giant space where water moved swiftly around the room and out a large opening at the north end of the chamber. In my vision, this space seemed big, but in reality, it was gigantic. Crates upon crates stood before us and seemed to go on for a few hundred feet. They were stacked high but appeared to be well organized. Every box was marked with the Knights Templar emblem and Latin symbols.

As we gazed to our right near a wall, we spotted a large crate the size of a coffin placed on a pure gold stand. It had been stored far away from the rest of the boxes and in a respectful fashion. It was laid on a large red silk cloth, and four tall, gold ornate pillars surrounded the coffin, and they were engraved with the Holy Trinity symbol with an ornate crucifix placed on the top.

Everyone stood their ground as they didn't dare approach the holy crate. We knew it was not our place. But we moved toward the rest of the boxes, wondering what they contained.

"Armie, what are in these massive numbers of containers?" Billie asked.

"It's hard to say. Generally, we stored gold, but it can be anything of value. Either holy or monetary. Whatever had been required of us. But the rest of these things don't matter now; the scroll is our only objective."

We returned to stand near the relic and waited for instructions from Armie.

There was a loud noise behind me, and I witnessed Maharis's eyes focusing, and he lunged in my direction, attempting to grab me. Grayson was caught off-guard, but even though he recovered quickly, he wasn't fast enough, and his charge got away from him. Maharis's eyes reflected rage as he reached for my throat. I tried to sidestep him but wasn't quick enough and was knocked to the floor near the outer wall. Because he missed grabbing me, he frantically stumbled and smashed against the coffin. We stared in horror as the outer crate tipped sideways, crashing to the ground, and shattered into many pieces. The body from the coffin slid out and rolled across the floor. It landed just a few feet from my position, but as I watched the blessed body roll, a scroll placed within his hands flew out and tumbled across the floor as well, but was headed straight for the gushing water channel. I heard Armie's warning yell, but my only thought was to rescue the holy artifact.

I instinctively reached out to save it from destruction, but Maharis realized what I was after, and he grabbed it ahead of me. He screamed in terror when he clutched the relic, and his entire body started to disintegrate before my eyes. Reaching over, I struck his arm, hoping to break his fateful grip on the scroll. I also screeched as I felt a horrifying jolt when my fingers brushed against his shirt sleeve.

CHAPTER 21

I blinked several times and realized I was on my knees. My left hand held my upper body upright against the cold floor, and my right hand reached out pleadingly. I moved both of my feet so they were under me, and I rocked back and balanced myself on the balls of my feet. As I tried to stand, it felt like gravity had me rooted to the spot. Even the air was stagnant and heavy, and when I slowly inhaled, I detected a whiff of ozone. When I gazed around the cavern, everything in the room was frozen in time—my team's faces fixed in horror as they stared blindly at me and what was left of Maharis. The demented man's body was gone, and all that was left was a blackened scorch mark on the floor.

For some reason, I couldn't move, and everyone and everything in the room was motionless—even the water channels were stock-still. As I crouched, I smelled roses instead of ozone and knew something spectacular was about to happen, so I waited. Within moments, she appeared before me, and it was the Virgin Mary—the Holy Mother of our Lord and Savior!

My eyes lit on her. She was exquisite and reflected purity, piety, innocence, and great knowledge. Her perfection was undeniable with her heart-shaped face and dark, clear penetrating eyes, and she was clothed in a luminescent blue robe that covered her from head to toe. I instantly lowered my eyes in respect, awe, and unworthiness.

"Look at me, my child." Her voice was soft, sweet, and undeniable, and I could hear her speaking clearly through to my soul. I raised my face and stared into her luminous eyes.

"My...Blessed...Holy...Mother." This was all I could think to utter as I lowered my eyes to the floor once more. My body trembled, and my hands shook. *How could this be?*

"Mara, my child, please look at me." Raising my gaze to hers again, I couldn't look away as I was drawn deeply into her penetrating eyes. "I know you tried to save a demented man from death. But what transpired was what was planned for him—to discover if Maharis, as you call him, would continue to follow the demon's bidding or finally turn to the Lord in Heaven. It was his choice and his alone, and unfortunately, he selected the former. I'm afraid he's now in Hell. His twin brother, Amos, went down to meet him at the entrance of Hell, trying to persuade Maharis to repent each of his heinous sins and call to my Son in Heaven. I even tried as well, but he's an obstinate man."

I stared at her sorrowfully and asked, "Then there's no hope for him?"

"I can't answer that question, Mara, not yet. There *is* one person that this soulless man admires and to whom he may take heed," she said.

"I didn't think he liked anyone, dear Holy Mother."

"Hmm, so you'd think." She stepped forward, knelt before me, and caressed my cheek. "That one person is you, Mara."

"Me? That's impossible. I...I mean no disrespect, Holy Mary, but he tried to rape and kill me."

"Be that as it may, he respected you. You fought him like a tiger when he attacked you, and when you confronted him later, you never let him intimidate you—which was the only way to earn his admiration. Which brings me to this—I have an immense favor to ask, Mara."

I continued staring at her in awed silence, and she continued, "Since you're the only person I know that could influence this soulless man, would you consider trying to persuade him to turn toward My Son and our Father?"

"Me? But how can I do this? He's dead and in Hell."

"Yes. But as you know, time is subjective—especially regarding Heaven and Hell. As you've noticed, we're currently on another plane. One that's not part of the current time on earth; I guess you'd say we're out of sync." She mused, then continued, "If you agree, I'll guide you to Hell and keep you safe within my sight and protection. But if you do this, you must work quickly. As the soulless man is descending to the lower realms of damnation, you'll also be pulled down. I can only protect you for so long, so you must work quickly."

Swallowing hard, I looked fearfully into her dark, penetrating eyes.

"Mara, you don't have to do this, my dear, and we would never hold this against you if you refuse. But I know your heart—and you, like me, wish to save as many lost and forlorn humans as possible. If he atones for his horrible sins and calls to our Lord, he'll be given the soul he'd never been granted when his parents and grandparents committed the mortal sin of incest. He'll then be forgiven his transgressions, although he'll still have to pay for them in Purgatory."

I understood her and knew what she said was correct. No matter what horrible things Maharis had done, he still had the chance to turn to God for salvation. *How could he possibly deny God and want to spend eternity in the horrors of Hell?*

"I'll do it, Holy Mother," I said. But the thought of entering such a terrifying place shook me to my core. She pulled me to a standing position and stared into my eyes. An immediate sense of peace and strength flowed through me just from her loving gaze. Nodding, I understood the grace she'd given me, and I thanked her through our quiet psychic communication.

"You will do well, my dear child. Remember, I'll remain with you, but as I said, try to work as quickly as possible. The lower you fall, the harder it'll be for me to protect you."

I nodded and felt another jolt—then blackness.

∾

FREEFALL. I feel myself dropping like a spinning boulder down an empty skyscraper elevator shaft, except I can't see anything nor distinguish if I'm facing left, right, up, or down. Even though I'm given the graces to attempt such an impossible feat, a fearful scream still echoes in my head. But, now I'm slowing and can see illumination ahead—though I can't say it's light. Just brighter than black—if that makes any sense. The flickering glow is reminiscent of a flame in a darkened cave, and there's an intense cold. I shiver in response, and then the icy frost changes quickly to a fierce heat. As I move closer to my destination, the space becomes larger, and I'm shoved unceremoniously through a swirling wormhole, and my descent comes to a bone-jarring halt.

For a moment, I smell roses and know my dear Holy Mother is staying close to me. A calm comes over my spirit as I gaze at my surroundings.

Below me, I see miles upon miles of a desolate, heinous, and burning landscape. It's covered in tall spires of fiery rock and winding rivers that have a combination of lava and what appears to be brackish blood. The deeper I look, the more monstrous the view. So many creatures, demons, and critters litter every crevice—hiding in wait for their next victim.

The air is mired with something—maybe ash from burning flesh and who knows what else. I look left and right, and the view never changes, but as I look up, I see the giant spinning tunnel from where I just exited.

The intense heat surrounds me, and I try to ignore it, but the smell is even worse than the suffocating swelter. The myrmidons reeked of this place, but they were mild in comparison. The stench is horrific and reminds me of rotting corpses and burning flesh among piles of steaming manure. I'm amazed I can smell when I don't have a physical body within this mire of Hell.

The sounds in this place are extreme, and I can barely hear myself think. There's a dark, constant rumbling like an endless earthquake, but I have no clue what's causing the deep, teeth-chattering vibration. I also hear crackling, grumbling, and growling, along with a plethora of vile words in every language echoing from each direction. But the most horrifying is the incessant screams—a torrent of alarming wails full of terror and unbearable agony. The din never ceases. I can't even ascertain if they are all human, though I assume some are not.

I hear a torturous shriek. Looking down again and to my right, I see Maharis, or Karl Runyun, struggling to escape the clutches of a hideous fiend. He finally gets away and pushes upward again, but he's still below my location.

"Mara! It's all your fault!" He bellows my name, blaming me for his predicament.

I shake my head, briefly ignoring his rant. What can I possibly say to this man to persuade him to turn to our Lord and Savior?

Maharis is grabbed by another demon who bites his tender flesh. I hear his agonizing scream, yet he's still calling to me, swearing at me, using vile profanity.

The Virgin Mary croons to me again, saying, "My dearest child, try and sway this soulless man from his dark and sinful ways. He must renounce his grisly transgressions and that of his ancestors. Then, he has to call to my Son, for this is the only way he'll ever leave the bowels of the doomed. This man will finally be granted a soul, and he'll be redeemed. But it would be best if you did this swiftly, child. If this perpetual sinner sinks too far into the depths, there's no chance of saving him." I hear and acknowledge her directive.

I must move lower to where Maharis is being held, but I feel great trepidation. Where I'm currently hovering, I'm still safe from the clutches of the demons. But if I descend, I'll be within the reach of their razor-sharp claws and teeth. Taking the chance, I move down but realize the evil ones fear me. As I near Maharis, a horrific creature is gnawing on him. This beast resembles a cross between an alligator and

233

an octopus. It doesn't appear to have an actual head, but there are many razor-like teeth along its tentacles, and two arms are wrapped around Maharis's chest. When I approach, it attempts to grab me with one of its appendages, but I swiftly dodge beyond its reach.

Another creature attacks the first, and as they fight one another, Maharis is thrown clear. I grab him and pull him near me.

"Do you wish to leave this place?" I ask, bellowing over the clamor of the demons and their minions.

"Of course I do, you twit!" He swears at me again in frustration and pain.

"Then repent all your sins and call on His name. Only the Son of God can save you here. Call on Jesus!" I roar at him in exasperation, hoping he'll see reason and save himself from damnation.

"I don't owe Him anything. What has He done for me?" Another demonic critter grabs at Maharis's leg and takes a large bite. He screams in agony and anger but still refuses to listen to me.

"Are you kidding? He's done everything for you, yet you still deny Him. You chose your life's path, and you could have followed Him, not the likes of Lucifer. God is giving you one last chance to repent and call to the Lord. Do you want to spend eternity here?"

I realize we've been slowly sinking farther into the abyss, closer to the smoldering heat, and the lower we descend, the more creatures appear. They're more vicious than what we've already encountered.

Maharis looks down at the horror below him, and I notice his clothes are gone, and his skin has begun peeling off his body.

"Maharis, we're running out of time. Repent your sins and call to our Lord and Savior!"

"No! I...can't."

We're falling farther now, and I scream as my skin begins to sear— but I have no body, so how can this be? Finally, I feel something bite into my leg and clench my teeth, fighting back a torturous wail.

"Maharis, He...will...forgive...you! Please, I forgive you, so ask God also to pardon you. You must do this to live in His love! This is

what God can give you for all eternity. I beg you, call to Him, and your soul will be restored, and you'll live forever in the glory of Heaven." We're sinking too rapidly, and communicating or thinking is a struggle. Something from above touches me, but it's gentle and comforting. Fighting the insistent pull, I beg for more time from my Holy Mother to save this obstinate man. But Her grasp is persistent. I look down and Maharis is staring up at me. Most of his face has been torn away, and I grieve as I gaze into what's left of his eyes. "Maharis, call to Jesus...."

As I'm lifted from this horrible place, I see a young man below the whirling tunnel over my head. I stare in wonder, discovering it's Amos Runyon, Maharis's developmentally disabled twin brother, who we had to kill at the farmhouse. Gazing at his face, I see he's no longer mentally and physically challenged, and it now reflects intelligence, kindness, and, most of all, deep sorrow and remorse as he stares at his brother in the depths of Hell.

Amos returns my gaze and I emote sympathy and understanding. "Amos, I'm so sorry. Your brother won't listen to me. As much as I plead, he refuses to acknowledge our Lord and Savior, and I can't change his mind." I feel overwhelming sadness, and Amos responds to my apology.

"Mara, it's not your fault. In Karl's life, God gave him many opportunities to come to Him, but the evilness held him fast. It's up to Karl now, and there's nothing either one of us can do. We both tried, and neither of us could save him from himself. It's time for us to return. Me to Heaven and you to Earth. May God bless you, Mara, and thank you for trying." He gives me a sweet smile, then vanishes into the swirling vortex.

I'm being tugged again and enter the spinning wormhole, but everything goes black once more.

~

THERE WAS an electrifying shock as I returned to my body. I was back kneeling, and the Holy Mother still faced me. Mournful tears ran down my face, from what I'd just seen and from my failure to persuade Maharis to repent and call on the Father.

"I'm...so...sorry, dear Mother. I have failed both You...and Maharis." I continued to sob.

"Mara, you haven't failed. Going to Hell was an enormous feat for you, and you can't blame yourself if that man doesn't come to my Son. On the contrary, my dear child. Mara, you planted the mustard seed, and that's a blessed accomplishment. What happens now is up to the soul-less man, so dry your tears and move on. It's time for you and your team to finish this task." She kissed my forehead, and I felt my fear and painful grief vanish. I thanked her for easing my burden, and she smiled with love and compassion.

I stopped crying and wiped away my tears. The smell of Hell lingered in my nostrils, and my stomach rolled. She touched my face, and when she did, the wonderful aroma of roses again filled the air, and my nausea passed.

"Thank you, dear Mother," I whispered with sincerity.

My ears popped, and everything and everyone around me began to move in real time. It was as if my body shifted from a vacuum and back into normal, earthly space. I heard the water running in the channels again, and my team gasped with surprise as they now saw the Holy Virgin and me. They stayed a few feet from us, seeming unsure whether to venture near our dear Mother of Heaven.

"Now, I ask you, Mara, and God's wonderful warriors to say nothing of what you've seen here—and I'm referring to the body of my beloved husband. The knights will take the Scroll of the Seven Seals and spirit it away for safekeeping, but I request the Templars also take my dear husband's body to his new resting place. God will bring Joseph's sainted remains to the forefront of humanity when the appropriate time shall come to pass, which is only known to our Father." She touched my shoulder again, and I saw a couple of images, but I wasn't sure what they meant.

"It will be done as you ask. But I don't understand the rest of what you showed me," I replied.

"You will, my daughter. Trust me."

I nodded, and she gave me the most soul-filling smile I had ever seen.

I kissed her hand, and after, she touched my hair. "Mara, I asked the Father if I could give you this long, curly red hair. I must say, it suits you." I returned her smile, and she vanished, but the delightful scent of flowers lingered in the room.

After her departure, I turned to see Finn's tear-stained face as he rushed over and pulled me close. After he released me, the look in his eyes was both fearful and relieved. I mouthed to him that I was fine and then caressed his face in assurance. He took my hand and gently kissed the palm. Smiling widely at him, I turned to look around the room. Beside the blackened mark that once was Maharis was the cloth-laden corpse that had been knocked from the coffin. As I gazed at the Holy body, I gently slid the cloth aside that covered his face. This man was perfectly preserved, and I was staggered by his perfection. His hair was somewhat long, dark brown with a reddish tint, and he had a full beard and mustache. His skin was deeply tanned but clear, and his expression appeared blissful. He looked as if he was only sleeping, not dead, for over two thousand years.

"I can't believe it's Saint Joseph," I whispered in awe.

The chamber was silent as no one moved or said a word. I only heard the gentle gurgling of the water running through the channels as they left the outer edges of the cavern.

"My Lord all Mighty. Doesn't that beat all? The Holy Virgin, Herself, and Saint Joseph too." Jasper finally broke the silence, and we all breathed a sigh of relief. He began pacing as he ran his hand over his face in disbelief.

"Dat sure does beat all, Jasper!" Leon replied, then hollered, "Hoo-whee, Jiminy Cricket!"

We laughed with joy and a touch of fear and awe, then hugged each other, reveling because of what we had witnessed.

"We actually met the mother of Jesus?" Grayson asked in shock.

"Yep!" Edison concurred.

After our brief celebration, I looked around the room but didn't see the scroll. Armie saw the alarm on my face and said, "Relax, Mara. It is safe, *chérie*." He padded a waterproof, oblong container connected to a long shoulder strap. It was wrapped crosswise around his body.

I sighed in relief, and our team dispersed and began looking through the other crates. There were shocked responses from everyone with each discovery. As Armie had said, there was an overabundance of gold. But we also found silver, bronze, gems of every size and color, paintings in gilded frames, vases, daggers, swords, and various expensive and luxurious fabrics. My crew even discovered books that were as old as time.

"Mara, we must depart this place and secure the scroll," Armie said urgently.

I was also feeling a pronounced sense of impending danger and agreed. "You're correct. We must leave, but it's such a shame, though," I replied.

"Don't worry. My people will return to remove the balance of these items," Armie said.

"We can't get the coffin out of here through the slide, so how can we remove him?" I asked.

Armie smiled, then strode toward a rear wall. There was more writing on the cement wall blocks, and he pushed several of them. There was a rumbling sound, dust fell from the ceiling, and a door shifted to the right beside the indented blocks. It led to a sizeable well-lit corridor. I still had no clue how the chamber was illuminated, but there was no time to investigate.

"This tunnel leads to a concealed exit—or so the printed tiles say.

There is only one to follow, but it should split into two exits. We must investigate which is the safest, so I suggest we take a test run, *n'est-ce pas?*"

Finn answered, "I agree. Let's send a recon team down the tunnel and make sure the coast is clear. Edison, Billie, and Jonas, you three move out and let us know what you find."

With a "copy that," the three team members entered the shaft.

After several minutes, we heard Jonas over our earbuds, "So far, we've walked another fifty feet and are now ascending upward. We'll check back in a few more minutes."

"Copy," Finn replied.

Our team waited with apprehension until we heard Jonas's voice again, "We've come to the end of the main tunnel, and now it splits off into two tunnels. One heading east and the other south. We'll take the east one first."

Waiting for another fifteen minutes, we heard Jonas again. "The east one stops at a stairwell. We're heading up."

"Stay safe, brother," Aaron answered.

"You got it."

We heard labored breathing as they traversed the stairwell. More noises that sounded like clanging ensued, then a couple of squeaks and another gentle metal clang. "Jonas here again. There are hostiles at this exit. It leads to a busy plaza that contains too many myrmidons and a couple of mercs. We're heading back down to try the south exit. Stay tuned, folks."

"Copy," Finn said.

We waited another twenty minutes, hoping to hear from them soon. After another seventeen minutes, Jonas was again whispering in our ears. "I'll be a monkey's uncle! This exit leads back to where we first entered, under the church through the old market. We never saw this door, you sneaky Templars. No offense, Armie and Leon."

"None taken," Armie replied, and Leon grinned wolfishly.

Finn said with a smile, "We have our exit. Jonas, you and your team make your way back to the cavern."

"Copy," Jonas replied. After several minutes, they returned to join us in the cave.

Armie said, "Let Leon and me put St. Joseph's body back into another crate. I don't know if you are allowed to touch him, so I guess it's better to be safe than sorry."

"Good thinking. I don't want to go to Hell again," I replied, using a tone of dread.

"What? Is that what happened? We had no clue what was going on with you as you were frozen to the ground, kneeling like a statue," Jonas said in surprise.

"Yes. I went to the outer perimeter of Hell, trying to save the soul of Maharis. It was horrific, and I'll provide more details when this mission is over." I then asked, "My body was frozen, huh?"

Aaron nodded, "Yup. After you touched that serial killer's sleeve, you simply froze like a statue. It was bizarre. We tried to approach you but could only get within a few feet. As Jonas said, we didn't know what was going on. Wow. I'm so sorry you had to see Hades, sis."

"Holy fire and brimstone, sweet pea. I'm sorry, too," Jasper agreed.

"Thanks, everyone, but I'm fine. Although, I certainly wouldn't like a repeat performance." I gave a shiver as if someone had walked over my grave.

"No kidding, doll." Billie slapped me lightly on the back and gave me a quick hug. She was embarrassed at her show of affection and shuffled off in another direction of the room.

After Armie and Leon placed the body safely back into the coffin and then into the crate, they sealed the lid tightly closed.

"We'd better move," I said in warning.

"I concur, love," Finn replied.

The rest of us heaved the coffin off the stand, and we almost threw it into the air. We grappled to safely bring the box back into our hands and sighed in relief.

"I thought it would be heavy," I croaked.

"Me too. Who knew?" Aaron responded.

The entire team trudged out of the cavern, and before we left, we said another prayer of thanksgiving and guidance and departed the chamber.

CHAPTER 22

Following the tunnels, we stayed vigilant, wondering when the demon's followers would attack. We stayed as quiet as possible and kept praying to the Lord to protect us in this narrow and unforgiving space of the passageways. With relief, we reached the stairwell and climbed to the top.

Pausing near the door, Edison cautiously opened the exit and peered to the other side. "All clear. The church apse appears to be absent of our enemies. Let's move, but keep your eyes open, mates."

We entered the large area behind the thrift store, and Edison went through the next wooden door to the shop. He motioned us forward.

Wary and suspicious, I asked my team, "Does anyone think this has been too easy?"

Everyone nodded in agreement, and even Jasper replied, "Yep. That job was slicker than cow slobber, which doesn't feel right at all to me."

"I agree," Finn said with a grim look on his face. "Yosef, we're in the apse with the package. What's your twenty? Over."

We waited for his response for several minutes but finally heard a breathless mutter. "Can't...talk at the moment. They found us...hold your position." There were loud grunts, and we heard knives clanking and several moans of pain.

"I know you're busy, but where are you, Yosef? We'll send reinforcements," Finn said.

"Hold on…"

Several minutes later, he finally answered. "We won this battle, but more adversaries are on the way. Our twenty is about a hundred yards north of your location as we led them away from your team. But Finn, move now. Be careful—those horrific things are everywhere! They definitely know we're in Acre."

Billie, Edison, Jasper, and I took the lead and led the way for our team. The covered trucks were still waiting where we'd left them, which was a relief. I stopped the team with a hand signal as we neared the vehicles—it was that awful smell. I nodded to Jonas, and he signaled the rest of the team the myrmidons were dangerously close. Moving near the first truck, I used my rifle to slowly open the draping at the rear of the military vehicle. Three were hiding inside. I made a hand gesture, urging them to come for me. They jumped out, waving their knives in my direction, and I set down my rifle and pulled out my two kukri blades. Taking the first demon monster by surprise, I cut his throat and the femoral artery in his upper thigh. He went down like a stone.

The second one circled me. The spittle dripping from the corner of his mouth gave me a definite clue regarding his resolve. He thought I'd be an easy kill. I leered at him and waited. But to my surprise, someone impaled him from behind, and the blade protruded from the myrmidon's chest. Thinking it had been one of my team who killed it, I was about to thank them, but then I saw who'd slain the demon thug. It was the Amazon woman—the mercenary who had tended to me when Jonas and I had been held captive.

"*Nein, liebchen.* The little troll doesn't get to kill you. That privilege belongs to me." She smirked with triumph, which held a hint of desperation. "You see my face, *fräulein*? I was given this because you got away from me. That she-demon punishes severely when you don't follow orders." The left side of her face had been sliced from her lower jaw up over her eye to her hairline. Her left eye was unseeing and opaque blue. The deep cut was red, puckered, and angry-looking.

She lunged at me, but I sidestepped her advance.

"You shouldn't have worked for her, hmm?" I asked in a condescending tone.

"Like I had a choice. One does her bidding or they die."

"I would have chosen the latter," I replied.

She growled and lunged again with her blade. This time, I swiftly cut her forearm and moved my body so I was directly behind her. I slashed two more times, cutting shallow slices across her upper back. She screamed in anger as she turned around, facing me once more.

"You are a spitfire, *liebchen*."

"Stop your endless chatter and fight. Or are you inept at combat and would rather talk me to death?" I taunted her.

That did it. She ran at me and I dropped, thrusting out my feet, and she tripped over my legs and slid across the dirt. I rose swiftly and jumped onto her back, and she tried in vain to buck me off, twisting her body around to dislodge my weight. But I grabbed her heavy ponytail, pulling her head back toward me with my blade held firmly at her throat. She laid dead still, knowing she was about to die.

"Listen, Broom Hilda—you have two choices. I can release you, and you hightail it out of here, or I can take your life. It's your decision," I muttered in her ear. Little did she know that I had no desire to kill her; she was neither a demon nor possessed by one.

"If I leave, that monster will find, torture, and kill me. So, do what you must," she said shakily, terrified of either choice.

"Mara, kill her and be done with it. We have to move," Finn said to my right.

"Are all the other lackeys dead?" I asked.

"Yes. It's just her that's left," he replied.

I turned my attention back to the Amazon and said, "You know I'm a Chosen One and a strong psychic. If you let me, I can place an impenetrable wall in your mind that even the horrible demon can't infiltrate. That way, you can live without fear of her. But if you come after any of my team again, I'll kill you with no remorse. What's your pleasure?"

She tried to struggle again, and I pulled harder on her ponytail, pressing my knife blade a little firmer against her throat.

"Okay…let up; I can't breathe." I loosened my grip, and she continued, "You can do that—put a barrier in my mind?"

"I can. But let me warn you…this wall will protect you from her, not me. I'll know if you commit a major sin against God even once. Do you understand?"

"Yes." She was silent for a moment, then said, "I agree. All I wanted to do was retire and be left alone, anyway."

"Mara, just knock her out and let's bug out of here," Finn insisted.

"Stop it, Finn," I reprimanded him, and when I tried to enter the German woman's psyche, it was blocked. "Woman, open yourself to me and think of nothing so I may come inside."

I tried again, and this time it worked, and I dumped three heavy walls around her psyche. But I also left something else…a small bell that would warn me if she dared to sin against the Father.

Releasing my grip on her hair, I stood up. Finn held his weapon on her, not trusting the woman.

The Amazon rose and turned toward me. She wrinkled her brow in puzzlement and shook her head.

"I cannot feel the demon. You are sure she will not find me?" she asked in her heavy German accent.

"Yes. Of course, she can still find you through ordinary means, so I suggest you leave this country ASAP and go off the grid. I'm sure she'll send other mercs to find you," I warned.

She stared at the ground momentarily, then grudgingly uttered,

"Thank…you." Then turning, she grabbed her knife from the ground and took off in the opposite direction.

I also picked up my weapons and turned to follow Finn.

"Are you sure you should have let her go, Mara?"

"Yes. I sensed kindness as well as being trapped and desperate. She wanted to be free from Xerkamedes. Is the rest of the team okay?"

Finn nodded and said, "Just a few bumps and bruises, but we have a long way to go. The trucks are loaded, and we have to get moving."

"Copy that."

Armie had the scroll on one truck and was accompanied by Leon, Billie, Aaron, and Grayson. The remainder of us had the body of St. Joseph in the lead truck.

Finn pulled out his satellite phone. "Xavier, we're about thirty minutes out. Are you and Chuck still safe, and are there any hostiles in your vicinity?"

"Xavier here, and yes, we're safe and have seen little activity once darkness set in. We're waiting for your arrival, and a couple of Yosef's team have been keeping a close eye on us."

"Good to know. We'll contact you when we arrive."

"Copy that. Xavier out."

We traveled along roads that held very little traffic, and they were rough and haphazard at best. The ride seemed to take forever, but we finally made it to the port, and Finn contacted Xavier again, notifying him of our arrival. We parked a few blocks away. We hustled toward our designated meeting place. It was more difficult for Aaron and Grayson as they were carrying St. Joseph's body in the crate. They did their best to travel near the darkened buildings and away from the street lights.

Jasper was leading the team, and we closely watched his signals. He stopped us twice as a few locals passed by. Aaron and Grayson laid the crate down, sat on top of it, and conversed casually in Hebrew. The passerby ignored them and moved on. When it was safe, they rose, picked up the crate, and moved again.

I whispered into my mic, "Thank the Lord for giving us the gift of speaking many languages."

"Amen," Aaron responded.

Finally approaching our appointed meeting location, we hid behind a large boatyard storage building. We waited a few minutes while Finn contacted Xavier, but the hairs on my neck stood in warning. Using the night vision goggles, I spied more myrmidons, moving randomly along the abandoned pier.

"Armie, hold up. Three demon goons are coming your way," I ordered frantically. "Finn, we need to hide the coffin."

"Go, Armie!" Finn said, and Armie quickly acknowledged his order. "You heard her—Aaron, move your cargo out of sight."

We watched Aaron and Grayson grab the crate again and scuttle behind an old grounded fishing trawler. Armie's team split up and moved quickly in the darkness. Armie and Billie entered the abandoned storage building, and the remainder of our squad hid behind a large, rusted shipping crate.

After several minutes, the myrmidons moved away and headed toward the next pier. Edison signaled the Interceptors' crew, who were waiting by the old, dilapidated fishing docks. Their return light flashes gave us the all-clear.

Finn spoke quietly into his mic, "Armie, you're good to go. Get your team and your cargo to the boat. Head to Interceptor Two." Armie, Aaron, Leon, Chuck, and Grayson would take Interceptor Two to escape with the sacred scroll and the body of St. Joseph. A Templar ship waited out in deep water for them to arrive. Finn and the remainder of our team would use Interceptor One, taking us to a freighter anchored at sea.

We stood by, listening for a response, but none was forthcoming.

"Armie, respond," Finn demanded.

Still nothing.

Looking through our night vision goggles, we spotted Armie and Billie coming out the door of the building. Their hands were held high, and two people were behind them with rifles aimed at their backs.

"You honestly think you can kidnap two of God's Chosen Ones?" We heard Armie's voice over our coms.

"Ha! We just did. She will be pleased and reward us greatly for bringing her the sacred scroll and two of the Chosen. Now move!" We recognized the first man, and it was Saalim Hadid. The second man we didn't recognize.

"Why don't you just take the scroll?" We watched Armie turn and lift the case from his shoulder as he attempted to hand it over to the mercenary. But the merc backed up in fear as if he was about to be burned.

"Keep that away from me! I know what that can do if the wrong person touches it. Now move to the third dock and get into the speedboat."

"How did you know we would be here?" Billie asked.

"We didn't. Today, we were told you were in Acre ahead of schedule, so we had to scramble to cover all contingencies. You would have to leave by land, sea, or air, so we knew you would show up at one of these places. No more talk, and get into the boat," Hadid ordered.

Our team approached the Interceptors. Grayson and Aaron secured the crate that held the coffin into Interceptor Two, and the rest of us piled into the boats and buckled in. I heard Finn contact Basheer and Yosef regarding our current situation.

We waited while Hadid's boat moved away before we started our engines. Hadid's boat's running lights were easy to spot, but we kept the Interceptor's lights off and used our night vision equipment and radar. While staying well behind them, we tracked their movements and direction.

"Finn, I hate this. They have the scroll, and we've no clue where they're being taken," I whispered in frustration.

"I know, Mara. We must follow their lead and keep praying for His guidance."

I clutched his hand while Xavier expertly drove the watercraft, and Finn diligently watched the navigation instruments. Our nav expert was supposed to be Billie, but since she was taken hostage, Finn took the station. We kept in touch with Aaron on the other boat Chuck was driving.

Finn turned around and said, "Jonas, check in with Basheer and confirm he's still tracking us."

Jonas concurred and contacted Basheer. He was still trailing both of our boats' movements using the Raider's equipment, and he told us to let him know when he would be needed.

The kidnapper's boat was slowing. As they turned around a point, it was then that we saw it—an imposing and dangerous-looking yacht, and even through our goggles, it appeared ominous and threatening.

I said into my com, "Team, do you feel it?"

"There's no denying it, Mara. Demons are up ahead," Jasper answered.

"Yup," was my only reply.

"Holy Hannah! That ship must be over four hundred feet from bow to stern. And is the entire hull black?" Jasper questioned in amazement.

Edison spoke up from the other boat saying, "Looks that way to me, although these night goggles make everything appear gray. The ship is as dark and vile as the demon herself. I would also say that yacht is worth over five hundred million of your dollars, mates."

Our boats were stopped, and we stared at the shocking vestige of this enormous watercraft. A bright light was turned on, and we watched as Armie and Billie were escorted onto the ship using one of the lower deck's docking ports. After the mercs dropped off our kidnapped team members, they returned to their boat and left—luckily heading away from us. After their departure, the yacht's bright searchlight turned off, and three other powerful beams continually scanned the water surrounding their vessel.

As I studied the boat, I knew who and what was on that yacht and said, "Finn, we have demons aboard, although I can't detect any unpossessed humans other than Armie and Billie. But as you know, we can't always sense them."

Finn nodded. "So, now what?" he asked me and the team.

"Beats me, Kemosabe," I replied. "I guess we better start praying and then get to work."

"Agreed, Tonto."

CHAPTER 23

We pulled our boats around to the other side of the peninsula so the yacht wouldn't detect us.

"I'm sure they have a couple of snipers up top, and they probably have the same night vision equipment we have," Edison said quietly.

Finn nodded. "I agree. Approaching them using a boat or chopper is out of the question. But we need a ruse and must also scan their ship with thermal imaging. This boat is capable, but there's no way we'd have enough time to scan their vessel without being detected." Finn turned to the rear of the boat. "Jasper, do you have a pair of thermal imaging goggles stowed back there?"

"Sure do," he answered swiftly.

"I have an idea. Edison, we need to contact Yosef," Finn replied.

After a half hour, we had a plan in place. We contacted Yosef, and he said he'd arrive at our location within thirty minutes.

"Anyone hear that?" Jonas asked.

"What?" Jasper inquired with alarm.

"A chopper. It sounds like it's coming from the northeast. Do we dare edge one of these boats beyond our cover to check it out?" Edison asked.

Finn answered, "I don't think we have a choice. Xavier, let's take a peek." The sounds of the helicopter grew louder, and as we edged out of cover, we discovered it was landing on the yacht's helipad.

"It's her. Xerkamedes," I told the team.

"No doubt. We can all feel her stench of evil," Jonas said in agreement.

After returning to cover behind the peninsula, our team prepared for Yosef's arrival. We pulled on dry suit gear and grabbed additional weapons from the storage areas at the back of the boat. Our team would be called the "A" team. The "B" team would be Yosef's men who would stay behind while Team A boarded the yacht.

"I can't believe one of these dry suits fits me. We're prepared for anything," I said.

"We try to be, love," Finn returned.

"At least we know Armie and Billie haven't been at the mercy of that major demon all this time. I wish we had time for Jonas to conduct a spirit walk. It would give us the intel for where everyone was on that boat. We better hope we get to them quickly before she starts her interrogation," I warned.

"I know. Time is definitely of the essence," Finn said. I nodded my agreement.

Because of my words of caution, we paused in our duties and said additional prayers for our teammates who were hostages of the demonic beings.

Jonas spoke quietly, "Yosef and his team are arriving." We heard the *putt, putt, putt* of the medium-sized, dilapidated fishing boat's arrival, which we would use to distract the security team aboard the demon's yacht. Yosef's pilot pulled alongside and threw us a dock line, and Jasper hitched it to our boat. After reviewing our plans once more, our team boarded Yosef's fishing vessel. We laid down along each side of the watercraft, staying out of sight. The hilt of one of my knives dug into my back, but I ignored the jabbing pain.

"We're nearing the yacht, but wait for my signal," Yosef said. He was dressed as a lowly and poor fisherman of the area. We saw a bright light shine on his face, and it also scanned our boat.

"Who are you? You need to return to where you came from, brother," a voice yelled at Yosef in Hebrew from the yacht.

"I am only fishing, my friend. The best catch in these waters is at this time of night. I would gladly share a portion of my catch with your crew if you wish," Yosef replied convincingly.

"No. But I need you to move along. This ship belongs to one of great power and doesn't like her privacy interrupted. So it would be best if you left quickly. Come back tomorrow night to resume your fishing."

"I understand, and I will do as you say, and I wish you an evening of many blessings," Yosef hollered back and followed his response with a friendly wave. During their exchange, Jonas had slipped his head just above the edge of the fishing boat and scanned the yacht using the infrared goggles. When he'd finished, he lowered back down, switched his goggles to night vision, and sketched the vessel, marking sections where people and demons were located.

The light kicked off, and we slowly and quietly slipped out of the boat, into the water, and down into its dark, murky depths.

"Good luck, my friends," Yosef told us. Now that he'd dropped us near the yacht, he'd return to pilot Interceptor One, and Chuck would remain the pilot for the boat containing the relics on Interceptor Two.

The swim was farther than I'd anticipated, and I prayed to the Lord to help me traverse this vast distance. I found it disorienting looking through the waterproof night vision goggles, and I tried to focus on Jasper and Finn swimming in front of me. When I entered the water, it hadn't seemed so far when I'd scanned the distance from the fishing boat to the yacht. Finn saw my distress and returned to my side to check on me.

I'm sure my discomfort was evident to him when he witnessed a hint of panic in my eyes and that I inhaled too rapidly. We couldn't speak as we wore scuba masks and breathed through the tanks, but I felt Finn's calming presence. He slowly raised and lowered his hands in front of his chest, indicating that he wanted me to calm my breathing and swim steadily.

I nodded, and he stayed with me until my quick breaths returned to normal. Finn remained beside me as I swam in the water with gentle, calm strokes. Before long, we arrived at the vessel. One guard patrolled this side of the yacht, and we treaded water as we waited for him to walk to the other end.

Climbing aboard at the swimming deck, Finn signaled, and we found an empty locker room area.

"This is convenient," Jonas said quietly. We stripped out of our dry suits and tanks and stowed them into the lockers. He grabbed some towels off a shelf and wiped up the water we'd tracked in. Pulling out our fatigues from the dry bags, we dressed, checked our communications and weapons, and split into two teams. There was enough light on the boat that we didn't need our night goggles.

"Jonas, what did you discover with the thermal imaging?" asked Finn.

Jonas pulled out his sketch and laid it on the floor. "We're lucky this boat doesn't have a full complement, but it's just as we thought. There are two shooters topside—one at starboard and one at port, midway between both sides, located here," he said, pointing at his drawing. "There are two demons at the helm, but they're not at attention, so they should be easy to eliminate. Two myrmidons are patrolling this deck, and two more are on the top deck. That's all that are topside.

"Down below is another story, but to our favor, everyone is two levels down at the stern of the ship inside the engine room here. Two are seated, so we can assume they are Armie and Billie. I noticed no myrmidons, but there are three minor demons and Xerkamedes. Exactly as Mara had said."

Edison said, "We need to take out those snipers, and I recommend we head upwards and take out the myrmidons on the way."

"Agreed," Finn replied. "Mara and Jonas, you're with me. We'll hightail it to the bridge and remove those two minor demons." Jonas and I nodded in agreement. "Edison and Jasper, that means you get to take out the myrmidons on this deck, and I'll leave the rest of them on the deck above to your team as well. Once you've secured the myrmidons on this level, contact us, and we'll head to the bridge. When these decks are secured, we'll meet near the top of the stern ladder and eliminate the snipers."

"Copy that," Edison replied.

Edison and Jasper moved out, and we waited in the dark in the locker room. It was only a few minutes later when we received his go-ahead, and we proceeded toward the bridge. When we reached it, we ducked down low, taking only a couple of glances inside through the windows.

I motioned to Finn and Jonas that the two evil ones were still there and not paying attention to their surroundings. We pulled our knives and entered the room. The two demons tried to grab their rifles, but there wasn't enough time. This room wasn't large, and fighting space was limited.

I faced the first demon. It was a woman who grinned with satisfaction at being able to fight a human—thinking her opponent didn't stand a chance. Sheathing my knives, I urged her to attack me. She lunged forward, and I swiftly jumped aside, then kicked off the window, slamming my body into hers. I heard Finn fighting the other demon, and I prayed he was doing well. Jonas guarded the room and assessed whether we needed help, but he watched our fight with a hint of amusement—the cad.

The she-demon returned to her feet and charged me again, trying to hit me with a karate kick to my midsection. I grabbed her foot, twisted it at a backward angle, and she growled in pain and frustration. Holding her in a vice grip, I shoved her backward, and she hopped on one foot, attempting to keep her balance. But she tripped over the captain's chair and fell to the floor on the other side. I pulled out two blades, jumped on top of her, and slashed her throat. Her body convulsed a couple of times, then the smelly black sludge spread across the floor.

I jumped to my feet as I heard a crash behind me. Finn was still fighting the male demon, but I could tell Finn was playing with him. My husband's face beamed with a brilliant smile as he thwarted the demon's every move with a playful countermove.

"Darling, just finish him, will you? We have work to do," I said as I cleaned the demon goo off my knives.

"Whatever you say, love." Finn moved and did a quick three-sixty spin, kicking the demon in the chest, which shoved him hard against the corner of the navigation center. The pain caused the fiend a moment of pause, which was enough time for Finn to push his blade into the monster's neck. He grabbed his gaping wound, trying to stem the blood, but it was useless. Finn then stabbed him once more in the eye. The demon slid to the ground and was finally sent back to Hell.

"Nice job, you two," Jonas said as he patted us on the back.

"Thanks for the help," I replied sarcastically.

"Any time," Jonas returned snidely.

The three of us hurried to the rear ladder.

Finn quietly spoke into his com, "Edison, are we clear to proceed topside?"

"Confirmed."

We met them at the ladder, and Edison and Jonas asked to take out the snipers.

"Have at it," Finn replied.

Edison and Jonas silently moved off in different directions, and we stayed discretely behind them but kept them in sight if we were needed. We watched as they snuck up behind the shooters and took them out without a sound by slitting their throats. Edison and Jonas returned to our side while wiping the demon blood off their weapons and returning them to their sheaths.

"You should have played with them as Finn did," I said with a snort, and Finn sent me a flirty wink.

"Very funny, sis," Jonas retorted with a bright grin.

"Let's get down to the engine room," Edison replied. "But watch your back—we never know if a demon has moved from the bottom deck of the stern and is wandering around."

After nodding, we maneuvered inside and down toward the yacht's hull.

CHAPTER 24

*W*e descended toward the engine room, not knowing exactly where the demons and their hostages were located. Splitting into two teams, we crept along the lower deck. With our rifles raised and ready, we cleared each room as we passed.

"The engine room should be ahead," Edison murmured.

We took a few moments as my brothers and I scanned this lower deck with our minds, and indeed, we sensed everyone ahead, which had to be the engine room.

"Edison, watch our six," Finn ordered in a whisper.

"Copy."

Finn sent us several signals as we neared the engine room hatch, which was ajar. Jonas crouched low just to the right of the door and took out a small object that looked like a camera, and there was a long, thin tube attached to it. He slid it around the hatch frame and moved it slowly to the right and left as he watched the small screen. Pulling the line out, he tucked the gadget back into his backpack.

We backed up several feet, and Jonas whispered, "There's one demon to the right guarding the door, and our team is zip-tied to two chairs, sitting side by side. I'm sorry to say Armie and Billie have been beaten, but not severely. They're conscious and alert. Xerkamedes is five feet to their right, and there are two other demons there as well—one standing behind each of our team members."

"Where's the scroll?" Finn asked.

"The container is across Xerkamede's shoulder, and I doubt she's opened it," Jonas replied.

Our team developed a plan and prepared to enter the engine room.

Jonas threw open the hatch and shot the demon guard in the face, killing him instantly. The two demons guarding our teammates lowered themselves behind Armie and Billie. Xerkamedes zipped behind a boiler.

"You're too late. I have the scroll, you imbeciles!" she yelled around the machines.

Armie and Billie looked at us with relief, and I cringed when I saw their black eyes, bloody lips, and bruised jaws.

"You may have the scroll, but only I can open the locked container," Armie hollered back to the demon.

One of the minor fiends behind Billie fired in our direction, aiming to injure as many of us as possible. We were hidden behind massive engine room equipment, and the bullet pinged, then bounced around the room, finally penetrating one of the high-pressure pipes on the port-side wall. Steam whistled from the hole, and I could feel the heat even from my position eight feet away.

I raised my rifle, carefully aimed, and returned fire, catching his exposed left shoulder as he tried to hide behind Billie. The demon screeched in pain, and the shock of being hit caused him to shift his stance so I could shoot him in the forehead. *Another monster was down, and good riddance!*

The other fiend stayed behind Armie and Billie, shooting randomly in our direction, and luckily, he was a lousy shot.

Armie tried again, "Xerkie, did you hear what I said? You can't open the container without me. Look, I'll make you a deal. You let

Billie go, and I'll open the container for you—that's the best deal you'll get."

I spoke to Jonas's psyche and he nodded in agreement. Taking a brief moment, I scanned the major demon's mind. After getting what I needed, I exited the demon's thoughts and relayed what I'd discovered to my brother.

"Xerkie? Do we have an agreement?" Armie asked again.

A few minutes passed, and she finally responded. "Your teammates will leave the room with Billie and you have a deal. But you'll give your life for this debacle, you putrid human," she replied.

I forced a "no" into Armie's mind, but he ignored my plea. He then sent me a quick message, and I knew what he had planned. I was stunned by what he told me and then answered him. We were blessed that Armie was a strong psychic.

Armie spoke up once more, "You have a deal. My life for theirs, and you get the scroll."

The demon guarding Armie released his bindings and made him stand, keeping his charge before him for protection. The guard reached down and cut Billie's ties as well. Billie rose and quickly, but gingerly, joined us behind the machinery. She leaned against me in relief.

Whispering to Billie, I asked, "Are you alright?"

She nodded but wrapped her arms around her torso. "I may have some bruised ribs, but I'm okay."

After gently squeezing her hand, I told my team what Armie had planned.

"The rest of you leave. If any of you show yourselves again, I'll kill you," the remaining guard warned. I continued to watch them through a small space between the machines.

"Mara, you better be sure about this," Finn muttered hesitantly.

"Come on, do as my slave says," Xerkamedes ordered.

My team and I moved out from behind the machinery in view of the demon guard. We kept our rifles trained on him in case Xerkamedes betrayed us or Armie was wrong about what he told me.

We maneuvered our way out the metal door and pretended to close it, leaving it slightly ajar once more. Jonas pulled his camera out again, placing the tubing around the door's lower edge, and we watched what transpired inside the room.

Sure enough, she moved out carefully and walked toward Armie. The minor demon made him stand but kept his gun trained on his prisoner. Xerkamedes pulled the scroll container off her shoulder and handed it to Armie. He took it carefully, then turned the canister around so the bottom faced the guard and the top was in the direction of Xerkamedes.

"This had better not be a trick, or I'll make mincemeat out of your friends," she said, sliding one of her sharp nails along Armie's cheek. We watched as a small trickle of blood dripped from the injury. The demon licked her long claw and moaned in delight.

"Do you want the scroll or not?" Armie asked with impatience.

She nodded, and he punched in a set of numbers on the small keypad. There was a click. *Boom!* Each end of the container blew out, and the guard was killed instantly as the explosion put a large hole in his midsection. The direct charge that hit Xerkamedes was more extensive and intense, and the blast impacted her head. The force of the bomb sent her flying against the hull. We charged in at that moment and began our assault on the horrendous demon. Although we repeatedly fired our weapons at her, she was stronger than anticipated. She used her mind to send a blast in our direction, and several team members were thrown against the opposite wall. Jonas and I drilled our minds into her, and she recoiled at the impact but then pushed off the wall and stormed toward us in rage.

As my brother and I fought her with our knives, kicks, and punches, it was then that we saw this demon's true form. What we viewed was over ten feet tall. The trunk of her body was the color of mustard, and it was massive. Four arms were set at different angles along the sides of her upper chest, and one giant spiked razor-like claw was at the end of each one.

Her lower body was elongated like a beetle, and her appendages were more of a military green hue. But what was so surprising was she walked on six huge legs. Slime and something I couldn't define dripped from every inch of her, and I heard a sucking sound as she moved across the floor. The slippery sludge seemed to have its own intelligence, which I didn't understand. Her movements were exceedingly fast and agile for having so much bulk. The head was even more terrifying. It protruded at a forty-five-degree angle from her chest, and her six eyes were piercing gold and set vertically along the upper half of her long, jagged skull. Her mouth and jaw randomly pushed out like an accordion as she swung her head back and forth while she scampered along the ground. When her jaw was open, there were many sharp, thick blades which I assumed were her vicious, deadly teeth. I didn't see a tongue, but then I spotted two long whips that slipped out of the sides of her head that coordinated with the movement of her mouth. The tongues were dark green and dripped with spines and acid, and she attempted to strike us with those grotesque protrusions. She missed me by a few inches but slashed a fine jagged line across Jonas's upper left thigh. But as she pulled this tongue back, he caught it with his blade and hacked it off at the root. Xerkamedes roared in anger and pain and attempted to slash at us once more.

The sounds emitting from this demon were a deep rumble and a high, piercing whine, and it caused debilitating dizziness. The stench of this monster was unparalleled, and it matched the ghastly stink of the odors from my visit to Hell. My brother and I had to pull away quickly as the atrocious smell and ear-splitting sound began to send us into unconsciousness. Blocking it, we pulled out again and faced the abomination before us.

We removed ourselves from seeing her true self and now viewed her again as the stunning female she portrayed to be. Her once gorgeous face was shattered and bloody, and she stared at us with the only eye that remained. The blast had removed the left side of her face and skull.

Her demon strength kept this body alive, even with half of her brain destroyed.

"You! You're the one who took my chemist. I needed him, you disgusting little witch, and I'll make you pay dearly for taking him from me. But mark my words, his absence won't stop me or my great plan. I'll still make you suffer for what you've done!" She pointed an accusing fingernail at me.

"Uh-huh. What are you going to do about it, termite?" I asked.

Her rage erupted, and she attempted to lunge at me and impale me with her vicious-looking, foot-long nail. I quickly dodged her and smiled at her failure.

"Tsk-tsk," I said, wagging my index finger at her in reprimand. "You need to go back to the mires of Hell. You're pathetic. Don't you think she's a pitiful little thing, team?" I asked my friends, and we laughed at her, trying to spur her anger even further. It worked.

As she stormed toward us, Jonas and I called to the Holy Trinity and the angels. We waved our knives and began an all-out assault on Xerkamedes. She seemed well aware she didn't stand a chance due to her severe injuries, and before we knew it, she did the unexpected. She retreated at such a breakneck speed that we never saw her move until she was back against the hull again. Her lengthy nails protruded from her fingers, and she thrust them into the wall, ripping out a huge section. The hull gave way, and water began flooding the engine room. Xerkamedes used all her strength to shove her body through the hole and into the dark waters. We turned swiftly and exited through the hatch. Jonas and Finn attempted to close the engine room door, but the previous gunfire must have damaged it, and the engine room was flooding fast.

We scrambled up the ladder and Finn called our team on the Interceptors. "Let's get up top and wait for them to arrive," Finn ordered.

"What about Xerkamedes? I feel her, so she's still alive. Albeit she's gravely injured, but not dead," I said in exasperation.

"Mara, we do what we can, when we can. We have to get out of here because the boat is sinking," Finn replied.

Yosef yelled over our coms, "Finn, we have bogies coming in. Several speed boats and two choppers are closing in on your twenty, and they'll be there in about eighteen minutes."

"Yosef, get out of here. This yacht will blow, and we need all of you safe, my friends, and we sincerely thank you for your assistance. May God be with you," Finn said.

"Copy that. You are welcome, and we are here if you ever need our services again. May He be with you as well."

We heard their boat move away at a high rate of speed. We felt the ship lurch as it began sinking, the aft slowly lowering into the sea. Our feet slid a few inches toward the incline, and we quickly climbed up the ladder to the main deck.

"Finn, we didn't check every inch of this yacht, and the demon may have had one of her labs located on this vessel. Even if it sinks, she could still come back and retrieve what she may need. What do we do?" I asked in trepidation.

"That's why we're going to blow the ship," Finn replied. "Mara, do you feel the demon anywhere around this ship?"

I took a moment, rescanning the area for any sign of her. "I'm not getting anything—thank the Lord. At least, not nearby."

"Edison, it's up to you and Jasper to dive down and plant the explosives on the hull of this ship. We'll wait just off starboard with the Interceptor for your return," Finn said.

"We can do it, but we'd have to move fast," Edison replied as he pulled the explosives from his dry bag.

Finn nodded, and Edison and Jasper left to take care of the bombs. Finn then contacted the two Interceptors to meet us off the starboard rail of this yacht.

"Let's move," Finn ordered. Hustling to the ship's rail, we waited for our team to arrive with the boats. We heard them as they joined us.

"Armie, you and your team need to hurry to your awaiting ship and get the artifacts to safety."

Armie nodded to Finn, then I looked at Armie questioningly and asked, "Where's the scroll?"

"We did the bait and switch, *Cherie*. Leon has it in his pack."

"You dirty dog, Armie. Well done!" I grinned back and hugged him. He kissed my cheek and climbed into Interceptor Two when it pulled alongside. We watched as Armie, Chuck, Leon, Aaron, and Grayson departed. The coffin that held St. Joseph was still secured at the aft of the vessel.

"We will contact you when our cargo is safe and secure," Armie yelled. He and his team saluted us and sped off into the night.

Xavier took the helm of Interceptor One. The rest of us climbed in and waited for Jasper and Edison. Jonas and I sent a loud psychic alarm to all the sea creatures, hoping they'd stay clear of the yacht's explosion. It wasn't long before Jasper and Edison appeared. The boat was now sinking fast, and it wouldn't be long before it was submerged. Edison pushed the detonator after we traveled a safe distance from the ship. I'd never seen God's holy fire go off underwater; it was a fantastic sight. Even under the guise of darkness, it was an incredible display. The water rumbled, then a resounding *"whump"* traveled under the water, and a giant blue fountain erupted from the ocean. It was spectacular. Even though we were half a mile away, we were inundated with heavy seawater spray from the underwater explosion.

The *thup, thup* of the choppers could be heard coming from the distance, and we had to get to safety. Then we caught the high pitch drone of several high-speed boats approaching our location. Finn contacted Basheer and Yosef as we moved at a whirlwind speed toward our desired destination.

"Are we going to get there in time, Finn?" I asked in desperation.

"I doubt it. Everyone get to your stations and prepare."

We moved to the rear of the boat and opened the hatch, donning Kevlar vests, helmets, and grabbing weapons. Jasper adjusted the fifty-caliber mounted machine gun at the stern, and the remainder of us stayed low behind the bulletproof exterior of the Interceptor, ensuring we were harnessed into our positions. As Xavier steered the boat, he deftly maneuvered it in swift and agile turns as he evaded our enemies. We would have been dumped into the dark, turbulent waters without being secured to the watercraft. Aaron stayed on navigation to keep us on course.

Jonas yelled to Finn, "They all appear to be heading toward Armie's craft. We need to get their attention, Finn."

"Copy that," he replied. "Jonas, turn on our lights and keep us bright until I say otherwise."

The Interceptor's lights were engaged, and we were lit like a Christmas tree.

"That should get their attention," I said over our coms.

After waiting several minutes, our pursuers changed course and headed right for us.

Basheer spoke over our coms, "Their two choppers are searching the area where the yacht had been located and are looking for survivors. Four speed boats are headed to your twenty, and two are still after Armie."

"Copy, Basheer. I need you to take out the two in pursuit of Armie," Finn ordered.

"Order confirmed. I'm on my way," Basheer responded.

We heard the demon boats approaching fast, but our boat was quicker.

"Cut the lights!" Finn yelled.

Everything went dark, and we donned our goggles that could switch from binoculars to night vision. We could see their boats' running lights.

I removed my goggles and aimed with my sniper rifle, but I had issues keeping my gun and gaze steady. The boat did well with its stabilization equipment, but there was still plenty of bounce with each hit of a wave. After clearing my mind, I stared through the scope, spotted the gunner in the first boat, and took the shot. *Phing!*

"You got him, Mara!" Edison yelled when he saw the demon go down. "You need to get the gunner in the second boat."

Moving my attention and aim to the second watercraft, the demons were getting too close for comfort. I fired another shot, and the second demon was hit in the head, and it wasn't a pretty sight.

"He's down too—good shot, Mara! They're almost upon us. It's now going to get up close and personal, mates!"

The enemy bullets pinged off our stern, and Xavier quickly maneuvered us to a quick forty-five-degree turn, then straightened out again.

I lowered my sniper rifle and took up the Israeli automatic weapon —the Tavor 7 with the bullpup configuration. It was loaded with our unique, "monkified" bullets that would take out any hellion within its long range. One demon boat tried to pull alongside, but Xavier swung the boat starboard, and we deftly left the monsters in the wake of our frothy, high waves. We fired so many shots into the first demon boat that it blew up when we hit their gas line.

The second, third, and fourth demon watercrafts tried to come alongside to flank and trap us within the configuration.

"Jasper, how long before we reach the freighter?" Finn yelled.

"Thirteen minutes."

Our enemy combatants were firing at us, and we had to hide below the bulletproof hull to avoid getting hit. We then fired over our heads, aiming at anything in their direction and praying we were shooting the demons. Xavier turned hard to port and smashed into the bow of the lead boat. The pilot lost control of his watercraft, and it went into a full flipping motion at an intense speed, causing the craft to splinter apart, and the demons flew into the dark, turbulent ocean.

"Enough of this crap. Jonas, get the Holy Fire missiles and prepare to send them over," Finn ordered.

"Copy that!"

Sitting on the boat floor, Jonas loaded the small missile launchers and handed one each to me, Billie, and Jasper.

"Cover us on the port side," I yelled. When we raised our heads, we realized the demons were also about to send missiles our way. Finn and Jonas continued firing their automatic weapons while the devils dived to the bottom of their boat. I heard a bullet whiz by my head, and I instinctively ducked. But I heard a groan and knew one of my people had been hit.

"Fire!" Finn yelled. My other teammates continued firing their weapons at the other boats while we launched the missiles.

There were three successive "booms," and their boats blew into giant balls of blue fire. *Good riddance!*

To my dismay, Jonas was down. I panicked, unbuckled my harness, and scrambled around several obstacles to get to his side.

He was bleeding profusely from his head, and I screamed his name, "Jonas!"

Checking his pulse, I felt a steady *thump, thump*, and tried to persuade him to open his eyes. "Jonas, can you hear me? Please look at me!"

Xavier was our medic, but he was busy driving the boat. So much blood was coming from Jonas's head, and even though I tried to staunch the bleeding, it still oozed.

"Finn, I need Xavier now!"

"Billie, take the helm," Finn ordered.

Xavier was immediately at my side and examined Jonas. He pulled some things from his medic bag and administered to Jonas.

"Finn, three choppers are heading your way. They'll be there in five minutes."

"Thanks for keeping an eye on us, Yosef." Finn turned to us and said, "We need a break, Lord."

We heard the enemy helicopters in the distance and gaped at each other in frustration.

"Mara, return to your post," Finn said.

"Finn…"

"Move it! That's an order!"

"Copy that," I replied while feeling torn because I wanted to remain at Jonas's side. But I also knew I was needed to defend the boat and its crew. Taking up my Tavor, I reloaded and was ready for the incoming evil.

"The freighter is five minutes out," Xavier said.

"That's not soon enough," Finn replied.

We saw the choppers' lights as they approached, and they automatically fired on us. Giving everything I had, I continued the onslaught on their helicopters, and my team did the same. But it just wasn't enough. Even after taking down one of the choppers, the other two were well-defended, and they also had machine guns that never stopped their continued offensive.

"Cover your behinds, my friends! I have no choice but to blow them out of the air even though they're too close to you for comfort." Basheer said over our coms.

There was a ferocious explosion of the second chopper, and then the third helicopter detonated in a fiery ball.

Debris, flames, gasoline, and body parts rained down on us, and we dove to the bottom of the boat to try and get out of the way. One large piece of fuselage hit the bow. Our restraints couldn't hold us and broke under the massive jolt. The collision sent the entire crew of the Interceptor flying into the ocean's blackness.

The impact of my body hitting the hard, unforgiving surface of the water knocked the air from my lungs, and I sank quickly. Struggling frantically, I broke to the surface, and it took me several moments to replenish my empty lungs. The gasoline fumes on the water's surface burned my throat and eyes, but it was still better than inhaling water. The weight from my vest and helmet started to pull me back under, so I promptly removed them but assured myself that my handgun and knives were still safely secured within my belt.

After regaining strength, I frantically looked around me, desperately trying to find my friends in the ocean's darkness. I thought I spotted a few of them and was about to call out when something unknown pulled me back into the inky, cold darkness of the sea. Punching and kicking, I tried to assault whatever had a deathly hold on me, but it seemed fruitless. I was being propelled deeper, and panic set in.

"Lord God, please help me! Give me sight so I can see my enemy and the knowledge to eliminate it," I prayed silently in desperation to the Heavens above.

Instantly, I could see everything around me as if the sun was shining from above, penetrating the ocean's blackness. I caught sight of what held me fast. It was Maccafor, Xerkamedes' lieutenant. Pulling my blades, I slashed at the vile creature. The demon appeared to me in his true form, and must they always be so gruesome? Maccafor had more of a human look as he had two arms and legs and one head. But beyond that, he was slimy, scaly, and had lethal-looking weapons of tendrils and spikes sprouting from his entire body. His eyes blazed with fire as well as areas of flames crisscrossing his chest. He attempted to throw spires of fire at me from the ends of his bony, pointed fingers, but luckily, the heavy sea water stopped them from reaching my skin. The ocean began turning dark and murky from every gash and cut I gave him, but I kept hacking away. Unfortunately, I was running out of precious air. But I made one final deadly move as he tried to attack me once more. Circling him, I sliced him from ear to ear and gave him a ferocious kick. An eerie and bone-chilling howl reverberated through the water as he screamed at me with rage and defeat. After that last assault, I witnessed him moving away from me, shock and death in his eyes as the current took him swiftly from my sight.

Darkness surrounded my vision as my air was almost depleted. I called quietly to anyone who would listen to save me as I began to descend deeper into the depths of Davy Jones's Locker.

As I sank, I felt a gentle yet persistent push as I was quickly and firmly raised to the surface. It felt like flying. *Was I dying? Was I being lifted to Heaven?*

I felt my body break the surface, and the cool ocean breeze brushed across my face. Quickly inhaling the precious oxygen that would save my life, I gulped, coughed, choked, and breathed in the precious air once more. I knew I was alive. Something still supported me, but I had no clue what had rescued me.

As I laid there, trying to breathe and gain my bearings, I heard a familiar voice whispering into my left ear. "You saved my soul, Mara, so I asked God if I could be the one to save your life tonight. This act alone can never repay what you did for me, even though I did nothing to deserve your kindness. Thank you, dear Mara, for showing me the path to eternal life with the Lord, and I hope to be of further service to you and your team if I'm ever needed again. I must go now, as I still have to pay for the heinous sins I committed on this earth. But knowing I'll eventually be with our Lord and Savior, it's worth every moment of penance I must suffer. Goodbye, Mara."

The voice that sounded so familiar vanished, along with the supporting arm. I was alone once more in the cold, dark ocean. Something bumped against me, and I thought it was a body. I screamed in fear, worried it was one of my beloved team, or worse yet, my husband or one of my brothers. But it was only part of a seat cushion.

I signed in relief, hoping I was now safe.

"Mara!" It was Finn, and he was frantic. "Mara! Dang it, answer me, love!"

"I...am...here!"

"Thank the Lord, sweetheart. I'm coming your way. Keep talking to me, babe."

I did as he asked, and he finally swam to my side. He pulled me close and kissed my entire face.

"Mara, I heard you in my mind needing help, but I couldn't find you. I thought you were dead, my love."

"I'm okay. Maccafor attacked me, but luckily the good Lord gave me sight and helped me kill the demon. I have more to tell you about... what happened...later." It wasn't easy carrying on a conversation while treading water.

He hugged me once more with great relief.

"I love you, Mara!"

"I love you too, Finn!"

"We better check on the remainder of our team." He turned away and yelled, "Sound off!"

I then heard every one of my extraordinary team answer the call. Their voices were breathless, but they still replied. Everyone but Jonas. He had been unconscious when we were thrown from the boat. *How could he have survived?* I said a quick prayer and asked God for his mercy. Even though I hadn't realized it, my face was wet with tears.

"Okay, team, swim toward my voice. The freighter is only fifty feet to the north, so help has arrived," Finn yelled in exhaustion.

"Xavier again...I have Jonas. He's...alive...but...unconscious."

"Keep calling, Xavier. I'm headed your way," Jasper answered.

"Finn, I...can't make it to you...I can't swim with these broken ribs...dang it!" Billie tried to yell through her pain.

"Keep floating on your back, Billie. We'll come to you," Finn ordered.

The freighter had sent out several boats, pulled us out of the water, and carried us back to the ship. We were bruised, battered, and drenched but alive. As soon as I saw Jonas, I ran and followed closely behind as he was led to sickbay.

Xavier said, "I think he'll be fine. The blood was from a two-inch cut on his skull; I believe he has a concussion. It was lucky the bullet only grazed him. We'll know more when he's examined in sickbay. This freighter has a top-notch medical facility, so he's in good hands."

"Thanks, Xavier." I kissed his cheek and checked on Billie. She was holding her ribs and was pale, but she said she'd be fine and was also led away to sickbay.

"Come on, mates," Edison said. "They have quarters for each of us, so get showered and changed. Then you can check on your injured team members when you're cleaned up."

CHAPTER 25

We were in sickbay checking on our team a couple of hours later. Billie and Jonas were both on the mend and would be fine. Jonas only had a mild concussion but would be under watch by the doctors for the next several hours. He had a massive headache which was controlled by medications. Billie's ribs were only bruised but still painful. She pretended they didn't hurt, but we knew better and insisted she take her pain meds.

The rest of us had to be examined, and luckily, we only had minor cuts and contusions. Finn and I returned to our quarters and were more than exhausted. I plopped on the bed and pulled the blanket over my body, even though I was still wearing the sweats they'd given me.

"That tired, love?"

"Yup. I don't care about pajamas, and I'm sleeping in this outfit. Come to bed, Finn."

He joined me and we both went out like a light.

The next day dawned bright and clear, and we checked on Jonas and Billie in sickbay. They felt better and could join us on our flight from the freighter's chopper to Athens, where we'd catch our plane back home.

Finn contacted Armie, and he and his crew were safe and on their way to an undisclosed location. Aaron, Chuck, and Grayson would meet us in Athens to return to Idaho.

Yosef would join us on our chopper ride to Greece but catch another flight back to his base.

WHEN WE RETURNED HOME to Idaho, everyone was quiet and exhausted. Finn ordered our team to rest for another twenty-four hours, and we'd meet on Tuesday at nine in the morning.

Gracie, Mom, and Asher were thrilled to see us when we entered the apartment. We received many hugs and kisses and were delighted to be home.

That night when Finn and I retired to our bedroom, he said, "Out with it, love. What's going on?"

"You can read me like a book, can't you?" I kissed him on the cheek, and he pulled me close.

"Tell me, Mara."

"I feel like we failed…Xerkamedes got away and will continue her assault on God's good people and whatever other evils she's working on. Frankly, it terrifies me."

"The way I see it, her getting away was meant to be. You should know by now, my sweet, that everything is in God's hands and under His will. We're His players on the chess board. Our current position is "check," and hopefully, our next encounter will be "checkmate.""

I gazed at him and kissed the cleft in his chin. "You're right. We won't win every time, and we must be thankful to the Lord that we made it out alive and no worse for wear." I held him close.

"Mara, there's something else you haven't told me. Come on, fess up," he said in an urging tone.

I backed away and turned down the bed, gently moving Asher aside while I did so. He gave me a loud chirp in protest and then resettled at the end of the mattress. Sitting down, I urged Finn to join me.

I was quiet for a moment, then said, "When the Interceptor was hit by the debris and sent us flying into the dark ocean, I was practically knocked unconscious by the impact, and I knew I was drowning."

Finn hissed in dismay and fear and pulled me into a fierce hug.

"Kind of...like...now. Finn, I can't breathe."

He loosened his hold and whispered, "Sorry, my sweet."

Giggling, I continued, "As I started to lose consciousness, something or someone pulled me to the surface and flipped me over so I was on my back. It was then that I heard his voice."

"Whose voice?" Finn asked in puzzlement.

"Simon Maharis."

"What!?"

"At first, I didn't know who it had been, but then I realized it was him. Maharis told me that God said he could return to help me. He actually repented and will go to Heaven—if you can believe that. Then he thanked me for saving his soul and helping him find the Lord."

Finn was quiet for several moments, then said, "You did end up forgiving a man who wanted to hurt you badly, then you went to Hell and tried to save his soul. You actually convinced Maharis to follow the Lord, and in turn, this serial killer saved your life. I'll thank God for allowing this man to rescue you from drowning. The thought that I could have lost you is beyond comprehension." He kissed my cheek and held me, stroking my hair and rubbing my back.

"I love you, Finn.

"I love you too, my sweet Mara."

I immediately fell asleep but began to dream...

I'M MOVING across the sky like a bird and watching the scenery below me. The vista is stunning, with blue lakes, wildflowers fields, and green forests. I watch deer, rabbits, and squirrels frolic across the ground and play with joy and freedom. But my vision darkens, and I'm approaching

a city's landscape. Moving downward, I settle into the street and watch in horror at the scene before me. Death and destruction are everywhere. Corpses of varying ages, races, and gender are scattered around and in different stages of decay. Vultures are pecking away at the rotting flesh, and the smell is putrid and overwhelming. A young woman comes running down the street carrying a dead child; its body looks as if its flesh has fallen away, leaving only a pulpy mass of muscle and bone. The horrified woman screams in terror, begging someone to save her precious baby. I try to run to her, but my feet are firmly cemented to the ground, and I can only watch in terror as she screams and pleads for someone to help.

The woman's movements slow, and I watch her stagger and then drop to her knees. Her eyes flit left and right as if trying to focus on her surroundings. But her gaze turns vacant, and she absently drops her dead child's body on the hard pavement. She kneels, seeming unaware of anything around her.

Turning her head, she looks at me and whispers, "You must stop this from happening. Please save us!" After her utterances, her eyes return to the vacant stare. Blood begins dripping from the corners of her unseeing eyes, and she's unaware it's happening. Then the blood oozes from her nose, ears, and mouth. I watch in horror as her body convulses, which throws her figure back and forth along the ground. She violently twitches and rocks as the virus viciously holds her hostage. Her body stills momentarily as her skin turns bright red, then shrinks and melts before my horrified gaze. The poor woman convulses again in the grip of agony before death finally and thankfully takes her life.

"Mara." I can hear the voice but can't rip my gaze from the petrifying scene before me. "Mara." The voice repeats in a more commanding tone. Turning my attention away from the poor woman, I now see the Holy Blessed Virgin. Moving toward her, I kneel at her feet. The sensational scent of flowers replaces the stench of the death and rot surrounding me.

"My sweet child, I know what you see before you is overwhelming, and I wish you didn't have to witness it, but this could happen if the Chosen doesn't stop Xerkamedes and her minions. But I have faith in those my Father selected to destroy the evils that roam and permeate the earth." She touches my face and wipes away my tears of despair.

"But how do we do this, Holy Mother? She's more powerful than any demon we've encountered thus far, and I'm unsure if we're enough to stop her in her wake."

"Of course, child. God knows what's needed, and none is more powerful than Him. Trust me when I say, His Chosen can overcome any demon they must face—no matter how fierce. My Son and Father are always with you in your battles and never leave your side. Tell the others what I've imparted this night. It will give them hope and strength to continue in their journey. I love you, child."

With her final words, she vanishes. But I again see the two images she'd shown me after my trip to Hell.

JOLTING AWAKE, I sat up and breathed hard like I had just finished a ten-mile marathon.

"Mara, are you alright?" Finn turned on the bedside lamp and rubbed his eyes.

"Yes. I think so. Finn, the Holy Mother showed me what this virus can do if we don't stop the demon. It was so horrific…you can't even imagine how bad." I sobbed, and Finn pulled me against his chest. I snuggled into him and told him everything I'd witnessed in the vision.

"I'm so sorry, sweetheart. The Virgin Mary said we can stop her—and we will. I promise," Finn whispered, rubbing my back and kissing my tears away. "We'll also tell the rest of the Chosen what she said. Don't worry, love."

"Thanks, Finn." It wasn't long before I fell back to sleep, feeling protected and cherished, as well as knowing God would always be there, no matter what we may have to face.

WE MET FOR OUR MEETING, and it was beautiful seeing all of our team, although they appeared to be quiet and reflective. Jonas only had a slight scar on his forehead, and Billie moved around easier. The team was subdued and discouraged, and I found it disheartening.

Once Edison finished his opening prayers, he said, "Okay, team, well done. As usual, mates, you're a fantastic group of God's soldiers, and I'm proud to serve with you. I know Xerkamedes got away, but we'll get her next time.

"Regarding what we think she and Maharis have been up to, it's pretty ugly. While we were away doing battle, our talented team of scientists was working on what Jonas had recovered from Maharis's farm lab. If you look at the overhead screen, these are the photos and documents Jonas pulled from the lab's computer. Our scientists have narrowed down Xerkamedes' work to three viruses."

We watched as Edison reviewed documents on the monitor, showing us several photographs of viral cells.

"Wait!" I retorted loudly. Then I stood and moved closer to the screen. "Go back, Edison, but move through them slowly." He did as I instructed, and when I spotted one that was eerily familiar, I yelled, "Stop!"

Finn asked in confusion, "What is it, Mara?"

"When I returned from Hell as well as from a recent dream, the Virgin Mother showed me two images, and at the time, I had no clue what they meant. But this is one of them. I'm positive this is one she gave me."

Edison pulled up the corresponding report on this viral cell and what our scientists discovered.

Several moans and groans echoed around the room as the team read through the information.

"Good Lord in Heaven! This is what they were working on?" Aaron asked incredulously. "It appears to be a hundred times worse than Ebola!"

I was still standing as I read the report, then said, "According to this data, Maharis created this monster virus. This atrocious thing is still in the developmental stages, but apparently, those infected will die within minutes, depending on the victim's immunity. Once contracted, it's ninety-four percent fatal. My recent dream showed me what could happen if we don't stop Xerkamedes' scientists from completing this virus. Trust me when I say it's something out of a horror movie with people dying in the streets. But the Holy Mother said we can stop the demon and will be given the tools to do so. But what these tools are, I don't know."

The team digested this information, then Jonas asked, "Is there anything in the data about an antidote or vaccine?"

Edison replied, "Not that we've found—at least, not yet."

"Do we know how far the demons are in completing their research and having a viable virus?" Billie asked.

"Our people think they're close; their estimate is around six months. But it's a crapshoot at best. There's no way to know for sure if their other labs are further along," Edison replied with remorse.

Xavier, who generally didn't say much, spoke up, "We need to find these labs post-haste."

Finn scratched his head in frustration, then said, "That's the plan. Mara had a vision regarding one of the labs, but we still don't have the location—though I'm sure she'll be provided one soon—God willing."

I sat down in my chair with tears in my eyes. "We failed to destroy Xerkamedes; now she could kill millions with this virus. In my dream, this appears to be the worst virus in the world's history, and millions could die a horrible and excruciating death. I'm so sorry, my dear friends. I should have done more to destroy her."

"Mara, it's not your fault," Basheer replied. "From the battle you reported, there wasn't anything else you could have done. Your hands were tied."

The team sat in silence, feeling utter defeat and not knowing where to go from here in stopping the major demon and her diabolical release of this heinous virus.

We looked up when the door opened. It was our fifteen-year-old prophet, Kaiko. She walked in, sat at the table, and waited a few moments as if she was listening to something only she could hear.

She finally raised her head and spoke calmly, concisely, reflecting an age far beyond her teenage years. "My dear children, St. Gabriel has a message for you. Do not be disheartened. The Lord is pleased with your work, and everything that happened has been ordained. He knows you think you've failed in stopping the powerful demon, but it was a significant accomplishment when you gravely injured Xerkamedes. The devil has gone into hiding to heal the damage you have bravely inflicted, but she will attempt to keep her labs running at full speed.

"St. Gabriel needs you to know this: stay strong and vigilant. This demon knows about your God-given skills and will try to use them against you. Therefore, some of you will be given additional skills during your final battle with Xerkamedes. Remember, my lovely children, that He is always with you." Kaiko stood and walked around the table. She stopped by each team member, laid her hand on their shoulder, closed her eyes, then moved to the next person, repeating the process. When she was done, she strolled to the door and turned, gave us a beaming grin, then departed as quietly as she arrived.

As I looked around the room, everyone smiled with joy and contentment. We were quiet for several minutes, basking in the peace Kaiko gave us.

"That was...intense," Jonas remarked.

"I'll say. She gave our hearts ease and removed our feelings of failure. I wonder what else she gave us?" I asked.

"Time will tell, I assume," Finn replied, straightened in his chair, and cleared his throat. "Let's move on, team."

As the meeting continued, I told everyone how Simon Maharis decided to follow the Lord and how he saved my life when I was drowning. There were several surprised questions and comments.

"That is amazing, sis," Jonas replied in awe. "Now that you mentioned it, it made me remember something. When I was shot, I distinctly recall being shoved aside by some unknown force before the bullet hit me. I recalled smelling roses before the shot. If I hadn't been moved just so, I know I would have been killed."

"Jonas, that's incredible!" I exclaimed.

Billie cleared her voice, then said, "When the fuselage of the downed chopper hit the Interceptor, I remember being grabbed by something or someone, then picked up and gently laid into the water several feet from the boat. I don't know how this happened, but like Jonas, I also remember the smell of flowers. I'm verklempt."

We smiled and thanked the Lord for saving us, and as Kaiko had said, God is always with us.

"What you witnessed, my team, are the Lord's constant miracles and love for us. We need to remember that, don't we?" Finn asked.

The team nodded in agreement and grinned with happiness.

"Now, an update regarding Armie and his team, plus the holy artifacts. The Scroll of the Seven Seals and the body of St. Joseph are now safely stowed away at an undisclosed location. Armie said the trip went well, and we can rest easy. He also said Leon has begun his Templar training. Leon sent us a message too, and I quote, 'I love y'all for taking care of me and my dawg, and I miss him to pieces. Please find my boy a good and loving home and tell him I'm sorry.' Poppy had been caring for him, and we hoped she'd be willing to keep the old, sweet dog.

Finn continued, "We'll continue to research this demon disguised as Aviana Ottswater and delve into Ottswater Pharmaceuticals as well. There's a lot of data on her and her company that we *do* know, but it's what she's hiding that we must discover, my friends.

"Thanksgiving is this week, and remember, for those of you who don't have a place to go, you're welcome to join us for dinner in the ballroom. Thank you, everyone."

CHAPTER 26

On Thanksgiving Day, we celebrated in the ballroom on the base. Everyone was invited, especially if they had no one to share it with or couldn't get away to be with family. The turnout was large, and we were thrilled to share it with our facility personnel, family, and friends.

After thankful prayers, the meal was delicious, and Mom was pleased to spend the holiday with her children and grandchild. It was a joyous affair, with plenty of laughter, camaraderie, and friendship.

After the feast, Finn set up the stage so attendees could provide entertainment. Many talented people were at our facility, including musicians, artists, comedians, and other entertainers. When those who desired to perform were done, Finn and I stepped on stage. There were several screens around the hall, and we chose to display photos of tonight's attendees enjoying the festivities. It was a big hit.

Finn stepped up to the microphone, and I stood beside him. The lights were bright and hot.

"I would like to thank everyone for coming today and also for your friendship and support. I know our last mission may have seemed like a failure, but I assure you, that creep of a demon is licking her wounds and hiding in terror from God's Chosen Ones! Trust me, we will take her down next time, and she won't know what hit her! What do you say, my friends?!" Finn's voice was loud and determined, and he removed the mic from the stand, raised his fist in triumph, and moved back and forth across the stage. "Let me hear you!"

Everyone screamed, "Yes!" "Heck yeah!" "She's going down!" and many other hoots in support of our people destroying the horrific demon.

My husband pumped his fist into the air and asked the crowd, "And what do we tell her?"

They all yelled in return, "Del Bellator! Warrior for God!"

"Amen, my brother and sisters. We will win the next round—we have no doubt!!" Finn hollered again into the crowd.

They loudly praised God and chanted that all demons would be destroyed.

After the crowd quieted, Finn stopped pacing and said sincerely, "We have an amazing group of people on this base, and I'm proud of every one of you. I wouldn't trade any of you for anything." Finn's words were choked with emotion, and I took his hand in support.

After a few moments, Finn turned toward me and smiled. I nodded, and he spoke into the microphone once more. "Jonas and Aaron, would you please join us on stage?"

My brothers looked a bit confused but smiled widely and came up and stood beside us.

Finn handed me the mic, and I said, "Finn and I would like to thank you, our dear brothers, for your endless bouts of entertainment. I know I can speak for Finn and me when I say we love you and appreciate what you do to keep us in stitches."

Jonas and Aaron stared at us in bafflement, but Finn and I applauded them, and the audience joined in. Finn and I were waiting for something to happen under the bright, hot lights of the stage's spots, and sure enough, it came to fruition.

My brothers grinned from ear to ear as they gazed at us and the audience, and everyone laughed in earnest. Jonas and Aaron were bewildered, but they kept smiling anyway. The hooting and howling filled the entire hall, and it was deafening. Then, Jonas looked at one of the screens and saw both of their reflections. He grabbed Aaron's arm and pointed to the large display. Their eyes grew as large as saucers, and their smiles faded. But they couldn't help themselves and guffawed with abandon.

My brothers' faces changed before our eyes and turned into hilarious caricatures. Jonas's lips were red and shaped like a pouting woman's cartoon character's mouth. His eyebrows were colored black as night and were about an inch wide and went straight across his forehead like a unibrow.

Each one of his cheeks contained two large, solid red circles of rouge, and his nose was painted brown and had large blue whiskers drawn dramatically from his nose to each ear. Along his chin and jawline were spots resembling giant warts, each painted with one black hair protruding from them.

Aaron's face looked like a twelve-year-old freckled boy. A black circle was drawn around each eye, resembling spectacles. His eyebrows were now near his hairline, thick red and shaped as if he was in continued surprise. Blotches of dots covered his cheeks and nose to reflect freckles, but we had drawn in a giant handlebar mustache that curled and moved toward his ears. His lips had also been dramatically moved to his chin, which looked like they were parted and showed white, large buck teeth.

Unbeknownst to my brothers, when we had an intimate family dinner the night before, Finn and I gave them a Mickey in their wine glasses after the meal. They had left early because they said they were tired and went to their respective homes. Finn and I waited for a half-hour, then went to each apartment and found them deeply asleep. We took turns painting their faces using non-toxic, brightly-colored disappearing inks that would only re-appear under hot, bright lights—such as stage lighting. Finn and I giggled and cried while we painted their faces, then left their rooms to let them sleep the night through. By the next morning, the paint had disappeared and would only reappear under these bright lights.

When the laughter quieted down, Finn cued the cameraman, and then the original photo of our seascape painting appeared on the screen for all to see. Luckily, Mom had printed a copy of it when I had initially e-mailed her the photo when Finn first gave me the seascape. Then Finn played the video of our brothers switching the painting in our apartment to the final hilarious one still hanging on our wall.

"That, my dear brothers, is payback. Yes, we caught you!" I roared, then smacked them on their backs. "Don't worry; the ink will disappear within twenty-four hours—it's not permanent."

The screens returned to showing my brothers' funny faces, and as good-humored as they were, they laughed until tears ran down their cheeks.

"Mara, you and Finn got us good!" Jonas replied, then gave us both a warm embrace. Everyone in the room smiled and cheered for Jonas and Aaron.

"We love you two hooligans, and we wouldn't trade you for anything," I said, my eyes tearing up as well, and hugged them again.

THAT EVENING, the entire family met in our apartment, and we settled around the living room, enjoying the pies Mom had made that day. We were "oohing" and "aahing" while we tasted her caramel apple and pumpkin pies.

Asher was voraciously eating the leftover turkey we saved for him, and his face never left his bowl until it was licked clean. When he jumped on the sofa to join us, his face and whiskers were covered with bits of turkey, and we laughed at his mess. Sadie smelled the exquisite meat and licked the cat's face with glee—much to Asher's disdain. But he tolerated it and then sat down for his after-dinner bathing ritual.

Gracie and Aaron were playing "Go Fish" on the floor, and she was winning. Aaron was a good sport and pretended she outwitted him at every move. He made several goofy faces which were accentuated by the painted artwork that was still vivid and bright.

Jonas said, "Finn and Mara, Aaron and I want you to know that your original seascape painting is still in perfect condition and stored safely on this base. We also kept all of the other paintings with each change that was made. So the original will be returned to you tomorrow if that's alright."

We turned to look at him and broke out in gales of laughter again. His face was still brightly colored and hilarious.

Jonas grinned too, then said, "Aww, knock it off, you two. You better be correct that this stuff will be gone by tomorrow. Poppy is returning from seeing her parents, and I don't know how she would take seeing her 'love bug' looking this way. It's certainly not manly."

I giggled, then snorted. "Sorry, Jonas, but we can't help it." I picked up my phone and took several photos of them. "That's for posterior." I giggled again at my play on words, and Mom "tut-tutted" at our antics.

"Children, you never cease to amaze me. However, I do appreciate you keeping your pranks clean—well, somewhat." Mom glanced at the seascape and raised an eyebrow regarding the naked old man standing on the beach.

I squeezed Mom's hand, returned to Jonas, and said, "Tomorrow would be fine. I have to tell you, that prank was ingenious, and Finn and I were impressed." I giggled again as I looked at my two brothers' caricature faces.

They both made rude noises, which made us laugh harder. Even Gracie joined in.

The remainder of the evening was fun, and after Jonas and Aaron left and Mom and Sadie retired for the night, Finn and I tucked Gracie in bed and returned to our room.

After we prepared for bed, I sat on the edge of the mattress and gazed at Finn with a grin. He stared at me, perplexed by my expression.

"You look like the cat that swallowed the canary, love. What's going on in that lovely head of yours?" He sat beside me, kissed my cheek, and began a trail of kisses down my neck.

"Well...I have something to tell you." I grinned again but didn't say anything else.

Finn pulled away to stare into my eyes. "Come on. You're torturing me."

"Remember that I've been exhausted and cranky these last few months? I assumed it was the stress of our jobs for the Lord, but apparently, it's something else entirely," I said and chuckled.

Finn's face became concerned. "Are you okay, Mara? Please tell me you're fine."

"Don't worry. I saw the doctor yesterday, and she said I was as healthy as a horse. But she did find something." I paused, drawing out the suspense.

"Mara, you're killing me!"

I pulled something from my robe pocket and passed it over to him. Finn stared at it with confusion, but his eyes widened with realization and wonder. It was a sheet of medical test results.

Turning to me with shock, he exclaimed, "You're...pregnant!"

I nodded, and he pulled me tight into his arms. "Finn...can't breathe...my caveman!"

"Oops! Sorry, love." He pulled away, and there were tears of joy in his eyes. "I can't believe it. We're going to have a baby...." Finn hugged me again, but I could inhale oxygen this time.

"Yup," I murmured into his neck. "The doctor told me I'm about seven weeks along. But there's one more amazing thing, Finn. Remember I told you about that dream I had recently?"

"Yes. The one about the possible pandemic. What about it, love?"

"At the end of the dream, our Holy Mother showed me the same two pictures again. Of course, the first one was of the viral cell, but the second one, I now realize what it was."

Finn stared at me, waiting for me to continue.

"Mara?"

"The second one was of an ultrasound. I now realize it was the image of twin babies—our babies, Finn. We're going to have twins!"

"Whoo-hee!" Finn hollered, stood up, danced around the room, and then hunkered down into his caveman stance.

"My woo-man is having my putt-putts. I am he-man—big man of tribe." He used his fists to beat on his chest, then jumped on the bed, and his look put me into a fit of endless giggles. His brows were lowered like a Neanderthal, and he clenched his jaw, gritted his teeth, and gave me a hilarious toothy grin. Then, he grabbed me and pulled me back off the bed, and picked me up into his arms.

His face became serious and intent as he gazed into my eyes.

"Mara, I thank God every waking moment for bringing us together. And now, He's blessing us with babies. I'm the luckiest man on the planet—even if we have to fight demons and see the horror of their deeds. But as long as we have each other and God on our side, we can do anything. My incredible, gorgeous wife, I love you more than life itself."

"I know, Finn, we're immensely blessed by Heaven above. Our dear Lord has been good to us, and now we're having two babies! I love you too, my handsome hunk. My being pregnant explains my exhaustion and moodiness. But I have no clue how this war will work when I have two buns in the oven."

A startled look came across his face as he contemplated what I had said. "Good Lord in Heaven. How will we continue our missions?"

"I don't know. But I'm not concerned about it, as God has decided to give us children. Of course, I doubt I'll be combat-ready when I become as big as a house. We'll take it one mission at a time and trust the man upstairs to help us with each decision."

"Amen. It sounds like a plan," he whispered in my ear. Finn's eyes filled with tears again, then he kissed me with such tenderness that it made me cry too. He then nuzzled my stomach and said, "I'm your father, little ones. Welcome to the McKenna clan, and when you come

293

out of there, be gentle with your mum." He grinned when he faced me again, then reclaimed me as his "woo-man."

To be continued…

W<small>AIT</small>. Don't go just yet. Please go to the next page and see other exciting books by Tamara Maudelle available at Amazon…

ALSO BY TAMARA MAUDELLE

"The Holy Warriors' Commission" Series

Book One

SEALING THE GATE

(If you're reading my ebook, click on the picture above and it will take you to "Sealing the Gate" in the Amazon bookstore.)

How would you like to start your life over again—and make the ultimate difference *this* time?

Mara, who has been ill her entire life, suddenly wakes up in a new, healthy, youthful body. But this new life comes at a cost. She and the others who are specifically chosen by God for this fight must find and destroy a formidable and horrifying enemy. They are given a unique set of skills to aid them in their quest, and their adventures also take them on their own personal journeys where they discover love, sorrow, heartbreak, and forgiveness.

Join Mara and her team as they travel to dangerous locations, encounter assistance from strange and surprising sources, then fight a terrifying and dangerous evil who can ultimately take their souls.

Can she and her team find the courage they need, or will they fail in their commission and pay the ultimate price?

NEW RELEASE

(If you're reading my ebook, click on the picture above and it will take you to "Storm Harbor" in the Amazon bookstore.)

Hannah is on the run. She must not only escape from her childhood nightmares but also from someone who's supposed to love and protect her. The lakeside cottage she's inherited is the saving grace Hannah so desperately needs. Now, with a new home and identity, she's hoping for safety and a place to heal.

Storm Harbor Cottage provides her solace and peace, but how long will it last? After meeting the handsome veteran renovating her new home, she wonders if he will be another person who betrays her.

As danger closes in, who can Hannah rely on to keep her safe? And how can she explain the bizarre occurrences that keep happening? Learning to trust might be the only thing that saves her, but confiding in someone might also get her killed.

Will Hannah ever break free from her gruesome past, or will it threaten her life once again?

www.ingramcontent.com/pod-product-compliance
Lightning Source LLC
Chambersburg PA
CBHW030940260626
47169CB00002B/547